9/17 PC 7- scan

## Praise for *The Lemoncholy Life of Annie Aster*

"No book can be all things to all readers—but *The Lemoncholy Life of Annie Aster* succeeds resoundingly in being many delightful things that one does not ordinarily find tucked into the same cover: mystery, time travel, history, and gentle social commentary. Slyly mysterious, cleverly imaginative, wistfully romantic, and truly unforgettable."

— Sophie Littlefield, national bestselling author

"Readers will adore this heartfelt, one-of-a-kind debut and the charming, quirky characters tramping through its pages. Written in sly, quick-witted prose and filled with soul, *The Lemoncholy Life of Annie Aster* will have you thinking, smiling, and wondering if you can find your own magic door."

—Michelle Gable, international bestselling author of *A Paris Apartment*

"An endearing, magical romp, this tale of a charming cadre of misfits has everything. A charismatic leading lady, her lovably awkward sidekick, a truly evil villain, a Victorian schoolmarm, a wise waif, one amazing door, and a great deal of deft wit. *The Lemoncholy Life of Annie Aster* is a pitch-perfect exploration of love, friendship, and the ageless desire we all have to belong, regardless of when and where we are. The deliciously droll narration is a delight for any century, any time."

—Rhonda Riley, author of *The Enchanted Life of Adam Hope*

# THE LEMONCHOLY LIFE OF ANNIE ASTER

*Scott Wilbanks*

*For Mike*

*First, Foremost, and Always.*

*And in Todd (Edmund)'s loving memory.*



Published by Sourcebooks Landmark, an imprint of Sourcebooks, Inc.
P.O. Box 4410, Naperville, Illinois 60567-4410
(630) 961-3900
Fax: (630) 961-2168
www.sourcebooks.com

Library of Congress Cataloging-in-Publication data is on file with the publisher

2014046051

Printed and bound in the United States of America.
VP 10 9 8 7 6 5 4 3 2 1

## LEM-ON-CHOLY

**noun** (lim-uhn-kol-ee)

*plural* lem-on-chol-ies

1. The habitual state in which one makes the best of a bad situation.

adjective

2. Affected with, characterized by, or showing lemoncholy.

**Related forms:**

lemoncholily *adverb*
lemoncholiness *noun*
unlemoncholy *adjective*

**Word Origin & History**

*circa*: yesterday, a fabrication of the author's twisted mind that combines the phrase "if life gives you lemons" with the word *melancholy* to represent the state of being in which one makes the best of a bad situation.

# CHAPTER ONE

## Pray for Me, Father

*May 16, 1895*
*San Francisco, California*
*Mission Dolores Basilica*

*Randall—*

*I've not forgotten our quarrel, but I'm asking you to put that aside for the sake of scholarship and the friendship we once shared. You were right, I fear. I meddled in something beyond my understanding. The time-travel conduit works—I've shaped it as a door—but not, I suspect, by science or my own hand. You are the only person who won't think me paranoid should I put words to my suspicion. Something slumbers within it. Something with designs of its own.*

*Words have power. You know that better than anyone. And I am beginning to suspect the ones the shaman spoke—and which I foolishly copied into my journal's companion piece, my codex—were an invocation.*

*Please come soon, I beg you. Or don't come at all. And if you don't come, then pray for me, Father. Matters are coming to a head, and my instincts say this will not end well.*

*David Abbott*

Cap'n—adolescent con artist extraordinaire, picker of any lock, leader of Kansas City's notorious sandlot gang, and unofficial mayor to all its throwaways—plucked a wilted lettuce leaf from her hair as she peered through a break in the pile of rubbish where she was hiding.

Fabian didn't look so good, she thought, but there wasn't much she could do about it. He was lying in the mud, his legs bent at odd angles, and was staring down the length of his outspread arm, his mouth opening and closing in a creepy imitation of a fish on the chopping block. She couldn't make out the words, but it was clear Fabian was telling her to flee.

He wasn't going anywhere. Danyer had made sure of that. Whether it was a first or last name, Cap'n didn't know. He just went by Danyer. He was Mr. Culler's hatchet man, and he didn't fight fair. Danyer wasn't interested in fair, though; he was interested in results, and Fabian had failed. Cap'n knew it was a bad idea to let failure go unanswered in their line of business, but she never imagined it would come to this. Fabian was a moneymaker for Mr. Culler, after all.

Danyer towered over him, a granite block with meat-hook arms, his legs straddling Fabian's belly. As his boots rocked in the muck, Danyer's duster swept back and forth across Fabian's chest. His voice reminded Cap'n of a humming turbine—deep and dangerous—as he read from the letter they'd filched. "'Please come soon, I beg you—'" Danyer crumpled the paper, lobbing it into the air. It bounced off Fabian's cheek and into the mud. "Where's the journal?" He squatted, grabbing Fabian's chin with his sausage fingers before slapping him lightly across the cheek. "Hmm?"

Cap'n said a quick prayer for her friend and started backing up. But it was too late. She stepped on a stick that lifted a crate at the base of the rubbish heap just a fraction of an inch, and she could only grit her teeth as a tin can toppled from its perch, tinkling down the pile of debris while making a sound like a scale played on a badly tuned piano.

She froze as Danyer pivoted to stare at the pile of rubbish. He turned back to Fabian, speaking warily. "And where's Cap'n?" he asked. "Where's your pet pickpocket?" She watched him slap Fabian's cheek one more time, the muscles in her legs tensing as he turned and started to walk toward her hiding place. Five feet out, Danyer lunged, but all he got hold of was the remaining head of lettuce as she bolted from the mound, racing down the alleyway in a flurry of muslin, freckles, and carrot-colored pigtails.

Three blocks later, she rounded a corner, waiting. When the crack of the gun echoed down the street, she ducked into a drainage pipe to collect herself. A cockroach crawled over her foot, its antennae waving. Fabian admired cockroaches, she remembered. He said they were survivors. Suddenly, a whimper broke from her throat, and she ground the bug into a mosaic of chitinous shards before huddling in on herself, sobbing. And just as suddenly, she sat upright, her mouth set in a grim line while she ran the back of her hand across her nose.

Tears were for kids, and she needed to make a plan. When Fabian turned up dead, and there was no doubt he would, Danyer would want to tie up some loose ends—namely her. She wasn't too worried about that. She knew every hidey-hole in Kansas City, and the gang would watch her back. She regarded what was left of the cockroach, one of its severed legs agitating as though not realizing the body it belonged to was already dead, and nodded to herself. It was time to put the shoe on the other foot, she decided. Something had to be done about Danyer and his boss.

# CHAPTER TWO

## Elsbeth Grundy

### MAY 17, 1895

A wheat field outside Sage, Kansas

Elsbeth Grundy was a loner, and an odd one at that, but company was headed her way whether she liked it or not. She lived in the plains of central Kansas, alone in a cabin that was, to use a charitable word, uncomplicated. It was an austere dwelling with a cast-iron stove, a table and chair, two cabinets, a fireplace, a rocker, and a small bedroom to the rear. Being somewhat prideful of her country habits, Elsbeth had a privy built out back, a decision she often regretted with a few choice words when the weather turned for the worse.

In her bedroom was a tiny closet, and in that tiny closet were three cotton work frocks, two pairs of well-worn overalls, an occasional dress appropriate for a schoolmarm, and a family of field mice that had taken up residence in the latter's pockets.

Elsbeth wasn't necessarily inclined to solitude. She'd been a happy woman once, but a bitterness had set in after Tom died and her daughter, Beth Anne, left to find healing elsewhere. The only company she kept these days was a tattered scarecrow she'd dressed in a seersucker suit, a Panama hat, a mop of white hair, and a thick mustache made of cotton to honor Mark Twain, her hero. There was a chalkboard hanging from its neck on which Elsbeth would occasionally scribble her favorite Twain quotes. Currently, it read,

"Go to heaven for the climate and hell for the company," proving that there were those among the God-fearing who weren't afraid to poke fun at themselves.

When, on occasion, the loneliness became too much to bear, she would wander out into the field to sit next to her scarecrow and, ignoring her chores, talk until she was tired of hearing the sound of her own voice.

El was not lovely. She was old and dusty. And she spent her evenings sitting in the wooden rocking chair by the fireplace gathering more dust. Inevitably, she had a book in hand, which she read through wire-rim spectacles that took delight in slowly slipping down the bridge of her nose. This was not an easy task for the spectacles, as El had a rather large hook on her nose that one would think obstructed their mischief. They managed anyway.

Beginning this particular day as she did all her days, El awakened to collect her spectacles and quietly changed from her nightgown to a frock. She said a quick prayer, ending it with an appeal for rain. Kansas was experiencing an uncommonly long dry spell, and she was starting to run out of patience with the good Lord. If he didn't answer soon, she decided she wasn't above stripping to her knickers and doing a rain dance in the pigpen to see if that would get his attention.

A croak broke through the morning hush, interrupting El's irreverent prayer, and she poked her head out the window to see a crow impudently riding the thermals. After hanging the nightgown in her closet, she pulled on her lace-up shoes and shuffled past the corral, pausing to rub Yule May's muzzle before heading to the well with an arthritic snap and a pop to draw water for cooking and cleaning. The crow hovered above—an inky kite harnessing the wind—only to veer left and disappear from view.

While lowering the bucket, El put her hand over her eyes and scanned the horizon. Something was amiss. Her stomach felt off center, leading her to wonder if a storm was brewing. To the right, everything was as expected. The horizon offered a straight line separating golden fields from an endless buttermilk sky, broken only by the outline of the single oak tree on a gentle rise that provided shade to Tom's grave marker.

To the left, well… To the left, something was *definitely* amiss. Rising above the wheat in the distance sat a purple-and-gold mountain of a house. El sullenly shook her head at the illusion, unhooked the bucket from its tether, and walked back to her cabin. The heat occasionally toyed with her eyes, but the air was cool and dry this spring morning. Just before stepping onto the porch, she set the bucket down, took a resigned breath, and turned around.

For the briefest of instants, something akin to wonder, or maybe hope, flowered inside her, but it was soon gone and she found herself glaring at the house, her lips pressed into a frown.

El was a practical woman. But she was equally a woman of determination. The appearance of the house was more than the affront of someone trespassing on her back forty; it was an insult to her understanding of how the universe worked. She gathered her skirt in her hands and marched through the wheat toward the offensive structure, only to pause at the gate in the picket fence to scowl at the profusion of roses growing on the other side. However much this bothersome addition to the landscape made her mind reel, she had to admit it had a certain charm.

Nonetheless!

El marched up to the house and stretched out her hand to knock on the door. Just as she did so, her stomach turned and the door began to spin. She closed her eyes to clear the vertigo and opened them to find that she was back at the gate in the picket fence. Infuriated, she stomped back to the door, convinced that her attempt to knock had lacked conviction. She raised her arm to give the door a good wallop—

And found herself plopped on her buttocks by the gate, legs sprawled, and with her skirt around her waist like some rag doll carelessly tossed in a bin. Just as the dirt started to chafe through her undergarments, a bird chirped close by. She looked up to find a finch perched atop a brass letter box that sat on the picket fence, pretty as you please. She stared at it for a moment before gathering herself up to head back to her cabin, where she immediately collected her ink pot and stationery and began making her objections known in no uncertain terms.

*17th of May, 1895*

*Greetings,*

*I am Elsbeth Grundy, a retired schoolmarm for Pawnee County, Kansas, and have lived in the same cabin for nigh on forty-six years now, with a good part of that stretch in solitude—a condition suitable to my temperament.*

*You can imagine my surprise then when I woke up to find that overbearing piece of conceit you might otherwise call a house sitting on my back forty.*

*Lacking the disposition for subtlety, I'll get directly to the point. Trespass is dealt with at the business end of a shotgun in these parts!*

*And while it may appear to the contrary, I am not by nature the quarreling type, though that sissy of a representative from the county tax assessor's office might beg to differ. Frankly, I think the reports of his limp are greatly exaggerated.*

*Sincerely,*
*Elsbeth Grundy*

# CHAPTER THREE

## Annie

### MAY 17, 1995

Mission Dolores, San Francisco

*In polite company, she was known as Annabelle Aster. Being a spirited woman, however, she wasn't often found in such company, as she'd determined it to be, more often than not, insincere. And also being a sincere woman in every particular, Annie chose her company for the quality of its character, not its rank.*

Those were quite possibly the finest words ever written. At least to the mind of her precocious, twelve-year-old self, Annie recalled. She rolled her eyes as she took a break from housecleaning to catch her breath—something she was out of more than she cared to admit these days—and reread the note stuffed between the pages of the book she found in a shoe box under the stairwell where she had been cleaning. It was meant as a tribute to Jane Austen—she'd read all her books by the age of eleven—and something of a personal manifesto for a young lady who absolutely refused to go downstairs, despite her godmother's persistent calls, to attend a birthday party where the participants were more interested in a boy's anatomy than syntax. The fact that she would be utterly ignored by her guests was in no way a contributing factor to her decision.

Eyeing a particularly offensive smudge on the banister, Annie broke from the memory and was leaning over to retrieve a dust rag from the floor when she noticed a red splotch blossoming over its cotton weave. A second splotch appeared next to the first, and she let out a sigh, pinching her nose as she sat down in the middle of the hall to wait out the dizzy spell that would inevitably follow.

Crossing her legs, Annie emptied her pockets of several wadded and bloodstained Kleenex before finding one that was unsoiled. She held it to her nose as the *Rick Dees Weekly Top 40* piped through the speakers, recalling something else from that long-forgotten day—the ache that found a home inside her, made up in equal parts of confusion and hurt, and the premonition that life was going to be an ongoing struggle with loneliness. She'd spent the remainder of that afternoon alone in her room, ignoring the knocks at her door, and had gone to bed all cried out.

Fitting in was never in the cards for Annie, unfortunately. Homeschooled by adoptive parents who were university professors and an extremely cultured godmother, she was too cerebral and strong-willed by half, and having no interest whatsoever in the latest release by David Cassidy, she simply wasn't wired like other girls her age. Except for Elizabeth, of course. She had been a childhood kindred spirit, a peer, being the great-granddaughter of Annie's godmother and therefore equally versed in all things Austen.

But with Elizabeth long gone, her adoptive parents dead two years now, and her godmother only a cherished memory, loneliness was a challenge for Annie. Not a day went by that she didn't miss them, but she had her childhood home—a lovingly restored Victorian Stick, all done up in purples and golds, within a stone's throw of Mission Dolores Park—her books, and the company of her best friend, Christian, and that was enough. Or so she told herself anyway.

"Coming in at number twenty-three is Annie Lennox singing 'No More I Love You's,' but first, more than a year after his death, a tribute to Kurt Cobain."

As the distorted guitar riffs collided with Cobain's harum-scarum voice, Annie smiled inwardly and blotted her nose one last time before pulling herself to her feet to test her balance. With a glance at her watch, she quickly cleaned the offending smudge and headed into the kitchen to remove a vial from the refrigerator. Tearing open a bag of thirty-gauge needles and alcohol preps, she loaded a syringe and injected its contents expertly in the fatty tissue next to her belly button. Disposing of the needle and tossing the swabs in the bin, she strolled down the hall and disappeared into a closet.

Her house had six of them, and each was fairly brimming with clothes that were either hung from or draped over every conceivable surface, since Annie was better with piles than hangers. And while she had the usual assortment of distressed jeans, cashmere sweaters, and Doc Martens typical of women her age, they were relegated to a single closet in the master bedroom to make room for her prodigious collection of vintage attire—corsets, flounced petticoats, crinoline, bustles, hoop skirts, and tea gowns, though she favored long sateen and velvet dresses of a cut popular at the turn of the twentieth century that, while clinging tightly to her neck, accentuated her figure.

Annie adored Victorian clothing. And while she usually bowed to modern convention when, say, grocery shopping or hitting the gym, she could be seen, more often than not, sitting in a café or walking through a park looking like a ghost from another age.

And speaking of age, determining Annie's would have been an aggravating exercise. If asked, she might respond that she was "twentysomething," but then again, she might not. She'd consider the question impertinent. And the closer she crept to the "thirty" side of "twentysomething," the more impertinent she'd consider it. But she was undeniably lovely, a fragile beauty, possessing a face that looked as though it had been lifted from a cameo.

She had honeypot eyes—the kind that could warm you from head to toe with a glance—and a smile to shame a politician. Her long auburn hair was often tied up in a bun that no one seemed to notice was a century out of date, but everyone who met her agreed she was a beautiful woman, made all the more so by her curiously clever turn of phrase.

While her natural charms were obvious at a glance, to know Annie intimately, to understand what made her tick, required two additional pieces of information. First, she possessed a rather obscure talent, having the almost singular knack for maintaining her bone china without chips, cracks, or breaks. Indeed, the set she inherited from her godmother—a remarkable woman who insisted on being called Auntie Liza—lacked a single flaw, if one weren't to count its outright ostentation.

The second thing, perhaps a bit more relevant than the first—though Annie would argue the point—had to do with her health. It was uncertain at best. The culprit, you see, was her bone marrow. It wasn't doing its job properly, spinning out just a fraction of the necessary number of red blood cells. Only Annie and her doctor knew the long-term prospects, and that was the way she liked it, pity not being her thing.

Her best friend, Christian, was beginning to suspect something was amiss from the little clues she couldn't help but leave behind, however.

Unaware that her unblemished record with all things porcelain, as well as a good many other things, was about to change, Annie emerged from the closet sporting a straw boater's hat, complete with ivory-colored tulle. She wandered into the kitchen to grab the cup of tea she'd left steeping before heading out back to her English tea garden. Stepping through her back door, Annie froze, too dazed to notice, let alone do anything about it, while her teacup slowly slipped from its saucer to break into three large pieces and a puddle of Earl Grey on the gravel of her garden walkway, a walkway with which she was unfamiliar.

She stared at the fragments with hardly a trace of emotion as a faint tingling stirred in her stomach and absentmindedly slipped the saucer into one of the pockets of her sateen dressing gown.

Leaving the pieces of the cup behind, she numbly walked down the path. There were roses everywhere—red roses, yellow roses, blue roses, and roses in every shade in between. There were shrubs and vines and carpets of roses. Roses were draped over trellises, bubbled from planter boxes, and piled over each other in beds like parfait rings. There were roses the size of her thumbnail that grew in clusters like grapes to roses the size of a dinner plate. And, blanketing the ground as if dabbed onto a canvas by Van Gogh were rose petals loosened by the breeze.

Annie cupped a blossom in her hand, scaring off a ladybug before she even thought to make a wish. Bewildered, she followed it down the path until she reached a picket fence bordering a wheat field. Weaving between its planks were roses as pink and pale as a baby's cheeks, and atop it, perched on the gatepost, was a brass letter box. She glanced at it while running her hand timidly along the top boards of the fence and looked uncertainly out over the field.

Gathering her courage with a quick intake of breath, Annie stepped through the gate and began to wade, waist deep, into the frothy terrain, pausing when she spied a little cabin on the horizon with a wisp of smoke floating from the corner of its roof. There were no cabins in San Francisco of which she was aware. But, then again, there were no wheat fields either.

Curiosity overcame her, and Annie made a giddy dash across the field in the direction of the cabin, only slowing long enough to admire a scarecrow that bore a striking resemblance to Mark Twain. Odd, she thought, but not nearly as odd as the wooden sign with hand-painted letters that she passed a few minutes later. It read: *Pawnee County, Kansas. Pop. 673. Five Miles Due East of Sage as the Crow Flies.* She stored that information for future consideration and arrived breathless and dizzy at the cabin.

Finding herself sitting in a rather undignified heap, Annie realized that, only seconds before, she'd been about to knock on the cabin's back door. Being a quick study, she didn't need to be taught the same lesson twice. She pondered the existence of the cabin, the garden in her backyard, the state of things in general, and made a decision. She chuckled drunkenly, dusted off her hat, and hurried home to compose a letter.

Gazing at the brass mailbox as she opened the gate to the picket fence, and feeling a little silly, Annie gave into temptation and opened the lid. In it sat a parched-looking envelope, the words *Greetings, Neighbor* written on its face. Prying open the seal, Annie headed inside, reading the letter with an intensity that had her lips forming the words on the page.

Once seated at her rolltop desk, Annie tapped her pen against her front teeth, chuckled once more, and began to write…

May 17, 1995

Dear Miss Grundy—

I was surprised to find your letter in my mailbox this morning, primarily because I was unaware that I owned one at all.

Let me address my alleged trespass on your property straightaway. I say "alleged" because, from my perspective, your back forty just landed itself in my garden.

The fact that I live in San Francisco, along with my garden, seems entirely relevant to this exchange, even if I can't immediately explain why, and is a matter we shouldn't take too lightly.

There's more, and you might want to sit down for this one, dear. It has to do with the date at the top of your letter. You see, today is May 17, 1995, for me. So, I'm left to wonder how my back door leads to your back forty with a century and half a country between them.

Let me introduce myself properly. My name is Annabelle Aster. It's a bit of a mouthful, so just call me Annie. I'm twentysomething (mumble, mumble), live for books, adore Jane Austen, can't bake to save my soul, and have a collection of Victorian apparel that would make Cora Pearl blush. While I'm not working at the moment, having decided to take a sabbatical for personal reasons, I do volunteer at the food co-op in the Haight-Ashbury three days a week. That's a start, but if there is anything else you'd like to know, simply ask.

I understand that you're upset. Perhaps I should be too. My reaction, though, has been altogether different. I'm over the moon! We have a mystery here. And until I find an explanation to our shared conundrum, I will simply offer my apologies. Though for what, I'm not certain.

Sincerely,
Annabelle Aster

# CHAPTER FOUR

## Again and Again

It was a curious thing, seeing the face again. Just last Saturday, as he was staring at the surf by Crissy Field, Christian had caught a glimpse of the face on the jogging path and was instantly struck by an uncomfortable familiarity, something akin to déjà vu. The moment was quickly forgotten. He saw the face again only yesterday when he entered the supermarket, spying it out of the corner of his eye as the automatic door opened with a pneumatic hiss. The prickly sensation returned like an itch under the skin with the rush of cold air. He hesitated, trying to get a better view, but was hurried forward by a chain of customers marching through the door like a giant ungainly centipede, its legs rippling inharmoniously beneath sweat and nylon-cotton blends.

And as he was crossing Church and Twentieth on his way to Annie's house, Christian saw the face for the third time. His own had been pressed, inevitably, in a book. Christian was something of a reading opportunist—science fiction, primarily. He read while he ate breakfast. He read on his lunch break. He read before he slipped off to sleep each night. He even read while crossing Church Street, ignorant of gathering rain clouds—not the most brilliant activity if his aim was survival. But Christian wasn't a survivalist. If he were, he'd work in any field but the one in which he found himself. He worked in finance.

Christian glanced up from his book just in time to see the face walk past. The street noises stretched, deepened, and slurred as he considered the face and struggled to determine what about it made him so uneasy. His mind kicked into hyperdrive, which had the strange effect of reducing all movement to one-quarter time. The face froze only a few feet away, an enigmatic smile directed toward him. The person who belonged to the face was wearing a T-shirt under an orange flannel button-down with faded brown corduroys. If not for his surprise, Christian would have laughed at the corduroys. If he had more time, he would have found himself tickled by the slightly off-center combination of pattern and color in the shirt and pants. But the moment, however strangely long, was still just a moment.

The cars crawled. A hummingbird inched forward like a slow-motion sequence in a National Geographic special, its wings undulating in the exquisite fashion of a Japanese fan dancer. A dog floated upward in the park across the street, a look of pure joy frozen on its face, eyes focused on a Frisbee hovering inches from eager jaws and spinning so slowly that you could read the word *Wham-O* on it. Then, whoosh...time repaired itself and Christian was walking all too quickly past the face with the secret smile.

Even after the man disappeared over a hill in the park, Christian wondered about the face and why it had muscled in on his consciousness. He'd never seen it before last Saturday. Or had he? Could the face belong to a spirit of his former life converging on his present? Did it belong to a Texas transplant like himself? That could be bad. Christian had left behind some painful memories. He loved the state of his birth, he really did. It just seemed evident to him that Texas's rugged landscape bred equally rugged people, and having judged himself as deficient in certain qualities essential to the tall and the proud, Christian had sought sanctuary farther west.

Regardless, the face seemed to belong to someone he should remember. But he didn't.

Feeling ignorant and insecure, Christian stared in the direction where the man with the secret smile had disappeared and wondered if trouble was brewing. As if in answer, a drop of rain splattered on his cheek. He glanced at the gathering clouds, all bloated and black, with a bemused shake of his head, then crossed the street, walked down the block, and trotted up the crisply painted stairs to ring Annie's doorbell.

"Annie?" Christian called, rapping on the door. "Annie!" He shuffled his feet and peered through the lead-glass pane, looking for a flicker of movement in the foyer.

As usual, on the days he had tea at Annie's, Christian had given up his customary T-shirt and jeans for khakis, a collared, short-sleeved pullover, and black lace-up shoes. It was starting to sprinkle a bit more earnestly, and he was quickly moving from damp to wet as the wind drove rain onto the front landing. He knocked, and after a moment he banged, but there was still nothing. As many times as Annie had told him that her home was his, he never felt comfortable simply barging in. It just wasn't a "southern" thing to do. But there was nothing for it unless he wanted to fill his shoes with water. Christian took out his keys, unlocked the door, and stepped inside, picking up the daily booty scattered on the floorboards beneath the mail slot. He glanced nervously down the hall before scanning the return addresses quickly, making a mental note of one from California Pacific Medical Center.

Tossing the stack on the console table, he walked through the foyer, shoes squeaking, and past the fainting room where local lore had it that Beverly Aster, Annie's bodacious great-grandmother, had briefly retired to loosen her corset during a formal dinner party (as was customary then). Thinking better of it, she'd tossed it and a few other "inconsequentials" aside in a snit as "devices of female subjugation" and had boldly strolled out to greet guests in little more than her silk undergarments. Needless to say, there had been more fainting throughout the remainder of the house than in the room designated for it that night. Christian paused before the door, recalling the story, and smiled to himself before quietly stepping in the hall to peer up the stairwell.

"Annie…you home?" He drummed his fingers on the banister a few times before hearing a voice drift thinly through the house.

"I'm in the solarium."

Christian walked briskly down the hall, slowing as he entered the living room. The grandfather clock that normally slumbered in the corner awoke to announce the hour with four tired gongs while he looked around. Despite being quite large, the room felt cozy with its oversize, overstuffed furniture and rich, dark woods. Below the enormous bay window was a built-in seat covered with a crimson velvet cushion that ran from sill to sill.

The room's central feature was an enormous Persian rug. It normally housed a coffee table sandwiched between a pair of matching sofas but was, on this particular day, overrun by a mound of cushions. There was also an empty wine bottle—Christian laid odds on Cabernet—a plateful of crumbs whose origins were betrayed by a bag of Pepperidge Farm Chessmen cookies, and scattered reading material, fallout from another of Annie's late-night reading sessions.

Christian took a breath and let it out, caught between a grin and a grimace. Though he wasn't sure that an entire bottle of wine was good for Annie's mysterious condition, it was her life, and there was something about the scene he found oddly reassuring. Annie was such a force of nature that it was nice to be reminded that she was also quite human. When he threatened to put her on a pedestal, all he had to do was take a quick peek in one of her closets or inside her fridge. Aside from her garden, which she maintained to perfection, Annie was, quite simply, a slob, and chaos followed in her wake. She would go on a bender from time to time, manically washing, cleaning, and organizing, but her natural state was dishevelment, and her home would soon reflect it.

Christian had recommended more than once as he put away dishes he'd found in the unlikeliest places—he'd found a teacup inside the grandfather clock once—that Annie hire a housekeeper, but she wouldn't budge. She was quite pigheaded about it. In fact, she was quite pigheaded about many things. But her stubbornness was balanced by her loyalty, her sloppiness by her style, and her self-indulgence by her generosity. To be candid, he found Annie's idiosyncrasies endearing. They made her more interesting and lovable, because without them, she would seem out of arm's reach. *Perhaps that is the way of friends, to love one another for their imperfections, not despite them*, he decided.

Rolling his eyes at this awkward philosophy, Christian gathered the cushions and arranged them on the window seat. He quickly collected the saucer, glass, and reading material and was assessing the need for a vacuum cleaner when he heard, "Dawdle all you like, Mr. Keebler, but I'm sticking to the solarium."

"I'm cleaning up your mess," he yelled, snatching up the last magazine. He ran into the kitchen to dump the dishes in the sink, doing a double take as his eyes wandered across the back door leading to her garden. *That's new.* The thought was a charitable one, to say the least, considering the door's appearance. Further evaluation was curtailed when Annie called out a second time, and he hurried into the next room.

As he closed the solarium door behind him, the doorknob came off in his hand. The thing had been broken for months, yet Annie had never gotten around to fixing it. He jammed it in place, made another mental note to get it repaired—which he promptly forgot—and turned around.

Annie was sitting in her wicker chaise beneath a riot of plants, staring out the window with a distant expression. Her left hand was resting on her cheek, and lying beneath her right hand on the arm of the chaise was a piece of odd-looking parchment. To Christian's surprise, Annie was still in her morning robe, and her hair, usually gathered atop her head in a chignon, was tied back in a simple ponytail.

He dropped the Simpsons comic with which he planned to tease her onto the wrought iron occasional table and looked at his watch. "Did I… Today is Wednesday, right?"

Still looking out the solarium window, Annie replied thoughtfully, "Yes, why?"

"You're, uh…" He pointed shyly, wiggling his finger in place of the words that escaped him. "Are you having one of your spells, Annie?" he asked finally.

He'd said the word before he could stop himself, and he rolled his eyes. *Spells.* Annie was endlessly amused by his southern colloquialisms. She said they were part of his charm, but he was always left feeling like a bumpkin, nonetheless.

After a quick assessment of her clothes and the impossible state of her hair, Annie wrinkled her nose, letting a flutter of laughter bubble from her throat. "No, I'm not having one of my *spells*, and you're just in time." She shifted in her chaise, adding, "I have a riddle that needs answering, and I don't think I can do it on my own."

# CHAPTER FIVE

## A Door

Annie glanced at the comic book, then turned and smiled at Christian, struck as always by his physical contradictions.

Indeed, it was the contrary nature of his eyes that first caught her attention. She'd been taking her morning walk through Dolores Park and was making for her favorite bench, only to discover that it was occupied by a young man reading a book. She'd found the situation annoying—that is, until the moment he met her gaze. His eyes—deep, dark, and blue, with lush lashes under heavy brows—clearly told a story that she found herself wanting to hear, yet they sat on such a boyish face.

"Good morning," she'd said.

"Good m-m-mmmmmorning," he'd replied, peering bashfully above the pages.

He was a stutterer. *And* socially awkward. She adored him instantly and invited herself to sit down.

They'd talked through the morning. While he'd stuttered quite a bit, his face locked in an expression of intense concentration as he struggled through the simplest of sentences, and spoke timidly, as if every word were an apology, Annie had found him irresistible and did something quite out of character. She invited him to tea the very next day. And on the same day the next week. And the next.

It was slow going at first, their afternoon teas, but by the third visit, his stutter had practically ceased altogether, though he maintained a habit of speaking deliberately as they talked sometimes into the wee hours.

Nothing was too sacred or too personal, and Annie found that Christian had a way of smiling with a certain sadness at the center of his eyes while telling heartbreaking stories of the bullying he'd suffered growing up in Texas.

And then, of course, there was the accident. What could be said about that? It had changed everything, though he actually couldn't tell her much about it. A head trauma had erased great chunks of his memory, willy-nilly, but she'd learned more than she'd cared to when her curiosity got the better of her one day. It nearly broke her heart to look at the photograph she'd found on microfiche at the library—Christian being lifted onto a gurney in the foreground, limp as a forgotten saint, his arm dangling over its side, and in the distance behind him, a spray of water arcing from a fireman's hose onto the blaze that had charred the light post around which his car was pulled like taffy. The article was titled "Miracle on Folsom Street" because no one could explain how he'd been found thirty feet from the site of the crash, unconscious on the sidewalk. By all rights, he should have been dead.

The constant bullying had weakened him, left him uncertain, while the accident had shackled him with recurring hallucinations—his word, not hers—and, of all things…a stutter.

She'd asked him once if he'd ever considered the possibility that his hallucinations were something more, but quickly backpedaled when she saw how the word *visions* affected him.

The sum total of this—his stories, his past—made her forget the thousand little hurts of her childhood but often left her weeping for his long after he'd gone home and she'd crawled into bed to stare at the ceiling.

A year after their first meeting, they were still taking tea every Wednesday at 4:00 p.m., and in that time, Christian had come to be very dear to Annie.

He pulled up the ottoman partnered to a wicker chair, plopped himself down, and waited patiently for her to explain herself.

Sliding her legs over the side of the chaise, Annie leaned toward him, her hands gripping the parchment. Standing abruptly, she placed her hands on her hips. "How's your mood?" she asked diplomatically.

Christian wasn't the only person who could speak in code. The appropriate translation of her question would have been "Have you witnessed any hallucinations today, and, if so, how many?"

He held up two fingers, as his lips curled into a sort of sidewise *S* tucked into the corner of his mouth, Christian's version of an eye roll, and one that couldn't help but tickle Annie every time he produced it.

"You okay?" she asked, fighting a twitch in the corner of her own.

When he nodded, she glanced toward the back, all business once again. "Good, because I need to show you something, and it might be a bit of a shocker."

He blinked.

Annie nodded at his confusion and led him through the solarium and to the kitchen. Casting a glance at the back door as if it had somehow betrayed her, Annie walked over and threw it open.

Christian wasn't looking at the door, however. He was watching her as he whispered, "Annie, it's raining outside."

She smiled. "Not where we're going," she said and took his hand, leading him into the back.

Thirty minutes later, she led him to the living room sofa and, when he was seated, disappeared into the kitchen. "This will help settle your nerves," she said, returning with a cup of tea. To his surprise, she carefully set a Xanax on the saucer next to it.

He glanced from the pill to Annie, quickly shook his head, and stared at the coffee table where the broken pieces of china—casualties of her early-morning adventure—were resting. After a moment, he lifted his cup. It rattled noticeably against the saucer, and despite the care with which he brought it to his lips, tea sloshed onto his face. He reached for a napkin while appraising Annie from under his brow. She seemed strangely unruffled by the experience, even though her pride and joy, her collection of china, had acquired its first blemish.

When he'd set the cup and napkin aside, Annie handed him the piece of parchment. As he started to unfold it, she put her hand over his. "It's from my new neighbor," she said.

Christian frowned, momentarily confused by her comment. Then his eyes lit with alarm, and he set the letter on the coffee table, shaking his head.

Annie nodded, then gestured to the letter. "Go on," she said.

He glanced at it with renewed skittishness, the look on his face suggesting that he expected the thing to explode at any minute, scattering shards of insanity all over the living room. Reluctantly, he picked it up and started reading. When he was done, Christian put the letter on the table, covered it with one hand, and reached for his teacup.

Annie watched him drain it. "Well?" she said.

"It's a j-j-j…jjj—" His shoulders slumped. "Joke," he said, grimacing.

Annie wasn't too surprised that Christian had stammered. Acute stress could be a trigger, and this situation certainly qualified. "No, I think not," she said.

"Annie," he said, drawing her name out. He pointed to the header, then his fingers began to flutter as his hand danced in the air, a sure sign he was going to struggle for words. "It's d-da-dated 1895, for C-Christ's sake."

"And *you* just walked through a wheat field in the middle of San Francisco." She watched in wry amusement as Christian considered her comment and attempted the tricky mental adjustments that would reconcile the last half hour with his prior lifetime of experience.

An incredulous chirp broke from his throat. "Eighteen ninety-five," he said after taking a few breaths. Repeating the number slowly, he visibly relaxed and looked at Annie in wonder. Chuckling, he added, "If Miss Grundy has lived there for f-fuh-forty-six years, then that cabin's been in your backyard since ..." His voice trailed off as he did the math in his head. "Eighteen forty-nine."

He looked at the ceiling, a bemused smile plastered on his face. But it didn't last long, slowly melting to a frown. Tensing again, he rounded on Annie. "Aren't you the least bit"—he tapped the table a few times, a trick he'd learned to avoid stuttering—"alarmed... by the fact that you're holding a century-old letter, and it's written to you personally?"

Annie shrugged. "I don't see why I should be. The sky hasn't fallen."

Christian reached for the teacup, grunting, then snatched his hand away as he was hit by another thought. "Or maybe this letter was written yesterday. If that's the case, you just received a correspondence"—he looked up, meeting her eyes before finishing his thought—"from a ghost." He stood and began to work up a real head of steam as he paced, all traces of the stutter gone. "This is creepy. I mean, really creepy. Ghosts and time warps. Like something right out of—"

"I'm not sure you're being helpful, dear," Annie said quietly.

He paused with his mouth lodged open to find her staring with a slight arch to her brow. There was a smile hiding behind the line of her mouth—just a suggestion, an upward curve at the corners—that calmed him right down again. That was the way their relationship worked. She was the rock while he was the breeze.

"Well, it *is* creepy," he said under his breath before dropping onto the sofa with a grunt. "And what about her not-too-subtle threat?" he asked.

"Miss Grundy's just a little hot under the collar," Annie said, seemingly unconcerned. "I suppose I would be too, if someone was trespassing on my land."

"She *is* trespassing." Christian paused, wrinkling his brow. "Sort of."

"Trespass or not, she just lost her back forty while I've added a wheat field. I'd say I'm getting the better end of the deal."

Christian shook his head, marveling at her unflappability. "Okay, let me think," he said, moving on. "You don't like the ghost theory then."

She shook her head.

"Well, was this the first…" Christian broke from his train of thought. "I mean, when did you first find Kansas in your garden?" Struck by the strangeness of the question, he blinked, then clasped both hands over his head, giggling.

"This morning." She kicked his foot. "And it isn't proper to titter like that in polite company," she added.

"How would you know? I'm the only company you keep." He threw himself back onto the sofa, laughing even harder as she aimed another kick in his direction. "What's different then?" he asked, hanging his arm limply over the armrest. "How about that—"

"Door!" Annie finished Christian's sentence for him, though he'd planned to use the word *monstrosity*. "Of course," she added, and darted to the kitchen, leaving him to collect the teacups and follow.

Annie was staring at the back door as Christian entered the kitchen. She turned, beaming from ear to ear as he leaned against a counter to give the door a more thorough looking over. It was a heavy, menacing thing, painted Radio-Flyer-red with intricate carvings, like characters from some ancient alphabet running along its perimeter. Carved boldly in the center were planets, constellations, and a variety of astrological symbols. It was, frankly speaking, the ugliest thing he'd laid eyes on in a long time.

"Hideous, don't you think?" she said, mercifully saving him from telling a white lie, as she ran her hand reverently over a series of runes. "God, I love it." She gave the door a quick pat, then strode to a buffet-style cabinet and started to rummage through a stack of papers on one of its shelves. "I had it installed yesterday. Bought it at that quaint little antique shop on California Street." She bit her thumb, looking around. "Now where did I put the receipt?"

"In the 'stupid things I buy without thinking' drawer?" Christian parked himself on a bench in the built-in kitchen nook and set the teacups on the table. "Just trying to help," he added, grinning when she gave him a look that dropped the room temperature a degree or two.

Annie turned back to the buffet and, glancing sideways at him, slowly opened the center drawer. "Ah." Holding up a business card with *The Antiquarian* written across the top, she decided to ignore his self-satisfied air and said, "Now that's interesting." She leaned back against the buffet. "The salesperson gave me quite a line. What was his name?" She tapped the card against her lips. "Adam. He said the door had been in the store's possession forever, and despite having been sold on three separate occasions, it kept finding its way back like a bad penny. There was also some rumor of a curse." She paused, frowning. "It was all so mysterious, and the door was so ridiculous that I couldn't help myself. I bought the thing on the spot."

Christian began running a finger along a line of wood grain of the table as Annie started digging through drawers again. In a sure sign he'd recovered from his earlier shock—Christian was blessed with a short attention span—he said offhandedly, "Oh, before I forget, I just saw 'the face' again as I was crossing Church Street."

"That's nice, dear," Annie mumbled. She continued to flip through a pile of papers until Christian's comment sank in. She looked up. "What face? The one from your past?"

He brought the empty cup to his lips, frowning. "The one that *might* be from my past," he clarified.

"This could be good," she said, closing the drawer. "Perhaps he's a missing half brother. Or, better yet, an archenemy with a score to settle."

"There's something… I don't know." His eyes flicked in her

direction before refocusing on the cup. "Maybe? I can't put my finger on it."

Her task forgotten for the moment, Annie dropped onto the bench across from Christian. He was peering beneath the teacup for the maker's mark, but she wasn't fooled. She poked him on the chest in a very deliberate manner. "You can't just drop that on me and clam up. Spill the beans."

"I just saw him crossing Church and Twentieth on my way here." He lowered the cup. "It happened pretty fast. And I had my face in a book, as usual—"

Annie smacked him lightly across the back of the head, having witnessed him flirt with disaster time and again as a result of that unfortunate habit. He continued without batting an eye, adding, "I looked up and there he was."

"What does he look like?" she asked.

"Sorry?"

"What does he *look* like, Christian?"

"Kind of comical, actually. He was wearing a T-shirt under an orange flannel button-down and brown corduroys like some weird seventies throwback."

"Don't be dull, dear. Him! What does *he* look like?" Annie smelled a rat. This was the third time Christian had seen the face, and he was being a bit dodgy about the entire matter. Christian wasn't dodgy. So something was up.

"I don't know," he said vaguely. "Just a face. But I can't shake the feeling that I'm supposed to know him. Or that he knows me."

"Christian."

"Hmm?"

Annie lifted her cup, raising an eyebrow. "I'm not kidding," she said, snaking the cup across the table to hover over his trousers.

Well, actually, she was—sort of. Even so, Christian cocked his head with a "you wouldn't dare" expression. Properly provoked, she leaned across the table, smiling coyly.

"All right, all right!" He pressed himself to the back of the bench, grinning. "Let me think." His eyes lost focus as he said, "Medium height. Trim. Blond hair cut short and turning to silver on the sideburns. Light blue eyes, maybe? Early thirties. I think he had a goatee. Umm…that's about it."

Annie leaned forward. "That's it?" She gave Christian a measured stare as he shifted awkwardly on the bench, then sat back with a nod.

*What an eventful day*, she thought as delight began to play around her eyes. *I break my teacup, first in the annals of my life. I find roses and a wheat field in my backyard. There is a cabin where the corner of Dolores and Eighteenth, by all rights, should be. I receive a mysterious letter from an even more mysterious neighbor. And, to put the icing on the cake, my Christian might have a mystery of his own.*

A most topsy-turvy, yet satisfying day, all in all.

# CHAPTER SIX

## Prudence Travesty's Vintage Clothier

### MAY 20, 1995

Haight-Ashbury is the one place where the only people to stand out are those who try not to. It is a crossroads where stragglers, clinging desperately to the Summer of Love's memory, rub elbows with their spiritual heirs—the goths, neo-goths, metalheads, hip-hop bandits, and drag divas—and is wrapped up in a psychedelic explosion of flower power, hemp, DayGlo retailers, and one lone woman walking down the block in cerise sateen.

Annie stepped out of the Green Grocer loaded with organic produce and promptly collided into another woman. They knelt, echoing apologies while scrambling for scattered avocados and butterscotch scones. Once her bag was refilled, Annie broke away with a nod and was strolling past the display window at Prudence Travesty's Vintage Clothier when an insistent tapping caught her attention. Looking up, she saw a petite older woman, turned out in Chanel, standing in the window and holding a gown up for her inspection.

Annie ogled the garment in obvious fascination and rushed into the store. "Mrs. Weatherall, what do we have here?" she asked as she hurried to place the groceries on the sales counter.

Eyeing Annie over her reading glasses, Mrs. Weatherall draped the gown across the counter and said in a clipped, New York baritone that sounded like she'd lit up her fair share of Virginia Slims, "You almost walked right by."

"The insolence." Annie whisked the gown from the counter to stroke the fabric. If she were a cat, she'd have purred. "Have you been saving it for me?"

Mrs. Weatherall nodded. "I hated to think that this one should end up at a costume party," she said. "And what was going on out there?" She nodded in the direction of the grocery store.

Annie held the dress against her torso and admired herself in the mirror before turning to face Mrs. Weatherall. Her expression reflected something between embarrassment and chagrin and sat strangely on her face. "A chance meeting," she said. "She bought the house three doors down."

"Has she moved in then?"

"Two years ago." Annie's face reddened slightly before she turned back to her reflection.

Fully aware of Annie's antisocial habits, and not surprised in the least by her confession, Mrs. Weatherall merely chuckled. She pointed to the dress. "It reminds me of the first time you came into the store," she said. "Do you remember?"

Still glued to the mirror, Annie's eyes crinkled as her lips curved into a smile. "The lace Easter dress. I was ten. Or was I eleven? Auntie Liza dressed me up with a bonnet, parasol, and matching gloves. It was to be a surprise for Mom." She glanced slyly at Mrs. Weatherall. "I seem to recall that she drew the line at the pearl choker, though."

"You were such a strange little creature. Seemed to live with one foot in another world. Came through my door that day sounding like Elizabeth Bennet from *Pride and Prejudice*. And you were absolutely infatuated with that dress." She strode to Annie's side and untangled some of the appliqué on the bodice. "What ever happened to your Aunt Liza? She was a formidable woman."

"Formidable?" Annie smirked as she rubbed the appliqué between her fingers. "Don't tell me you're still smarting over that little dustup after all these years? What was that about, anyway?"

Caught off guard by the question, Mrs. Weatherall turned a trifle pink herself before replying, "I chided your aunt for letting you play hooky, and she..." She paused, searching for a diplomatic explanation. "Well, let's just say that she taught me to mind my own business."

Annie blinked, looking scandalized. "Did she even bother to tell you I was homeschooled?" Seeing Mrs. Weatherall's look of consternation, she burst into laughter. "Apparently not." Annie smiled sadly. "Auntie Liza died the following year," she said as she stepped back to admire the dress in the mirror. "She wasn't really my aunt, you know. She was my godmother."

"No, I had no idea." Mrs. Weatherall reached for Annie's hand. "Look at you now," she said. "All grown up, as strange as ever and even more beautiful." Secretly, she also thought that Annie looked too pale, but she wasn't about to say so. "You've been popping into my store for, what, fifteen years now?"

"Something like that."

"And I bet you wouldn't know a pair of jeans if you tripped over them."

Annie danced several steps of the waltz, then twirled in circles, causing the dress to fan out around her before collapsing in a rich melody of tinkling beads. Short of breath, she placed the dress on the counter and wiped the sheen of perspiration from her forehead. What little color she had was quickly draining away, and Mrs. Weatherall couldn't help but notice that Annie's hand was trembling.

By the time Annie had stirred through the contents of her bag to pull out a packet of cheese and crackers, her hands were shaking so badly that she couldn't get a proper grip on the cellophane wrapper.

Alarmed, Mrs. Weatherall snatched it from her hand and tore

the packet open, watching as Annie quickly downed a couple. "Are you all right, my dear?" she asked.

Annie tried to smile reassuringly as she nibbled on the last cracker, but it wasn't very convincing. She grabbed her cell phone, a novel thing forced on her by Christian, and punched in some numbers as she stepped across the room, talking quietly into the receiver. "I'll never remember that," she said, striding back to the counter to grab a pen from her purse.

One step ahead, Mrs. Weatherall reached into a tray to grab a piece of paper, but set it aside to stare at the pen in Annie's hand.

Annie looked from the pen to Mrs. Weatherall and spoke into the phone. "Can I call you right back?" she asked and disconnected the line. She sighed, glaring at the pen as if it were gossiping out of turn—the California Pacific Oncology logo stamped on its surface in white lettering. "This will be our little secret, yes?"

"But, my dear—"

"Please." Annie put the pen away. "And would you mind terribly calling me a cab?"

Elsbeth pried open the door to her cabin and stared suspiciously at the letter box sitting at the end of the footpath leading from her front door. It had been three days since she'd heard from her new neighbor and she still wasn't sure how she felt about the silence. Certainly, she was glad to be left alone, but three days without communication did more than push the boundaries of propriety. It was simply bad manners. And the letter box appeared entirely too smug, as if teasing her by saying, "You haven't lifted a finger. Why should she?"

Exasperated by her own peevishness, Elsbeth determined that a quick peek inside was, in no way, an indicator of her eagerness for more correspondence, and a walk would do her good. She wandered to the end of the path and brushed a spider from the lid.

May 20, 1995

Hello!

I apologize for the delay, but I've been a bit under the weather and, to be honest, thought it best to give you a few days to adjust to the change in our mutual circumstances.

It was a fair enough beginning, Elsbeth thought. There's not much you can do about a cold. She waded through the letter like a guilty pleasure, torn between annoyance and enchantment with Miss Aster's obvious enthusiasm. Regardless, she read each line carefully, only pausing to sniff when asked what led to such an early retirement and at Miss Aster's suggestion that an ongoing correspondence might prove to be of some interest to both parties—not for the suggestion, but for having the presumption to natter away as if Elsbeth's acceptance was a matter of course.

There was the requisite polite chatter, and Elsbeth begrudgingly admitted that her new neighbor's diction was surprisingly adequate, despite the occasional odd turn of phrase. There was also some talk about a door that El found curious. Then Miss Aster advanced a number of peculiar philosophical questions and general folderol regarding Elsbeth's existence, which served only to elicit another sniff. As if El needed to confirm she existed. The fact that her life was unremarkable made it no less real. And to suggest she may be a ghost! Bristling, Elsbeth prepared to toss the letter aside when her eyes lit on the final paragraph.

I've enclosed a recent photograph. My friend Christian took it as I was sitting on a bench in Dolores Park.

Delightedly,
Annabelle Aster

P.S. I offer a topic for discussion. The past is nothing more than the present romanticized, while the future is history with imagination. Any thoughts?

El swayed gently in her rocker and shook the envelope until the photograph in question fluttered out to land in her lap. One glance at the uncanny image, and she froze—an unexpected pinprick of delight lighting in her chest. Tearing her eyes away, El snatched her spectacles from their perch on her nose and stared at the walls to regain the comfort of her natural belligerence. When her spine became as rigid as her resolve, El replaced them to dare a second look.

To her nineteenth-century eyes, this was not a photograph. It was a window.

And on the other side was Annabelle. She sat on a wooden park bench with a panoramic cityscape, unlike anything in Elsbeth's experience, in the background. The park opened behind her like a fan, sloping downward before easing itself onto an expanse of lawn in the distance. But it was the church bell tower at the base of the park, its dome almost pulsing off the photographic paper in brilliant turquoise, that did Elsbeth in.

The cityscape spread out behind the tower, and something about its complex geometry of cubes and rectangular prisms reminded Elsbeth of a geode. There were glimpses of a bay showing between the buildings in the distance, and the sun was just breaking through the trees in the foreground to scatter whipped-cream dollops of light everywhere.

Elsbeth turned her attention to the figure on the bench. Annabelle was wearing a high-necked, champagne-colored dress that shimmered in the dappled sunlight. Her hat had a large brim and a diaphanous wraparound scarf. She was relaxing with her elbow on the park bench arm rail, her fist resting on the side of her head, obviously flirting with the camera.

Annabelle was beautiful. And her eyes, most especially her eyes, revealed a woman of character. Rubbing her thumb across the edge of the photo, Elsbeth reluctantly decided that something about Annie appealed to her.

Despite that admission, however, she did not intend to make things easy for her new correspondent.

*20th of May, 1895*

*Dear Miss Aster,*

*Well, truth be told, I'm a bit of a suffragist who was coaxed into early retirement by the powers that be when, during a class discussion on that very topic, I cut off an unenlightened (and smelly!) young man by saying, "Johnny! Didn't your mother ever teach you not to speak with your mouth full of stupid?" We have an informal three-strike rule in Pawnee County, which I managed to exceed with that single sentence, apparently. (Nobody told me Johnny's father was on the school board.) When, during the inquiry, it was suggested that my pension be halved, I announced I would be writing my memoirs, complete with anecdotes on my former students. The matter was dropped.*

*All that being said, I have yet to decide whether your letter is welcome, as, frankly, I remain more comfortable thinking of you as a burr in my stocking. In truth, I originally hoped you were nothing more than a bout of mental indigestion and would disappear with a good dosing of baking soda and apple cider vinegar. It appears, however, that you are here to stay, and through no fault of your own.*

*And while it is possible I was a bit hasty in my original assessment, and even less circumspect in making my feelings known, I'm not thrilled with the prospect of sharing my damn wheat field!*

*I'd like to start again by stating that your diction is surprisingly tolerable for an interloper. Before you think I'm one to toss compliments about cavalierly, however, let me caution you. I am not. But language is dear to me and I appreciate its elegant employment.*

*The door you mentioned intrigues me and bears investigation. Logic leads me to wonder if, while you found it there, it may not have been made here. I can think of nothing else that explains your presence.*

*Am I a ghost, you ask? I'm certainly old. Perhaps even a bit dusty. But I think not. How can one be sure, however? Would a ghost know itself to be such? What a poor state for one, if it is required to carry into the beyond every ache and pain earned in life. I snap and pop with every movement, an uncongenial condition for haunting.*

*Thank you for the "photograph." I was quite taken by it. Enclosed is one of me at the state fair a few years ago.*

*As to your question in regard to past and present, I must admit to a decided lack of an opinion, being no philosopher.*

*In Your Confidence,*
*Elsbeth Grundy*

Setting the letter aside, Annie shook the faded envelope and a small photograph—more brown and yellow than black and white—fell out. That the photographic paper wasn't worn by time seemed significant, though she didn't know why. *El, State Fair, 1889* was written on the back. A large splotch of black ink sat just below the number nine with another drop at the bottom. Annie turned the photograph over. She was simultaneously drawn to and taken aback by the diminutive figure in the foreground. Elsbeth was standing proudly, if not defiantly, before the camera in a field just outside the fairgrounds, bearing an uncanny likeness to the spinster daughter in the painting *American Gothic*.

Her eyes spoke of hidden knowledge, yet the line of her mouth was hard, curving neither up nor down, and Annie wondered what type of life had left Elsbeth unable to smile at a fair.

Couples were promenading in the background between booths, food stalls, and other amusements. Overall, the photo felt harsh, its austerity matched by Elsbeth's clothes. She was wearing what appeared to be a dark cotton dress with long sleeves and lace around the neckline and cuffs. The dress had no other ornamentation except for a row of three large wooden buttons running down the bodice. Elsbeth held a slim book close to her side. Annie pulled out a magnifying glass and could just make out *Common Sense*, by Thomas Paine.

She reached for the letter. By the end of the first paragraph, she'd slumped into the sofa, giggling. Elsbeth was certainly a no-nonsense character, and Annie took an instant liking to her. More than that, however, Elsbeth's compliment had challenged her, and she was determined to live up to it. Blowing a wisp of hair from her eyes, she drummed her fingers on the sofa's arm before making her way to the desk. Pulling out paper and pen, she began to write—tapping into her inner Jane Austen, as Christian would put it.

May 20, 1995

Dearest El,

Thank you for the compliment, and do please call me Annie, for heaven's sake. We'll never get anywhere with this "Miss Aster, Ms. Grundy" routine.

Both my parents were writers who taught me to appreciate

prose in all its forms. But it was something my Auntie Liza said many years ago that changed forever the way I thought of words. "If the command of language dictates the elegance of our thoughts," she said, tapping my nose for attention, "then those which people think today must be dull, indeed. There is very little pride in written or spoken words, Annie, and people wield them like a sledgehammer rather than a brush. I am raising you to be an artist, not a construction worker."

From that point on, I was hooked.

I must admit to occasionally "dumbing down" for public consumption, and on those occasions I don't, Christian, my best friend, pokes fun at me for putting on airs.

Your letter would've had him in stitches.

There was something about your photograph that left me feeling as if I've known you forever, and while you won't be so quick to come to the same conclusion, I'm beginning to suspect that we are kindred spirits, Ms. Grundy, if for no other reason than our predilection for beginning sentences with a conjunction.

*And* in the spirit of our budding friendship, rest assured it never entered my mind to accuse you of being a flatterer—unreasonable, maybe; cantankerous, certainly; and perhaps a little trigger-happy—but no flatterer. To be honest, my early imaginings had run wild, as I pictured an ascetic spinster who milks the cows, feeds the pigs, and finds entertainment in trapping and drowning orphaned kittens in the well out back. Your letter shows you to be much more substantial (though I still fear for the kittens).

As to your indisposition, I do regret it. But if the apple cider vinegar and baking soda is intended solely for my disposal, do leave off, dear. I'm here to stay. More to the point, we have a mystery to solve.

Sincerely,
Annie

Across the wheat field and into a bygone era, El read the letter and jolted with surprise. Her spectacles fell from her nose to land unceremoniously in her lap. She stared in the direction of the house on her back forty, frowning. Then she huffed so quietly it could have gone without notice. The huff was followed by a giggle. The giggle by a laugh. The laugh by a wheeze and a guffaw so profound that El began to cough. Slapping the rocker while she tried to catch her breath, El thought, *Fine. Annie, it is.* Wiping her eyes before replacing her spectacles, El got up from the rocker with her customary snap and pop. She began to whistle reedily and ambled over to the stove to put on some hot water for her evening tea.

# CHAPTER SEVEN

## A Book, Antihistamines, and a Scheming Universe

### MAY 21, 1995

The universe is not immune to surprise. Every now and again that perfect combination of gravity, oxygen, dust particles, hydrogen, stellar winds, neutrinos, the kitchen sink, and a good dash of radiation converges in a single, unique instant that results in a big *KABOOM*! A hole is torn in the fabric of space and time. Sometimes a similar convergence, no less profound in the strategies of the universe, can lead simply to two people meeting at the intersection of Castro and Eighteenth Streets. This particular confluence of events involved, among other things, a book and antihistamines.

It was Sunday, and Sundays spelled errands for Christian. He was off to Walgreens, not that he knew why. It was just that he always ended up there eventually when running errands, and he figured he could get a jump-start on things by heading there straightaway. His peculiar logic dictated that, although he didn't know what he needed at the drugstore, there must be something (as there always was), and he would recognize it once he got there.

An unacknowledged but very real corollary to this line of reasoning was the sad fact that were he not to run these errands he didn't need, Christian would have no excuse to leave the house at all.

So, grabbing his keys, wallet, and a book from the counter, he whisked out the door and began meandering down the street in that particular way of his, paying more attention to the book in his hands than the sidewalk beneath his feet.

He looked up only once, as he passed the copy shop on Market Street, to see a thing he knew wasn't really there. It sat atop the awning, looking like a cross-legged angel, and watched his every step. They were well acquainted, Christian and the thing that wasn't really there, and he did what he always did. He ignored it.

Just over the hill from Christian's home and two blocks to the left, Edmond, known at this point only as "the face," was stepping from his door to run errands as well. In stark contrast to Christian, however, he had a list. His first stop would also be Walgreens. It was allergy season, and Edmond was going to stock up on antihistamines. From there, he planned to head to the nursery, where he would buy annuals for the small garden behind his apartment. It was doubtful he'd buy impatiens. He'd planted them the year before, and while they did very well in his garden, Edmond was ready for a change.

Walgreens was a five-block walk from Christian's house. Coincidentally, it was also a five-block walk from Edmond's apartment. Were Edmond's apartment, Christian's home, and Walgreens to be marked on a map and the dots connected, a perfect isosceles triangle would be formed. The significance of that fact was, at this particular moment, unknown.

Ignorant of the influence geometry would soon have on his life, yet confident that he would meet the day on his own terms, Edmond stepped from his door at the exact moment Christian stepped from his. Unlike Christian, however, he walked down the street with the certainty of someone who was an old hand at navigating the neighborhood. Indeed, Edmond had lived there for more than four years, though he had found himself in San Francisco completely by chance.

His original intent had been to pursue a career on the stage, and San Francisco was only meant to be a weekend excursion. But he'd fallen in love with the city and decided he could as easily pursue his dream in Baghdad by the Bay. The universe had other ideas, however, throwing him a curveball in the form of laryngitis the night before his first big audition.

After a period of sobering introspection, Edmond had switched professional gears, becoming a landscaper. It wasn't a big occupation with big rewards, but Edmond didn't have big aspirations at the moment. He was still healing from choices he'd made in a prior life that led to unexpected and undesired consequences. Little aspirations suited him well at this time. He would no doubt aspire to more when he had healed.

While affected by this turn of events, Edmond was ever the optimist who was certain the universe had a plan, though he often questioned whether its successful execution required these little miseries.

Frankly, such thoughts were far from his mind as he made for Walgreens, a little blue dot on the radar image being watched at that moment with particular interest by none other than the universe itself.

And Christian was a red dot.

The two dots simultaneously worked their way, with fits and starts, to an end point where they merged as a single, blazing spot of bright purple at a fire hydrant in front of the drugstore.

Christian was leaning against it, squeezing in a few more pages from the chapter he was reading before going inside to purchase what he was yet to determine he needed, when someone tapped him on the shoulder.

"Excuse me."

Christian turned.

"This yours?" The "face" calmly returned his gaze while its owner held out the frequent-reader card Christian used as a bookmark, causing the uneasy itch of misplaced memory to surge like a word on the tip of his tongue. Christian hiccuped in surprise and slipped off the fire hydrant.

"Careful!" Edmond scrambled to break the fall but missed. He shrugged cheerfully as Christian landed in a heap on the curb, saying, "And down he goes." He hauled Christian up. "You all right?" he asked.

Christian rested his hand on the fire hydrant, massaging his back and nodding stupidly. "That's my"—he blinked several times before managing to say—"b-b-bookmark."

Edmond handed over the item in question with a lopsided grin that trailed away quickly as he gave Christian a closer look. "I know you from somewhere," he said. This was typical of Edmond. While anyone else in a similar circumstance would have asked, "Do I know you?" Edmond made a statement of fact. He was never uncertain.

Unnerved by the intensity of Edmond's gaze, Christian felt his vocal cords start to tighten—a bad sign—but as he struggled for a response, Edmond took the lead, firing off, "It's you! From Crissy Field. And...hold it"—he snapped his fingers twice—"the supermarket! And I'm pretty sure I saw you crossing Church and Twentieth yesterday." He stared at Christian and said with a hint of mischief in his voice, "If I were the suspicious type, I'd think you were tailing me."

Missing the joke entirely, as was often the case, Christian fired back with something less than his usual rhetorical genius. "I li-li-li-"—he closed his eyes and swallowed, wrestling with the word, then raised his hand, moving it as if in benediction—"live...here."

"Neighbors then." Edmond nodded knowingly. He leaned forward in a manner that suggested he would unveil a singular truth, impart the one inimitable law that bound the universe and everything within, and said, "I was kidding, by the way, about the 'tailing' thing."

Having gotten that off his chest, Edmond crossed his arms and declared, "Well, the universe is telling us something, isn't it?" He said this with confidence because, unlike Christian, he had come to believe the universe had a plan. Since he also believed in guardian spirits and dream catchers, that shouldn't come as much of a surprise. And best not to even get him started on karma. He lifted an eyebrow as Christian continued to nurse his back. "Maybe you should sit down," he added.

"I'm good," Christian said as he slapped dust off the back of his pants.

Interrupting his attempt to tidy up, Edmond extended his hand, offering his name.

Christian took it, sharing his as he looked to the clear skies, certain he'd heard the rumble of thunder. He glanced over to see Edmond doing the same before examining his own hand as if it were somehow to blame. He looked at Christian, puzzled.

"Well, Christian, nice to meet you," he said, glancing at the heavens a second time. "By the way, you have a doozy of a stain on your pants." He waited for a response, but getting none, shrugged. "Take care," he said, before turning to walk through the entrance of the drugstore.

Christian waved noncommittally and headed to the street corner. He decided that heading to the hardware store before going to Walgreens would be best, even though he was dead certain there was nothing there he actually needed. Glaring skyward, he let out an exasperated woof of air and opened his book to the next chapter as he entered the crosswalk.

Shouts. Screeching wheels. The blare of a horn. Christian felt a violent tug from behind, yanking him to the curb as a car went screaming past.

"Wake up, dumbass, before you get yourself killed!" yelled a shadow from the passenger seat of the passing car, its engine roaring like a sour note of a tuba.

Floundering at the edge of the street only to trip on the curb, Christian ended up next to the fire hydrant in an all-too-familiar heap. Doing a quick inventory, he decided nothing was broken and gingerly propped himself up on his elbow before reaching across the sidewalk to rescue his book. He sat up, Indian style, rested his forearms on his knees, and began to breathe in and out very slowly. Having collected himself, Christian scanned his surroundings to note with acute embarrassment that a small crowd had gathered and that Edmond was standing over him with a belt loop dangling from his upraised hand.

Edmond stuffed the belt loop into his pocket and said, "Sorry, grabbed the first thing I could reach. Mind if I ask..." He paused. Looking at Christian's stricken face, he seemed to realize that this was not the time to discuss traffic hazards. Instead, he extended his hand. "Okay, up with you," he said, hauling Christian up for the second time that day. "Let's get you out of the monkey cage." He turned to face down the crowd. "Show's over, people!"

As the crowd dissolved into the complex rhythms of urban sidewalk traffic, Edmond helped Christian brush himself off, noticed a stain to shame the first, and overheard him mumble, "Annie's going to k-kill me."

Christian was examining a nasty scrape on his elbow when Edmond gently pushed him on the back to set him in motion. "There's a coffee shop down the street. I want to get that cleaned off."

Edmond sipped his coffee and watched as Christian picked at a slice of pound cake. His elbow was cleaned up and forgotten, and he was making a mound of crumbs that he lined up in rows by scraping the tines of the fork through the pile, though he'd yet to take a single bite. "You don't say much, do you?" Edmond said.

Christian stole a glance at him before fixating once more on the cake.

"The conversation's going to suck if I have to do all the talking," Edmond added, clearly amused despite the narrowing of his eyes.

Still nothing.

Just as Edmond was about to give up, Christian slumped back in his seat. "I'm sorry," he said, the words coming out as little more than a breath of air.

"It's okay," Edmond said airily. "Want to tell me about the death wish?"

Christian reached for the fork and shoveled some cake in his mouth, then took a deep breath as if preparing himself for a monumental effort. Speaking deliberately, like a third grader reading in front of class, he said, "My best...friend says that books are my ah-ah-"—he raised the fork, moving it in a complex series of gestures like he had with his hand outside Walgreens—"armor, b-but evidence suggests I'm just a garden-variety misanth-th-th-th—" His eyes blinked with each repetition, and he raised the fork again. This time, though, he wrote the rest of the word in the air: "—thrope." After a stretch of silence, he realized his attempt at humor might have generated a certain ambiguity. "I stutter," he added, shrugging. He set the fork aside.

Edmond smiled, charmed by Christian's admission of the obvious.

"M-m-muh"—Christian's hand waved restively, moving his words along—"mainly... around people I don't know. So I keep my w-wo-wo-"—he paused, grimacing, before forcing out the word—"*world* pretty small. There's Annie and my books."

"That must be very lonely for you."

Christian furrowed his brows and grimaced, an expression that seemed to say, *You think?* "There are certain d-d-duh-deficiencies in my social skills," he said.

"Do you always talk like *that*, though?"

Not sure that he'd heard Edmond correctly, and afraid he was going to be the butt of yet another in a lifetime of jokes, Christian blinked. "Like what?"

"Like a person with too many smarts and not enough experience." Edmond glanced at the clock on the wall and jumped to his feet. "I've gotta run. You going to be all right?"

Christian nodded.

As he turned to leave, Edmond dug into his pocket, pulling out a business card. A few pieces of paper scattered to the floor. Picking them up, he placed the card on the table and tapped it. "I'm a bit of a loner myself," he said. "And you know, you're kind of interesting—in a weird sort of way."

Christian picked up the card with a start, trying to figure out if there was intended insult in the statement. He looked at Edmond carefully and decided he was sincere enough. He nodded, not knowing what else to do.

At that, Edmond barreled out the door with the same conviction with which he had entered it, leaving Christian to wonder if the man laced his breakfast cereal with testosterone. He banished the thought with a shake of his head and opened his book to page forty-seven.

He'd only begun to be transported into the world of Middle-earth when the waitress walked over to pick something off the floor by his foot, something that Edmond had missed, and placed it on Christian's table with a nod.

# CHAPTER EIGHT

## Candid Conversations

At the exact moment Christian watched Edmond disappear, minus a hundred years, Elsbeth was busy responding to Annie's latest correspondence.

*21st of May, 1895*

*Dear Annie,*

*I'm certain it will come as no surprise that I read your letter with some measure of incredulity. Drowning orphaned kittens, indeed! Clearly, you must realize that you've laid down the gauntlet with your anemic attempt at humor. I have never drowned a kitten in all my sixty-three years.*

*I may have dined on a few, however.*

*Sincerely,*
*Elsbeth Grundy*

*P.S. While not being familiar with the phrase "dumbing down," I certainly understand its intent. Never lower yourself for others. Make them rise to you. Whether they can or not is their burden, not yours.*

*P.P.S. Were you aware that Shakespeare originated the term "in stitches" in Twelfth Night? "If you desire the spleen, and will laugh yourself into stitches, follow me." He was a clever man, Shakespeare.*

Elsbeth read the letter and grunted in satisfaction. She placed it in an envelope and made her way across the field to Annie's picket fence. Like yesterday, and almost every day recently, it was warm and sunny in Kansas. She stopped at the gate and considered the house. What a fascinating turn of events for her rather ordinary life. She'd found a friend—an unexpected treasure. She waved at the door self-consciously before dropping her hand to her side, then placed the letter in the mailbox and slowly made her way home.

As Elsbeth closed her back door, Annie's flew open in an orchestration of precise, yet serendipitous timing. Annie swept through the rose garden in a swishing pile of sateen to collect her mail, returning to her rolltop desk to read in comfort.

And she was thrilled! Elsbeth had met her pound for pound with her drollery. Who would have thought she'd find a friend in such an unlikely place? And one who shared her sense of humor, no less. She placed El's letter in a cubicle of her rolltop and rested her hand on it affectionately before closing the drawer.

On a whim, she grabbed a bonnet and whisked out the back door to stand before the picket fence. A light breeze sent tendrils of stray hair swirling over her face. Annie gazed fondly at the cabin on the horizon, then, as a declaration of her budding friendship with El, lifted the bonnet and scarf over her head like a banner before slowly turning around and going back inside to the future.

May 21, 1995

Dear El,

Shakespeare. Whether he "sets your teeth on edge," or you love him "like the dickens," you can't escape borrowing his phrases. (Smirk)

It's high time we became better acquainted—a little "girl talk," to coin a phrase. To start, you may be surprised to learn that Annabelle Aster is my adopted name. I don't know my birth name, having never bothered to learn the particulars. The only testimonials to my prior life are some documents gathering dust in my safe-deposit box.

My adoptive mother and father raised me with prodigious assistance from my godmother—Auntie Liza. I've mentioned her already. Mom and Dad passed away two years ago, and I still live in the home they built. It's too much house, but I can't bear to part with it.

I'm not married, having found no one possessing a disposition that is consonant with my own. There were one or two who might have possessed a congenial makeup, but they lacked what I considered to be the requisite constitution. I'm told that I can be quite willful, but I prefer to think of it as knowing my own mind.

I suppose that's enough for now. It's your turn to "spill your guts," as people say. There must be quite a story behind your solitude.

Sincerely,
Annie

P.S. Are your traps in good repair?

P.P.S. Just reread my letter. Miss Austen is turning in her grave.

*21st of May, 1895*

*Dear Annie,*

*Spill my guts? Is this where the English language is headed?*

*And solitude? If we are to be friends, I will require you to speak precisely. To wit, you wish to know why I behave like a spinster. Do not deny it! No one knows better than I the image I present to the world, and I accept the mantle even though it is an ill fit for a widow.*

*You are surprised? Yes, I was married once. And happily. His name was Tom. I recommend the institution, should you find it convenient. We had a daughter named Beth Anne. We loved her dearly, and she repaid us threefold with joy.*

*Tom died of sepsis from a plowing accident. And I lost my heartbroken Beth Anne to wanderlust. There were letters from her in the beginning, but we lost contact many years ago. I can only hope she made it to Chicago as she dreamed.*

*Regardless, they are both memories to me now, and I occupy my days with pigs and wheat. At night, I sit in my rocker and think. Occasionally, I read.*

*I have had twenty years to forget love. But I don't think I am loveless.*

*Sincerely,*
*El*

*P.S. Traps are fine. Sadly, supply is low.*

*P.P.S. I want to know more about that door you mentioned.*

# CHAPTER NINE

## A Peculiar Door

### MAY 26, 1995

Annie waited patiently as the gaunt owner of the Antiquarian spoke into his cell phone, his voice as scratched and tinny as the music coming from the gramophone by the door.

"Yes, yes… That's fine," he said, eyeing her warily for the third time. Flipping the phone shut, he turned on his heel and walked briskly to the sales desk where he settled onto a stool, his elbows and knee joints collapsing upon themselves in a disheveled pile. As he poured a cup of coffee and arranged his features into a well-practiced blank stare, a faint electric buzz signaled the imminent demise of the fluorescent light overhead, stuttering Morse code across the patina of his bald pate. To the knowledgeable the message read, "Approach at your peril."

Annie placed the ghastly jade ashtray she'd been ogling on a table and walked to the sales desk. Ignoring the signal and feeling a bit perverse, she simply stared at the man.

He tried to ignore her at first, but her silence was off-putting, and the stick figure of a man finally pursed his lips as a single leg unfolded in sections to rest on the floor. "I'm on my coffee break, ma'am. Perhaps—"

Grinning, she interrupted him. "Yes, you were most eager for it," she said.

"Pardon me?" The jig was up, and he knew it.

She flicked her wrist, a gesture that might have been construed as saying, "It doesn't matter," but contained enough condescension to also be interpreted as "You're dismissed." She ran a finger over the counter and flicked away imaginary dust, hammering her point home. "Is Adam available?" she asked.

Startled speechless, the man blinked his amphibious eyes and lifted a bony finger, looking like the Ghost of Christmas Yet to Come in an Alexander McQueen knockoff as he pointed to a door at the far end of the sales counter.

Before she'd taken three steps in the direction indicated, the door in question opened, and a young man walked out. "Miss Aster!" he said, looking delighted. "How lucky! I have something for you." He disappeared inside, returning with a file labeled *Abbott's Door*.

Following Annie's gaze, he watched the store owner retreat into his office, along with his cup of coffee. "Is it just me, or does he dislike women in general?" she asked, nodding at the recently vacated space.

"Women?" It took Adam a moment to follow the thread of her thought. "He adores them!" Seeing her skeptical look, he started to tick off a list of names. "Barbra, Judy, Bette, his mother..." He looked Annie up and down impudently and added, "He'd adore you too, looking like you just walked out of a Victorian novel, but—" He shrugged, sliding the file across the counter. "Some interesting stuff in there," he said, tapping it. He looked across the room. "I'd better go soothe some ruffled feathers. Give me a holler if you need anything."

Stapled inside the file was some Antiquarian letterhead, but the insignia was unfamiliar. A closer inspection revealed that the original Antiquarian was located in Kansas City. "Well, it appears that all roads do lead to Rome," Annie whispered. She scanned the list before withdrawing a yellowed, water-stained newspaper article tucked into the sleeve on the opposite side.

The hairs on the nape of her neck stood up when she saw that the article was dated May 30, 1895. Reading the contents as quickly as possible, she learned that the door had been designed as a prop for the stage show of David C. Abbott, a professional illusionist. While she was a bit spooked that the designer of her magical door was a magician, the next bit of information caused her to gasp.

Adam stuck his head out the door. "Everything okay?"

"Someone just walked on my grave," she said. Seeing his blank look, Annie waved him off with a smile, too impatient for further explanation. Waiting until he closed the door, she read on. David Abbott appeared to have cut quite a swath in Kansas City until he met a rather untimely end. He was murdered in his home, stabbed repeatedly. Several of his belongings—including the door—were slated to be auctioned the following day, a bizarre coincidence stemming from his recent purchase of a new home. The article mentioned that there was a suspect but no known motive. Stuffing the clipping back into the file, Annie glimpsed yet another hint of yellow. A second article.

Feeling the need for air, she stepped outside and started to pace as she read. This one was in dreadful shape. It appeared to have been printed the following day, but most of the contents had fallen victim to whatever substance had stained the first article. Only one section was clear enough for her to make out.

> A money clip engraved with the initials "AC" has been found at the scene of the crime, leading law enforcement to seek Ambrosius Culler, the business partner financing David Abbott's show at the Coates Opera House, for questioning.
>
> The rumor that Mr. Culler paid a visit to the officer in charge…

Annie chewed on her lower lip for a second before flipping open her cell phone and typing a quick message: Christian, call me.

May 26, 1995

Dearest El,

From the moment we "met," I have suspected there were larger forces at work. I am not fond of words like "fate"—my independent nature rebels at the notion—but I simply can't put our meeting down to chance.

And if some agency does have a hand in promoting our friendship, then I may have stumbled upon its motive. I think it's very possible we have been brought together to save a life.

I'm babbling. Let me start over.

I've just returned from the store where I purchased the door. Everything comes back to Kansas City, as you suspected.

Two news clippings, obviously forgotten, were tucked away in the back of a file the store proprietor provided me. The articles were dated the thirtieth and thirty-first of May, 1895. It seems that the person who made my door was a stage magician by the name of David Abbott. He was murdered in his home in Westport on the twenty-ninth, apparently by his business associate (a Mr. Culler), and the door was auctioned off the following day.

The math frightens me, El. May 29, 1895, is ninety-nine years and 362 days ago for me. For you, it is in three days!

We can't simply ignore the fact that there is going to be a murder. I think we should do something about it, don't you?

Your confederate,<br>
Annabelle Aster

P.S. If you decide to go to Kansas City, please take care. The articles were water-stained so I could not read everything, but the first article did mention that there was a suspect. My alarm bells are ringing, though I don't know why.

*26th of May, 1895*

*Dear Annie,*

*You do like to test your friendships early, I see. And I'm guessing that you'll continue to pester me until I agree to this crazy idea. It is an unfair comment, I know, as I have no doubt that, were our roles reversed, you'd be hopping off to Kansas City without a second thought and without a plan.*

*I'll go. Knowing what you've found, I suppose I can't do anything else. The next time you decide to share the future, however, make it something useful, like next year's alfalfa report.*

*David Abbott is a magician of some renown in these parts and is currently performing, I believe, at the Coates Opera House in Kansas City. I will go, and I will speak to him.*

*I wonder, however, if you have considered other implications of this potential misadventure? Should I succeed, Mr. Abbott's door will not be auctioned off, and the series of events leading it to your possession will be altered.*

*Let me just say it now and get it over with. I have become fond of our correspondence—there you have it. Indeed, I have become fond of you. And my life will be made less for the loss.*

*Still, I will go.*

*Affectionately,*
*El*

"The series of coincidences is eerie," Annie said.

While she was relaying her discovery and the news that Elsbeth had agreed to travel to Kansas City, Christian was eating a burned oatmeal cookie, a vacant expression on his face.

"Strange, don't you think?" she asked.

Suddenly aware of a pause in Annie's monologue, Christian looked up, and seeing that she expected a response to a commentary he wasn't listening to, his ears colored slightly. "Hmm?"

"I said, 'Strange—' Never mind. You evidently have something more pressing to deal with."

"I'm a little distracted," Christian said apologetically.

"Clearly." Annie watched as he politely nibbled at the edge of his cookie. She, on the other hand, had given up on her gastronomic nightmare after one agonizing bite. "And I'll hazard a guess it isn't my culinary tour de force that has you so preoccupied."

"Actually, it's not ba—" Realizing he wasn't fooling anyone, Christian dropped the cookie onto his plate and started to laugh. "Annie, it's terrible!"

The comment was so honest and the laughter so infectious that Annie joined in, against all attempts to the contrary.

Resting his chin on his fist, Christian pressed the thumb of his other hand on the cookie until it broke into three pieces. He looked rather detached as he said, "I met him."

"You met whom? Oh! Well, this *is* significant. Is he a third cousin twice removed? Or, better yet, have you been marked for"—she wiggled her eyebrows—"liquidation?"

Christian glowered at her. "We're talking about Texas, Annie. Those options don't have to be mutually exclusive."

Grinning at his riposte, Annie glided onto the empty bench across the kitchen nook from him. "Start from the beginning," she said, tucking a pile of sateen behind her knees.

"Well, he sort of-of-of..." Despite appearances, Christian wasn't stuttering. He was balking. "Well, he pulled me off the street before I could get splattered on a car's bumper." Wincing, he added, "I might not have been paying attention to where I was going."

She blinked. "Were you...?" She didn't even need to finish the sentence.

Knowing full well what was going to happen next and determined to speed up the inevitable, Christian handed Annie the entertainment section of the newspaper, waiting patiently as she rolled it into a tube before whacking him lightly on top of his head. He grinned as she reached over to comb her fingers through his hair. "Continue," she said.

"Not much to say, really. I was pretty shaken up, so he dragged me off to a coffee shop. We talked a little...very little." Christian glanced at Annie from under his brow to see if she caught his drift, then changed the subject. "I banged up my elbow," he said, proudly displaying his scab. "He gave me his card. I don't think he has many friends, you know? It was something he said. Oh! And I have his driver's license. It must've fallen out of his pocket."

"He'll be wanting that back then."

Christian tried to frown, but his fist was pressed against his cheek and he could only manage half of one. "I called him." He dropped his head to the table with an audible thump and looked at Annie from the corner of his eye. "We're meeting at Gill's later—for drinks."

"You don't sound very eager."

"Can I just mail his stuff and call it a day?"

"No, you cannot."

"But I'm a disaster when it comes to actual conversation, Annie!" He shrugged, causing his head, which was still resting on the table, to slide across its surface, getting cookie crumbs in his hair. "Let's examine the facts." He sat up, lifting a finger with each piece of information. "I stutter. I'm socially inept. I have an anxiety disorder. And I strongly suspect that the diagnoses of ADD and OCD were intentionally overlooked by an *understandably stressed-out diagnostician.*" He practically barked the last four words before dropping his head back onto the table. "Aside from taking an eternity to get a word out, I'll end up saying something stupid—the phone call was chock-full of classics—then I'll get embarrassed by whatever it was I said and say something else stupid, on and on, ad nauseam." He took a deep breath while scratching at a ketchup stain on the table with his index finger. "And if that's not bad enough, I'll spend the following day—the entire following day, mind you—replaying and wincing over everything I said, while beating myself up for what I wish I'd said. It's exhausting."

"You forgot to add Asperger's to the list."

Christian straightened, obviously giving Annie's comment more consideration than intended.

"And hypochondria."

His shoulders slumped as he looked at her from beneath his brow. "Funny," he said sullenly.

"You're going." Her eyes flashed in a way that brooked no argument. She brushed the crumbs from the side of his head. "Your problem is that you have no idea how charming you really are. And you need to make a few friends—besides me."

"That's rich."

She waved off his insinuation that she suffered from an equal shortage and softened her tone as she scooped crumbs onto a saucer. "I'm worried about you, Christian."

Somehow, without her intending it to, the comment hit a bull's-eye. Christian's features blurred and became barren, and his eyes locked onto the table.

"What?" she asked.

He looked up, not quite meeting her eyes. He shook his head, but she wasn't fooled—not by his air of indifference nor his milquetoast smile.

"What?" she demanded as she set the saucer aside to sit across from him.

Realizing she hadn't been duped, he relented. "We've been seeing more of each other lately."

For anyone else, the comment would have made no sense. But Annie understood immediately. This was about his hallucinations. This was about the angel. Annie didn't know if the angel was one of mercy or ill will, but her visitations began after Christian awoke from his coma. She disturbed his sleep, a golden-haired beauty wrapped in a radiant nimbus who also appeared at his regular haunts, sitting quietly in the cafés he frequented or dangling her feet from tree limbs above the sidewalks of his beaten paths. Thousands of dollars in therapy and buckets of psychobabble provided no real answers, at least not to Annie's mind.

The trauma from the accident had scrambled his brain beyond the memory loss, apparently. No matter what anyone said or the evidence presented, he swore that his mother, a Jayne Mansfield look-alike, had pulled him from the wreckage and had stood guard over him until help came—all this despite the fact that she'd died many years prior. He wouldn't budge from that position. His therapist said that the angel was a "protective bubble," a coping mechanism that his mind retreated to when some stimulus in his environment threatened to trigger a flashback, and that it naturally took the appearance of the person that made Christian feel safest—his mother. But if the angel was a protective mechanism, why were her features always locked in an expression of terror?

Fully aware that his comment would keep Annie's head busy, and in the lack of any response from her, Christian collected the plates and took them to sink, giving himself a moment to reflect. He was about to tell her not to worry when another thought crossed his mind. He turned, curiosity scribbled across his features. "Annie, what is the Serenity Prayer?"

"Why do you ask?"

"A slip of paper fell out of Edmond's pocket with a prayer written on it. Does it mean anything to you?"

"Yes," she said.

Despite Christian's mastery of interpreting the nuances of Annie's expressions, this one left him baffled.

Finally, she smiled. "It means we have a rescue project."

# CHAPTER TEN

## David Abbott

### MAY 29, 1895

Elsbeth boarded the train, stowed her satchel, and settled into her seat, all the while thinking of Yule May. That damn horse could read her like a book every time.

She'd been grousing as she loaded her buggy for the trip, looking for any excuse not to go to Kansas City but knowing she would, regardless. Promises were meant to be kept, most of all to a friend. And Annie, as sad as it seemed, just might be her best friend in the world. There was Amos at the Hay and Feed, but she'd kept him, along with everyone else in Sage, at a distance since Tom died and Beth Anne left. The memories they stirred up were too painful. Eventually, the invitations stopped coming, Elsbeth ran out of reasons for leaving the farm, and she settled inevitably into a solitary existence. That is, of course, until Annie came along and stirred up a hornet's nest.

It had happened when Elsbeth was stowing her luggage on the buggy. She'd stepped away to glance across the wheat field and back to the cabin, suddenly aware of the price she'd paid the last twenty years. *This isn't a life*, she recalled thinking. Before she could get too sentimental, though, Yule May had taken three lazy steps in her direction, dragging the buggy behind, to give her a good head butt, snapping her into the present.

And then again, when she was winding her way down the

seldom-used path leading from her front door, that crazy animal had actually tossed her mane and started to gallop like some fool thoroughbred and not the fossilized plow horse she was, almost as if she recognized Elsbeth's need to shed her burdens and put her past behind her.

As the train pulled from the station, Elsbeth started to chuckle, thinking what a sight it must have been with that crazy horse galloping down the road and her thrown over her heels into the wagon bed, cussing up a storm.

Several hours later, she woke to the sound of the train's whistle as the porter walked down the aisle saying, "Next stop, Kansas City. Kansas City in twenty minutes." She snorted and pushed her spectacles up the bridge of her nose, gathered her satchel, and stuffed the *Kansas City Star* inside. The locomotive took a good ten minutes to grind to a halt at the railroad station, where Elsbeth emerged onto the platform from a wall of steam, a little soggy but none the worse for wear.

The general clamor, clang, and congestion unnerved her, and she made directly for a horse-drawn trolley that eventually dropped her at the front steps of the Broadway Hotel.

Safe in her room, El examined the ticket she'd purchased for a matinee performance of Abbott's production through the concierge in the lobby. She'd decided that the best course of action was to seek out the man in his dressing room after the show. How she would do that she didn't know, but that was the sum total of her plan, despite how she'd bedeviled Annie for her own lack of one.

With the show hours away, El retrieved a penny dreadful from her satchel—part two in a series called *The String of Pearls* that introduced her favorite character, Sweeney Todd, to the world—and wandered into the bathroom. She'd worked her knickers down to her swollen ankles and situated herself on the toilet, preparing to get her fill of the demon barber of Fleet Street when her eyes strayed to the eagle-claw tub.

Tugging at the porcelain chain pull, she resituated her knickers and wandered over to give it a good once-over before switching her attention to a shelf containing an assortment of scented bath oils and soap bars. She tested a few and stared at the tub with renewed interest. It would be a shame to waste the opportunity, she decided, turning on the tap.

El arrived at the theater with twenty minutes to spare—cleaned, combed, and smelling, regrettably, like a French whore. She looked up at the gilded, honeycombed ceiling as she stepped through the lobby doors and stopped dead in her tracks. Receiving a sharp word from the gentleman behind her, El moved farther into the lobby. Obstreperous to the end, she glared at him witheringly before heading to the stairs and into the theater proper—a colossal, cloisonné jewel box, if ever there was one.

An usher helped her to her seat while she studied the other patrons. The sheer volume of satin and brocade was astonishing, and she found herself glancing down at the course fabric and roller-print floral pattern of her calico dress. She sniffed at her sleeve, catching a whiff of mothballs, and looked across her shoulder at the peacock sitting next to and staring at her. "What?" she barked and turned to face the stage as the woman switched seats with her none-too-happy partner.

Music drifted up from the orchestra pit, the curtain rose, and the social politicking wound down as people took their seats. Abruptly, floodlights panned over the audience. The hush evaporated to silence as a man walked across the empty stage, the click of his heels echoing throughout the auditorium, to sit on a stool placed front and center. He was wearing a tuxedo, a top hat, and white gloves that he slowly and methodically peeled from his hands as if oblivious to the thousand eyes watching him.

David Abbott looked out over the audience for the first time as though startled. With a flick of the wrist, he gave the gloves a good shake, and a white rubber ball appeared in each hand. He rolled them expertly between his thumbs and index fingers, then between his index and middle fingers, on down the line, and back. Then, grasping the balls in his palms, he threw them sharply to his feet where they bounced off the floor into the air above his head. At the peak of their arc, the balls disappeared in a puff of white smoke to emerge as a pair of doves that flew over the audience and into the rafters, leaving a trail of downy feathers. A scattering of polite applause followed. The show had begun.

David Abbott was a fine fiddle of a man, elegant and commanding, for all that he was a powerfully built, ruddy-skinned brunet. His beard was neatly trimmed and black as tar, framing a handsome, if not swarthy, face. He was built to pitch hay, Elsbeth decided, and from the look on the faces of the female patrons, clearly they wouldn't mind if he took a roll in it.

Saying little and using simple props, Abbott engaged in his craft. As entertaining as he was, though, Elsbeth found her thoughts drifting. She was wondering how to arrange a private meeting with the man when the flash of a bulb coming from the press box distracted her. She stared at the journalists scribbling notes, and, just like that, she had a plan.

When a prop was rolled onto the stage—a large, red door—she sat erect.

David Abbott took another rubber ball from his pocket, rolling it between two fingers as he motioned for silence. "I would like to take a moment, if I may, to discuss the physical universe," he said. He raised his arm and made as if to place the ball on an invisible shelf above his head. When he removed his hand, the ball remained frozen in place. Nodding, David pulled out two smaller balls.

"As humans, we have a voracious appetite to understand it, to conquer it. The study of matter, energy, motion, force..." As he lectured, he suspended the smaller balls on each side of the larger one. "Do you know what an electron is?" He looked out over the audience. "No?" He returned his attention to the balls and, with a light tap, sent them orbiting around the larger one in opposite directions. "You will." He chuckled, as if at an inside joke.

"Our most brilliant minds are using the Galilean principle of undetectable motion, or relativity, to understand the nature of time and its relationship to our physical universe." He clasped both hands behind his back. "Time. An interesting concept. How do we define it? Can we define it? We can certainly describe it." He paused, his eyes trailing over the audience as he recited, "Time is the sequential relationship of an event that has the property of past, present, and future in continuous duration."

He began to pace. "Past precedes the present, which precedes the future. These concepts are immutable and cannot be interchanged. There is no present without a past, and the two certainly cannot occur simultaneously." He stopped abruptly as if struck by a thought. "Or can they?"

Baffled by the speech and where it was going, several audience members shifted in their seats. Mr. Abbott regarded them somberly. "Bear with me," he said. "Certain civilizations such as the Mayans, the Aztecs, and even Native American tribes like the Cherokee do not believe in the linear relationship of past, present, and future. They live by different laws and seek to define time and space in different terms. The Cherokee specifically are rumored to have permeated the veil of space to travel what they called the 'spiritual plane.' My labors into these mysteries, however, show that the Cherokee are misled. What they think is a door to a different plane is, in fact, a door to a variant time in this world."

He gestured toward the door behind him. "This is my masterpiece. The culmination of my studies in the mystical realm of temporal translation." He looked back to the audience, raising his voice. "Ladies and gentlemen, through this door, I can traverse time, bend space, and redefine the relative 'now.' I can dissect past, present, and future so that they are experienced in any order. The distant future is merely a step away, which I will demonstrate tonight, not in principle, but in action."

He ran his hand across the framing that held the door erect. "This is no trick, ladies and gentlemen," he said. "It is no counterfeit prestidigitation. It is real."

Having said that, David merely opened the door and walked through it to a blinding flash from the floodlights. When they dimmed, the stage was empty. A stagehand emerged and turned the door around three hundred sixty degrees. There was no one behind it. David Abbott had vanished, but in a spectacularly uninteresting way. The stagehand then turned the door another ninety degrees so that it was facing to the side.

A knock came from the door, causing the audience to stir. The stagehand opened it and exited to the side of the stage as a bizarre profile began to emerge from the door frame, distending from the prop. It swelled, and a slick, man-shaped outline, both hideous and hypnotic, began to take shape. As more of the profile appeared, extruding farther and farther from the frame like a soap bubble from the oily film clinging to a hooped wand, Elsbeth was struck by a thought.

It was as if the door had eaten Mr. Abbott on one side and was now spitting him out on the other. Locked onto this notion, she could not shake the image of the door as a huge, gaping maw from which Mr. Abbott—or an oily likeness—was regurgitated. Once separated from the frame, the oily integument covering David evaporated, and he turned to face the audience, holding a newspaper in his hand.

Uncertain what they had witnessed, the members of the audience sat in stony silence until they realized that something defying explanation *had* just occurred. A scattering of applause awoke them, and the remainder of the audience joined in, confused. Abbott hushed them with a simple gesture before walking to the edge of the stage. He peeled off a section of the newspaper and offered it to a woman in the first row. "Madam, could you please tell the audience what this is?"

She took it, saying, "It's the financial section of the *San Francisco Chronicle.*"

"And what is the date of the paper?" Abbott queried.

"May twenty-ninth. Today's date," she said matter-of-factly. "How did you—" She was going to ask how Abbott managed to get a copy of today's paper from halfway across the country in one day when he interrupted her.

"Take a closer look."

Looking offended, she pursed her lips and glared at the print. She squinted her eyes, then gazed at Abbott incredulously. "Nineteen sixty-five?" she whispered.

"I'm sorry, madam. I couldn't hear you."

Louder, she said, "It reads 1965."

The man sitting next to her gasped, snatching the paper from her hand as whispers radiated outward until, in seconds, the place was in an uproar.

Unperturbed, Mr. Abbott quieted the assemblage, holding out his hand. "Sir, would you kindly return the newspaper? Knowing what is written on these pages, knowing from where I just returned, knowing the future, I assure you, will only provoke discontent." Since the man was reluctant to give up the item in question, Abbott had to lower himself to the edge of the stage and gently pry the paper from the man's hand. Their eyes locked as Abbott stuffed it in his coat. Standing, he looked over the audience, then walked to the door, ran his hand across its surface, opened it, and disappeared for the second time.

A minute passed, then two, then three. The crowd looked about in confusion, slowly coming to the realization that the show had come to a rather unorthodox close. They surged to their feet, some obviously angry, others shouting, "Encore. Encore."

Elsbeth, however, didn't budge. This was confirmation of Annie's suspicions, and she knew what she must do.

She remained seated as the audience fanned out of the exits while engaging in a hundred distinct conversations that converged on two questions: *Who did Abbott think he was?* and *Was it real?*

Half an hour later, the lights went down in the theater with a clunk and a trailing hum. Elsbeth got up from her seat and walked through the lobby to a door labeled with the sign *Personnel Only*. Looking about, she stepped through and wandered down a hall, where she confronted a man tossing around directions as stage-hands scurried to oblige. After a brief exchange, he motioned for her to follow him.

"Mr. Abbott, you have a visitor," the theater manager said as he knocked on a dressing room door. "A *Kansas City Star* reporter, sir."

David Abbott opened the door, clearly preoccupied with the bow tie he was trying to loosen. His shirt was unbuttoned, giving Elsbeth an eyeful of a deep, muscular chest with an even coating of coarse black hair. The bow tie slid from his neck and he looked up, catching the first glimpse of his guest. He froze openmouthed for a heartbeat before hastily buttoning his shirt. "I'm so sorry! I would never—" He glared at the stage manager before meeting Elsbeth's eyes. "I assumed you were a man."

"Quite all right, Mr. Abbott." Her response was brusque, businesslike.

"And your name is?"

"Elsbeth Grundy."

David gestured for her to enter and hurried to finish rebuttoning his shirt. As she stared about the dressing room, he apologized. "It's a bit of a mess, I'm afraid." He removed several items of clothing from a chair, and Elsbeth seated herself, accompanied by a noise more like a creaking wheel than her customary snap and pop. Holding her purse primly in her lap, she fixed both feet on the floor and waited for Mr. Abbott to be seated.

"I'm a bit surprised. I've already been interviewed by the *Star*."

"I'm not with the *Star*, Mr. Abbott," Elsbeth said. "I'm not even a journalist. I said that to get past your little watchdog outside." She looked apprehensively at the dressing room door, then back to Mr. Abbott. "Listen here, young man, I haven't much time and neither do you, so I'll get right to the point. You're in danger."

David stared in open astonishment. He started to lift himself from the chair but, flustered, seated himself again. "Danger?" His expression turned grim. "Miss Grundy, I've had a long day and I'm very tired."

"This is not a laughing matter, and I'm no schoolgirl to be intimidated by your churlishness." She brushed a crease from her skirt before continuing. "As a gesture of my sincerity, I will begin by saying that I am aware that the properties of the door used in your act are, for lack of a better term, real. How I have become aware of this fact is of no consequence. However, because of your door's properties, I know you'll be murdered tonight in your own home unless we take precautionary measures."

David rocked back, almost toppling his chair. He took a moment to collect his wits, then stood stiffly, grabbed Elsbeth by the arm, and led her forcefully to the door.

"Mr. Abbott!" Elsbeth's face flushed as she reached for her cane.

"I don't know what your game is, and frankly, I don't care."

He slammed the door just as Elsbeth blurted out, "Tonight. Culler. Do not invite him into your home!"

She looked up and down the hall, then back to the dressing room door. "Stupid, stubborn man," she said while stomping her foot. Hiking up her skirt, she marched out of the theater and into the night, pausing to look at a billboard with David Abbott's image on it. "I plan to save your skin whether you like it or not!" she said, then whacked the poster with her cane for good measure and stormed off.

Back in the dressing room, David tossed a few items of clothing into a trunk. Tonight's performances were the last of a sold-out run, and he was not pleased that his high spirits had been interrupted. He had twenty minutes to spare before the second show, after which he would be meeting Mr. Culler for a celebratory drink in the café. He pivoted, staring at the dressing room door. She'd said "Culler," he realized.

A knock at the door interrupted the thought, and he threw it open, scowling.

The stage manager froze midknock and, seeing the look on Mr. Abbott's face, cleared his throat. "Twenty minutes, sir. And I have a message from Mr. Culler, sir. He apologizes for the inconvenience, but he will not be able to meet for a drink. It seems that Mr. Danyer is back in town and the two must attend to some urgent business."

"At this time of night? Well, thank you, Stan." David closed the door and stared at the floor. In a way, he was relieved. While he found Mr. Culler entirely acceptable, David didn't care in the slightest for his associate, a reclusive man named Danyer who was lovingly dubbed "Hatchet Man" for some reason David preferred not to speculate over. Danyer didn't seem to care for the company his employer kept and always managed to make himself scarce. When asked about his associate's odd behavior, Mr. Culler would only shrug and say, "Three's a crowd."

David fetched a clean shirt from the rack, reliving his first interaction with the enigmatic Mr. Danyer. It was in the alley behind the theater. He'd stepped out back for a smoke when a shifting shadow so startled him that he'd choked on the fumes, dropping the cigarette into a fold of his waistcoat. He'd looked up in alarm, slapping at the embers, as a silhouette broke into the filtered light coming from a window to convey a message from Mr. Culler in a low hum of a voice before walking away without waiting for a reply—not that he was prepared to give one anyway.

David had caught a glimpse of what he thought was a cowl, and a shudder ran down his spine before he realized the figure was simply wearing a duster with the collar pulled above his ears and a cowboy hat pulled low over his brow.

# CHAPTER ELEVEN

## In the Closet

Down the block and across the street, Elsbeth stormed into her hotel room and snatched a Kansas City directory from the desk. She looked up the name Abbott, David C., finding a Westport address as Annie had mentioned in her letter. Turning to the map in the back of the directory, Elsbeth plotted a path to Mr. Abbott's home. The journey would require a good amount of walking, but time was on her side—his second performance had only just gotten under way.

She gathered her cane along with her handbag, stomped out of the hotel, and took a trolley to the third stop on the Westport line. After a thirty-minute walk down streets lined with massive oaks and magnolias, she found herself standing where David Abbott's drive met the street.

The sun was setting over his house as Elsbeth leaned against a lamppost, staring at his front door.

After only a minute or two, a gleam like the glow of a cat's eye caught her attention. She ignored it, but another flash of light teased at the edge of her sight, and she traced the source to a boy standing under an oak and examining three silver dollars in his open palm. He practically jumped out of his overalls when she appeared from a bend in the hedge.

"Holy—" The boy quickly pocketed the coins, his eyes trailing everywhere but at her. "You scared me, ma'am."

"What's a little thing like you doing out here at this hour? Stirring up mischief, are you?"

"I ain't stirring nothing, ma'am! Just taking a shortcut home." He nodded toward the house. "Are you staying at Mr. Abbott's? I'm sorry for cutting across his yard. My pa don't shine to that."

Since she was a schoolmarm of vast experience and knew a thing or two about the inexhaustible font of children's mischief, Elsbeth's instincts told her there was more to the story, but she really didn't have the time to ferret it out. She nodded. "You run along then."

"Yes, ma'am."

Elsbeth watched the boy bolt across the lawn, then made her way back to the streetlight just in time to see a carriage pull up to Abbott's drive.

Focused on the carriage, she didn't notice the boy circle back along the line of a hedge to the oak tree, where he was joined by a shadowy figure, the two of them watching her with great interest.

She did notice, however, that Mr. Abbott was in a mood.

David stepped from the carriage with a sour expression on his face and made his way slowly up the gravel drive to his front door. Fumbling for his keys, David opened it and headed directly for the bar to pour a scotch—a hint of red playing in the corner of his eyes. He looked up to find his stage prop in the corner of the room. Taking a swig from his drink, he dropped onto the divan and stared at it for a moment, his thoughts troubled.

He was beginning to wrestle with a throw pillow when he noticed a tiny baseball mitt resting among porcelain figurines and a metronome on the side table. He picked it up and smiled for the first time that day, looking toward the bedroom off the kitchen.

A woman, red cheeked and thick as a beer stein, entered the

room while he toyed with the mitt. She waited grim-faced as he placed it back on the side table.

"Yes, Hannah?"

She motioned to the glove. "That baby ain't one year old, and already you have visions of Cy Young's second coming."

David looked at the glove, then to the nanny.

"You're setting everybody up for a world of hurt when that child don't want to play ball, is all I'm saying."

David took a quick swallow, looking over the top of the glass. "Experience has taught me that when a woman says, 'That's all I'm saying,' I'll never hear the end of it."

Hannah put her hands on her generous hips, refusing to take the bait. She cocked her head toward the door sitting by the bar. "Stan dropped that by earlier, and the baby's fast asleep."

David grunted. "Anything else?" he asked.

"There was a bit of a mess. The blanket is drying on the line."

"Thank you, Hannah. You can head on home."

David heard her leave through the back door and held the cold glass to his head, feeling a headache build.

The doorbell chimed. Irritated, he got up and slowly made his way to the front of the house. He'd only cracked it when the source of his headache barged into the living room, turned, and faced him, looking like the very devil.

"Miss Grundy! I'm sorry, but—"

Whatever David had been about to voice lodged in his throat when Elsbeth cut him off. "Please, no need to apologize. I was so delighted with our earlier encounter that I simply had to drop by to see what you'd do for an encore—those being your specialty." Having said that, she gave him a look that would singe the fur off a cat.

David blinked and cleared his throat. "I must insist that you leave before I am forced to contact the authorities."

"Call them," Elsbeth barked. "That will provide a tidy solution.

And it is *Mrs.* Grundy," she added while poking him in the chest with her cane. "Mr. Abbott, I will be only too happy to leave. But not before you hear me out. I will be brief."

After calculating the effort necessary to remove the woman from his home against the effort required to listen to her story and let her leave of her own accord, he dropped onto the divan, again pressing the glass of scotch to his forehead.

Elsbeth sat in the chair next to him, waiting for his full attention. He set the glass down with a sigh.

"This isn't even my idea," she said. "I'm only trying to save your neck for a friend." She gave him a look that suggested he think twice before asking who and took a breath, clearing her head. "As I attempted to explain to you at the theater, you are in danger, though why I should care at this point, I don't know. Your friend, Mr. Culler, will be coming to your home tonight, presumably for your door. The visit will end with you deader than a doornail. Do I have your attention now?" She emphasized the last word by slamming her cane on the ground. Having said her piece, Elsbeth laid her hands in her lap and waited.

David took a gulp from his drink and grimaced. "I apologize for my coarse treatment of you at the theater," he said. "And I can't claim Mr. Culler's friendship. We are business associates. That is all. I doubt he even knows where I live."

"And I did?" Elsbeth quipped.

Abbott muttered several words under his breath before speaking aloud. "Can you corroborate your accusations?"

Elsbeth glared at him, thinking she should just walk right out the door and leave him to his fate, but she knew what Annie would say to *that*. She put her hand over her purse.

Abbott pointed to the handbag and was about to say something when she snapped, "Don't test me, young man!" catching him off guard. "I'll show you 'corroborate'! You'll end up wiping your soiled drawers with the corroboration I've got!" She lifted her handbag to the side table and began to rummage through it while muttering to herself.

"It'll serve you right and prove to be a damn sight more entertaining for me than being kicked out of your"—she looked Abbott in the face and said sharply—"pigpen of a dressing room!" before continuing with her muttering diatribe. "Some people wouldn't know help if it came wrapped in a pretty bow. Better to let it bite them on the ass. But I said I'd do what I can, and I will..."

Precariously balanced, the purse fell to the floor and its contents scattered left and right. El stared at the mess. "Well, sonofabitch," she whispered and gingerly bent over to begin shoveling loose items into her bag.

David tried to assist her and was rewarded by having his hand roundly smacked. Too tickled to be offended, he retreated to save himself from another tongue-lashing and took stock. He found his commitment to loathing Mrs. Grundy wavering and, given enough time, could see the two of them making the pub rounds together—smoking, drinking, and cussing like sailors. Caught up in that entertaining notion, he didn't notice a slip of paper that had fallen from her bag to flutter momentarily on the lip of the Garnkirk vase resting at the base of his table before tumbling inside.

Having retrieved the last of her articles, Elsbeth obstinately waved off David's hand and used her cane to get to her feet before slowly insinuating herself back into the chair. She glared at him, reluctant to part with a letter held firmly in both hands.

Having learned the hard way not to press her, David glanced out the window, giving her a moment. Standing abruptly, he craned his neck, utterly dismayed to see the root of her accusation walking up the block to pause under the canopy of a magnolia tree. Mr. Culler appeared to be engaged in a heated conversation, but the play of the shadows hid the other party from view.

"Mrs. Grundy," he said. "I suddenly find myself believing you entirely." Realizing that time was short, he hauled her up by the elbow for the second time that day. Elsbeth looked out the window, then turned to David in alarm. "I assure you," he said, "I will get to the bottom of this. However, I think you are safer here." David guided Elsbeth to a nearby closet, opened the door, and roughly deposited her inside.

He started to close the door when she barred it with her foot. "Don't be a fool!" she said.

David stared at the front door, then turned to Elsbeth. "Listen to me," he whispered. "It is clear that you know things you shouldn't, but that is a mystery for another day. You must understand that I cannot risk the door falling into the wrong hands. The result would be disastrous. I created it. It is Pandora's box, and I am the guardian. I know its potential for runaway mischief, and I alone am responsible."

"You will fail!"

"I assure you, I will not." Taking a deep breath, he continued. "Please understand. The safety of the door is of the upmost importance. Everything else is secondary." He stole a glance at the front door, adding, "One way or another, I don't intend to end up 'deader than a doornail,' as you so eloquently put it."

David closed the closet door and leaned against its frame as he considered his next move. His gaze drifted to the back of the house, and he hurried past the kitchen and through a door. Rushing to the crib in the corner, he lifted a child from the bed and wrapped it in a blanket. It gurgled happily and grabbed his nose. Holding the tiny hand in his, David kissed the baby's cheek before putting it in a bassinet sitting on the bureau.

He threw a drawer open to retrieve a stack of documents. With them in hand, his eyes darted about, and he stormed across the room, grabbing another that was pinned to the wall with thumbtacks. As he yanked at it, a large piece tore loose, fluttering to the ground. The rest he put in the bassinet with the baby.

In the other room, Elsbeth peered apprehensively through the closet's keyhole as David entered and exited her narrow line of vision. Quite suddenly, he loomed before her in front of the red door. She was stunned to find him lowering a bassinet, of all things, to the floor in front of it before running his hands across the door's surface. Then, kneeling down, Abbott pulled what appeared to be a tiny baseball glove from his pocket and wrapped it in the blanket that spilled over the top of the bassinet.

He remained on his knees for a second, whispering words just outside Elsbeth's hearing. Standing, he opened the door and, before she could protest, pushed the bassinet through. She watched, blinking in confusion, as both David and the child appeared to evaporate into the door frame. A moment later, he reappeared in the living room empty-handed and dropped to his knees.

Elsbeth's mind raced and she took a step back, tripping over a shoe before catching herself against a wall. Abbott had a baby? A boy? Annie hadn't mentioned a child. She cleared her head with a shake and put her eye back to the keyhole.

David Abbott looked tormented. After a moment, he stood abruptly to study the carvings on the door's surface.

He seemed indecisive to El, reaching for the doorknob only to drop his hand to his side. Finally, moving his hand rapidly across the surface, tapping one icon after another, he opened the door and melted yet again into the frame. Less than a heartbeat later, he reappeared, looking strangely haggard. The set of his shoulders and a haunted expression left him looking like a man burdened by the weight of the world, and it led Elsbeth to wonder not what he was doing, but what he had just *done.*

When a knock sounded on the front door, Abbott whirled to face the stage prop. "I didn't—" He shook his head, speaking barely loud enough for her to hear. "Ah, you are a fickle friend. What game are you playing at?"

Elsbeth hadn't a clue what Abbott's words meant. She watched him stride across the living room in the direction of the entryway. He slowed as he passed the closet where she hid, staring at it in a very peculiar fashion before raising his hand in a gesture of acknowledgment. It was odd of him to do that, she thought. Something important had just happened, but she was at a loss as to what it might be.

David's voice carried from the entryway, almost as if he wanted Elsbeth to hear what he was saying. "What an unexpected surprise. Please come in..."

# CHAPTER TWELVE

## A Conversation No One Heard

Quit toying with it, Mr. Danyer. It's dead already."

"Yes, Mr. Culler." Danyer's voice, more moan than hum, still managed after all these years to scrape the inside of Mr. Culler's skull.

"I simply don't understand your fascination with death."

"I admire its purity."

"Yes, okay... Well!" Mr. Culler gestured toward the Abbott estate at the end of the block, picking up where the conversation left off as they made their way down the street. "I've been meaning to ask, has Fabian acquired Mr. Abbott's journal for us, yet? It's been, what, two weeks now?"

"I had to...fire him, Mr. Culler."

"I'm not sure I like your tone of voice."

"Hmm."

Frustrated, Mr. Culler massaged the back of his neck. "Mr. Danyer, you can't simply dispose of everyone with whom you have a disagreement."

"It needed doing, Mr. Culler. Unfortunately, Cap'n witnessed his dismissal."

"That *is* a shame. I'm assuming you're handling matters in that regard?"

"It's being dealt with."

"Be careful. That kid's wily. Do you agree with the strategy we discussed yesterday?"

Danyer merely grunted his assent—a primitive, apelike sound.

"But David is a man of scruples. He has rigid ethical boundaries. Persuading him will be no easy task. Any thoughts?"

"Ah, Mr. Culler, you know me. I prefer direct inducements, lacking your finesse."

"Yes, you have always had a simple philosophy. But sometimes it rubs against the grain, don't you think?"

"I will admit that I am not one to let principle overshadow prudence."

"You're bloodthirsty!"

"I make the hard choices. If it weren't for me, you'd still be wasting your talents making Mr. Raven wealthier. Our business prospects have thrived since his convenient demise."

"True, but I still say it wasn't necessary to suffocate him with his own fist, you know."

# CHAPTER THIRTEEN

## A Wolf in Jackal Skin

Mr. Culler stepped into the dim light of David Abbott's porch, set a valise at his feet, and adjusted his tie. He still wore his finery from the evening's performance at the opera house. In stark contrast to his clothes, the valise was oversize and tattered. While it might have seemed an odd supplement to his tuxedo, Mr. Culler carried it with him everywhere.

After rapping on the door, he looked over his shoulder at Danyer who was holding back a few paces, almost lost in the shadows of an overgrown oleander bush.

Suddenly, the gaslight of the living room bathed Mr. Culler in a lurid glow, and he turned. "Good evening, Mr. Abbott," he said. "Should I have called first?"

David smiled at him from the doorway before peering thoughtfully in Danyer's direction. He looked back to Mr. Culler. "What an unexpected surprise. Please, come in." He stepped to the side, so deep in thought that he lost track of time and was caught off guard to find that Mr. Culler had already worked his way to the far side of the living room and was calling his name.

"Oh, pardon me." David closed the door and, ignoring Danyer, strode across the room, studying Mr. Culler's face. Even away from the harsh porch light, it was completely unreadable, but David had expected that. Time and association had proven to him that, aside from the eyes, Mr. Culler had a talent for making his face bland, a putty mask over which his emotions would occasionally and violently churn from the least provocation, almost like a child preparing a tantrum, before quickly returning to a state of utter complacency. These episodes were so fleeting that David was left to question what he'd actually seen.

The eyes, however, told another story. They always seemed a little wild, yet detached, as if they were out of touch with Mr. Culler's humanity. David could explain it no better than that. The little "tremors of change," as he called them, were unnerving to witness but harmless enough. Even so, his first encounter with this phenomenon was so vivid that he was left with the mistaken, yet lasting, impression of disfigurement in Mr. Culler—a scarring of his face with pockmarks. So he was always mildly surprised to note that the man's skin was unblemished.

But tonight was different. Mr. Culler's eyes were not flashing. They were eerily focused. David had seen that look before, but never on a human. Mr. Culler was sizing him up, like a fox that had cornered a chicken in the coop.

"Please, make yourself comfortable," David said, motioning to the sitting area. "Can I offer you a drink?"

"Allow me." Mr. Culler walked past the divan to the bar before David could protest. He set out three tumblers and poured bourbon into two, while motioning with a subtle tilt of his head for his associate to seat himself in the farthest chair opposite the divan. "I believe you are a scotch man," he said to Abbott as he filled the third. He wandered back to the divan, handed the scotch to David, and placed a tumbler of bourbon on the side table for his associate before dropping into the remaining empty chair. "Fine house you have here, Mr. Abbott," he said, lifting his glass.

David didn't respond immediately, his eyes focused on the tumbler Mr. Culler intended for his associate, watching as water beaded on its surface. He blinked several times, as though Mr. Culler's voice had pulled him out of a trance, and looked up. "It's a bit spare, I'm afraid, without the items the auction house collected," he said. "To what do I owe the pleasure?"

"I have a bit of a proposal, actually," Mr. Culler said. "The show has run its course, and it is time to move on to other ventures. One has become immediately obvious. It may surprise you to learn that it involves that most unusual door of yours."

David put down his drink. "I'm intrigued," he said.

"Yes, so am I, by your door. While I find it difficult to understand, there is no arguing that it has…unique properties." Mr. Culler noticed that Danyer was about to interrupt and silenced him with a quick, steely glance.

David missed the exchange but noticed anger flare across Mr. Culler's features for an instant, only to quickly melt into a placid smile, and was left to wonder what had just transpired.

"It's a brilliant deception," Mr. Culler continued. "This pretense of a magic show to disguise the fact that the door is indeed magical." Pleased that David didn't interject or prevaricate in any way, he added, "It's the ultimate sleight of hand and a deception that can be turned to our economic gain, I think."

"How so?"

Mr. Culler cleared his throat. "Is it not obvious? Let's not be coy, Mr. Abbott. This door is of inestimable value for those with the courage to seize upon its advantages."

David returned his gaze without comment, noticing a slight compaction along Mr. Culler's jawline.

Mr. Culler glanced one more time at Danyer who became fixed in place, still as stone, before turning back to face David. "You are going to require me to be blunt, I see," he said. "It is only too obvious that a person, or persons, armed with"—he searched for an appropriate term—"foreknowledge…can formulate strategies to their economic advantage." He picked up a porcelain figurine of a wolf and examined it while he spoke. "The proposal is simple. Plainly stated, you use the door to collect information that will guide investment decisions to our benefit. Another partnership, if you will—uncomplicated and profitable." He set the porcelain figurine on the table next to that of a lamb and rested his elbows on the arms of the chair. Slowly, he leaned forward to rest his chin on his knuckles.

David set his scotch on the side table. "I'll not deny that the door has 'unique properties.'" He tugged at a chain pull, illuminating the table lamp. "There are natural laws that run parallel to those properties that I do not fully comprehend, not unlike electricity, I would guess, and I'm beginning to suspect that meddling with them can have disastrous consequences."

Agitated, David stood and walked behind the divan. Grasping its backrest with both hands, he leaned forward, causing the muscles in his shoulders to knot. He continued speaking as much to his own conscience as to Mr. Culler. "There are so many unknowns," he said. "Surely my forays into the future must have consequences. And those consequences lead to other consequences like dominoes knocking one another over as they race back and forth through time.

"We are talking about a chain reaction of inconsequential actions that lead to monumental changes, sir. I don't think the natural laws have a place for someone who does that, and still I do it twice a night to provide us a tidy profit. Isn't that enough?" He shook his head. "Frankly, the door should never have been made in the first place, but I was proud and it was a challenge. I'm afraid I've become overly sentimental and cannot conceive of destroying it, though that may be best." The divan scraped an inch or two across the floor as he shoved himself erect. "To be honest, I do not trust myself. And I wonder if I can trust it."

"You're talking in riddles, Mr. Abbott."

David's eyes turned to the door sitting in the corner. "I know," he said.

Mr. Culler's cheek twitched, a flicker of a movement that rippled across his face. While it faded rapidly from view, David could read the signs. Things could go very wrong if he was not careful. As Mr. Culler stood and started to dust his pants, David glanced at the closet. "It must be kept secret," he said.

Mr. Culler paused. The ghost of a smile played over his features as he reseated himself, motioning discreetly for Danyer to do the same.

David's eyes trailed to the untouched drink sweating on the table. "This door is no trifle, you understand."

"Completely," Mr. Culler said, his eyes straying to Danyer, watching as he shook his head for only his boss to see.

David rubbed his forehead. "Tomorrow then," he said. "Come back tomorrow. I need to think."

"Much more to my liking, Mr. Abbott."

David nodded grimly, stepping around the divan to extend his hand.

Ignoring it, Mr. Culler stepped forward and wrapped his arms around him in a clumsy embrace. After a very awkward moment where David struggled to reciprocate, Mr. Culler stepped back, muttering to himself, and glanced over his shoulder at Danyer. He nodded. Silver flashed in the light of the room as a hand shot out. Then again. And a third time.

David huffed, as if the air had been knocked out of him. He stared at Mr. Culler in wonder before staggering back to raise the hand he'd placed over his stomach in front of his eyes. He began to shake, causing the blood that soaked it to trail down his wrist, dripping ruby-colored pearls onto the carpet. The shock of the image left him disconnected, and he stared at the large dagger buried in his midriff, almost as if it were embedded in another man.

Mesmerized, he touched the bone handle, noting that it was etched with the image of a clipper ship capsizing in a storm. A crimson stain blossomed over his shirt, running down his leg to collect in a small pool on the wooden floor around his feet. He tugged at the knife feebly before stumbling forward, reaching for Mr. Culler.

Amused by his struggle, Mr. Culler held him upright. "You're a better magician than actor, Mr. Abbott," he said. "It appears that our partnership is at an end."

A movement tickled at the periphery of Mr. Culler's vision, and he looked up at a watercolor painting on the near wall. David's struggle was reflected in the glass pane, showing the man draw him close to whisper in his ear. The image of a third man materialized in the glass as if from thin air, and Mr. Culler tried to turn, but David's grip was unbreakable, so he could only watch from the corner of his eye as the newcomer raised a knife, lazily drawing it across Mr. Culler's throat to peel it open as if it were made of wax.

He watched in horror as blood pooled in the lip of the painting's frame before overflowing to pour down the wall in a burgundy-colored sheet. The scream that was building in his throat died as the illusion vanished, and he looked back to David, shaken.

Blood began to bubble on the side of David's mouth as he struggled to speak. Spent from the effort, he sank slowly to his knees before toppling backward like a marionette whose strings had been clipped.

Mr. Culler frowned while wiping blood from his ear, then looked back to the painting—roses wilting in a vase, their petals accumulating on a wooden table, and nothing more. He shook his head and squatted down to examine David's body, taking his time and breathing evenly to slow his pulse. Mr. Culler thought he should know the third man in the mirror, but his mind was a blank. He glanced at Danyer suspiciously, then reached into his pocket to pull out a pair of surgical scissors. Lifting David's left hand, he knelt, placed the scissors over the top joint of the man's pinkie, and snipped, the flesh and bone resisting until that last moment before detaching with a satisfying pop.

Dropping the end joint of the pinkie into a handkerchief, Mr. Culler looked up to see Danyer staring at him, a strange expression on his face, and answered his question before it could be asked. "He said that even death could be an illusion." Mr. Culler stood, stuffing the hanky into his pocket. "Odd that. Unexpected." He didn't like the unexpected. "Messy business all around," he said, watching with some apprehension as Danyer studied the expanding pool of blood, its surface gleaming like molten copper in the gaslight. The man was unpredictable, and Mr. Culler didn't put it past him to wallow about.

He motioned for his associate to take a few steps back and placed a foot on David's chest for balance as he extracted the knife, after which he went to the kitchen to turn on the tap, lecturing Danyer as he rinsed off the dagger. "If we dispose of the body, Mr. Abbott will be presumed missing," he said, reaching for the soap. "And the last thing we want is for the authorities to freeze his assets." He rubbed a drop of blood from the counter with his fist and turned to Danyer, smiling at his own cleverness. "Did you know Mr. Abbott scheduled an auction of selected pieces of furniture in advance of his move to the McFarlane mansion?"

Danyer followed Mr. Culler into the living room.

Studying Abbott's body one last time, Mr. Culler glanced at the side table and, on an impulse, released the latch to a metronome. Watching the arm sweep to and fro, he said, "Tomorrow." He turned to his associate. "His death couldn't be more timely, don't you think? I'm sure we can pull a few strings to have the door added to the catalog."

Letting Danyer think that one over, Mr. Culler turned out the lights and made his way to the foyer to collect his bag before he stepped outside.

They'd closed the door and stepped off the porch when two things happened simultaneously. Danyer said, "The journal," even as a light appeared in a window next door.

Mr. Culler pulled Danyer into the shadow of the oleander and peered through the foliage at an older woman who appeared on the porch of the house across the lawn. He shook his head. "We'll have to come back for it."

As they made their way up the street, Elsbeth stuck her head out of the closet. "Mr. Abbott?" she said, looking left and right before seeing him lying on the floor. "Mr. Abbott!"

Hobbling across the living room, she leaned over to check his pulse even as blood enveloped his outstretched hand. Rising as quickly as she was able, Elsbeth staggered backward. "Ah, Mr. Abbott," she said. "If only you had taken me more seriously. My fault, I suppose. What do I tell Annie?"

She turned to face the mysterious red door and thought of the child Abbott had carried through it. A few tentative steps later, she had her hand on its doorknob. Gently prying the door open, she peered through to the other side. Cool air stirred against her cheek as her eyes widened, and she slammed the door shut, before stepping back a few paces.

Unsure of what to do, Elsbeth shuffled toward the back of the house, passing a small shelf lined with books, titles displayed on their spines in fine, gold lettering. There was a tattered volume sitting abandoned in the corner, completely at odds with all the rest.

Even while telling herself to quit being a first-class fool and leave, Elsbeth reached for it. Some liquid had spilled on the book's cover and had leached between the pages—coffee, she guessed. The pages were matted, and many of the notes obscured. Fully aware that time was of the essence, Elsbeth skimmed a page and made out the words *wife* and *Florence*. She gathered from another entry that David's wife had died in childbirth. She dropped the diary in her handbag, knocking over a framed photograph with her elbow in the process.

Righting it, Elsbeth confronted an image of David standing behind a seated woman. She picked up the photo for closer study, and her lower lip began to quiver. A single tear stained her spectacles. "Hello, Florence," she said, brushing her hand across its surface.

Suddenly angry, she dried the lens with the cuff of her sleeve and hurried out the back door.

CHAPTER

# FOURTEEN

## The Hen House

Westport, Kansas, was a community of thoroughbreds, where proper breeding was not only expected, but also required. Decorum was the air the town breathed, and the first commandment of local society was "mind your own damn business." Privacy was considered so sacred to the good people of the township and so jealously guarded that—and this should come as no surprise—there were no secrets there at all, human nature being what it is. Everyone was taught reconnaissance at their mama's knee and went on to become an agent provocateur. In Westport, secrets were scandal, and scandal was sport.

Even those who survived the carnage of the rumor mill learned that Westport was anything but an egalitarian society. A pecking order existed. The big hens pecked at the smaller hens that, in turn, pecked at the even smaller hens on down the line until they reached the last unfortunate soul with no one to peck.

That lonely little hen would be the widow McCready, who was standing on her lawn, staring at the Abbott estate when the staccato beat of hooves interrupted the night.

A light appeared in the window of a home. Then another. And soon another. Within minutes the neighborhood windows looked like the lights of a phone company switchboard. Doors opened and people appeared in the soft glow of their porches to look for the source of the commotion.

Policemen rushed onto the grounds of David Abbott's house, and neighbors were quietly yet sternly told to return to their homes without explanation, much to their dissatisfaction. Reconnaissance would follow. Then the gossip.

Only the widow McCready was allowed to remain. She stood in her nightgown, slippers, and hairnet while speaking to a pair of officers—having found just enough time to put in her false teeth. The officers took notes and tried not to wince at her shrill, somewhat nasal tone.

"I was settling in for the evening when I noticed the strangest thing at David's home." She sighed, her eyes losing focus, and said, "Such a lovely man, David."

The officer tapped his pencil on his notepad.

"Oh yes. As I was saying," continued Mrs. McCready, "I stepped onto my porch to investigate." She leaned forward, whispering. "There was an older woman at his back door who looked about in what I can only say was a calculating fashion before making her way quickly to the gate. She disappeared down the service street." Mrs. McCready waved vaguely toward the back of the house.

"And what was the approximate time you saw this woman depart?"

"Well, I'm guessing an hour or so ago. Perhaps 9:30 p.m.?" Mrs. McCready's mouth tightened as she did the math in her head, leaving her upper lip to look as if it were pleated. "Yes, that would be right."

"Were you able to get a close look at this woman?"

The widow's smile faded. She appeared offended by the question, pressing her hand to her chest as she said, "Well, not really. I didn't get a close look at her at all. We mind our own business here in Westport, you know."

Mrs. McCready let out a quick huff of breath while tapping her forefinger to her neck. "Let me see what I can recall. It was dark, mind you," she said. Her eyes narrowed as she dredged up a shocking amount of detail for a woman who minded her own business. The officer took notes on everything from Elsbeth's spectacles to the number of wooden buttons on her dress while thinking that Mrs. McCready had the eyes of an owl.

"And that dress! So unfortunate," she said, placing her hand over the neckline of her gingham nightgown. "Oh! And her bones clicked when she walked!"

"Clicked, ma'am?"

"Yes, quite noticeably. Obviously arthritic, bless her soul."

*Eyes of an owl, ears of a fox*, the officer thought as he asked, "Can you tell us anything else?"

"Well, after I saw her depart through the alley, I thought to myself, 'Evillene, there is something strange going on at the Abbott residence.' I'm not the prying type and almost decided to let matters lie, but I was concerned for David's welfare. We're on a first-name basis, you know."

Mrs. McCready went on to describe in a mountain of words and without taking a breath how she knocked on David Abbott's door and, receiving no response, peered through a side window to see a figure lying on the living room floor.

The three walked over to the window in question. Evillene pressed her head against the windowpane and cupped her hands around her eyes. "Can you see him?" she asked. Tapping it, she added, "By the divan."

At first, the two officers could see very little in the darkness. Eventually, their eyes adjusted, and they were able to see a form lying at a peculiar angle in the middle of the living room. They looked at each other, then turned to Mrs. McCready. "Thank you for your assistance, ma'am. We'll handle it from here."

Evillene wasn't taking the hint and remained rooted in place, forcing the officers to usher her toward her home while she squawked in protest. "Don't forget about the baby!"

"What baby?" yelled the first officer from across the lawn.

"David's baby! The nursery is at the back of the first floor."

After the officer held up his thumb in acknowledgment, Mrs. McCready cut across the hedge separating her property from the Abbott estate, quickly straightening her hairnet when she saw a pair of bored-looking reporters loitering on her front porch.

As Evillene began to repeat her story for the press, Officers Franklin and Kearney tested Abbott's front door. They could hear her unmistakable voice peal across the lawn as they disappeared inside. "Well, I'm sure I don't know what, but there's something amiss in that house!"

A quick sweep revealed one corpse, no evidence of forced entry, no signs of a struggle, and no baby. They did find three drinks—one scotch and two bourbons.

Sergeant Kearney pulled out a notepad. Aside from the obvious question, he wanted to know how an elderly woman, purportedly not even five feet tall, could stab a man of Mr. Abbott's size to death. And why three drinks? He wondered drily whether the old woman's poison was scotch or bourbon as he jotted down the question. And, if this was a murder-kidnapping as it appeared, why was the suspect not seen leaving with the baby in her arms? If Mrs. McCready could make out wooden buttons on the suspect's dress, she certainly would have noticed a child, he thought.

Lieutenant Franklin walked back into the room and broke Kearney's train of thought. Looking about the room, he made a decision. "Clay, the lighting's too poor. Let's seal off the room, place a team at the front and back of the house, and come back tomorrow. The last thing I want to do is taint the crime scene. Can you oversee the placement of security?"

"Yes, sir." Sergeant Kearney headed for the front door.

Franklin took a final look around, turned down the gas lighting, and followed him out.

Soon after, there was a stirring near the stairwell, and a shadow separated itself from the darkness, gliding through the den. The brief intersection of moonlight and a mirror captured a flash of wild, vividly focused eyes. A shuffle, a bump, and the scraping rasp of wood on wood followed as the divan lurched an inch or two. The revenant froze, melting into the shadows. After a pregnant pause, it reappeared to circle in front of the divan and hover over David Abbott's corpse. Through it all, the officers on duty outside remained blithely oblivious.

# CHAPTER FIFTEEN

## The Chase

### MAY 30, 1895

"You must first tease away a small fragment. Then, if you incise the skin precisely, you can peel it away from the meat in a single piece, almost like stripping the hide from a squirrel."

Danyer's words rang inside Mr. Culler's head as he attempted to shuck the boiled egg. Despite his best efforts, however, the result paled in comparison to his associate's almost inhuman ability to resurrect the egg's shape from the shell alone.

He dropped the failed attempt onto his platter, daring Danyer to comment. When he didn't rise to the bait, Mr. Culler flagged the waiter to top off his coffee and grabbed a clean plate, only to freeze, certain that he'd caught the reflection of something that shouldn't be there. He angled the plate this way and that until the same man he saw reflected in the glass of David Abbott's painting resolved onto its surface. The man threw back his head to laugh, all the while pulling clumps of hair from his head. Mr. Culler dropped the plate, threw his napkin over it, and, with a quick glance to Danyer, opened his newspaper.

"Seeing things that aren't there again, Mr. Culler?"

Ignoring the question, he scanned the page. An article had caught his attention. He frowned, folded the paper, and passed it across the table.

Danyer began to read about David Abbott's murder but was caught off guard by a particular paragraph.

> Mrs. McCready states that she was on the porch enjoying a cup of tea when she noticed an elderly woman exit Mr. Abbott's back door. She describes the woman as being in her midsixties, a bit less than five feet tall, with steel-gray hair tied up in a bun and a slight stoop…

He looked up, startled, and Mr. Culler nodded. "A loose end," he said.

A rumbling at the back of Danyer's throat signaled his understanding. Loose ends were unacceptable.

Mr. Culler picked up a fork and began stabbing at his pancakes, thinking out loud. "It might be prudent to talk to the detective in charge of the investigation. Find out what he knows." He tapped the article with one hand while scooping a helping into his mouth with the other. "There's more," he said.

> What makes this brutal slaying all the stranger is the absence of Abbott's one-year-old baby.

As if he'd read Danyer's mind and found it lacking, Mr. Culler waved his hand in irritation. "Forget about the baby. Read further," he said.

> Local authorities confirm that the auction of Mr. Abbott's personal belongings will proceed as scheduled.

"The door, yes?" said Mr. Culler, grinning at Danyer's primitive, predatory murmur. "The door, indeed." Suddenly ravenous, he stuffed the napkin back in his collar and dug into his breakfast, thinking to himself how rewarding it was to have a plan. Find the loose end. Kill her. Buy the door.

He looked across the table to see Danyer lift the eggshell with a fork, the corner of his mouth rising. Clearly, his associate was thinking along the same lines.

It was not unusual for there to be common ground between their thoughts. Culler and Danyer were almost always in sync. Ironically, the creature at the intersection of their deliberations was, unbeknownst to them, sitting three tables down.

Elsbeth was occupied with the same article. She sat up with a start upon reading her description, causing her spectacles to fall into her oatmeal. Plucking them from the melted butter that pooled in the middle of the bowl, she cleaned the lenses with a dampened napkin. Despite the fact that they were somewhat the worse for wear, she placed them over the hook in her nose and finished the article.

Annie had warned her to take care. And despite the warning, she'd walked right into a passel of trouble.

Elsbeth signaled for her check and glanced around at a room filled with people, many of whom were enjoying the morning paper. Suddenly feeling like a "sitting duck," though she wouldn't be familiar with the term, Elsbeth let loose a shockingly colorful stream of expletives under her breath. Roughly translated, they fell into one of three categories—body parts, barnyard animals, and, in the most extreme cases, body parts of barnyard animals.

Having exhausted her supply of non-liturgical rhetoric while fishing change from her purse, Elsbeth decided a disguise was in order. She reached into her bag for a scarf to cover her steel-gray hair and removed her spectacles before making her way through the resulting fog toward the front door. Bumping into a patron, she exclaimed, "I do beg your pardon!"

Mr. Culler merely grunted his acknowledgment as he fished change from his pocket to settle the bill. He signaled to Danyer, and the two made for the lobby doors to hail a hansom cab for Westport.

The day already promised to be unseasonably hot, and Mr. Culler stood in front of Abbott's home, patting the shine from his face. He stuffed the soiled handkerchief in his breast pocket and turned to his associate. "I'll do the talking, Mr. Danyer," he said.

They made the long walk up the drive, only to be stopped just shy of the porch by a duty officer who was escorting a journalist out the front door. "We have a crime scene here, sir," the officer said as he crossed their path. "I'm going to have to ask you to move along." He booted the journalist to the curb. "Pull one more stunt like that, Thaddeus, and you'll be meeting tonight's deadline from the hoosegow!"

"I might be able to help you with that suspect," Mr. Culler said, offering his card when the officer stepped back onto the porch. "The late Mr. Abbott was my business partner."

Caught off guard by the comment, the duty officer took a quick look at the card. "Wait here, sir," he said.

At length, the front door opened and a large, balding man sporting a mustache fit to sweep coal stepped out. "Ambrosius Culler?" he asked.

Righting himself from the brick wall where he'd been leaning, Mr. Culler extended his hand.

The man stuffed a notepad in his pocket before sizing Mr. Culler up. "I am Lieutenant Franklin. Come in and don't touch anything." He disappeared inside, leaving Mr. Culler and Danyer scrambling to follow him into the living room.

"I understand you may have some information that relates to this case?"

"I'm not certain," said Mr. Culler, picking at a thread hanging from the divan. "Possibly."

Impatient and not amused by Mr. Culler's coyness, Lieutenant Franklin simply turned to walk off. "Get back to me when you are," he said, looking over his shoulder.

Unperturbed, Mr. Culler didn't let the officer take two steps before saying, "Mr. Abbott had a stalker fitting the description of the suspect in the paper."

The comment had an immediate and desirous effect. Lieutenant Franklin turned, scowling. He shoved his hands in his pockets, waiting for Mr. Culler to continue.

"She was seen several times backstage at the Coates Opera House where he was performing. A very determined woman."

While Mr. Culler spoke with one eye to the lieutenant, the other scanned the room. An officer, taking measurements of the bloodstain surrounding Abbott's body, knocked over a vase sitting at the base of a side table, leading to an unfortunate series of events.

Called into a quick powwow, the officer failed to see a slip of paper dangling from the vase's mouth. Mr. Culler, on the other hand, did.

Minutes later, having completed his business with the police, Mr. Culler said his good-byes, collected Danyer, and made a hasty exit.

Sergeant Kearney, half a dozen paces behind, stepped onto the porch to have a quick word with the duty officer, feeling uneasy. Something about Mr. Culler set his teeth on edge. Returning to the living room to find the man on his knees by the side table was disturbing. He was just too...satisfied, despite holding up a pocket watch he'd supposedly dropped.

Kearney examined the table after Mr. Culler left and found nothing suspicious, but he remained ill at ease. Failing in the struggle to put words to his concern, Kearney shrugged and turned to speak to Lieutenant Franklin through the open door. "Arthur, there's nothing more to be done until the medical examiner arrives. Let's take a break and I'll spot you a cup of coffee."

Lieutenant Franklin nodded. "Let the duty officer know," he said and followed the sergeant out the front door, even as Messrs. Culler and Danyer turned the corner at the end of the block.

"Did you find the journal?" asked Mr. Culler. He pulled the slip of paper from his pocket even as Mr. Danyer shook his head. It was from a piece of stationery embossed with the Broadway Hotel logo and read:

*May 29*

*Mrs. Grundy:*

*Your ticket is confirmed and waiting for you at will call.*

*Concierge Desk*

Mr. Culler checked his timepiece. "Fancy a coffee at the Broadway, Mr. Danyer?"

Having navigated the lobby without incident, El quickly packed, then sat on the bed with her satchel at her feet. She yanked her spectacles from her nose and began to clean them, starting with the stems and working her way to the lenses, a habit of hers when she was anxious. Realizing that she was just killing time, Elsbeth hobbled to the desk, where she found hotel stationery and a pencil in the drawer. She wrote the date in the upper left corner, then stared at the wall, her mind a blank. The ticking of the desk clock insinuated itself into her consciousness like a fly buzzing around her head that she couldn't wave off.

El scowled at the stationery, trying to focus, but the insistent palpitation left no room for words to emerge in her mind. Dropping the pencil in frustration, she wrestled the clock into the closet and slammed the door. She returned to the desk, but the unrelenting sound was only muted, making it all the more aggravating. As she considered taking a mallet to the clock, El realized she was simply loath to report her failure. Having diagnosed the problem, she mulishly began to write. And once started, she became so consumed by her task that she didn't notice the ticking from the closet had begun to slow. Time apparently was running out.

*30th of May, 1895*

*Dear Annie,*

*I have much to report.*

*Let me start by saying that I watched David Abbott's final performance and am now certain that the door is the latchkey that links our worlds.*

*However, there is sad news. I am sorry, but I have failed. He is dead.*

*My plan was simple. I met with him in his dressing room, but I'm afraid my damn temper got the best of me. I was dismissed out of hand. Undeterred, I went to his home. There were more words before I managed to get through to him, but I was too late.*

*He was killed while I strained to see through a keyhole in his closet door. I could hear very little, but what I did made it clear to me that he was killed for his remarkable red door. I've seen death before, but murder is another thing altogether. It is evil.*

*I wish I could have prevented his demise, for your sake and for his. He seemed to me a good man who held himself accountable for his actions.*

*There is something else I wish to report. Mr. Abbott*

*has a son. He deposited the child through that queer door of his. I suspect he thought it to be the safest place while he dealt with the intrusion.*

*It seems that my failure is double. I came to save a life. Instead, I lost two. There is nothing I can do for Mr. Abbott, but I have a duty to that child. If he is alive, he may well be somewhere on your side of the door.*

*It's now your turn to intervene. Enclosed is Mr. Abbott's diary. You may find it useful, although it is in disrepair. There are references to Florence, his wife, and a birth in June of 1894 at Our Lady of Lourdes Hospital in Kansas City. I scanned several entries regarding the door, but they are fragmented, resulting from the diary's poor condition.*

*There is one last thing. Your warning about a suspect, unfortunately, was in vain. I was seen leaving Mr. Abbott's home and am now, apparently, the suspect mentioned in the article. I will make my way home cautiously.*

*I have learned some things of use, suspect even more, and have never found myself so completely at a loss.*

*Apologetically,*
*El*

# CHAPTER SIXTEEN

## Down the Rabbit Hole

Elsbeth had just settled into her seat when the train bound for home lurched into motion. With a quick glance out the window at the receding platform, she rummaged through her satchel for some crackers, only to come across the bars of soap she had taken from the Broadway. She experienced a twinge of guilt, not for their acquisition—it would be a cold day in Kansas before Amos carried scented soap at the Hay and Feed—but because they reminded her that she hadn't settled her bill. She was preparing to check out when she spied the man she'd bumped into at breakfast approach the counter and had ducked behind a potted plant, feeling foolish.

Uncertain why, she'd determined he was trouble. He'd settled into a lengthy conversation with the receptionist, rudely ignoring the line waiting behind him. But when she heard him mention her name, she'd decided she could just as easily settle her bill by mail and had made herself scarce.

The trip home was uneventful, and Elsbeth found herself at the picket fence surrounding Annie's house several hours later. She placed the letter she'd written at the hotel inside the brass letter box and was turning for home when, remembering the diary, she retrieved it from her pocket and dropped it inside as well.

She and Annie had stirred up a hornet's nest together, that was certain, yet she was surprised by the realization that she had no regrets. *Your garden needs pruning*, she decided. Pulling a rose from its stem, she breathed in the aroma and smiled, causing the dark, downy hairs that had recently taken over her upper lip—a light dusting of charcoal—to tickle at the base of her nose.

Snatching a hankie from her pocket, Elsbeth sneezed violently, a response that seemed to indicate her body was allergic to any expression remotely associated with happiness. She gave the letter box a pat and made her way home, imagining Annie sitting at her desk writing a letter when, in fact, she was sitting in one of the window seats in her living room.

Annie was relaxing with her bare feet propped up on the cushion so she could look out the window onto the park while she pressed Christian for details about his pub crawl with Edmond the evening before. There was a rose from the mystery garden in her hand and a Cheshire grin on her face that came from hearing what he was saying and listening to what he was not.

"Nope, no insight on whether we've crossed paths before," Christian said, speaking with his usual broken tempo, something Annie hardly noticed anymore. "He's a little cagey about his past, but here's something for you. I'm pretty sure he's holding on to a secret—something painful. I don't know what it is, though." He plopped down on a chair, threw his leg over the armrest, and grabbed a magazine from the coffee table. Flipping through the pages, he added, "Apparently, I'm a complication."

Annie had been watching a Yorkie circle a Great Dane in the park. The Yorkie was running round and round as fast as its little paws could carry it. The Great Dane, by contrast, was standing still and merely turned its head back and forth while watching the Yorkie's antics, radiating amusement in an almost human way.

"A complication?" She held the flower to her nose and inhaled, unable to bottle up the smile that was beginning to play around her eyes. "What do you mean?" she asked.

Christian shrugged, unaware that she was baiting him. "Something he said." He flipped through a few pages before dropping the magazine onto his lap. "I have a headache," he said, massaging his temples.

"It's called a hangover, dear." Lowering her feet to the ground, Annie added, "You're long overdue. My first was with a bottle of cheap port at the tender age of fourteen. Trust me when I say you're getting off lightly." She shuddered at the memory. "Now, back to being a complication."

"We were just talking, you know. I began with my usual brilliant exposition on genetic m-markers and environmental triggers for stuttering."

"Riveting, I'm sure."

Christian looked up from under his brow, smirking. "Not nearly as riveting as when I told him how you slipped me a Xanax to see if what you'd read about the benefits of dopamine suppression for stuttering were true."

"Did you also tell him about our experiment..."

"With sentences comprised solely of cuss words? Yeah, I even gave him a demonstration."

Annie burst into laughter. "He must have loved that."

"Him and half the bar," said Christian. "The conversation was moving along fine—I learned he was an orphan, and boy, did I stick my foot in my mouth with that one—but he suddenly got the queerest look on his face and started talking about needing to keep his life simple."

Christian went on to relay, as best he could, the part of the dinner conversation that had him confused, hoping that Annie could shed some light on the subject, but he stopped abruptly when he found her looking out the corner of her eyes at the dogs playing in the park and appearing terribly pleased with herself.

"But he's still planning to make those planter boxes for your entryway?" she asked.

"Yeah." He tossed the magazine aside. "Am I missing something?" he asked suddenly.

Annie broke into an ear-to-ear smile. "I'm just..." She turned to face him. "I'm happy for you, that's all."

"Huh?"

She wagged her hand playfully and stood. "I want to meet him," she said before disappearing into the kitchen, dropping the rose in his lap on the way.

"What are you doing?" he yelled after her.

"Checking for mail!"

Six blocks away, and oblivious to the fact that he was the immediate topic of conversation, Edmond was reshelving books in the science fiction and fantasy section of the library, where he worked part time. The task was mind-numbingly monotonous, so he made a game of it. He stepped onto the bottom rung of the library ladder and positioned it at the end of the shelf with a book in hand. Gauging the distance with a keen eye, he shoved the ladder down the length of the rail attached to the top of the shelf in an attempt to get it to rest in the exact spot where the book should be deposited.

The objective of the game was to collect ten points. If the book's slot rested between the poles of the ladder, Edmond collected a point. If not, he lost one. If the book's slot was even with one of the poles, Edmond determined whether a point was added by flipping a coin. After all, there must be some element of chance in the game.

Edmond knew his fantasy authors by the amount of force needed to get from the end of the shelf to their slots. A little push to get to Asimov—that one was almost a gimme. A bigger push to get to Tolkien.

He had accumulated six points and decided his effort merited a five-minute break. Sitting on a stool, he sipped a diet soda as his thoughts drifted to the night before. A patchwork quilt of images floats through his head—bread crumbs, infectious laughter (following an expletive-laden demonstration), compassion, and charity. As the thoughts advanced into uncomfortable territory, Edmond leaped from the stool to wander restlessly through aisle after aisle of books.

Christian was a frustrating young man. There was no denying that, but those frustrating characteristics were precisely what made him so, well...frustrating! And charming. And aggravating! And sweet. And wrong. And maybe right. But definitely exhausting.

Moments later, the drink was half finished and Edmond found himself on the third floor. He turned into an aisle and caught a glimpse of someone placing a book on the shelf at the far end before disappearing around the corner.

"Ken? That you?" He hurried to the end of the row. "Would you mind handling my shift next Tues—" Edmond broke from his request when he realized he was speaking to thin air. He peered down the aisle, looking this way and that before drumming his fingers on the corner of the bookshelf.

He looked up at the header hanging from the ceiling and discovered he was in the applied sciences section. Running his index finger along the ledge, he paused at the spine of a book titled *Hidden Doors: Hidden Magic*. Books on magic certainly didn't belong in the science section of the library. Edmond pulled it from the shelf to look for the Dewey decimal code, but there wasn't one. There was also no library card. And while the book was bound, it was not printed.

He took a closer look. The pages were handwritten in black ink, leading him to wonder if the book might belong in the archives. The ink looked surprisingly fresh, though. He flipped through the pages to find strange symbols drawn in the margins in brownish ink. Perhaps it was more red than brown. Regardless, the color made him uneasy.

Edmond scanned several pages, reading how the author had made a scientific study of rituals and ceremonies from various civilizations. The common thread involved purported journeys to the spirit world. Fascinated, he sat on the floor cross-legged and propped the book in his lap, the soda still in his hand.

> It is my belief that these civilizations developed an approach to science that is, in some ways, more advanced than our own. Our science is purely quantitative and stands alone. We separate it from philosophy and religion. In doing so, we are restricted by our senses. If we cannot see, feel, or touch something, it does not exist in our world and explanations are left to the Church. To coin a phrase, religion fills the void that science has no answer for. American Indian, Mayan, and Egyptian cultures, however, explored science in harmony with their culture's philosophy and spirituality and, as a result, were freed from such constraints.
>
> Of particular interest, and the focus of my study, are the "spirit walks" of the Cherokee. I believe that through an extraordinarily complex ceremony that has been passed down from teacher to student and using an arcane combination of distillations, symbols, rituals, and mental exercises, they discovered how to dislocate time. Their spirit walks do not take them to another realm but, more significantly, reach beyond the three dimensions with which we are familiar to another time within our own.

From the first word, the writing struck a chord with Edmond. But as interested as he was in the text, a strange drowsiness took hold and the words began to blur on the page.

His head dipped, and he became aware of a mechanical hum that had no external source pulsing from within his ears. His body began to vibrate while an oddly soothing light bathed him in rapid bursts like a strobe. Just when he was certain the mounting vibration would disperse his body into a billion flecks of potential, the hum, the light, and Edmond were sucked into a pinhole and vanished.

# CHAPTER SEVENTEEN

## The Unintentional Orphan

The infinite complexity of the universe can be boiled down to two simple forces—pushing and pulling, creation and destruction. And the war between the two is evident in even the tiniest interactions.

Consider the universal building blocks. Protons, neutrons, and electrons are irresistibly pulled together to create the atom. From there, the atom goes on to build, well…everything. Despite the obstacles that impede the particles' attraction, the drive to construct the atom out of its component pieces is relentless. In the end, the atom, and creation, always win.

"Mail call," Annie said as she reentered the kitchen waving a letter. She had what appeared to be a book in her other hand.

"From Elsbeth?" Christian asked, startled out of his thoughts. His mind was still locked on her obscure responses to his retelling of the conversation with Edmond. He hated it when she was obscure. Usually it was because he was left with the vague feeling that she knew something he didn't. *Why can't people simply say what they mean?* he wondered.

"Who else?" Annie sat in the kitchen nook and ripped open the envelope. Her smile disappeared as she read. "Oh…no." So quietly that Christian could barely hear her, she added, "No, this is not what I intended at all." She rested her head in the palm of her hand for a second before glancing out the window, clearly upset.

Christian eased the letter from her hand and began to read as she picked up the book, flipping furiously through its pages.

Putting the letter aside, he massaged his forehead. "You can't blame yourself," he said. He waited until her eyes meet his. "You tried to stop a murder. Your intentions count for something."

Annie was unconvinced but touched his hand in thanks before returning to the book.

Not happy with her response or lack of one, he grabbed her arm and squeezed. "Maybe nothing you could have done would have changed the outcome. The article reported a suspect. Isn't it likely that your actions were already accounted for?"

"But that's just it," she said. "Don't you see? I *did* cause this unholy mess. By convincing El to intervene, I created the circumstances that led to her being implicated in the very crime I urged her to prevent."

"Annie, Elsbeth is a grown woman."

"She's also my friend."

The way Annie made the last comment, almost inviting him to contradict her, chilled Christian. "Yes, she is," he said. "And like you, she obviously knows her own mind. You may have brought the murder to her attention, but she made the decision to act."

Annie's gaze had drifted back to the book during Christian's last comment, and he wondered if she was even listening to him. Christian knew better than anyone how Annie could lock on to an idea. He asked himself a simple question. *What would Annie do if she felt she'd created the problem?* The answer came to him all too quickly, and he let out a little moan. *She'll try to fix it.* Christian didn't like the idea of what fixing the problem would entail, but just as he was about to voice his concern, he heard Annie quietly say, "Good Lord."

"What now?"

"His diary," she said. She held up the book. "This is his diary. David Abbott." She flipped through the pages with increasing excitement. "It describes how he made the door. And there are instructions..." She looked at Christian in awe. "We have David Abbott's blueprint for time travel here."

Christian peered over her shoulder as she flipped through the diary. The title on one of the pages commanded their attention. It read: *How to Triangulate Location*.

"Does that mean..." Annie tapped her finger over the title, looking to Christian for some sort of confirmation. She slid the book in front of him as he eased into the nook next to her.

He wrapped his hands around it and looked over his shoulder, suddenly fixated on the door situated not six feet from where they sat. "It looks as if Mr. Abbott is telling you how to set a location, Annie," he said. "This isn't just a door to 'when,' it's also a door to 'where.'"

Even as Christian confirmed her suspicion, the implication of the discovery sank in, and Annie knew what she had to do. She tabled the thought, not ready to share. There would be time to consider it later when she was alone. Instead, she went to a cabinet over the stove, pulled out a directory, and started riffling through its pages.

Christian followed her across the room. "Annie, what are you doing?"

"Genning uh ummer for uh hoshpiral," she said with a pencil between her teeth.

"What?"

She took the pencil out of her mouth and repeated. "Getting the number for the hospital. El asked me to do something. I don't intend to let her down. Besides, aren't you even the least bit curious about Abbott's son?"

Christian put his hand over the directory. "For one thing, that's the wrong directory, and let's be realistic. Do you really think you're going to be able to get records on a child born in 1890? In Kansas?"

"It's 1894 and why not?" She gently moved his hand and went back to riffling through the pages.

"Stop, stop," Christian said, taking the phone book and holding it to his chest. "It amazes me how people choose to take the longest route to get from A to B. You have a perfectly good computer in your study upstairs." Annie blinked, so he added, "I linked it to the Internet for you."

"But it's dial-up!" she said as she followed him upstairs.

Christian booted up the computer and dialed into AOL, patiently waiting out the electronic touch tones, burps, and feedback. "What's the name of the hospital again?" he asked.

She looked at El's letter. "Our Lady of Lourdes."

He opened a browser, typed in "Our Lady of Lourdes, hospital, Kansas City," then hit the Enter key. A list of references appeared. It included several hospitals, but none of that name.

He was about to try another search when Annie grabbed his hand. "Wait!" She pointed to the screen. Under the heading of "Saint Luke's Hospital," a subheading read, "Since purchasing Our Lady of Lourdes Hospital in 1943, Saint Luke's has become the region's leading nonprofit provider."

Christian grinned. "Let's see you find that information in a phone book." He clicked on the icon even as Annie gave him a quick kiss on the cheek.

An internal directory for Saint Luke's appeared. Among the numbers listed was one for the records department.

Christian tapped the screen. "Bingo," he said, then slumped back into the chair.

Five minutes later, Annie had completed a phone call to the listed number. "Now we wait," she told Christian as she hung up the phone. "The records for Our Lady of Lourdes are stored off-site. But the lovely man I spoke to is going to ask a friend who works at the archives to give me a call."

They headed down to the kitchen to get some tea. Annie had just put the ice in the glasses when the phone rang. "Annabelle Aster here."

After a brief exchange, Annie put her hand over the phone and mouthed, "He has them by year on disk."

Christian was not surprised. This was part of the magic of being Annie. Things simply fell into place for her. He'd witnessed it time and again.

Annie hung up the phone and turned to him. "He's emailing the information as we speak." She sipped her tea and hummed tunelessly until her eyes wandered to Christian's face. He was grinning.

"What?" she asked.

"You're a flirt."

She rolled her eyes, feeling disinclined to comment on the obvious.

Even so, Christian watched her take a few more sips before leaning forward to whisper, "What are you waiting for?"

"Oh!" Annie sprinted upstairs with Christian following more slowly. By the time he arrived, she had downloaded an eleven-page attachment from Our Lady of Lourdes Hospital and pulled up the barely legible image of a birth certificate for a Beatrice Lansing, born June 16, 1894. She stared at it curiously before scrolling through two more birth certificates. Neither was an Abbott. The screen came alive with the next birth certificate, one for a Walter Moore, born June 19, 1894, causing Annie to start.

"Find it?" asked Christian while looking over her shoulder.

"No, but there's something familiar about them. All of them. Something…" She shrugged, at a loss for words, and scrolled to the next.

Christian decided this might take a while and settled himself on the floor. The next document was reluctant to appear, and Annie made an impatient sound as it stubbornly refused to resolve on the screen. When it finally did, she leaned in to get a closer look, hit a key, and walked out of the room without a word.

Over the clack and hum of the printer, Christian heard Annie throwing boxes around in the bedroom closet down the hall. He lumbered to his feet and retrieved the document.

Born June 23, 1894
*Annabelle Abbott*
to
*David and Florence Abbott*
at *Our Lady of Lourdes Hospital*
Kansas City, Kansas

"Sweet Jesus," he whispered. Dropping the printout, he chased Annie into the bedroom. "Your birthday, it's the twenty-third of June, right?"

She appeared from the closet with a piece of torn parchment clutched in her hand, her knuckles white from gripping it so tightly. She flashed it at him and nodded before hurrying back into the study.

He found her kneeling on the floor beside the printout.

After a moment, she murmured something unintelligible and laid the parchment she'd retrieved from the closet on the floor beside the printout. The artwork and cartography were identical, that was plain to see, but the top right side of the parchment was missing. Annie started to chew on her thumbnail as she studied the documents. She shook her head, then slid the printout over the parchment and held the two to the light of a table lamp. The words from the original merged seamlessly with the copy—the number "1894," as well as "lle Abbott" and "id and Florence Abbott" now filled the remaining areas that were torn away.

Reaching numbly behind her, Annie pulled herself into the desk chair. She started to say something but instead cupped her forehead in her hands atop the desk.

A sound like a quick intake of air, or perhaps a hiccup, escaped her as Christian stood, taking two uneasy steps to reach for the wall. He leaned with his back against it and blinked, his features frozen in disbelief, before sliding to the floor with a thud as he tried to make sense of their discovery. He could rule out coincidence; the matching birth certificates made that clear. The only reasonable explanation, if reason could be applied in any way, was that his best friend had been born before the turn of the century. Beyond that shocking bit of news, they'd also learned the identity of Annie's birth father and that he'd been murdered.

It was almost too much to take in, and from the look of things, Annie was not faring any better. Christian knew he needed to snap her out of her thoughts before she sank too far, so he got up. Tucking a forlorn strand of hair behind her ear, he whispered, "He never intended to abandon you, Annie."

She looked up, clearly startled. As the implication sank in, she put her hand over her mouth.

Christian nodded. "He was trying to protect you all along."

Despite the certainty of his comments, Annie needed to speak the words aloud to lock them to the truth. "Elsbeth must have been mistaken," she said. "The baby wasn't a boy." She looked from the birth certificate to Christian, speaking slowly. "I was that child. He—" She stopped, collected herself, and started again. "My father moved me to the only safe place he could think of. The future."

She gazed at the wall behind the desk, her eyes unfocused. Amid the torrent of thoughts that followed, one bubbled to the surface. "I wasn't supposed to be an orphan." Saying that, putting the thought to words, suddenly lifted a weight she'd never known existed. And once that weight was lifted, the hole was filled by guilt. "But I love my parents," she whispered.

"Of course you do!" Christian said, dropping on his knees beside her. "This has nothing to do with them." He squeezed her leg.

Just as she nodded, her eyes widened again. "Elsbeth!" she cried. "I have to write her!"

She lurched upright, perhaps a little too quickly, and lowered herself back into the chair, her skin going white as soft-paste porcelain. The loss of color seemed understandable under the circumstances, but a slick, roseate bubble flowered and burst at the base of her nose.

Cursing under his breath, Christian flew into the bathroom for some tissue, returning only to find Annie already holding one to her nose while nibbling on a cracker. Her expression made it clear that questions were not welcome.

He waited out her silence and did the only thing he could think of when she stood. He wrapped her in an embrace before she could take a step. They rocked back and forth until he felt her body relax. "Would you like me to stay with you tonight?"

She hugged him a little tighter before disengaging, her features unreadable. "No, I'll be fine." Christian tilted his head, frowning, so she added, "Really, I will. But I need to wrap my head around this. I'll write El and try to rest my head a bit." She squeezed his hand and headed downstairs.

Christian followed, watching as Annie took a seat at the roll-top desk.

Before writing anything, she turned to him. "This changes nothing..." Looking a little surprised, she added, "... and everything."

Christian was about to ask her to explain her meaning, but it seemed clear enough. This knowledge did not change the way she felt about her parents, but it changed everything in the way she felt about herself. He wandered to the sofa as she started to write.

May 30, 1995

Dear El,

I got you into this mess, and I intend to get you out of it. At the moment, I haven't the foggiest idea how. The challenge is made all the more complex by the not-so-insignificant factors of geography and time, but I now have the door's instruction manual in my hands.

Christian suspects my intent, of course, and is worried. He knows how single-minded I can be. But you're my friend! And I do not abandon friends.

I have done as you requested by investigating the mystery of David Abbott's child and must regretfully inform you that, despite what you thought you saw, Mr. Abbott had no son.

He did, however, have a daughter.

It's me, Elsbeth. As crazy as it sounds, I'm the child you witnessed disappearing through the door.

My mind is a tangled mess, and you will not be pleased to read that I find myself struggling with dueling motivations. The first is as I've already mentioned. I plan to get you out of this mess. The second is more primitive.

Revenge.

Sincerely,
Annabelle Abbott Aster

The letter delivered, Annie walked arm in arm with Christian back up the stairs and to her bedroom, while trying to contain her growing anger. She disappeared into the bathroom and came out wearing a dressing gown.

"I'm not comfortable leaving you like this," he said, as she pounded a pillow into submission.

"I'm fine," she lied.

Christian looked doubtful, so she shoved him lightly on the shoulder. "Go on," she said. "Don't you have plans with Edmond?" She dropped back against the pillows, began to smooth the covers with a quick glance in his direction, and said quietly but firmly, "Go on."

"Annie?"

She looked up to see him standing in the doorway.

"What are you up to?" he asked.

"Just sleep," she said, smiling. "That's all."

Despite her assurances, Christian knew that Annie was anything but fine. How could she be, after everything she'd learned? An aura of distress surrounded her, but knowing better than anyone that some demons were best tackled alone, he nodded reluctantly. The bloody nose and its implications would have to wait.

She listened to his tread on the stairs, saddened that she'd taken advantage of Christian's trusting nature, but he would only get in the way. Sighing, she reached under the covers and pulled out the diary.

*February 3, 1893*

*There is more magic in the natural world than any one person can imagine—magnetism, crystallization, photosynthesis, gravity, and now this. I have been able to confirm that the earth's surface is dotted with countless discrete, interconnected resonances, tiny folds in the time-space horizon that can be tapped and manipulated. These "interruptions" are apparently caused by variances in the topography as they interact with mineral content in geological structures. I can't take credit for this breakthrough, however. Mayan and Aztec civilizations discovered them before me. The Cherokee have mapped a few locations but have mistaken them for bridges to the spirit world.*

*My divining rod will flush out these "hot spots." I'll shape it as a door. The image of stepping through one to another time and place satisfies my taste for showmanship.*

The pages were pruned and much of the writing muddied, but Annie worried through the entries as best she could, trying to capture the spirit of her father's life.

She read on to learn how he had stumbled upon the possibility of time travel. He had been researching Indian lore, especially that of Cherokee shamans, looking for a link between it and Mayan astrology, when he came across a compendium on the hidden power of Celtic runes. He was certain that there was a link between the three and began experimenting in a shed he'd built in the backyard.

The diary "sketched out" the steps he used in the making of the door, along with vague references to a collaborator. Annie was mesmerized. Even the paint was integral to the door's function. The ingredients that went into its making were numerous and bewildering, not the least being David's own blood.

*March 9, 1893*

*I am done. The door is made—as well as its codex. But I am tired. I will dare it tomorrow.*

Her father tested his "divining rod" the next day and found himself in San Francisco, of all places, uncertain how he came to be there. He described his panic, the rolling waves of vertigo that left him retching before he composed himself enough to explore, all the while describing sights of a future place that he could barely comprehend. These visits were repeated, his handwriting scrawling manically across the page as he rushed to describe a sight or sound before his attention was diverted. He scribbled pages and pages of notes, for the first time sounding almost incoherent—that is until he talked about the girl.

Her name was Florence. He'd met her at a lecture by Mark Twain a month prior.

Annie couldn't help but giggle at the outrageous language that followed—"tawny-haired sylph" being a start—that is until it seeped into her brain that he was talking about her mother. The romance was whirlwind, and a date was set for the wedding.

*July 16, 1893*

*Mother is here for the nuptials. Today I swore both her and Florence to secrecy and showed them the door. Florence came back through the door trembling but bubbling over with excitement. Mother had a go. For some reason, the door did not work. I was beside myself with fear that the magic had been undone until I stepped through it. Still, it will not operate for Mother. She said that she felt as though the door was rejecting her. I must think on this. It appears that bloodline is at issue. One thing is clear, however. A strange alchemy is at work. This magic is strong, but blood, I think, is stronger still.*

Annie repeated the last sentence, wondering what it meant before reading on.

*January 21, 1894*

*I have mastered the door's cipher. It now delivers me where I command. Also, I can make the door slumber so that it does not operate at all. Mother roused it, though she could not make it work. Curious.*

Even though her father delighted in the door, he began to have reservations, suspecting that his actions had consequences altering outcomes within the stream of time. And then he met a Mr. Ambrosius Culler, who made an offer he couldn't refuse. From the outset, it was clear that her father was leery of the man's reputation and disliked his reclusive lackey intensely, but their financing drove the success of his magic show.

Ambrosius Culler. It was the name from the article Annie had found at the Antiquarian, the man suspected of killing her father. Her first thought was that her father should have chosen his friends more wisely, but it was soon replaced by a slow-to-boil hatred. This man, if he did kill her father, had completely altered the course of her life. She tabled her anger and read on.

*February 11, 1894*

*I have made a most unusual discovery. I calibrated the door to send me to a particular place and time. It performed perfectly. However, upon returning and checking my calculations, I was alarmed to note that I'd made an error. I should not have ended up at the preset destination. It's strange, but I have always felt a rapport between my door and me. I have decried it as the hubris of invention, a Geppetto syndrome, with the door as my Pinocchio. Now, I'm not so certain. It's almost as though the door has a life of its own and responds to my wishes. Clearly, something marvelous is at work here.*

*May 30, 1894*

*I have solved the problem of bloodline and more. So much more! The answer eluded me due to its simplicity. It was within my grasp all this time. I must keep this secret safe. But where?*

The first of the two comments suggested that "intent" had as much to do with operating the door as the mechanical process of setting time and place, which her father described in great detail over the next several pages. The second, discussing the perils of his bloodline, merely left her feeling uneasy.

The next several pages of entries focused on her parents' life together but were barely legible. Annie could only make out that her mother was expecting in late June.

*June 23, 1894*

*Florence is dead. The doctor said it was the result of complications from an amniotic fluid embolism. But only a few hours ago, she was alive and well, cradling the baby in her arms as we argued over names. The doctor explained that fetal cells breached the placenta, entering her bloodstream and causing a cardiac arrest. This is torture. I know it's insane, but I can't shake the irrational thought that this child, my daughter, killed my wife.*

*June 25, 1894*

*I am smitten all over again, but it's so bittersweet. I held little Annabelle yesterday, walking around the nursery as I bounced her in my arms, telling her stories of her mother. Since that moment, I can hardly bear to be without her. Somehow, she has reached inside and taken hold of my heart. That she will be beautiful is obvious. But I have plans. She will also be a great lady, for I intend for her to be educated, and I will show her…the future.*

The entries were beginning to wear at Annie's composure. She flipped through the remaining pages, but there was only one more legible entry, and only partially so.

*I can no longer pretend otherwise. Something is trapped—*

She strained her eyes, trying to make out the remainder of the sentence but couldn't. Giving up, she rubbed her itchy eyes and closed the diary, overcome.

Too much. It was all too much, and she knew that sleep wouldn't come. Sitting on the side of the bed, she slid into her slippers and made her way downstairs with the diary in hand.

# CHAPTER EIGHTEEN

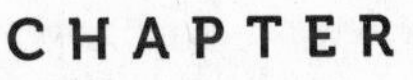

## The Chosen One

There was nothing but void, and Edmond wondered if he was dead. In the time it took for him to form the thought, though, the emptiness he occupied was filled with tiny soothing lights. Twinkling ruby stars. Thousands of them. Millions. Like bioluminescent shrimp in a deep, dark ocean, they drifted gently around him before condensing into a single image.

Confused at first by what he was seeing, Edmond realized the image was that of a door, red as raw liver. As could only happen in dreams, he felt that it was scrutinizing him, evaluating options.

A clattering sound interrupted the dream, and he woke with a start to watch his soda can rolling across the linoleum floor of the library, leaving an effervescent trickle of cola in its wake. Edmond stared at the book in his lap, curious. A possibility tickled his brain, and he deliberately picked it up and continued reading.

> Only the spiritually enlightened are initiated and taught the rituals and formulas for spirit travel. And while they are held in great esteem, even more prized are those very rare individuals who are gifted with the talent to take others on a journey with them. The name attributed to these gifted souls roughly translates to "the key" or "chosen one."

Edmond's eyes fluttered and eventually shut. Again, he found himself staring at the door. Only this time, he was standing in a kitchen. Something was wrong with his vision, however. It was grainy, pixilated, almost as though he were standing within a two-dimensional construct or, perhaps, a memory. The kitchen was large and a little too warm for comfort, with granite countertops and redwood flooring.

Feeling flushed, Edmond took off his sweater and tied it around his waist, taking in a cozy, little breakfast nook. He was curious as to why the dream would add that detail. The door itself throbbed with a deep red glow, and Edmond noticed for the first time that it was covered in strange carvings that appeared to be astrological symbols and arcane script.

This was a purpose-driven dream, and Edmond opened the door.

On the other side was a bleak, achromatic landscape—a stark contrast to the warmth and color of the kitchen. There was no vegetation on the ground. The earth was lined with a montage of cracks, and enormous clouds boiled across the darkened sky. At random intervals, all motion froze as though the memory bank providing the image had been interrupted. Then, after a stutter, the frenzy was renewed.

Edmond's eyes were drawn to the brilliant yellow of a flame—the only color in this freakish world. A circle of men sat cross-legged around the fire. Like the landscape, they looked as though all the color of life had been bled from them. There was something else, however. Edmond's depth perception was out of whack. The faculty of near and far had been erased. Only the fact that they appeared to be the size of toy army men suggested that the men were distant. To confirm his impression, Edmond stretched out his arm in an attempt to touch them as if they might be on a TV screen.

One of the men from the circle stood to stare in Edmond's direction, then blinked in and out of his vision with three alarming flashes. The man multiplied in size with each reappearance until he blocked almost all of Edmond's view of the landscape. It took Edmond a moment to realize that the man hadn't simply enlarged but was standing not more than a few feet away. He squawked in surprise and stumbled backward into the kitchen, but the man was not threatening aggression. He radiated calm and stood still as a stone, inviting Edmond's inspection.

He was dark-skinned with long, straight black hair, but almost all his exposed skin was coated in white chalk, with black-and-white stripes covering his torso. He wore leather breeches—his only adornment being a large piece of carved stone hanging from his neck by a strip of hide—and exuded energy as potent as the flashes of lightning in the churning atmosphere.

Extending his arm, the man pointed to Edmond and barked something clear yet throaty that seared into Edmond's brain. "*Nay he ooo ha he ha es dee ee es dee!*" Having spoken, the man became still once again. More than still. He froze. Edmond saw no indication of breath, not even a subtle pulse from his neck. The man's skin became slick. At first, Edmond thought it was the sheen of sweat, but there was a shine to it, almost as if a glaze had seeped through the man's pores.

Edmond dared a single step through the door into the barren dreamscape, and, without warning, the man exploded into countless shards and pinpricks of light. Its brilliance left Edmond's eyes watering as he shaded them and tried to adjust to the roseate brightness.

Little by little, he was able to focus and found himself staring down the point of his nose at a red rose stirring in a gentle breeze. He looked around, blinking. The desolate wasteland was gone and he found himself standing in a garden full of roses. Behind him, the door rested quietly on the back wall of a large, purple Victorian house.

Edmond walked warily down the garden path between vines and bushes rampant with blooms and stopped before a brass mailbox on a picket fence. He reached out to touch it, and the mailbox oscillated into a blur as if it was losing signal reception. The closer his hand, the more distorted the image. He retreated, and the image of the mailbox stabilized.

He looked up and over a wheat field. Across a gentle curve in the landscape, he spied a wisp of smoke trailing up into the sky.

Edmond grabbed the bookshelf and hoisted himself to his feet, staring at the book in his hand. He'd been circling a small cabin—its mailbox sitting off a dirt road had the name *Grundy* written on it—and had come across an old wooden road sign when a piercing noise cut across the wheat field, sucking him back through the void and into the applied sciences section of the library.

The sound still rang in his ear—a lone police car, its siren blaring as it raced down Sixteenth Street to some unknown destination. While its siren faded into the rumble and hum of the city, the memory of his experience did not.

Edmond made a dash to the languages section of the library. The book mentioned Cherokee culture, so he decided to start there, combing through shelves of reference materials until he found a Cherokee-to-English dictionary that, not surprisingly, seemed to have been little used. Grabbing a pen and scratch paper, he parked himself at a counter and flipped through page after page, jotting down words as he did so. It was a tricky exercise, because the discrete phonetic sounds didn't match up word for word with English counterparts. Eventually, though, he had what he was looking for. *You are the key.* The specter had said, "You are the key." Edmond recalled from the text that gifted travelers were called "the key," and his spine began to tingle.

Looking around to make sure the coast was clear, he took both books and headed downstairs to quickly shelve the rest of the inventory, his game long forgotten. Then he grabbed his backpack from the employee lounge, shoved the books inside, and ducked out the employee entrance.

It was a little chilly outside, so he unwrapped the sweater from his waist and…froze. *Didn't I take the sweater off in my dream?* Uncertain, Edmond lifted the receiver on the library's pay phone, dropping in a quarter when prompted. He needed some help sorting this out, and he could only think of one person to call. Unfortunately, he was rolled to voice mail because Christian had yet again forgotten to turn on his cell phone.

Even so, it was bouncing around in Christian's pocket as he walked the familiar route home. He had been uneasy since leaving Annie's house, uncertain how she was holding up under the weight of the recent discoveries—not the least of which was that she was born in 1894.

He turned on his phone to check in with her and was surprised by the stutter tone indicating he had a message.

"What's the point in having a cell phone if you never turn it on?" Edmond asked.

Ignoring the comment, one in the litany of jibes he had so far received during his brief association with Edmond, Christian said, "I got the potting soil."

"There's been a slight change of plans," Edmond responded.

The comment took Christian off guard. While he was processing the information and trying to determine the precise reason why the comment felt like a body blow, Edmond chuckled, breaking the silence. "I'll pick you up in front of your place at a quarter to seven. Bring a coat."

"Quarter to seven, out front, coat. Got it. Anything else?"

"Just the usual. Cure the common cold. Save the planet."

"Adopt a highway?"

# CHAPTER NINETEEN

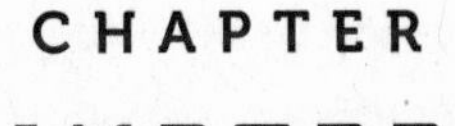

## The Thinking Spot

Edmond pulled around the corner to find Christian sitting on the front doorstep of his house with a coat in his lap, staring at nothing in particular. Seeing him there, looking so withdrawn, struck a chord, and Edmond idled his truck at the end of the block, trying to understand why he found it so touching. After a moment of reflection, he thought he had it figured out. Unlike himself, Christian was content with solitude. Suddenly feeling like a Peeping Tom, Edmond threw the truck into gear and pulled up to the curb. "Step on it," he said from the open window.

Christian worked his way into his coat and hurried over. "Where are we going?"

"Across the bridge. We're chasing the sunset."

The truck groaned in distress as Christian hopped in. He glanced at Edmond who shrugged indifferently. "Can't afford new shocks," he said as he shifted to first gear.

Christian pulled a Polaroid from the visor over his head as the truck worried its way down the block. He studied it before tapping the image of a clean-cut man who looked to be in his midtwenties. "Is this you?"

Edmond shook his head. "That's my brother." He snickered as Christian furrowed his brow while scrutinizing the remaining figure. The lopsided grin was there, but it was overshadowed by a horseshoe mustache—Edmond informed him that it didn't last the summer—and a siege of shoulder-length hair.

Crossing the Golden Gate Bridge, Edmond took the last exit before the tunnel leading to Sausalito and circled back to a road that wound along the edge of a cliff wall above the bay. The air was cooling rapidly, and the aroma of sap and sea got under their skin like a shot of espresso. Christian, who'd said nothing since inquiring about the photo, shook off whatever seemed to be bothering him and joined the conversation. His stuttering had vastly improved, Edmond noticed, though he still tripped over a word here and there and peppered his sentences with odd breaks.

Also gone were the elegant hand movements Christian had employed to help him move words along—the air scribblings, index finger raised as if offering divine sanction.

Traveling up an incline, the truck rounded a corner to come face-to-face with the top half of one of the bridge's towers peeking over the hill. The bay was hidden from this angle, and the tower looked as if it had burst from the landscape. Christian was captivated, pointing it out to Edmond, who responded by hitting the gas, a nasty grin plastered on his face.

Careening along the cliff wall, the truck lost contact with the road as it passed over a rise, offering a perilously breathtaking view of the rocks below. Once the wheels found asphalt, Edmond glanced sideways at the passenger seat to find Christian pressed against the backrest, eyes tightly shut and murmuring under his breath. Edmond floored it for good measure, laughing when Christian slugged his shoulder as the truck ground around another curve, spraying loose rocks over the ledge.

"Hey!" He eased up on the accelerator to pull into a makeshift parking space at the base of World War II bunkers that looked like metal boxes unceremoniously shoved into the ground and peered over the dash at the horizon. "Just in time," he said. Throwing the door open, he took in a deep breath before wandering to the back to open the tailgate.

Leaving him to it, Christian gingerly ascended a set of cement stairs on the side of one of the bunkers and stopped to ponder monstrous iron bolts jutting from the ground—all that remained of turret guns that once guarded the bay. He wandered to the edge of the cliff. A seaborne gust rocked him, and he wrapped his arms across his chest, craning his neck over the edge to catch a glimpse of the beach far below. From that angle, the sun appeared to float on the open water like an inflatable ball. Chuckling, he cocked his finger as if to thump the glowing orb, then looked over his shoulder to find Edmond lugging a couple grocery sacks and a blanket around the front of a bunker.

"Christian! A little help?"

Christian blanched. "Not now," he whispered, banishing the angel that was dangling its legs directly above Edmond's head, and dashed over to scoop up the grocery sacks.

The flame that had bathed the angel was slower to dwindle, and Christian wondered if Edmond could feel the residual heat as he leveraged himself onto the roof. He seemed no worse for wear, however, as he slung plates, sandwiches, tabbouleh, and deviled eggs over the blanket with a reckless abandon that seemed on the verge of—but never quite meeting—disaster.

When Christian settled onto the blanket next to him, Edmond pulled the cork on a bottle of wine and poured two glasses. "What were you looking at?" he asked.

Having dismissed the angel, Christian had to take a second. He shook his head.

"You were looking at something." When Christian seemed unwilling to respond, he handed him a glass. "Okay then, here's to the city by the bay, the most beautiful city in the world."

"To San Frannn-cisco," Christian said. After a quick sip, he put down his drink, his eye drawn to a poppy growing from a crack in the bunker's roof. He pulled it and stared across the water at the skyline, determined that the uninvited guest wasn't going to ruin his fun.

The sun was a copper-colored sliver sinking into the bay by this time, its waning glimmer leaving the lights of the city to look like a fine spray of luminous paint on the far shore.

Five pelicans soared along the rise of the cliff in a broken vee formation.

Edmond nudged Christian with his foot. "Did I catch you *praying* in the truck?" he asked. His question was meant as a joke, but it flustered Christian nonetheless.

He shook his head. "No, I'm not much for prayer anymore," he said as he set the flower aside. "Used to, but not anymore."

"Used to? Why did you stop?"

Christian shrugged. "When I no longer understood what I was praying for," he said, as if the answer should have been obvious.

Edmond stared openmouthed, waiting to see if more was forthcoming, but Christian simply turned his gaze skyward as stars broke around them one at a time—phosphorescent cherry blossoms pinned to an indigo silk sky. The Big Dipper glimmered just over his shoulder, ladling out just enough mystery to leave Edmond scratching his head. "Beautiful, aren't they?" he said.

Like a kid caught stealing a cookie, Christian broke from his trance, grinning to mask his embarrassment. He leaned back on both elbows with his legs splayed out in front of his body. "This is nice," he said. "Down there"—he gestured toward the skyline with his foot—"it's almost as if the plane I live on is out of alignment and I disappear." He looked across his shoulder at Edmond. "Know what I mean?"

"No, but I don't understand half the things you say, to be honest." Shoving his plate out of the way, Edmond lay on his side, his head braced in the palm of his hand, and watched Christian flick the flower off the side of the bunker. "However, in spite of the fact that we seem to speak two different languages, I think I'm beginning to figure you out."

Christian watched the flower tumble into the weeds below and, after a moment, returned Edmond's scrutiny. "What happened, Edmond?" he asked, the question coming out of nowhere like a pint-size stealth bomber.

"What do you mean?"

"To you. Something bad happened, and you lost your way, I think."

Edmond's instincts fought against his flair for sarcasm. It was a fair question that deserved an honest response. But how could he explain his past to an innocent? For that's surely what Christian was. Some people were locked into innocence by their very nature. How then could he explain the rebellion against his strict, Catholic upbringing in a way Christian could understand? And how that rebellion was alchemized through a dare and a joint, taking him down a perilous road of ever-greater risks, and how *that* led to something, something terrible—something he didn't think Christian could understand.

Everyone had secrets; he knew that. But his demanded atonement and explanations he wasn't ready to offer, so he simply said, "I made some mistakes. I'm paying for them now."

Christian seemed to worry the statement around in his head for a moment. "I'm…I'm sorry."

He sounded so sincere that Edmond could only shake his head, almost undone by such gentle clemency. "Don't be. I'm fine." Struggling for composure, he shifted the focus back to Christian. "What about you?" he asked.

"What do you want to know?"

"Tell me something you've never shared with anyone." He shoveled some tabbouleh into his mouth before waving his spoon at Christian. "Why did you leave Texas, for instance?"

"Oh." Christian rocked his head back between his shoulder blades and stared heavenward. "I suppose I ran away from expectations I couldn't live up to," he said, palming his napkin before a gust of wind could carry it away.

"Because you stutter?"

"In part." Christian picked up his sandwich and took a bite. His eyes widened, and before he could ask, Edmond said, "Fennel." He watched Christian chew in silence.

The piercing call of a hawk sounded somewhere behind them.

"I miss the hand gestures."

Christian paused midchew, blinking, and Edmond cleared his throat. "You know, when you stutter?" he said. "It's beautiful. Your hands…they write in the air, and you move your fingers like this." He twiddled his and gave up. "I…I can't do it like you."

The comment was so unexpected, so sweetly outrageous, that Christian laughed—a reflexive bark that ended on a note of incredulity. His cheeks flooded with color, red as rouge. And in the awkward hush that followed, when he needed a distraction, Christian did the strangest thing. Setting the sandwich carefully on his plate, he grabbed a toothpick and started jabbing at it, a behavior Edmond remembered from their first encounter that seemed to indicate Christian's emotions were very close to the surface. "No one's ever said that to me before."

"Well, they should," Edmond mumbled.

The sandwich was a sad shadow of its former self by the time Christian was through with it. He balled his hand around the toothpick, staring at the damage as he struggled to make sense of the random comment—the idea that someone, anyone, could make him feel almost at ease with his strange affliction, and that it ended up being the very person who'd so unsettled him to begin with.

He would have liked to share that insight with Edmond, but he knew it was wound so tightly with a net of conflicting emotions that the words would come out in a nonsensical pile. Instead, he decided to attack an even trickier problem. "I n-n-need to ask you some…thing." He resumed jabbing in the hope that the repetitive nature of the exercise would clear his mind and lubricate his voice.

"And it would really help if you took it seriously." He waited for Edmond to lower his spoon. "Have we…have we met before?"

Edmond shook his head, not understanding the question.

"Before we met, I mean." Christian grimaced, knowing full well that the last remark only made sense in his mind. He stood and shoved his hands in his pockets. And just as quickly, he sat back down, crossing his legs in front of him. "There are some…" He looked over the water, his legs bouncing—up and down, up and down.

Alarmed, Edmond reached over to place a hand on his knee.

Christian smiled. "There are some gaps in my memory, you see. I had an accident." He shrugged, as if happy to get the words out, yet at a loss to explain why they had been so difficult for him to say in the first place. "Would you mind if I don't talk about it?" He shook his head. "I…I don't like talking about it."

Edmond lifted his brow before wisely popping half a deviled egg in his mouth. Something clicked inside his head as he chewed, however, like connecting that crucial dot to reveal a disastrous picture, and an involuntary intake of air left him choking.

Christian sprang to his side, pounding Edmond's back as he rolled onto his hands and knees. Edmond tried to talk, to wave him off, but it only left him with a coughing fit so intense he retched. Exhausted, he rolled onto his back to peer at Christian with a fresh set of eyes. "My God," he whispered, blinking. It was more a verbal spasm than anything else, breaking from his mouth like speaker feedback.

It was that moment, as nitro blasted in his belly, when Edmond knew the stakes had been raised and that he was on a collision course with a confession. He sat up, stymieing the impulse to walk off, to deal with the rush of insight and its implications in peace and quiet. If he did, he'd have to come back and explain why his reaction seemed out of proportion to Christian's disclosure, and that was out of the question.

To his credit, Christian seemed to take it all in stride, settling back onto the blanket a few feet across from Edmond—a distance that might as well have been a mile for all that had just occurred.

Edmond shoved the other half of the egg into his mouth, consciously forcing himself to chew as he looked for a topic that would bring them back to safer ground. Not certain what that would be, and with the silence becoming unbearable, he simply took a punt. "Tell me about your family."

Christian reached for the toothpick, but Edmond saw the signs and got there first, snatching it from the plate.

"You"—he shook a finger—"stop that!"

Christian started, and Edmond sighed, regretting his outburst. "You're so comfortable with loneliness. As if you think you deserve it." He shoved the toothpick in his own mouth, assessing the situation. "That's not right." Getting back to the immediate topic, he said, "Your family?"

"I don't like talking about that either—"

"Well then, what do you want to talk about?" Edmond barked, exasperated. He put a hand over his mouth and breathed. "I'm sorry. I'm sorry." After a moment, the hand fell to his side, seemingly of its own accord. "You can be really frustrating, you know that?" he said. "Open up a little. You're safe." When Christian made eye contact, he nodded. "You are."

The plea was so earnest that Christian relented. Fighting against his instincts, he offered up a little piece of himself. "I'd like to be a writer," he said quietly.

Edmond looked up. That was not at all what he expected. "Write? Write what?"

If ever there was a time for levity, this was it, so Christian gave it a whirl. "Obituaries, Hallmark jingles, fortune cookies, maybe even a satanic verse or two." He shrugged. "Failing that, I might try my hand at a…book."

The ploy succeeded. After the initial shock wore off, Edmond reeled his head back and howled. "A joke? Christian's first joke!"

Jerking his leg out of the way just as Christian attempted to kick it, he added, "Who would have thought that quiet little Christian would be hiding such ambition?"

He laughed so hard he almost choked on his food a second time as he unsuccessfully tried to dodge another shot while adding, "And—ow!—here I am laying manure—shit, that hurt!—on roses for a living. But gardening is a noble cause, nonetheless." He waited breathlessly for Christian to settle down, then slapped his thigh and nodded toward the crescent moon rising over the water. "You have the floor."

"What?" Christian recoiled. "Nooooo," he said and sat up, crossing his legs—all business. "Uh-uh. I'm not drunk this time. Thanks for the hangover, by the way. It was my f-first."

Edmond gazed under his lids at Christian. "Wasn't it Hemingway who said there's nothing to writing? That all you have to do is sit at a typewriter and bleed? Consider me a blank page. Go on, I can take it."

Clearly, that hit a nerve. Christian let out a breath of air and lay back on the blanket, crossing his hands behind his head.

As Edmond settled in, Christian shifted his gaze to the stars littering the night sky. Then, in a strange gesture, he swept his hand above his face as if to collect them in his closed palm, then flicked his wrist as if to scatter them about, creating a pattern more to his liking.

"Annie—our heroine—lives in a beautiful Victorian just off Dolores Street in San Francisco. This is no ordinary house, however. It has a secret. Walking in Annie's front door is one thing. Walking out her back door is something altogether different. Do so and you will discover that hers is not surrounded by other houses, as one would expect in a city like San Francisco. Instead, you will find that her home floats in a sea of wheat." He broke from his narrative long enough to take a sip of wine. "Nearby, a dirt road runs through the wheat, and on the road is a sign. It says 'Pawnee County, Kansas. Population 673. Five Miles Due East of Sage as the Crow Flies.'"

Immersed in his tale, Christian didn't notice Edmond stir, propping himself up on his elbow.

"Annie has a neighbor in this wheat field. She lives in a little cabin on the horizon with smoke continually floating up from a corner of its roof. Annie's never met her neighbor, but they've exchanged many letters. And always, Annie's neighbor dates her correspondence in the year 1895. Her name is Elsbeth—"

"Grundy?" Edmond interrupted, wide-eyed, effectively shutting Christian up. "Mind if I interrupt with a story of my own?" he added, when it became clear Christian couldn't continue.

Christian shook his head emphatically, then seeing the expression on Edmond's face from the corner of his eye, slowly nodded.

"It begins with a book I found in the library—"

# CHAPTER TWENTY

## Bearer Bonds

The sun was setting, and Elsbeth sat in her rocker, reading Annie's letter a second time. Key words seemed to lift from the page and flutter like moths in the mustardy light of the lantern sitting on the table. *Mess. Daughter. Revenge.*

She finally settled on one sentence, reading it over and over again. *But you are my friend!* Annie didn't know the half of it. And neither had she, until she read Annie's news. For the second time that day, Elsbeth reached for her writing set.

*May 30th, 1895*

*Dear Annie,*

*That cotton-picking diary! I had a feeling it would be nothing but trouble. Now listen to me before going off to do something half-cocked!*

*I'm quite possibly more shocked by the news than you because of something I chose not to share in my last correspondence. It was, I thought, nobody's damn business but my own! But I see I was wrong.*

*Before exiting Mr. Abbott's home, I came across a photograph of his wife. He called her Florence in his diary, but I knew her by another name. I mentioned it in a previous correspondence. Beth Anne. She was my daughter.*

*If the natural consequence of this is not immediately clear, then let me state it simply.*

*Annie, you are my granddaughter! And Beth Anne was your mother.*

*I'll grieve for her as I may, but, truthfully, I did most of my grieving long ago. We did not part on good terms, your mother and I. It was a case of my infamous temper butting heads with her colossal stubbornness. I loved her fiercely, and that, I'm afraid, drove her away. I was overprotective and smothered her after her father died.*

*You should know some things. She loved honeysuckle, having gotten it in her head from some foolishness her father told her that all honeysuckle vines were gates to the fairy kingdom. Chess was her favorite game. She and Tom would play for hours with a set he carved for her. And crows were her favorite birds. She told me they were her "totem," her guardian angels.*

*There is much more than coincidence happening here, Annie, and in some strange way, it's beginning to make sense. We were meant to find each other. It comforts me to think there is some agency looking over us, giving me a second chance to love someone more perfectly.*

*Love,*
*Your grandmother*

*P.S. Stay put, damn it!*

Elsbeth reread the letter and stepped outside to deliver it. It was dark, but she didn't need the light. El knew the way by heart.

"You're still up," Christian said as he bounced into Annie's kitchen, throwing a spray of wilted poppies onto the counter. "Sorry I'm so late, but Edmond's rear bumper came off on the Golden Gate Bridge. If you ask me, it was a botched suicide attempt. That truck's time has come and it knows it." He shook his head, chuckling at his own joke. "Edmond's in mourning. What?" That final word—*what*—flowed from his mouth so seamlessly it could have been mistaken for the last syllable of the prior word. Mourningwhat. But it was actually his knee-jerk response to the fact that Annie was pacing back and forth with her father's diary in one hand and a letter in the other.

After a second, she handed Christian the letter and wandered to the sink to rinse out a mug.

"Good God," he said, collapsing onto a bench in the breakfast nook. "This changes everything."

Annie nodded as she reached for a dish towel. "Murder was a hanging offense in Kansas at the turn of the century."

Christian paused, slowly connecting the mental dots that led Annie to make that statement. "That's not what I meant," he said. As she turned to glare, he added quickly, "Yes, that's terrible, but there's something more important at stake here."

"What could be more important than my grandmother's life?" she demanded.

"Yours!" Realizing he'd just opened a can of worms, Christian withdrew, running his finger over a dent he'd put in the table during their first tea together more than a year ago. He'd been terribly nervous that day, stuttering so badly he'd resorted to using a pen and pad to write down an occasional, stubborn word that Annie would promptly decorate with hearts and flowers using a pink felt-tip.

He'd managed to topple a teacup within minutes of being served. That would have been bad enough, but he'd jarred the table as he leaped to right it, and a pewter candleholder had overbalanced, stringing a line of wax across the plate of biscuits while gouging a moon-shaped dent into the tabletop.

Annie had only just managed to grab his hand before he could start mopping up the mess with one of her prized linen napkins. She'd whisked out a roll of paper towels and shooed him from the table. With words lodged in his throat, Christian had quickly scribbled a note that evolved somehow from offering to pay for its repair to buying her a new table altogether.

When she'd wiped up the tea, replaced the biscuits, and covered the dent with a lace doily, Annie had coaxed him from the corner where he was desperately trying to disappear. "Just a second ago it was a dent," she'd said, laying the note aside to pour him another cup. "Now it's a story you and I will be laughing over for years to come. Do you think for one minute I'd trade that for a new table?" When he'd shyly pointed out that her cuff was swimming in the mustard bowl, she'd cussed like a sailor and dashed to the sink, knocking over the second candleholder in the process.

Coming back to himself, Christian said, "Remember this?" tapping the dent.

She nodded, though her expression indicated that she was on high alert. "I saved the note." Relenting a little, she added, "Did I really say 'shit on a stick'?"

"Among other things."

They stared at one another, at a bit of a standoff.

Christian spoke first. "Annie…Elsbeth's your family," he said quietly. "The two of you share a bloodline. And that means a potential bone-marrow donor is just across that wheat field in the back."

The room stilled as if the air was sucked out of it, then rushed back in when she rounded on him. "How can you possibly know about—" She stopped midsentence. Guilt was written all over his face. "You've been snooping," she said.

"I didn't go rifling through your d-drawers, if that's what you mean. But I considered anything you left on the console t-t-table fair game." Without moving a muscle, he gave the impression of melting into the bench he was sitting on. "You don't tell me anything, Annie," he added.

"It's nobody's business."

"It's *my* business!" he said, slamming his fist on the tabletop and causing Annie to jump. "Mmm… Damn it, n-not now!" He let out a lungful of air, calming himself. "M-mine," he finished, more quietly. "You're muh-muh-my friend, my best friend."

Annie cut him off before he could continue. "For heaven's sake, if we're going to fight, I want it to be fair," she said. "Turn around until you're back in control. That always seems to help."

She stirred the air with her finger, and Christian twisted in his seat, looking at the wall. "Let's be honest—my only r-r-r-real… friend, though Edmond seems to have some potential." He sighed and turned around to meet her gaze, his eyes as big as a pair of peach pits whose juice had worried a sour-sweet trail down the bridge of his nose. "I have no one," he said. "With you gone, I have no one." Having said that, he turned back, facing the wall, but not before she caught a fleeting, tragic glimpse of pain in his features.

Annie tried to muster up some anger over his little betrayal but found that she couldn't. Over the course of their relationship, she'd never once heard Christian express a selfish sentiment. It frightened her. And the pain in his face was making it clear just how much her silence had cost him. So, she filled the cup she'd just washed with coffee and wandered over to stand next to the table. Setting it down, she took a deep breath and exhaled slowly, placing her hands on her hips. "What do you know?" she asked.

"Well…" He paused, noticing a hint of crimson collecting in the cleft between her nose and upper lip. He fished a tissue out of his pocket and handed it to her, his words limping along as he spoke. "Aside from figuring out that you're on a list for transplant donors, I know the obvious. You're an orphan, making donors hard to come by. You haven't asked…me, which kind of hurts." He looked up, adding, "I'd say 'yes,' by the way."

"I know." She pressed the tissue under her nose, slid into the nook, and leaned back against the bench's upright, closing her eyes. "You're not a compatible donor," she said.

"You don't know that."

Her eyes sprang open, but her expression was guarded as she peered at him from above the wad of tissue.

Suddenly, he understood. "You too?" he asked, realizing that Annie had been doing a little snooping of her own.

She blotted her nose a couple times before tossing the tissue in a bin. "I might have slipped a note to Nicki along with a twenty-dollar bill when we donated blood together in February," she confessed. The corner of her lips pressed in a moue of distaste as she added, "It was tacky. I know."

"You could've just asked."

"Yes," she said. "And you would've asked why." She reached into her purse for a compact to touch up her nose and cheeks. "We had our blood type tested as part of science class when I was in third grade. I was AB negative. Less than one in a hundred, my teacher told me. How very special." Annie leaned forward, resting her cheek in her hand. "Now it feels like a noose around my neck."

"But Elsbeth…"

"One out of a hundred, Christian," she repeated, reaching for her cup. "It's been five years. Hope hasn't worked out so well for me, so I live by a more practical philosophy." Before the panic in his face could find a voice, she added, "I'm not dying. It's just inconvenient… and, I'll admit, awful at times."

"You can't give up."

"Do you think for one second that I want to be sick?" she asked, bristling as she set the cup aside. "Constantly measuring what I want to do against what I can? Misunderstood by those who don't know me and pitied by those who do?" She snatched the compact off the table and dropped it in her purse. "It's just easier to be alone. Less fuss."

"But it's not about pity. This isn't, anyway."

"It's not? Are you sure?" She gazed at Christian quizzically. "I think it is," she said.

Christian's forehead creased as he thought about her question, a gesture that somehow made him look even younger. "I don't pity you," he said finally. "But every time I pretend to suddenly notice something new on the pathway we've walked each day for the last year just so you can catch your breath, I want to—"

He started rubbing the dent in the table with his thumb, swallowing before glancing at her from the corner of his eye. "Do you know why I always carry my cell phone on our walks even though you're the only person who ever calls it?" Letting her think about that, he picked up the sugar spoon, scooping and pouring, scooping and pouring. Finally, he said, "Maybe it is a type of pity after all, but it comes from my absolute devotion and sense of utter helplessness."

At that, Annie grabbed a tissue and reached across the table to dab at his eyes. "And that's why I love you," she said, smiling. "Because occasionally, and quite unexpectedly, you sound like a sonnet."

He swatted at her hand as she tweaked his nose, the barest hint of a smile replacing the misery that had clouded his eyes a moment earlier, and started tracing the wood grain on the table.

Annie watched in silence until the secret festering inside her needed lancing. "There's more to it than that," she said. "You're right. It *was* the first thing that crossed my mind when I read Elsbeth's letter. I didn't like that. We're talking about my grandmother. I may not have known her long, Christian, but there's a seed of love there. She's not a young woman, and a bone-marrow transplant can be a tricky proposition. If I indulged in those thoughts"—she lowered her voice—"I'm afraid I'd choose myself over her." She shook her head, looking miserable. "And I don't know what that says about me."

And that was that. All that needed to be said between them had been said.

"Now go home," she insisted. "I have a difficult letter to write and a lot of thinking to do."

As she pushed him toward the kitchen door, he turned, looking suspicious. "You're up to something."

"If I am, not even I know it yet. And I always win these arguments, so let's simply pretend that it has reached its natural conclusion and save some time." She shoved him out the door and turned to stare at the diary. Waves of emotion washed over her as the implications of her recent discovery, Elsbeth's disclosure, and Christian's insight demanded attention. Her mind ricocheted from one thought to another but ultimately kept coming back to Elsbeth. Suddenly, she fixated on the line from the diary that had unnerved her earlier in the day. *This magic is strong, but blood is stronger still.*

The words took on a new meaning, and Annie began to suspect that she and El were doomed never to see one another because the same blood ran through their veins. The speculation led to other questions. How could she use the door at all then? Didn't she share her *father's* blood? Annie tucked the thought away for later examination because she needed to explore something more immediate. Reaching for notepaper and a pencil, she opened the diary to the page titled *How to Triangulate Location* and seated herself in the breakfast nook.

A few hours later, notes were scattered across the table, and an impressive pile of wadded stationery was spilling over the top of the trash can at Annie's feet. She laid her head against the back of the bench, wearily reading through a set of notes before crumpling up the piece of paper on which they were written and tossing it over her shoulder. She flipped through the diary to reread a particular section, then wandered over to the door to stare at a set of engravings. Going back to the breakfast nook, she quickly scribbled some final notations before slamming the diary shut with a most unladylike grunt.

Standing, Annie rubbed her lower back with her fist, then arched backward until her vertebrae gave three satisfying pops. She turned out the kitchen lights and headed upstairs to bed, determined to sleep, but the audacity of her plan kept her staring at the ceiling through the night.

As the sun crept over her windowsill, Annie finally gave up and got out of bed. Sitting at the bureau, she brushed her hair out and coiled it into a chignon that she secured with pearl-drop bobby pins, all the while doing her best to ignore the dress draped over the back of the easy chair in the corner—the one she'd purchased at Prudence Travesty's. Pulling a couple strands of hair loose to frame her face, Annie disappeared into her utility closet, reemerging with an off-white dress in one hand and a pair of matching pumps dangling from two fingers of the other. She glanced wistfully from the dress in the chair to the one in her hand and sighed.

Dressing quickly, she assessed her image in the mirror. The dress was a contemporary take on Victorian fashion—spaghetti strapped, ruched, with an empire waist—and not quite her thing.

Throwing a shawl over her shoulders that was so sheer her alabaster skin showed through, Annie went downstairs to the rolltop in the living room, searching through the center drawer until she found the key to her safe-deposit box. That done, she sat at the breakfast nook, nibbling at a scone while reviewing the notes she'd prepared the prior night. When the grandfather clock rang the hour, Annie snapped out of her preoccupation, downed the last of her coffee, and set the dishes in the sink.

Moments later, the garage door opened and she pulled her 1986 Mercedes W123 onto Dolores Street and sped downtown, parking in a spot directly in front of the bank. While most people in San Francisco prayed to their personal parking saint for such luck, Annie came by it naturally. Little bits of magic—perhaps a gift given at birth by her father—surrounded her.

Throwing some quarters into the meter, Annie retrieved a hat from the backseat and placed it atop her head. It was the one concession she offered to her eccentricity this morning—an outrageous thing, chalk white, with a brim the size of a garbage can lid (though she would have shuddered at the reference) and a delicate white scarf draped around the crown, its tail flowing down her back to her waist.

Nodding at her image in the rearview mirror, Annie walked briskly into the lobby and, with a quick wave to the security guard, headed down a set of circular stairs into the cavernous vault—an unforgiving space of steel, gunmetal gray marble, and bleak lighting. She signed the register and handed the custodian her key before following him to her lockbox. He inserted the master key as well as hers—both were required to open her lockbox—then pulled out a recessed surface for her convenience and excused himself.

Annie lifted the lid off the box. Inside was a stack of twenty documents. She knew nothing about them except that they were her property, accompanying her when she was adopted. Her father—her adoptive father—seemed to know a little about them, but he was annoyingly vague on the one or two occasions they were referenced, simply telling her to ignore them and that they'd be there for her "when she was ready."

She collected one and placed it in her purse. She started closing the lockbox lid when she noticed something tucked away in its corner—something she'd forgotten about long ago. Like the documents, it had never held much meaning for her, just an oddity from a past she knew nothing about.

She reached inside, picking up a tiny, hand-stitched baseball glove. Sitting down, she cupped the mitt in her hands, staring, her face not giving a clue as to the emotions it stirred. Looking around the vault a moment later, as if she'd momentarily forgotten where she was, Annie replaced the glove, closed the lockbox, and headed for the elevator to call on her personal banker.

The elevator door closed with her inside, looking very determined, only to open an hour later to a much less steady version—Annie clutching at the handrail, her face drained of color. She'd never seen the man speechless before, but then again, it's hard to talk when you've just choked on your coffee. He'd stared at the document like a teenage virgin ogling his first Trans Am.

"Are you getting out, ma'am?"

Annie blinked, noticing that she was holding up a crowd waiting to enter the elevator. She mumbled apologies and strode through the lobby thinking about what she'd just learned.

The instrument was an Edison Electric bearer bond dated 1894—the year of her birth. Apparently, Edison General Electric had merged with a company called Thomson-Houston the very next year to form General Electric, causing the value of the individual bonds to skyrocket even back then.

"A hundred years and countless mergers later, this piece of paper will be worth a small fortune," her banker had said. "As a historical document, however, it'll have Sotheby's wetting their pants."

That comment had her fanning her face before she realized, to her horror, that she was doing so with the bearer bond itself. But it was his next comment that hit her like a brick.

"Whoever bought this couldn't have made a more clever pick had they been able to see into the future."

See into the future. No doubt her father had.

The meter had long expired by the time she reached her car, yet there was no parking ticket on her windshield, even though those on the cars immediately in front and behind hers sported one each. This wasn't new. Annie always chalked it down to luck. Christian, however, called it magic.

Arriving home, she made straight for her bedroom to quickly change into the dress draped across the occasional chair. She packed an old leather suitcase with a change of clothes, the diary, the article, and the bearer bond she'd taken from the lockbox. She also grabbed a vintage handbag she'd purchased from Prudence Travesty's, her favorite "utilitarian" hat, and a couple of scarves to wrap around its brim for variety. Lugging the suitcase to the kitchen, Annie scribbled a note to Christian and attached it to the refrigerator with a magnet. Lastly, she selected one of her favorite wines, uncorked it, and poured herself a glass.

Annie peered at the note on the refrigerator as she savored a sip and, on impulse, attached Elsbeth's last letter to it. Another thought entered her mind. She opened the diary to the entry on the thirtieth of May, 1894, and laid it on the counter. Then she pulled the note from the refrigerator and scribbled a postscript.

> P.S. Okay, you win. I'm starting to hope again. My father solved the bloodline mystery. Note the entry dated May 30, 1894. You love riddles, Christian. Solve this one for me.
>
> P.P.S. Oh, and don't forget that we have tickets to see "The Bridges of Madison County" this weekend.

Carrying the suitcase to the back of the house, she reviewed her notes one last time before laying them aside. Then, pulling a pin from her hair, she pricked her index finger so that a small bubble of blood welled up. The diary didn't necessarily call for this exercise, but Annie wasn't taking chances. After wiping her blood on the door frame, Annie tapped the runes and the astrological carvings in a complex order as directed by her notes and, gathering the suitcase, stepped through the door...

# CHAPTER TWENTY-ONE

## Annie Meets a Throwaway

### MAY 29, 1895

And into Kansas City. Or so she hoped.

Annie found herself in a meadow. There wasn't a stir of wind or a whisper of sound, and she panicked for a moment, wondering if she'd gone anywhere at all but rather was locked in some imaginary place created at the whim of her door.

She turned to confirm that it was still behind her, and her stomach lurched when it was nowhere to be seen, apparently having been replaced by a pair of large stones that resembled giant arrowheads partially buried in the ground, their points facing skyward. A buoyant, flutelike trill broke the silence as a meadowlark landed on one of the stones, chirping at her in mild reproach.

Annie's panic dwindled at its arrival, and she took a closer look at the stones. They were covered in markings and surrounded by a thick wall of foliage. Night-blooming jasmine, flowering not only out of season and its nightly cycle, but also in a climate where it had no right to exist, snaked along the outer edges and across the top, creating a natural roof with deep-red altissimo roses blanketing the space between. It looked like a secret. Perhaps it was the roses' particular shade of red or the familiarity of the markings on the stones, but Annie was certain she was looking at her back door, albeit incognito.

A placard at the base of the stones stated that they had been donated to the parks and recreation service of Kansas City in 1889 by the Cherokee Council. Noting a cluster of buildings just off the horizon and satisfied that she could find her way back to the stones and home, Annie stepped onto a path and made her way toward them.

Having been reassured by the meadowlark, Annie began to notice other things as she walked. The air was warm and so heavy with the fragrance of grass and wildflowers that it left a sweet taste on her tongue. A quiet little pond stood a stone's throw away. Mallards drifted between clumps of reeds, their wakes breaking the still surface in crisscross patterns that looked like a veil of plaid floating atop the water. A turtle's head broke through the surface, following her progress, while swifts and swallows darted about overhead.

To her left was a little rivulet that gurgled over a rock bed to empty into the pond. It gave the impression of water running uphill, and Annie paused to work out the illusion, which turned out to be the result of the pathway dropping more steeply than the streambed. Across the pond, a small panorama of buildings peeked quietly over the tops of the trees at the edge of the park.

Coming to a fork, she chose the leftward path cutting through a grove where she had an encounter so surreal it stopped her in her tracks. It began with a sound from her childhood that made her think of banana seats, training wheels, and handlebar streamers—the metallic chime of a bicycle bell. An apparition glided into view from a bend in the path, and the man sitting atop it dipped his bowler hat politely as he drew near. She stepped to the side, riveted by the sight of the delicate front wheel towering over her head. Annie imagined calliope music playing as it drifted past like a ghostly image from a kinetoscope. The man sitting atop it pedaled so slowly compared to the speed he was generating that the penny-farthing seemed to float over the surface of the path.

Suddenly aware that she was staring, Annie clamped her mouth shut and started to acknowledge his greeting when little black spots began to swarm in her vision. She touched her index finger lightly to her nose. It came away red, and she simply sat down in the path on the off chance she might faint. The cyclist circled around, but she motioned him on with her thanks and dabbed her nose with a tissue while schooling herself to greater caution. That one step through her door erased a century, give or take, and she realized that her twentieth-century mind was grossly out of tune with the times.

A piece of airborne paper, weaving back and forth in a herky-jerky motion, broke her train of thought. Standing, she tested her balance and, deciding she was fine, wandered over to retrieve it from the grip of a small bush before the wind could carry it away. It was from the evening edition of the *Kansas City Star* and was dated May 28, 1895—the day before her father was to be murdered. Whether or not it was an old paper remained to be seen.

Heading east, she entered the bend from which the penny-farthing had emerged and happened across an expanse of lawn. It was littered with people lounging on quilts, enjoying the morning air. The day's theme apparently was bonnets, baskets, and bow ties.

While she was deciding whether to interrupt the conversation between the nearest couple, a dog whisked past her and down the path in the direction from which she came with, of all things, a top hat in its jaws. Following in the dog's wake with a look of utter dismay plastered on his face was a man wearing a dark twill suit and matching vest over a starched white shirt. He managed a breathless "Pardon me, ma'am" as he sprinted past, yelling, "Rupert! Slow down, boy."

Annie watched their progress with wry amusement, decided that the hat was a lost cause, and continued down the path with a shake of her head. She hadn't gone more than a few steps, however, when the dog streaked past her again. The gentleman was not far behind, churning up the gravel beneath his feet. This time he gasped, “So sorry,” as he flew by and disappeared around a curve. You certainly had to give him credit for politeness under fire, Annie decided.

As the dog appeared in the bend for the third time, Annie crouched with her hands on her knees and said, “Here, Rupert! Here, boy!”

Immediately slowing to a trot, the dog wandered over, tail wagging, to drop the hat on the gravel at Annie’s feet and sat with his tongue lolling out. “Good boy!” she said, rubbing his head. She was dusting the hat off as the man came into view.

Seeing Annie with the top hat in her hand and Rupert sitting on his haunches next to her, the gentleman slowed. He tried to marshal his composure and say something, but Annie beat him to the punch.

“Is it fair to assume this is yours?” She held out the hat while attempting unsuccessfully to keep the amusement from her voice.

“Oh!” The man glanced at the meadow and the rapt picnickers. “I don’t suppose I could deny it’s mine and pretend this never happened?” he asked as Rupert trotted over to lick his hand. He looked down at the dog, and a reluctant smile formed across his face. “You rascal!” He squatted to massage the dog’s ears in both his hands before attaching a leash, giving Annie a moment to make a quick appraisal.

Jet-black hair covered his head in lazy swirls and tumbled over his ears to rest on broad, spare shoulders. And while his jaw was firm, he had a delicate, straight nose and a wide mouth with a full lower lip. He was somewhere in his midthirties, Annie guessed.

He glanced at her, grinning as he rubbed Rupert behind the ears, and she noted that his eyes were the color of smoke. He was handsome to the point of being pretty.

Standing up, the man accepted the top hat with surprising grace, considering the circumstances. “Thank you for salvaging what little remains of my dignity.” He cocked his head toward the picnickers in the meadow. "Though they no doubt will make short work of it."

"Certainly." Annie tipped her head lightly and turned to make her way down the path.

"Surely there is some way I can return the favor."

Lowering her baggage, Annie turned, looking at the gentleman critically. "There is, actually," she said. "If you could direct me to the nearest bank?"

He scratched his head, not the most elegant of gestures. "I can do better than that. I'll escort you." He strolled forward and picked up her suitcase with one hand while tipping his hat with the other. "The name's Nathaniel Goodkin."

Taken aback and not at all certain she was ready for the company of a stranger, handsome as he was, Annie protested weakly. "Thank you, but that's really not necessary."

Looking at Rupert, who chose that moment to whine, Mr. Goodkin said, "But Rupert insists. The matter is out of our hands, I'm afraid."

Annie smothered a smile and considered her options. She noticed several people strolling in the distance and decided the situation was safe enough, but she wasn't going to allow Mr. Goodkin the satisfaction of corralling her without a suitable riposte. "I'll accept Rupert's kind proposal then."

Taking the leash from Mr. Goodkin's hand, she started down the path with the dog trotting happily beside her. After a few steps, she paused, looked over her shoulder, and turned to say, "I suppose this won't do at all, will it?" She sighed. "If Rupert has no objection, you…could…join us." She knelt to address the dog. "What do you think, Rupert? Is he safe enough?"

Dropping to his belly, Rupert rolled on his side and continued to pant without comment.

Glancing back at the obviously stunned Mr. Goodkin, Annie shrugged. "I must admit his response is open to interpretation, but…" She rubbed the dog's belly, then stood, offering her arm. "Annabelle Aster, from San Francisco."

Accepting it with a bemused shake of his head, Mr. Goodkin directed Annie down the pathway of the park and in the direction of the buildings that could be seen above the tree line.

As they broke from the park onto city streets, Annie's mind began to rebel. A tree looks much the same from one century to another, but a city is another thing altogether. Nothing was right, despite everything being familiar. And the women strolling through the boardwalks—all the oddities of past were drowned out by the sight of them.

They crowded the streets, walking in one another's company or chaperoned, but never alone, and Annie was acutely aware that, for all her sartorial eccentricity, she still stood out like a sore thumb. The amount of clothing piled atop any single body was staggering. There were corsets, bodices, undergarments, overgarments, "mutton leg" sleeves, opera gloves, parasols, and bonnets—all on show in a variety of silks, velvets, and satins.

Despite the flamboyant display, however, there was a uniform bleakness to the women that puzzled Annie. They were pale, paler than her, and looked as if the little light that animated them had gone out. Upset, though not certain why, she whispered to herself, "So dreary."

Overhearing her, Mr. Goodkin leaned in as if sharing a distasteful secret. "Arsenic," he said.

Annie nodded knowingly before gazing at a particularly wan pair, but as his inference sank in, she stopped dead in her tracks. "You can't mean to say they are trying to look that way intentionally!"

Taken aback by her vehemence, Mr. Goodkin said, "The consumptive 'look' is quite fashionable with the upper class…" He paused, looking her up and down, clearly confused.

Annie rolled her eyes, exasperated that he'd lumped her in with this lot. "I come by it honestly," she said, then stared about, aghast. "You would think they might take up something healthier, like jogging."

"Jogging?" Mr. Goodkin looked at Annie as if she'd lost the plot, then broke into a smile. "I suppose it would do them some good, but whoever heard of such a thing?" He chuckled, shaking his head at the joke he was certain she'd made. "If I may inquire, Miss Aster, what would you have done if Rupert said no?" he asked, artfully changing the subject.

Annie thought about the question for a moment before responding. "What better test of a man's character than how he treats his dog?"

"Hmm, I see. And if he isn't my dog?" The look on Annie's face made him rush to add, "I feel a sudden need for a disclaimer, not wishing to put my character in further question." He grinned, his cheeks dimpling. "He belongs to Mrs. Woolvey, my housekeeper."

Annie laughed, while Rupert, who seemed to be aware that he was the topic of conversation, wound his way between Mr. Goodkin's legs before sitting on his shoes and panting.

"I take it that you're an attorney then."

"I was rather afraid the word *disclaimer* would give me away," Mr. Goodkin said as he pulled a business card from his coat's inner pocket and handed it to Annie. He pointed to a large Greek Revival building. "We're here."

"Thank you for the company, Mr. Goodkin," Annie said, retrieving her luggage.

He tipped his hat, hesitating briefly. "If you find yourself in need of an escort..." His face colored.

"Yes?" Annie asked.

"Well," he said, suddenly at a loss. "You...you have my business card."

Annie gave Rupert a quick pat on the head while offering Mr. Goodkin her most winning smile. She reached for his hand and squeezed, then entered the building, the click of her heels echoing sharply throughout the entryway.

The banking floor was cool as an icehouse and, aside from her footsteps, quiet as a mouse. Unperturbed, Annie strode to an empty station next to a gentleman who looked like he'd just come off the range, needing only a lasso to add to his duster coat and cowboy hat. The bank clerk behind the counter was wearing a visor, a pin-striped, button-down shirt, and a pair of dark wool pants held up by suspenders. He stood so still that the occasion seemed to have robbed him of expression and movement, like a statue over which someone had impudently thrown a set of clothing. Then he moved. "How may I help you today, madam?"

"If it's not too much of an inconvenience, I would like to speak to the bank manager."

The clerk frowned. "I'm certain I can be of help."

Annie reached into her handbag, pulled out the bearer bond, and slid it across the counter. "I would like to redeem this, please."

The clerk examined the bond resting on the counter. "If madam will wait here, I will locate a manager," he said, looking almost offended when he handed the bearer bond back to Annie.

As he disappeared through a door, Annie turned, nodding to the gentleman at the adjacent station who made no bones of his interest in whatever caused such a commotion.

Moments later, the clerk returned with a manager. One glance at the bearer bond and the manager's nostrils dilated. "Do you have an account with us?" he asked.

"Unfortunately not. I would like to redeem it for cash."

"But the amount will be considerable!" Noticing patrons looking in their direction, he opened a side door, guiding Annie down a corridor to his office—an efficient little space with plastered walls and mahogany wainscoting. Offering her a seat, he rounded the desk, rocking back in his chair with his hands steepled over his chest, assessing her.

Amused by his body language, Annie copied his posture. "I'm attending an auction, cash only," she said.

The nape of the manager's neck started to color, and he cleared his throat. "I see. Might I suggest you open an account and simply withdraw the necessary funds for the auction?"

All business now, Annie said, "That depends, I suppose, on how much I'll receive in exchange for the bond."

The manager flipped open the lid of a wooden box sitting to the side of his desk. Inside were several compartments containing linen stationery, nibs, elaborately pearlized barrels, caps, and fillers. He quickly assembled a pen, pulled out a sheet, and began scratching notes.

An hour later, Annie walked out of the bank with a thousand dollars in cash and a book of checks with an account balance of $4,488, having reduced the service fee from eight to two percent, while leaving the manager scratching his head over how he came up for air at the shallow end in the war of the sexes. She also had the date, directions to the nearest hotel, and the rudiments of a plan, having decided the simplest course of action would be to shift suspicion from Elsbeth to the man she read about in the article. It took her a moment to remember his name—Ambrosius Culler.

She stepped outside, looking for the trolley rails, as per the bank manager's instructions. A paperboy, identifiable by his knickerbockers, flat cap, and wooden crate, was more than happy to point north for a nickel, and she wandered toward the downtown section of Kansas City, past billboards for such oddments as Dooley's Yeast Powder and Mrs. Winslow's Soothing Syrup. But she was stopped in her tracks by a billboard advertising Eno's Fruit Salt, illustrated with the image of a dapper gent and a winsome lady separated by Cupid.

The caption read, "Riches, Titles, Honour, Power, and Worldly Prospects Are as Nought to a Deeply Rooted Love!" Apparently, Mr. Eno was selling a love potion, and the advertisement was so pretentiously fraudulent, so delightfully hucksterish, that Annie had to restrain herself from applauding. A horse-drawn carriage rolled by, kicking up dust, and she reached for her handkerchief before sneezing violently.

"Bless you, ma'am."

It took Annie a second to understand the words' meaning, as they rolled across her ears in a lazy drawl that, in keeping with the southern style, added an extra syllable or two and sounded more like "Bless ya, may-um." She turned to find a little soot-covered scarecrow of a boy wearing a ball cap and grimy overalls staring at her from the front doorsteps of a brownstone. He couldn't be more than eleven or twelve, she thought, and looked almost fragile despite his pert grin. "Thank you," she said.

"Looks like you got a bleeder."

"A what?"

The kid tapped his nose.

"Oh!" Annie pressed the handkerchief to hers.

"No, no!" the kid said, hopping up. "Put it in your mouth and chew on it, hard-like. That does the trick every time."

Annie laughed but did as he suggested, feeling a little silly as she chewed on the cloth. After a minute, she pulled it out, testing her nose. "Well, I'll be," she said.

The kid stuck his thumbs in oversize pockets and, without an ounce of sheepishness, said, "Now, ain't that worth a coin or two?"

Tickled by his chutzpah, Annie set her suitcase down and made an act of glaring at him disapprovingly, while taking stock of the blue eyes and freckled nose. She reached into her purse, pulled out a dollar, and winked.

Clearly not expecting such a response, the boy took a moment to collect the offered bill, looking at Annie all the while as if trying to decide whether she was an earthbound angel or simply had a screw loose. He shoved it in a pocket while looking up and down the street warily before taking her by the arm and saying something completely unexpected. "You better come with me, miss."

He tried to pull her around a corner, but Annie stood her ground. "My hotel is that way." She pointed in the opposite direction.

Glancing in the direction from which she'd come, he shook his head and started tugging at her arm again. "If you want to make it there in one piece, you best come with me."

The frankness of the comment made Annie follow his gaze, but she saw nothing beyond a game of kick-the-can being broken up by a passing trolley. She glanced across her shoulder at the kid, the corner of her lip coiled in a look that clearly said "Are you trying to play me?"

He looked at his shoes before glancing at Annie from the corner of his eyes. "Do you know you got a shadow?" he asked.

Perplexed, Annie quickly peeked behind her back. Noting nothing out of the ordinary, she asked, "A shadow?"

"A tail."

Annie shook her head, not understanding.

"You're being followed!" he hissed. "I noticed it when you come up the street." The kid cocked his head. "He's standing at the corner of that building yonder."

Annie started to turn but stopped when the boy barked, "Not so fast!" He added quietly, "Make it look natural. He's wearing a duster. You can't miss him."

She made a show of setting her suitcase down to adjust the laces on her shoes while glancing down the street from under her brow. She scrambled to her feet, trying not to stare. "I believe that's the gentleman who was standing next to me at the bank!"

"Do you know who he is?"

"I haven't the foggiest."

"Well, I do. He's Ambrosius Culler's buddy. Name's Danyer, though some folk simply call him Hatchet Man."

For a split second, Annie thought she heard him say *killer* and *danger*. But she didn't have time to consider the irony before her mind registered the name like a slap to the face.

"I see you know the name," the kid said flatly.

Annie risked a second look at the figure in the distance. "It's familiar to me."

"Thought it might be," the kid said, looking up and down the street, lips pursed in concentration. He nodded to himself and took Annie's arm. "Come on," he said, leading her up the street past Gwinn's Dry Goods and around another corner to a sandlot.

"Wait here," he said before wandering past the dugout to the side of a large wood-framed building with the words *Womack's Hardware* over the door to have a muted conversation with a pair of kids loitering against the wall. One disappeared inside while the other, after a quick glance at Annie, made his way back up the street in the direction from which they came.

Returning to take Annie's hand, the kid led her to the corner, sliding open the door to Crane Brothers' Carriage Company. He ushered her inside, then followed, peeking his head back around the door frame. He looked up at Annie and cocked his head. "Wait," he said before lowering himself so she could peer over his shoulder.

A girl with carrot-colored pigtails and a muslin skirt stepped out of the door of Womack's, froze at the sight of the man in the duster coming up the street, and rocketed down an alleyway next to the hardware store with the man in quick pursuit.

Puzzled, Annie turned to her companion and asked, "What just happened?"

Arching his brows, the kid grinned. "I just bought you some time. Come on."

Before Annie could argue, he started working his way through the building, past a room where leather hides were draped over dozens of wood rails, into an assembly hall past a rack loaded with spoked steel wheels and what appeared to be leather-covered box springs, and station after station of elegant carriages in various stages of completion, each labeled with names like Saratoga Phaeton or Imperial Surrey. An occasional worker in a leather apron would look up and nod respectfully to the kid, leading Annie to wonder exactly whose company she was keeping.

Taking her out the back and down an alley, he guided her into a deserted building, up a set of questionable stairs, and into a derelict room before heading to a lone window to peer out onto the street. After a minute, he turned, looking rather smug.

"Now that you've dragged me off to God knows where, can you at least tell me who the girl is?" Annie demanded.

"Wrong question," he said. "You should be asking who Danyer *thinks* she is." He took his cap off, and a pair of carrot-colored pigtails tumbled out. "He thinks she's me." Stacking a couple crates atop each other, the kid gestured for Annie to sit down. "You can call me Cap'n, and I think we should have us a talk, miss."

Annie's mouth formed a perfect O as her fists dropped from her hips. She lowered herself uncertainly onto the makeshift chair and began fussing with her skirt while taking stock of this interesting change of affairs. She studied Cap'n from the corner of her eye. Her initial assessment had put the girl around age eleven, but now Annie wasn't so sure. There was something in her manner that was altogether too mature for a child of that age. When the silence became uncomfortable, Annie broke down and simply asked, "If you don't mind me asking, how old are you?"

Chuckling as if at an inside joke, Cap'n asked, "Why? Think I'm playing hooky?"

"The name's Annie. Speaking of which, why *aren't* you in school? And where are your parents?"

Cap'n shook her head. "No parents, no school, and no one cares. I'm a throwaway, miss." She walked to the corner and leaned against the wall, rubbing her chin before getting down to business. "But we got more important stuff to talk about, you and me. Why is Danyer following you?"

Annie stared at the girl in dumb silence, attempting to digest her sad account while simultaneously shaking her head at the improbability, the crazy chance that she'd be followed by anyone even remotely associated with the man who murdered her father. "I honestly don't know," she said.

"Then how come you looked like you seen a ghost when I said his name?"

"It wasn't *his* name I responded to," Annie said, more severely than intended.

Cap'n's eyes flashed in understanding, and she stared at Annie with a look that began to mingle respect with her earlier skepticism. "Just so you know, this one's old man Culler's henchman. Does his dirty work. I don't know why he's tailing you, but I do know it don't add up to no good."

"Dirty work?"

"Aside from his legit businesses"—Cap'n said the word *legit* in a manner that suggested they were anything but—"Culler runs the grifts in Kansas City. No one can as much as pinch a penny without he gets a piece of the action…or Danyer pays them a visit." She paused. "You don't want Danyer paying a visit," she added. The strange intelligence, as well as the girl's cool self-possession, caught Annie left-footed, but the girl pressed on. "You got something against Culler?" she asked. "If so, we just might have something in common."

Annie held up her hand, her mind a riot. She wasn't certain, but Cap'n seemed to be proposing an alliance of some sort. She chose her words carefully. "While I can't see the appearance of that dreadful man as anything more than a coincidence, it is feasible that my business here involves Mr. Culler."

"You friends?"

"Quite the opposite."

Annie's inflection left no debate as to her opinion of Mr. Culler, and Cap'n rubbed her hands together. "All right then." She grabbed a crate and sat across from Annie. "He got it in for you too?"

"'Got it in for me'? I honestly don't..." Annie puzzled over the comment for a moment before exclaiming, "Good lord! What have you done to cross the man?"

"I didn't *do* nothing. Maybe saw something I oughtn't, though." Cap'n chewed on her lower lip before meeting Annie's eyes. "Danyer killed a man, you see... My friend Fabian. Beat him to a pulp in an alley while I watched from behind a pile of rubbish. Then he shot him."

"But why? Why would he do such a thing?"

"We botched a fleece job."

Annie absorbed what she could of the girl's story, but it created more questions than answers. She looked around. "And you...you live here now?"

Cap'n nodded.

The gesture silenced Annie. This hovel—she couldn't think of a better word—was the girl's home. More to the point, she was in desperate trouble, and from the same man who had killed Annie's father. Yet there Cap'n stood, a defiant, brave little throwaway living in a condemned building, hiding from an obviously ruthless man, and stubbornly refusing to give in to everything life threw at her.

Annie wasn't certain how long she was struck dumb, but it was long enough to witness Cap'n dealing with an internal struggle of her own. The poor thing must be desperate for allies, Annie thought, and her initial shock on hearing Cap'n's story began to give way to a surprisingly tender feeling. She wanted to help her. And given what she knew about Cap'n's story, Annie thought it was quite possible that she'd never been the beneficiary of a sympathetic heart—in an adult, anyway. She looked for something to say, something that Cap'n wouldn't mistake for pity, certain the girl would have too much pride for that nonsense.

But she waited too long and lost the opportunity when Cap'n sat down again, saying impatiently, "Your turn."

Annie sighed, regretting her silence. She could hardly blame Cap'n for her wariness and decided to trust in the truth, at least a part of it. "Mr. Culler has caused injury to two members of my family," she said.

"What did he do?"

Annie considered her response but quickly realized anything she said would lead to other questions she wouldn't know how to answer.

Undeterred by her silence, Cap'n tried a different tack. "Is that why Danyer is tailing you?" she asked.

"Strangely enough," Annie said, standing up, "that just seems to be pure, dumb luck on his part. Neither he nor Mr. Culler know who I am."

"Well, who are you then?" Cap'n asked.

*Who am I, indeed*, Annie thought. She walked to the window and looked out at the backdrop of dreary buildings. "Someone unexpected," she said. Catching a movement below, she craned her neck to seek the source of the disturbance and almost missed Cap'n saying under her breath, "Yes, you are." She looked over her shoulder.

The girl returned her regard, her eyes narrow and uncertain. It angered Annie that Cap'n should be forced into such unfair decisions as to whether to trust her, and it angered her further that, ultimately, she felt judged. She turned that anger against its source, Mr. Culler, and surprised herself by saying, "Let me help you."

If she expected some visual cue, a change in Cap'n's features indicating she'd heard the comment, she was disappointed. Not a muscle twitched in Cap'n's face, and her gaze never wavered. If anything, she gave the appearance of looking through Annie at the wall behind her. After a moment, however, her cheeks budded with tiny pink explosions. But as quickly as her skin colored, Cap'n's eyes hardened and the blush faded away.

*Well, it's a start*, Annie thought.

"What are you going to do?" For the first time, Cap'n sounded like a scared little girl.

"I'm going to start by getting you out of here. Someplace safe," Annie said. "Then I'm going to put a fly in Mr. Culler's ointment."

Cap'n's gaze trailed to the floorboards. "There ain't no safer place for me." She pivoted on her crate to face Annie. "And begging your pardon, but I think it's you who'll be needing my help."

"That's out of the question."

"Look, I don't mean to sound ungrateful, but you really don't understand what you've gotten yourself into, Miss Annie." As quickly as that, the scared girl was gone and Cap'n was back in business. She stood up, planted her feet apart, and folded her arms across her chest, leaving Annie with the vague impression of a rooster scratching in the dirt. "Truth be told, I don't know what to make of you. But I have a stake in this, and you're going to need my help."

When Annie appeared unconvinced, she continued. "I'm Cap'n," she said. "That makes me the eyes and ears of this here city. Nothing happens I don't learn about it, and there ain't one square inch of this place I don't know like the back of my hand. Besides, we've been itching to get in a dig with those two."

Despite being pleased that Cap'n had used her name for the first time, Annie managed only one word in response. "'We'?"

Cap'n nodded in smug satisfaction. "The sandlot gang."

# CHAPTER TWENTY-TWO

## Pure and Simple

Those who think boys are made of snakes and snails and puppy dog tails have misjudged the condition of being one. Boys are made of mischief and mayhem, pure and simple. Adding Annie to the mix makes a double dose. And the unfortunate souls who think that girls are made of sugar, spice, and everything nice have obviously never met Cap'n.

Cap'n rearranged the crates, plopped herself down, and pulled her knees up under her chin, gesturing for Annie to join her. "I get a bead on people pretty quick, and there are three things I already know about you," she said. "One, you're a decent lady. Two, you're in way over your head. And three, you *know* something."

The comments were so perceptive—the last two, at any rate—that Annie needed a moment to regroup. Finally, she met Cap'n's eyes. "You're a child," she said.

"I can handle myself."

Annie had to admit that the evidence was on the girl's side. Nothing about Cap'n fell within her experience. The girl was obviously resourceful. More than that, she had a rough and ready grace beyond her years. There had been hints as to what forged it, and Annie found herself wanting to know more about the circumstances, but her curiosity would have to wait. She stared at Cap'n silently, weighing her conscience.

"What's it going to be?" Frustrated by Annie's uncertainty,

Cap'n added, "Look, it's pretty simple. My problem ends up with me dead if I don't solve it. You say you want to help, and it's kind of you not wanting to mix me up in your problems—tells me the kind of lady you are—but I don't have time for that kind of thinking. Either we work together, or we shake hands and go our separate ways. No hard feelings."

Annie could think of no argument so after a moment she acquiesced, saying, "There are secrets I must keep for now, things I won't be able to explain. Can you live with that?"

Cap'n scratched her ear, thinking. Finally, she slid off the crate and walked over to peer out the window. "I don't like secrets," she said.

"I don't blame you. My entire life has been built on secrets that I'm only now uncovering."

Leaning with her hands on the sill, Cap'n raised her index finger to scribble on the dirty window.

Annie could see she'd written the word *trust* and wandered over to write something next to it.

Cap'n peered at the writing, then turned to search Annie's face. She nodded, extending her hand. Annie shook it, and the two wandered back to the crates, leaving anyone who happened to see the window from the alley to wonder what *em tsurt* might mean.

"There is going to be a murder tonight," Annie said. She paused, waiting for Cap'n's reaction, but there was none forthcoming. "I can't tell you how I know this to be true, but I can tell you that the murderer will be your Mr. Culler, no doubt with the aid of his loathsome associate."

Annie folded her hands together in her lap. "My grandmother is going to be accused of his crime."

She looked up to see Cap'n making a show of adjusting the straps to her overalls. She took her time and, once satisfied, looked up thoughtfully. "It seems to me that you know a lot more about what's *gonna* happen than a person oughta."

Annie chose not to defend her comments.

"Okay," Cap'n conceded. "And who's going to be murdered?"

"David Abbott."

"The magician? The man who travels to the future?" That didn't sit too well, and Cap'n's expression reflected it. "Wait a minute! Don't he and Culler work together?"

Annie recalled the article she took from the Antiquarian and nodded.

Cap'n took a long breath before letting it out. "Well, that's an earful." She wandered around the room, running her hand lazily along the wall. At one point, she stopped. "You can't go to the Grunts?" Realizing the word hadn't registered, she tried again. "Police?"

"What would I tell them?"

Cap'n thought about that and began to wander again, tracing patterns in the faded wallpaper. She reached into her pocket and pulled out the dollar Annie gave her, turning it over in her hand. "Do you know where this is going to happen? This murder?" she asked.

"In David Abbott's home."

Cap'n looked up, searching Annie's face. "And we can't stop it?"

Annie shook her head.

"You sure?"

"That's already been attempted," Annie blurted out. Grimacing, she collected her thoughts. "I know that makes no sense. Frankly, I don't think the murder can be stopped, but I'll be damned before I allow my grandmother to be convicted for it."

Cap'n let out a breath of air, sounding tired when she said, "Already been tried? How could you have already tried to stop something that ain't happened yet?"

"Remember that I said there are things I can't explain?" Annie struggled to find something more to say but gave up, looking deflated. "Cap'n, if you want out of our agreement, I certainly understand."

Looking as though she had been slapped, Cap'n exclaimed, "No! I made a promise, and I'll keep it." She began to pace again but with greater determination, muttering to herself all the while. "If we can't stop it, then we have to point the finger at them who done it." She closed her eyes, thinking, before smacking her fist into her palm. "A plant," she said.

"A plant?" asked Annie. "I don't understand."

"We're going to plant something on Abbott's body that points to Culler and Danyer."

Annie rocked back, almost losing her balance. "Are you suggesting that we break into a private residence and...and *violate* a corpse?"

"Yup." Cap'n broke into a grin. "And I know just the thing." She sat across from Annie, looking very pleased with herself. "This solves both our problems, don't you see? It gets Mr. Culler out of my hair and the heat off your grandma at the same time." She caught Annie's look of distaste and tried to mollify her by adding, "If the man's dead as you say, he won't mind."

For the briefest of moments, Annie had a vision of a cat smugly dropping a mouse at her feet, but despite her queasiness, she had to admit the plan was a good one. "This thing..." she asked slowly, uncertain whether she wanted to know the answer. "How are we going to acquire it?"

Hooking both thumbs in the bib of her overalls, Cap'n looked sideways at Annie and said, "I'm gonna pinch it."

"Oh."

"You might as well know, Miss Annie. I do what I need to get by. Learned to pick pockets and locks from Johnny Parker before Fabian took me in. Then I got pulled into Mr. Culler's racket—another reason he's out to get me. I was a pretty good moneymaker, not that I saw much of it." She reached over to touch Annie's knee, then removed her hand. "I'm not proud of what I done, but pride ain't really something I can afford."

Looking properly ashamed, Annie asked in a subdued tone, "Do you know what you are getting yourself into?"

"Do you?"

*Checkmate*, thought Annie. She leaned forward, resting her chin on her entwined hands, her eyes narrowing. Unexpectedly, she asked, "Do you know where Mr. Culler's office is located?"

"Sure. It's just three blocks up the way. Why?"

"Well," Annie said carefully, "it would be a shame to waste these talents of yours."

Cap'n blinked, snickering when Annie broke into a grin. She clapped her palms against her thighs and stood. "It's a little after noon, now," she said. "Mr. Culler's lunching at Ma Maison. Same thing every day. Breakfast at the Broadway. Lunch at Ma Maison. Now that Danyer's in town, he'll probably be in tow. I'm going to skedaddle. You might want to wait for me here. I'll have one of the gang check in on you." She retrieved the dollar bill from her pocket one last time, staring at it before asking, "By the way, how's your handwriting?"

CHAPTER

# TWENTY-THREE

## A Flimflam

While Annie and Cap'n were wrapping up their strategy session, Messrs. Culler and Danyer were eating a meal at Ma Maison.

Mr. Culler was, for the most part, quiet. He was thinking primarily of loose ends, but Abbott's door wasn't far behind. Danyer... Well, it was hard to fathom what Danyer was thinking. "You were uncharacteristically late for lunch today," Mr. Culler said, breaking the silence. "Were you delayed at the bank?"

Danyer issued his usual grunt and shoveled a pile of beans into his mouth as he shared the story of the woman with the Edison Electric bearer bond.

Mr. Culler winced as if Danyer's voice had irritated his inner ear. "Well, that is interesting. But must you talk with your mouth full?"

At that, Danyer shoved another helping in his mouth for spite, while relaying the details of his thwarted attempt to tail her between chews.

Immune to Danyer's vulgarities, Mr. Culler sat back in his chair and began shuffling a dollar coin between the knuckles of his right hand. "There is no accounting for people," he said, as if the fact that the woman did not allow herself to be caught was proof of her low character. He dropped his napkin on the table and motioned for the tab as the waiters scurried to clean up the mess, wisely ignoring Danyer in the process.

They exited the restaurant, right into the path of a freight train barreling down the sidewalk on eight little legs.

"It's mine!"

"Is not. I found it!"

"No you didn't. Tommy did!"

"Then how's it yours?"

A mousy-haired girl dressed in overalls bounced off Mr. Culler's leg and into the three boys who were chasing her. Before the tornado of motion could regroup, Mr. Culler dropped his bag and grabbed both the girl and the largest boy by the scruff of the neck as Danyer held his hands up and danced out of the way of the remaining two.

As is the way with most evil men, Danyer had his Achilles' heel—children. To him, they were unformed, intractable, and quite possibly the repositories of disease, so he refused to expose himself to them unless absolutely necessary. Certain that Mr. Culler had a handle on the situation, he was content to step to the side.

The two captives were swinging away at each other with little discipline but plenty of commitment, while the other two, having taken sides, were egging them on. The girl continued to swing away as she looked up at Mr. Culler and yelled, "Lemme go. I didn't do nuthin'. Lemme go!"

"What is all this fuss?" Mr. Culler asked as he yanked at their suspenders. When they didn't respond as quickly as he would like—that is to say, immediately—he shook them again.

The boy he was holding gurgled, "She took Tommy's dollar."

"I did not! He found that dollar on the street, then he dropped it! Finders keepers, and you're a snitch, Marty Flannigan!"

The boy took a swing at the girl, who turned scarlet and threw a few punches and one impressive kick of her own that missed the mark only because Mr. Culler had the two separated.

"I did not drop it. You knocked it out of my hand!" Tommy yelled from the sidelines. There was a new burst of kicking and screaming.

"Enough!" Mr. Culler took it upon himself to shake the two

kids so hard their heads rolled. "Who presently possesses this dollar bill?" he demanded.

The question was met with stony silence. After a quick shake, the kid named Marty Flannigan pointed resentfully at the girl.

"Will you kindly show me the item in question, little miss?"

Looking sullen but whipped into obedience, the girl pulled a dollar bill out of her overalls and showed it to Mr. Culler. He released her and took the proffered bill for closer examination. "Why, I can't believe it!"

Danyer, possibly concerned that he could get the dropsy from direct contact with the children, peered at the bill from a safe distance.

"This is the very dollar bill that I dropped on my walk this morning. I'm sure of it!"

"Hey! What are you talking about?" the girl shouted.

"Look here, young miss." Culler pointed soberly at the bill. "It says 'This Note Is Legal Tender' on the face."

"All dollar bills say that!"

The girl drew back when she witnessed the sudden upheaval of Mr. Culler's face, a violent ripple that relaxed almost as quickly into a more amiable expression. He looked at her, his eyes flaring. "Are you claiming that I wish to deceive you for the sake of a dollar?"

She bit her lip, suddenly terrified, while her companions looked on disconsolately—not witnessing what she had. "No, sir," she said as Culler pocketed the bill.

"I would like to thank you for returning my property. I'd reward you, but unfortunately I have no change." Culler gave the girl a gentle shove on the back. "Now be on your way."

Not thinking twice, she took off like lightning, leaving the boys to trudge down the street behind her. "Told ya'll not to grab it from me," the smallest boy said as they retreated. "Now look what you done. He nicked our buck!"

Mr. Culler watched them round the corner and turned to Danyer. "Did those brats look familiar?" he asked. When Danyer didn't respond, he said, "No matter. They're of an age to learn that trust is a commodity they can ill afford." He picked up his valise with a light heart. "It's been years since I've run a con of my own. Quite invigorating, really."

While Mr. Culler was busy congratulating himself, the kids ducked into an alleyway, forming a huddle around the smallest boy. He rapped on a door, his eyes dripping innocence as it opened. He pulled something out of his pocket—a money clip holding four crisp twenty-dollar bills—and gave it to the hand snaking out from inside while the other kids patted him on the back.

Cap'n peered out the doorway, staring at the little girl as she pocketed the clip. "You all right, Emma?"

"Careful with that one, Cap'n," Emma said, shaking her head. "There's something bad inside him, and it wants out."

Cap'n paused, taking in Emma's words. Like most street kids, Emma had wisdom beyond her years, so it would be wise to listen to her warning. Cap'n stepped out of the doorway to peer around the corner at Mr. Culler's back and nodded at Emma before handing the money to the largest boy. "Put this in the general fund. There's something else I gotta take care of."

As the gaggle turned to leave, the largest of the four faced Cap'n. "I'm guessin' you told Emma to call me Marty Flannigan?"

Cap'n's lip twitched. "Maybe."

"Funny," he said. "In case you ain't noticed, I'm black as pitch."

Cap'n burst into laughter. "Have someone tail Mr. Culler. I'm heading to his office and need a good hour."

The kid saluted, then bolted down the sidewalk, keeping an eye on—but a good distance from—the target that was whistling as he strolled down the street.

Mr. Culler practically bounced on his feet as he walked. "I think I'll have it framed," he said.

Danyer grunted, the sound as much a question as Mr. Culler was going to get.

"The dollar," he said. Sliding his hands into his pocket, Culler managed several steps before he found himself frowning. He stopped bouncing and, after a few more steps, stopped walking altogether. Dropping his valise, Culler began to pat his pockets. Unhappy with the result, he turned them out and watched as a lone dollar bill fluttered to the ground. His face turned scarlet. "Those kids!" He reached down to retrieve the bill and waved it in Danyer's face. "We've been outmaneuvered by professional cons in diapers!"

Once again, his face went through a rabid metamorphosis as he walked around punching the air with his fists. A minute later, he took a few even breaths, looked back in the direction from which he came, and said with a hint of admiration in his voice, "One would almost think I'd trained them myself." Having said that, his eyes glazed over as he connected the dots, and he bellowed at the top of his voice, "*Cap'n!*"

He turned to Danyer, his face flushed. "That little ingrate! How dare she use my own tricks on me!" He started to stuff the bill in his pocket when he noticed something odd. There was a bit of handwriting on the back. *Today's lesson examines the advantages of being underestimated. Thank you for being so predictable, Mr. Culler.*

He grunted, then after a brief pause said, "Very clever." He showed the bill to Danyer before tossing it in the air. "If it *is* Cap'n, she has help." The dollar caught in a wind eddy, lurching down the street. Mr. Culler watched its progress, then removed his bowler to smooth back his hair, yanked sharply at his lapels, and, with as much dignity as he could muster, said, "I hate kids." He signaled to Danyer before picking up his valise. "We're going to the bank."

# CHAPTER TWENTY-FOUR

## Mr. Culler's Curiosity Cabinet

Cap'n walked into the room and plunked herself down next to Annie. She was all business as she reached into her pocket and pulled out the money clip, placing it carefully in Annie's hand.

The clip was made of gold, and the letters *AC* were inscribed on the surface with elaborate strokes. Cap'n punched playfully at Annie's arm, then, seeing the blood drain from her new friend's face, asked, "You all right, Miss Annie?"

Words from the newspaper clipping Annie had found at the antique store scrolled across the back of her eyes like ticker tape. *A money clip engraved with the initials* AC *has been found at the scene of the crime.* She ogled it in disbelief, laboring against the possibility that her plan of action had already been scripted.

The comfort Annie took in the immutability of time had been threatened, but she decided not to concern herself with the ramifications of her meddling. Now was not the time for such introspection. Elsbeth needed her.

"I'm fine, dear," she said. After a moment, a smile broke out on her face. "I feel as if I'm contributing to your delinquency, though."

Cap'n grinned at the comment and stood up. "We should head on down to Mr. Culler's office while the coast is clear."

"Clear? He won't be there?"

"If I were one to bet"—Cap'n glanced at Annie—"and I'm not," she added quickly, "I'd wager he's halfway to Denver by now."

"Denver?"

"Mr. Culler don't go nowhere with an empty pocket. He'll head to the bank, so I've planted a gang member out front to buy us some time. Mr. Culler's gonna be chasing that little jackrabbit all over town."

She gave Annie a quick rundown of the noontime activities as they made for Culler's office. "It won't take him too long to figure out I had a hand in it." She stopped, pointing to a solid, unimpressive building. "We're here," she said.

Annie motioned with an exaggerated flourish for Cap'n to lead the way, following her little companion through the entrance hall and up a set of stairs to the second floor. They stopped in front of a door midway down the hall and across from an emergency exit. The sign on it read *Culler Enterprises*.

Annie stared at the sign thoughtfully. "Isn't Mr. Abbott his business partner?" she asked.

Cap'n shook her head. "Mr. Culler practically owns Mr. Abbott. Paid for his production, you see."

Annie *did* see—much more than she ought, but that was what came of thumbing her nose in the face of time. She considered the door. Espionage not being part of her skill set, she was uncertain how to proceed. Feeling somewhat foolish, she pressed her ear to it, lurching back as if stung when she heard a click and the door inched inward. Her heart pounding, Annie looked down in time to see Cap'n pocket a metal pin, then stand to face her. She shrugged. "Like I said."

Annie gave the door a slight shove with her index finger, half expecting to see the knucklebones and knee joints of small mammals tumble out and around her feet, but the only thing that greeted her was the musky odor of disuse, cigar smoke, and an acrid tang that reminded her of a high school biology lab.

Cap'n inched around her and disappeared into the room, exclaiming in a hushed tone, "Oh my God."

Annie stepped in behind her. Even before her eyes adjusted to the dim light, she got the sense that there was something dreadfully wrong with the place. However, a first glance revealed nothing more than a rectangular room approximately twenty or so yards across its length. It was wrapped floor to ceiling in felt wallpaper of the Regency style that might have been purple at one time, but the color was so obscured by soot it was hard to tell. A shabby Oriental rug lay over the dark wood floorboards, with identical oak desks lining the room's farthest and nearest walls. Annie looked up, getting a nasty shock when she saw stuffed birds in horrible disrepair, as well as a mildewed crocodile carcass, hanging from the rafters. Tintypes, dressed in ornate gilded frames, hung from every vertical surface not occupied by shelves and cabinetry.

Cap'n was examining one on the far wall and motioned for Annie to join her. She pointed to the placard at the base of the photograph. It read *Joseph Carey Merrick—The Elephant Man*. The image, grainy and water-stained along the borders, was of a hideously deformed man with a bulbous head and a freakishly enlarged hand. He was standing in profile, wearing a well-cut Victorian suit and, despite his unfortunate physical state, still managing an air of dignity.

Hanging from the wall to its left, they found another tintype of a young lady wearing a lace blouse. Her hands were planted on the ground, and her knickers were cinched above a pair of knees that were so hyperextended that they gave the illusion she was standing on all fours like a dog. The placard read *Ella Harper—The Camel Girl.*

A good half a dozen more freak-show images covered the walls, but Annie, numbed by the grotesquerie, left Cap'n to ogle the remainder and slowly made her way to examine a floor-to-ceiling, glass-encased panel hanging on the wall that showcased a variety of nightmarish insects—the centerpiece being a foot-long atrocity that was all bristles, digits, and fangs. The label read *The Goliath Birdeater*.

Shuddering, she moved on to a cabinet, quickly discovering why she was reminded of her biology lab. The dusty shelves were covered with row upon row of specimens preserved in formaldehyde—among them an enormous toad with no eye sockets, the fetus of a lamb with what appeared to be a stalk protruding from its stomach, and a ghastly preserved head with an enormous spire-like horn growing from the top of its bald pate. *Wang—The Unicorn Man* was written on the placard.

Annie was both revolted and fascinated by the gossamer sheets of skin that had sloughed away from the man's face and were suspended in the solution. She tore her eyes away to pick up what appeared to be a boar's tusk, holding it in the palm of her hand as she examined a variety of horns, skeletons, and other forms of macabre bric-a-brac—among them the head of a monkey that was too obviously sewn to the body of a small dog.

For all the room's freakishness, it was just that until Annie stumbled across the icing on the cake, shifting the room from the ghoulish to the sinister. It was a wax figurine of Jack the Ripper disemboweling a woman. The kernel of loathing that had been lying dormant in Annie's gut suddenly ruptured, spreading icy roots throughout her body, and she began to be afraid.

Cap'n reached out, causing Annie to jump. "Sorry," the girl said, letting go of Annie's wrist. She glanced about the room soberly. "Let's do what we come to do and get out of here."

Annie nodded, but there was one last place to look. While Cap'n wandered over to a coatrack and snatched up a bowler hat, reshaping the brim to her liking, Annie walked over to the closet. She studied the door, almost giving in to her impulse to walk away and leave it be. Doors were no longer simple things—that illusion had been shattered a week or so earlier when she stepped into her backyard. And this particular one seemed to concentrate all the wrongness in the room. So it surprised her to discover the closet was empty except for a few spiderwebs and a box with a duster and a Stetson carelessly heaped on top. Next to the Stetson was what appeared to be a matted pile of fur the size of a small bird's nest.

Annie carried it gingerly to the closet door and looked at Cap'n, one eyebrow raised.

Cap'n wrinkled her nose, shrugging.

Tossing it on the box, Annie wiped her hands on her skirt several times and closed the closet door. She went to the nearest desk, ignoring a specimen jar containing an enormous tapeworm, and started sifting through the papers that littered its surface. There were unpaid invoices, a smattering of correspondence regarding David Abbott's show, and a note from Mr. Culler approving a transfer of funds. She looked from this last item to a pair of filing cabinets.

"Got an idea?" asked Cap'n.

"Getting one." Annie scanned the headings on the file cabinets and opened a drawer. She withdrew a file, then sat in one of the chairs with her feet propped up on the desk. "Well, Cap'n. What do you think we have here?"

Cap'n tilted her head back to peer out from under the bowler's brim.

"It looks to be Mr. Culler's financial ledger. Danyer's also." Annie scanned it. "Well, well, they have been a pair of busy bees. Their investments are nicely diversified, and it looks like their funds are managed by"—she shuffled through the file—"New York Life."

Annie rested the file under her chin and closed her eyes. Snickering under her breath, she wandered back over to the filing cabinet and began opening more drawers.

"What are you looking for?" Cap'n asked.

"Order forms. It seems that Mr. Culler and Danyer will be selling quite a large portion of their assets today."

"They will? Ohhh."

*Sharp kid*, thought Annie. She turned her attention back to the file. "And they are going to place the proceeds in..." Annie considered various options, and a malevolent grin oozed onto her face. "Tesla Electric! Oh, yes, I think Tesla Electric will do quite nicely." She rummaged through a drawer full of documents and held up a stack of order forms. "Here we are. Now, let's see." She glanced about the room. "Cap'n, have you seen anything with Mr. Culler's signature on it?"

Cap'n got up from her lookout station and began to leaf through the papers on the desk opposite the one occupying Annie's attention.

After reviewing the forms, Annie looked across the room to see if Cap'n had any luck and immediately sensed that something was not right. Cap'n was sitting in front of an open drawer. As Annie got up to join her, Cap'n reached inside and removed a tray, placing it on the desk. She turned to Annie, her face blanching.

Annie hurried over to see what had ruffled the girl's feathers. From across the room, the tray appeared to be a smaller version of the entomology board resting on the wall, this one containing a rather spare collection of small insects pinned and on display. A closer look, however, proved to be confusing. *Eraser heads?* she wondered. *Colored eraser heads?* As odd as it would be to find insects pinned to a board, this was altogether stranger. She took it from Cap'n's hand to examine it more closely, and her stomach lurched.

"Emma was right," Cap'n said.

Pinned to the board and painted in a comical variety of pastel colors were the end digits of pinkie fingers. They were in various stages of decomposition, but all swollen and monstrous, and below each specimen was a name. Annie only registered a few—Fabian, Raven, even a Culler—before her eyes fixed on two labeled pins that lacked specimens. They read *Abbott* and *Cap'n*, respectively.

She threw the board back in the drawer, which she slammed shut. "We're leaving." She reached for Cap'n's hand, shaking violently, but the girl had other ideas.

"No."

"Cap'n!"

"No! This don't change nothing." She glared at Annie, repeating, "It don't change a thing." She handed Annie a piece of paper.

It was a letter from Mr. Culler to a client demanding $320 by the end of the week lest he confiscate property. His signature at the bottom of the correspondence was an ostentatious display.

Annie stared at Cap'n for a second, giving the adrenaline time to dissipate, then took the demand notice to the far desk and sat down with a blank piece of paper to practice his signature. Half a dozen efforts later, she glanced up to see Cap'n sitting at Mr. Culler's desk with an open box before her and a cigar protruding from her mouth. Her nose was furrowed, and she was searching through the pockets of her overalls.

"What on earth are you doing?"

Cap'n lifted her index finger, pulled a cigar from her pocket, and held it up for inspection. She carefully pulled the cigar ring from the one in her mouth and slid it over the other. Placing the counterfeit in the box, she closed the lid, dropped the box back into the center drawer, and slid it closed.

Taking the cigar from her mouth and putting it in her overalls, Cap'n grimaced while smacking her lips and returned Annie's gaze with an expression so steely that it startled her. "Payback" was all Cap'n said. She picked a fleck of tobacco from her tongue, adding, "Fabian was my friend."

"What was it?" asked Annie, pointing to the drawer.

"I rolled gunpowder pellets in the center."

Annie opened her mouth to protest but, thinking better of it, shook her head and practiced a few more signatures.

Holding her scribbles next to Mr. Culler's signature, Annie grunted in satisfaction and reopened the financial ledger to confirm the accounts he would be liquidating. She filled out a stack of order forms and forged Mr. Culler's name at the bottom of each.

Nervously tapping the pen against the edge of the desk, she looked about the room once more before turning to Cap'n. "Let's get out of here," she said.

They tidied the room and left through the fire exit, looking back in alarm as a voice boomed through the hallway.

"Miserable brat!" shouted Mr. Culler from the lobby downstairs, his voice echoing down the empty corridor. "Who would have guessed he was part greyhound?" He locked one hand into a fistful of hair on the top of his head while the other clawed at the back of his neck and looked as if he was about to unleash a wail before kicking a trash container that spilled over with a deafening crescendo.

Forcing his rage into his belly, Mr. Culler turned to Danyer. "Find that kid," he said quietly, a surprisingly delicate smile softening his features. When Danyer didn't immediately comply, Mr. Culler's eyes began to bulge from their sockets, a pair of eggs hard-boiled by his anger. "*Now!*" he yelled. He left Danyer on the stairwell and, wishing a pestilence on all youthful things, stormed up the stairway to his office, sending another trash can to the lobby floor with a swift kick on the way.

Muttering to himself, Mr. Culler stormed into the office and dropped his valise by the hat stand. Completely out of sorts, he sat at his desk breathing heavily when a tiny stirring caught his eye. He slammed his hand on the desk, cupping it around a cockroach. Picking it up carefully between his thumb and index finger, Culler examined the insect under the desk lamp, fascinated by the translucence of its carapace and the rows of spines running down its legs like a shark's teeth. He stifled the impulse to put it in his mouth, pulled his macabre collection from the desk drawer, and impaled the cockroach on the pin labeled *Cap'n*, instead.

Lighting a cigar, he rested his forearms on the desk and placed his chin on the back of his hands, waiting for the insect's legs and antennae to stop churning. Suddenly, he yanked the cigar from his mouth, making a moue of distaste. Looking from the cigar to the cockroach, he carefully burned the insect's legs off one by one, delighted by the slight popping sounds made by the burning chitin in the exoskeleton, and threw the cigar in the wastebasket.

Outside, pressed against the building directly under his window, Cap'n jolted at the sound of the explosion and turned to Annie. "That didn't take long," she said.

# CHAPTER TWENTY-FIVE

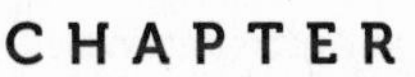

## A Plan in Full Swing

"Pardon me."

The secretary for the investment division of New York Life glanced up from a pile of papers on her desk, looking somewhat put out. "Yes?" she asked.

"I have some order forms for Culler Enterprises that need to be dropped off."

The secretary started at the word *Culler* and lowered her pen. "Your name?" she asked.

"Miss Aster."

"Make yourself comfortable." The secretary gestured to the seating area and hurried down the hall, only to return a moment later with an account manager in tow. She couldn't hightail it back to her seat fast enough when she saw him take one look at the lounge's occupant and run his fingers through his hair before arranging a pleasant and, to her mind, completely alien smile on his face.

"Miss Aster?" he asked, stepping into the lounge.

"I apologize for coming without an appointment, but my employer, Mr. Culler, insists that I deliver these order forms to you immediately."

The secretary looked up with a start at the change in the woman's inflection, and her mouth settled into a smirk as she watched from the corner of her eyes, torn between amusement and disgust while the woman proceeded to play the account manager like a violin.

Handing over some order forms before leading him to a corner, the woman said, "Mr. Culler has received news from a *very* reliable source and is trusting to your discretion—"

Abandoning even the pretense of work, the secretary strained to overhear as the manager mumbled something, prompting Miss Aster to reply, "Yes, the highest regard. He also said that you might wish to *share* this information with your more discerning clientele."

More heated murmuring was offset by perfectly timed laughter, and the secretary felt a bubble of grudging admiration for Miss Aster, who was making optimal use of her appreciable assets without any appearance of impropriety. *He hasn't got a snowball in hell's chance*, she thought.

She was right. In the end, Miss Aster and the natural order proved to be too much for the manager, and he escorted her past the secretary's desk and to the exit. "I will personally attend to the details," he said.

"You're my angel," Miss Aster purred.

After they had shaken hands, the secretary looked at the account manager's retreating back with contempt. She smelled a rat but had no intention of telling him so. While men thought they ruled the world, she knew they were simply there to do the heavy lifting for women like Miss Aster.

As if reading her thoughts, the woman met the secretary's eyes. Smiling faintly, she tapped her finger to her nose before holding it over her lips and stepped out the door.

The secretary watched Miss Aster's progress as she passed from window to window on the front of the building and wondered what she was up to, hoping it added up to a little mud in her boss's face.

She went back to separating carbons as Annie navigated a few blocks before slipping through the door at Crane Brothers, nodding to the workers who followed her every step while pretending not to. She stepped into the alleyway and made her way into the derelict building where she found her confederate taking, of all things, batting practice. Cap'n had cleverly attached a rope to a support beam and was swinging away at a baseball wrapped in some netting secured to the rope's end.

Cap'n dropped the bat and wrapped the cord around the pole. "How did it go?" she asked.

"I'm afraid Mr. Culler not only lost a lot of money today, but quite a few friends as well."

Cap'n snorted, then got on her hands and knees to lift a couple boards from the floor, exposing a cavity. Reaching down with both hands, she began tugging at something inside, falling back onto her tail end with Annie's suitcase landing between her straddled legs. She adjusted her cap and looked up. "We should get you settled in at the Broadway," she said.

Annie helped her up, then took the suitcase and headed for the door. She turned to find that Cap'n hadn't moved. "Aren't you coming?" she asked.

Cap'n ran a hand across her nose. She tugged at the strap of her overalls, clearly bothered by something, then walked to the far wall, leaning against it with her arms crossed. "I can't figure you out," she said.

Annie lowered her suitcase.

"You know I pick pockets to get by." Cap'n suddenly became fixated on a piece of loose wallpaper, picking at it while she spoke. "You gave me a dollar!" The words came out almost like a sob but more nearly like an accusation. "I was testing you," she said, glancing at Annie from the corner of her eye. "When we met. I figured anyone who crossed those two was either stupid, rotten, or both. Either way, I figured I could handle it and get something on Mr. Culler I could use. But you weren't either. I didn't expect that."

Annie walked across the room and braced herself against the wall next to Cap'n. She leaned her head back and closed her eyes, saying nothing.

"You don't fit, you know." Cap'n sniffed, rubbing her nose again before looking over to meet Annie's eyes. "I see things. Everything about you sticks out—the way you walk, talk, even the color of your skin." She reached over to finger Annie's dress. "You're too pretty by half, and you wear expensive clothes, but they smell old. Really old. And I've never seen nothing like this."

Annie looked at the zipper Cap'n had exposed.

"There are two worlds, Miss Annie. The one I live in and the one you live in. There ain't much trust between the two."

And that was the crux of it, Annie realized. Cap'n was struggling to cross the border between need and trust, between a business arrangement and friendship. She reached out to touch the back of the girl's hand. "I'm not asking for anything you aren't ready to give."

"I know, and that's just it," Cap'n said. She walked across the room to lift Annie's suitcase. "We should go."

Annie stood in the lobby of the Broadway, where Cap'n had left her with a promise to meet out front at 6:30 p.m., and tried to shake the impression that she was in the middle of a dream. Nothing, not even the bank, had impressed upon her so completely that the world she now inhabited was a century behind the world she'd left. It wasn't simply the hotel's ornamental excess—the elaborate trim applied to every conceivable surface, the ponderous marble fireplaces, the grand mirrors—but the buzz, the general persona of the hotel and the people that occupied it. It was alien and completely up her alley.

Delighted, Annie pivoted and the lobby responded, spinning slowly about her like a carousel until she almost lost her balance from an unexpected dizzy spell. She walked to the registration desk and wrote a check for her accommodations from the book given to her at the bank. A second spasm of vertigo rocked her as she turned, causing her to drop the room key on the counter. She dabbed her nose with a handkerchief, but there was no need, and reached for the edge of the counter to steady herself.

"Are you well, madam?"

She collected the key with a wan smile. "I think I forgot to eat today," she said.

"There is a fruit basket in the room. Shall I have a bread board sent up?"

Shaking off her dizziness, Annie thanked the receptionist and walked up the two flights of stairs to her room on the third floor, oblivious to the crowd of people collecting in the lobby on their way to a magic show.

She opened the door to her quarters and hesitated, certain she'd been here before. But that, of course, was impossible. Then she made the connection. The room was a dead ringer for the parlor in a custom-made Victorian dollhouse her godmother gave her for her seventh birthday. They'd spent hours playing make-believe with it, and Auntie Liza had used any excuse to buy Annie new "appurtenances." Her favorite was a tiny wooden table clock whose gigantic likeness was sitting on a shelf in the hotel room's shallow entryway.

Annie dropped onto the bed, munching an apple. That little bout of vertigo in the lobby was nothing like the wooziness she felt when her illness was acting up, she decided. In fact, it reminded her of a day not so long ago when she tried to knock on a cabin door. She sat bolt upright. Could it be that Elsbeth was nearby? Should she seek her out? Was it safe?

That the blood she shared with Elsbeth was stronger than the strange alchemy of the door had been made painfully clear when she first attempted an introduction. Her father's diary compared the phenomenon to corresponding poles of two magnets violently repelling each other.

Lying back, she closed her eyes and found herself trying to

remember the term used when matter contacts antimatter. Annihilation? Her eyes popped open. Uncertain whether her imagination had trespassed into the terrain of pure science or the ridiculous, Annie made a decision. She couldn't risk contact with Elsbeth and would take precautions to avoid the possibility.

Having made that unhappy decision, she attempted to quiet her mind, but it continued to race ahead of her. She rolled a word around in her mouth—*daddy*—and fussed with a pillow while thinking that somewhere out there, at this very moment, he was preparing for his show. Her throat constricted when she realized that she would never get to know him because he had died—would die?—while saving her life.

Two hours later, she stirred and looked about the room in confusion. She may not immediately have known where she was, but she definitely knew where she was not. She wasn't in her own bed in San Francisco. Slowly, she came to herself and looked at her watch. It read 8:15 p.m. She glanced at the clock on the shelf beside the bed, which read 6:15 p.m.

Annie closed her eyes for another moment, then, with a start, sprang out of bed and into the bathroom to wash her face and tidy her hair. While she made herself presentable, part of Annie's mind was wondering at the curious irony of time. The clock in 1895 was off by two hours. She found that oddly unsettling.

Bolting out the door, she headed downstairs and outside while, concurrently in time, Elsbeth was watching in trepidation and fascination as David Abbott disappeared through a door at the Coates Opera House.

Annie found Cap'n sitting on the steps, holding a paper bag full of peanuts. She looked tightly wound, cracking the husks with her front teeth and chewing purposefully. She chucked a husk into the gutter when Annie appeared over her shoulder.

"You got the plant?" Cap'n asked. When Annie handed it to her, Cap'n motioned for her to follow and scrambled after a passing trolley, hopping on board with practiced ease. She reached back to lend Annie a hand. Making eye contact with the conductor, she jerked her head toward Annie as if to say, "She's with me," and led her to a seat toward the back.

Cap'n latched the money clip to the top of her bib, then sat in silence, watching the sunset wash over the cityscape like a sheet of honey. Annie looked up to see the trolley had entered the park and started casting about for familiar landmarks. As she did so, she began to talk quietly, almost as if to herself. She talked about her grandmother and how they'd never met, only communicating through letters. Of course, she avoided the not-so-insignificant issue of time, choosing instead to focus on how quickly fondness had grown from their mutual uncertainty.

She talked about how she delighted in her grandmother's testiness and her independence, and how she was growing to rely on her wisdom. She talked about family and responsibility. And, finally, she talked about love and how it had come upon her so quietly that she didn't recognize it for what it was until its grip was unbreakable.

She wasn't certain why she shared all this. Perhaps it was to provide context, or perhaps it was to throw Cap'n off balance so she wouldn't question Annie when, without any indication that the subject had changed, she launched into the series of events that would take place later in the evening, as she had pieced them together from El's letter and the two articles from the antique store—Abbott's return home, Elsbeth's confrontation, the interruption by Mr. Culler and Danyer, and the nosy neighbor.

"Elsbeth is at Coates Theater attempting to warn Mr. Abbott of danger right now," Annie said. "She'll fail, but that won't stop her. She'll go to his home to try again. It's imperative that she not see us." She closed her eyes, listening to the chatter of the wheels on the tracks.

When Annie finished her tale, Cap'n tucked her feet underneath the bench and stared at her for a stretch. "You're a mystery, and that's a fact," she said. The corners of her mouth dimpled. "Here's what we're going do," she added.

# CHAPTER TWENTY-SIX

## Cadavers and Spiders

See where the end of the street seems to go right up that drive on the other block?" Cap'n asked. "The house at the end belongs to Mr. Abbott."

The house in question sat in the middle of a block forming a T junction with the one Annie and Cap'n were on. She took stock of a majestic, plantation-style house at the end of a drive bordered on each side by hedgerows. White columns lined its porch and supported a second-story veranda. "I didn't realize we were so close," she said, feeling a little panicky. She stopped, trying to estimate the remaining distance. A hundred yards, the length of a football field, she decided. That's all that separated her from the place where she had spent the first year of her life, the place that would have been her home had things played out differently on this very night.

Cap'n tugged at her sleeve, looking concerned.

Annie wrapped her hand around Cap'n's and squeezed before motioning for her to lead the way.

Being a smart kid with a healthy dose of intuition, Cap'n decided a distraction was in order and began a running discourse on the neighborhood's inhabitants as they closed the distance. "That house yonder belongs to the widow McCready," she said, lifting her head to indicate the house directly to the left of the Abbott estate. "We call it the 'goose.'" And it was, a goose among swans—an unremarkable home on a large plot of land with a few live oaks set off by another hedge that divided the properties. Cap'n grinned. "Tater's ma is best friends with Hannah, and she has lots to say about Mrs. McCready."

"Who's Hannah? Wait, who's Tater?"

"Tater is one of the gang, and Hannah's Mr. Abbott's housekeeper. All Tater's ma hears about from Hannah is how handsome Mr. Abbott is and how that old Mrs. McCready makes any fool excuse to visit so she can make doe eyes at him, knocking on his door day and night, asking for a cup of sugar or bringing him dessert, and never giving him a moment's peace. Tater's ma says it's embarrassing how the widow McCready goes on and that she should be ashamed of herself for behaving like that around a man half her age and whose wife ain't even been in the ground a year yet."

"Tater's ma sounds like a God-fearing woman." Annie didn't even try to keep the humor from her voice.

"I don't think she holds much truck with church, to be honest," Cap'n said. "Runs the bordello on Main Street, you see."

Annie wisely declined to comment, being perfectly scandalized by the breadth of Cap'n's experience, though she wasn't able to muzzle her grin. "Well, perhaps we should find a place to settle," she said, pointing to the hedge between the properties. "How about over there by the oak trees?"

"I'll take a look." Cap'n scampered out of sight, only to reappear a moment later. "Follow me," she said. "There's a likely spot in the back where the hedge curves around an oak. We can see the Abbott and McCready houses, but I don't see how no one will spot us."

Annie settled in with her back against a tree, her dress hogging most of the clearing. She tucked the excess out of the way to make room for Cap'n, who hunkered down and made herself comfortable. She pulled some peanuts from her pocket and held them out. When Annie shook her head, Cap'n began to shell and pop them, one by one, into her mouth. One bounced off her upper lip and rolled down her overalls to the ground between her crossed legs. After a brief search, she gave up and reached in her pocket for more. "You should eat," she said.

"I don't have much of an appetite, I'm afraid." Annie leaned her head against the tree and rested her eyes. She chuckled, a drowsy sound, when Cap'n stuck a peanut between her lips. She began to chew. Suddenly ravenous, she held her hand out for more.

Cap'n poured the remainder into Annie's palm, stuffed the bag in her pocket, and rocked back on both elbows, looking skyward. A cicada started to stridulate, breaking off when Cap'n said, "My dad left Ma just after I was born."

Annie cracked an eye open and encouraged Cap'n with a nod before closing it again.

"Then when Ma died, I was supposed to be sent to the orphanage." She reached under her hip, eyeing an acorn for a second before tossing it over the hedge. "I had other ideas." Then she began to talk in earnest, sharing with Annie what it was like to live on the street, scavenging for food by the most wretched means, sleeping through winter in boxes stuffed with newspaper, being constantly alert to violence. Worse than all that, however, was the utter indifference she encountered.

"It was like, all of a sudden, I was invisible. People didn't want to see me. I made them uncomfortable, maybe even a little angry. Fabian says"—she paused for a second before correcting herself—"*said*...they resent the fact that I make them face their own pettiness." She shook her head. "He was the closest thing to a pa I ever had."

As best Annie could tell, Fabian had taken it upon himself to look after the children caught in Mr. Culler's grift. He taught the new kids the ropes and created the code of conduct for the gang—a lowbrow system that, based on Cap'n's description, was more Robin Hood than West Point, though no less honorable in its own way. It was based on three simple, unbreakable rules. Don't take if it harms. Defend the gang. And, when honor demands it, even the score.

"Fabian made me Cap'n because I have street smarts and I'm good with the other kids."

While they were settling in, Cap'n chronicled the gang's history, complete with descriptions of some of its more colorful characters. "Andrew actually went on to pitch for the Cleveland Spiders. He was before my time, though."

Cap'n narrated Andrew's exploits in the professional league as the night's smoke doused the last light of day, but not without a fight. The lawns, hedges, trees, and all their green things were banded with gold for a glorious moment before fading into shadow. And shadows within shadow. The day sounds turned into night sounds. The clippety-clop of hooves on dirt and the crunch of wheels on gravel turned into the chirrup of crickets and the peeping of frogs—all this as spring's clean perfume piggybacked on a whisper of air that tiptoed across their skin. It was an altogether bewitching night in Westport.

"... The gang called Andrew 'Pepper' because he threw a mean fastball." Cap'n eyed Annie, counting off names. "There's Tater, Bit, Bean, Checkers..."

Cap'n's voice blended into the backdrop of night noises, soothing Annie. She closed her eyes and took a deep breath, giving in to a rush of fatigue. She rode a languorous wave inside her head until her eyes suddenly flashed open. Recognizing the sensation, she shook off her lethargy and peered over the hedge to see a diminutive lady walking stiffly down the street in the distance, wearing the same dress Annie recalled from a photograph.

The older woman walked over to a streetlight and pulled out a handkerchief to wipe her brow as if she too had a touch of vertigo. She looked about in confusion, then began to stare intently at Mr. Abbott's home.

Cap'n followed Annie's gaze. "That her?" she asked.

"Yes," Annie said. "That's Elsbeth. That's my grandmother."

Cap'n rested her hand on Annie's arm in silent support.

"She's coming this way," said Annie.

"What?" Cap'n's head jerked around.

Elsbeth was indeed walking directly toward them. Looking around to determine what had given them away, Cap'n's eyes rested on the bib of her overalls. The money clip was aglow like a cat's eyes, reflecting the light from Mrs. McCready's porch and flickering as she moved. Cap'n turned to Annie. "I'll handle this."

"She's a character, your grandma. Asked me if I was stirring up mischief," Cap'n said, returning from her encounter with Elsbeth. She settled back down behind the oak, her lips canting to one side as she shook her head. "She don't know the half of it." Cap'n pocketed three silver dollars and cocked her thumb over her shoulder. "I saw Mr. Abbott as I was circling back."

Annie scrambled to her knees, peering over the hedge to catch a glimpse of her father disappearing into the house with Elsbeth following unnoticed.

Moments later, Elsbeth knocked on the door and Abbott reemerged. Annie and Cap'n couldn't hear what was being said, but they could tell Mr. Abbott was not pleased. They watched as the little woman pushed her way past Mr. Abbott and inside the house.

"Gotta hand it to her. She's got pluck," Cap'n said.

Clearly flustered, Abbott followed her inside, closing the door.

Cap'n tapped Annie on the shoulder before pointing down the length of the hedge. "I think we should head to the back of the house. It won't do for the widow McCready to see us." She kept a worried eye on Annie as they settled around back. She'd hardly said a word since her grandma showed up, though her eyes looked as though they were full of them, Cap'n thought. Peering over the hedge, Cap'n tried to imagine what was happening inside. Having met Annie's grandma for only a moment, she was certain that it involved a good tongue-lashing.

Abbott's front door was out of their line of sight, so Cap'n sat down next to Annie, waiting. A dog bayed, but a sharp rap at Abbott's front door cut it off. Cap'n's eyebrows rose as she heard the murmured exchange of voices. "Culler?" she mouthed. Annie nodded. Minutes ticked by, one after the other.

Without warning, Abbott's back door opened and Elsbeth stole down the pathway, disappearing into the alley. Their turn was coming.

As scripted by Annie, a lady in a nightgown and hairnet walked across the lawn directly in front of them and knocked on Abbott's door. When there was no answer, she looked around and sneaked to the side window, her head bobbing up and down as she strained to look inside. Lurching back abruptly with one hand clamped over her mouth, the widow McCready shuffled quickly back into her house. The brittle clank of her screen door shutting cracked across the lawn.

"It's time," Cap'n said. "I'm going on the roof before the cops get here. You got hold of yourself?"

Not trusting her voice, Annie only nodded.

"You need to signal when the coast is clear and I can go inside." Not waiting for a response, Cap'n sprinted across the yard and began shimmying like a squirrel up a vine wrapped around a corner column. She grabbed a drainpipe and pulled herself past the veranda and onto the roof where she clambered over to sit in the shadow of a dormer window, settling in with her elbows crossed over her knees—a pocket-size gargoyle.

Hearing horse hooves on gravel, Annie peeked over the top of the hedge. A pair of police officers were looking down at Mrs. McCready who was gesturing wildly at the Abbott home. Leaving her behind, they wandered to Abbott's front door, opened it, and vanished inside.

Annie melted under the hedge as two more walked past, stationing themselves directly under the dormer window where Cap'n was sitting.

One light after another went on in the house.

Annie muffled a gasp, reaching for the trunk of the oak, when she realized why the house was being searched. The police were looking for the baby. They were looking for her. Time was out of joint. The future, past, and present were entwined for an infant thrown forward and a woman traveling backward in the stream of time.

A light poured through the dormer window next to Cap'n, bathing the shingles below in a luminous strip. Annie collected herself and peeked through a gap in the hedge to see a man's face in the window casting a long shadow over the roof. Cap'n sat next to him, frozen, her eyes aglow. An anxious moment later, the shadow disappeared from view, and the incandescent band below the window vanished as a light was extinguished.

When the downstairs lights went out a short time later, Annie counted to ten and peered down the road leading away from the house. She was just able to make out a pair of shadows moving down the drive. The police had completed their search.

She peered at the rooftop, racking her brain on how to signal Cap'n without alerting the duty officers, when she saw a silhouette separate from the shingles and open the window. Obviously, Cap'n had seen the flaw in their strategy and had taken matters into her own hands.

Perched on the windowsill like a tattered crow, Cap'n scanned the darkened room and tried to get her bearings. She looked over her shoulder, thinking she'd signal to Annie, but she could only make out the glow of fireflies blinking in and out of the hedge like a parched strand of Christmas lights. She dropped onto the floor and huddled in the corner of the room, waiting for her eyes to adjust.

The moonlight breaking from the window outlined shadows that swayed on the wall opposite her, a particularly ragged one bubbling from the headboard of the room's sleigh bed. It descended onto the comforter, moving against the breeze. Too late, she threw herself back against the wall as it launched onto her shoulder and pricked the side of her neck. She stifled a scream and rolled into a ball, but it was up and out the window with an indignant mewl before she could cover the back of her head. Her heart pounding, Cap'n scrambled up and poked her head out the window in time to see a black tail disappear in a drainpipe. She grunted in exasperation and stole to the door to peer down the hallway. The house was quiet as the dead.

Cap'n sat on the top step of the stairwell, rubbing her neck as her eyes adjusted to the poor lighting. When her heart stopped racing, she started downstairs, testing each step before putting her weight on it. Where the stairs turned the corner, she paused to scan the living room. There was no one to be seen, but she could just make out a large red door resting in a frame toward the back. She'd heard about David Abbott's stage prop. Everyone had. Still, it was a strange thing to keep in the house, she thought.

Finishing off the remaining steps, she made for the shadows of the living room, only to bump into the edge of a divan, freezing as it scraped across the floor. Flustered, she looked up and into a pair of eyes, gasping even as she realized it was her reflection in a mirror. She glanced toward the front of the house. When no one responded to the sound, she knelt down and began to crawl on all fours.

Rounding the divan, she caught an unnerving whiff of something in the air—a salty, electric tang that almost but didn't quite register on her tongue—even as the fingertips of her right hand met something cold and sticky. Cap'n settled back on her knees and lifted her splayed hand to her nose, taking a quick sniff. She choked on air, wiping her fingers on her bib, as she caught her first glimpse of the body.

The reality of it sent her scuttling backward to rest against the divan, her own blood pumping so hard that it made her eardrums throb. She examined the stain surrounding David Abbott's corpse as the gruesomeness of her task finally began to sink in. It didn't help that his upper body was framed in blood. There was no way she could make the plant without stepping in the blood and leaving a trail for the police to follow.

Cap'n sat down, watching a spider scuttle across the bridge of the corpse's nose and into its mouth.

An idea squeezed through the din in her head, an idea she wanted to discard, but she didn't see any alternative. She gritted her teeth, took off both her shoes, and positioned them on the rug close to Abbott's knees. Then, standing on her toes, she took two mincing steps into the puddle, feeling a slight resistance when she lifted her feet, as if the blood would glue them to the floorboards, given the chance. Blood soaked through her socks, an oily, nauseating sensation. Swallowing bile, she started to squat over the body when a hint of movement brushed across her peripheral vision.

Cap'n jerked her head around, her eyes settling on David Abbott's stage prop, when the room began to tilt. Arms gesticulating wildly, she wobbled, just on the verge of catching her balance, before crashing forward to land on the cadaver's chest with her arms extended in front of her.

The force of her fall caused the cadaver to wheeze out a froth of blood while its head lifted off the ground to spit the spider onto her cheek. She squealed shrilly, registering both the look of surprise on its face—Abbott's face—and her own horror reflected in his eyes for a gruesome instant before his head dropped back with a thud. Her cap fell from atop her head and onto his chest. She snatched it between her teeth and, in an adrenalized frenzy, pushed herself to her feet.

Breathing raggedly, Cap'n crammed the cap atop her head and

examined the corpse. Abbott's hand rested by his shoulder, palm up and open. The spider floated in the pool next to it, the segments of its legs tucked in like a parasol. More than happy to end the grisly exercise, Cap'n leaned over, closed the hand around the clip, and turned back to the edge of the pooled blood.

Shifting her balance to one foot, Cap'n lifted the other to remove the wet sock, before slipping her bare foot into the shoe resting outside the stain. She repeated the exercise with the other foot and stood outside the pool. Folding the length of the socks' leggings around their blood-soaked feet, Cap'n shoved them in her pocket before hurrying to the kitchen to wash her hands and the tips of her hair.

As she did so, her eyes trailed across the room to rest on the strange door. A man—tall, thin—stood in its frame, clear as day, watching her. At first, her brain didn't want to acknowledge his presence, then shock went straight to her knees and she dropped like a stone against the kitchen cabinetry, banging her head against a handle. When she opened her eyes, he was gone—as quick as that. She scrambled to her feet, looking everywhere for him, but he'd vanished so completely she began to doubt she'd seen anything at all. Regardless, it was time get out.

She grabbed the first thing she could find, a silver ladle, and made for the base of the stairs as quickly as she dared, her finely tuned instincts insisting that her every move was being watched. A floorboard creaked in the corner and she bolted. By the time she reached the bend between the first and second floor, her heart was in her throat. Another creak, and the thump of something dropped. Muffled laughter? She wasn't sure.

Petrified, she bounded up the steps, three at a time. Clearing the landing with a leap, she tore down the hallway and into the master bedroom to throw herself against the side wall, her eyes locked on the doorway—waiting for what, she didn't know, but it—he—was out there.

She glanced at the ladle and threw it aside in disgust. The percussion created by a thump on the wall behind her threw her forward, and she got the hint, racing across the room on all fours, sliding out the window, and scrambling out of arm's reach at the side of the dormer. She knew the duty guards were below, but if it came to a choice between them and whatever was in the house, she'd take her chances with people made of flesh and blood.

For her part, Annie watched Cap'n appear on the roof with a sense of profound relief. She started to lower herself against the tree trunk to wait for the duty-officer shift change, but a disturbance caught her attention. The pair of policemen stationed at the back of the house wandered toward the source of the noise, only to watch a raccoon emerge from the hedge, stand on its haunches, and wave its front paws over its head while sniffing the air with its delicate, damp nose. Seeing the two men, it hissed and scampered off on paws that seemed too tiny to carry its bulk. By the time the guards returned to their post, Annie saw that Cap'n was gone.

Catching up with her at the street corner, Annie watched Cap'n pull the balled-up socks from her pocket. The girl trembled as she threw them down a sewer and turned to Annie, shaking her head. "I made the plant. The rest is up to the police."

They made their way through Westport while quietly discussing strategy. Cap'n had several obligations in the morning but agreed to meet Annie afterward to take her to Pierson's for an auction.

Their conversation was interrupted by an ear-splitting catfight that ended with the crack of a gun and a pair of tabbies streaking across their path. Suddenly, Annie smacked the palm of her hand against her forehead. "I'm not thinking! He'll be on his way soon. I've left a road map and practically dared him to follow," she said.

"Dared who?" asked Cap'n. "We're here," she added.

"Hmm?" Annie looked at the hotel marquee in surprise, then back at Cap'n who was trying to stifle a sneeze. "Oh!" She pulled a tissue from her pocket. "Christian," she said.

Cap'n wiped her nose as she tried to make sense of Annie's cryptic comments. "More trouble?"

"Only the well-meaning kind. A friend with a big heart and, unfortunately, bigger thumbs." She searched her purse for the room key, then paused, turning to her confederate. "Cap'n, are you familiar with the stones donated by the Cherokee Council at the duck pond in the park?"

"Yeah," Cap'n said uncertainly.

"I have a rather unusual favor to ask..."

# CHAPTER TWENTY-SEVEN

## The Money Clip

### MAY 30, 1895

The sun was still on the rise when a squirrel poked its head out from behind the trunk of an oak that bordered the Abbott and McCready homes. Raising its head and testing the morning breeze, the squirrel fixed button-black eyes on something at the base of the tree. Scampering down the trunk, it dashed across a root and ran clever paws through a pile of peanut husks until it found a prize.

The squirrel began to chew while continually spinning the nut round and round between its paws like a lathe whittling down a block of wood, looking over with a twitching tail as the widow McCready walked out to her porch and gazed at the Abbott home. Still in her nightgown and cap, she sipped her tea without taking her eyes off the house. Mrs. McCready was deep in concentration.

Setting the cup down, she walked across the lawn to confront an officer standing guard by the front door. "Have either Officer Kearney or Franklin returned from their coffee break?"

The duty officer looked at her wearily. "No, ma'am. They should be here shortly."

"Well, I'd like to speak to them as soon as possible."

The officer's cheeks twitched. "Yes, ma'am."

Mrs. McCready nodded to him and shuffled home in a pair of oversize slippers to her rapidly cooling tea. Taking it inside to forage for a biscuit or two, she failed to notice the objects of her inquiry making their way up the block.

"Thanks for the cup, Clay," said Lieutenant Franklin as the men walked up the drive to the Abbott estate. He pulled a pack of Black Jack from his pocket, popped a piece of the licorice-flavored gum in his mouth, and handed the rest to his partner. Waving to the duty officer, he added, "Do you mind waiting inside for the medical examiner? I didn't get a chance to speak to the men in the back earlier." Not waiting for a response, he was starting across the lawn to the back of the house when the duty officer called out.

"Mrs. McCready would like to speak with you when it's convenient, sir."

Franklin waved his hand in acknowledgment without breaking stride, then rubbed his forehead. He could feel a headache coming on. Turning, he walked across the remainder of the yard to the back door. "Anything to report?" he asked the pair of officers standing watch.

One shrugged. "Got a visit from a raccoon."

Nodding, Franklin sent them home and walked to where the hedge met the sidewalk. Seeing nothing interesting, he began to walk along the hedge line. As he neared a second oak tree, a startled squirrel scampered up the trunk, chattering at him indignantly. Squinting his eyes against the late-morning sun, Franklin looked up into the canopy, then down to the ground, noticing a pile of peanut shells. Kneeling down, he picked up a husk and rubbed it between his index finger and thumb while gazing back at the house.

"Officer Franklin! Officer Franklin, one moment please!"

Franklin wiped his palms together and turned to face the little figure that rushed toward him. "Good morning, Mrs. McCready."

"Thank goodness I found you," Evillene said, breathing heavily. "I was afraid that the officer to whom I spoke would forget to deliver my message. Is there any news?" She smiled, shifting her feet while waiting for his response. When none was forthcoming, she continued, "Well, with all the commotion from last night, I do expect some follow-up from the press."

For all that she was a nuisance, Franklin felt sorry for Mrs. McCready. He'd seen people like her before—ever so slightly ridiculous and, as a result, lonely for company that rarely called. "Nothing yet," he said, tapping the brim of his hat with his finger. "Good day, Mrs. McCready."

Evillene watched him head to the Abbott home and step inside as she tried to decide whether or not she had been put off. Clicking her false teeth, she cut through the hedge, kicked some peanut shells in exasperation, and headed home.

Inside, Franklin's conversation with Kearney was interrupted when an officer knocked and stepped inside the hallway while closing the door behind him. "The medical examiner is here, Lieutenant."

"Show him in."

"Yes, sir." The officer left through the hallway door, and Franklin could hear a muffled exchange at the front of the house.

The medical examiner, a portly, balding man who barely came up to Officer Franklin's lapel, wandered into the living room holding a large leather satchel. "Morning, gentlemen."

"Morning, Doc."

"What have we got?"

Kearney pointed with a pencil toward the body. "Probable homicide. Stabbing."

The examiner walked over to the edge of the bloodstain, set down his satchel, and peered at the body.

Franklin strode over. "Doc, before you get busy with your end of the investigation, do you mind if I ask you a question?"

Without taking his gaze from the body, the medical examiner nodded. "Shoot," he said.

"Our primary suspect is a woman—small, elderly. She was seen leaving the scene of the crime by a neighbor. Any opinion there?"

Without hesitation, the medical examiner responded, "I'd start looking for another suspect."

Franklin nodded. "I was afraid you'd say that."

The medical examiner rubbed his chin. "She couldn't have done this…unless she had a lot of cooperation from the victim." He waved a finger over the corpse. "Cutting through the abdominal muscles and perforating the stomach on a man of this size requires a lot of leverage." He broke from his monologue and squatted to appraise the body more closely. "Lieutenant, are you aware that the victim is holding something in his right hand?"

Kearney's head snapped up from the side table he was examining. "What?"

"And that the tip of the little finger on his left hand has been cut off?" the medical examiner continued.

Setting down a figurine, Kearney joined Franklin beside the medical examiner.

Franklin turned to him. "Has anyone examined the body yet?" he asked.

"No, they were waiting for us…" Kearney's voice trailed off. "This isn't the first homicide we've seen with the end finger cut off, you know."

"I know." Franklin rubbed his forehead as his headache mounted. "Well, let's not get ahead of ourselves."

Looking at the body and the sticky sheet of blood surrounding it, Franklin crossed his arms. He looked around the room, strode to the fireplace, and grabbed a poker. Stepping to the edge of the pooled blood, he squatted and used it to slowly pry open the extended hand, flinging the money clip across the room with a quick flick of his wrist.

Kearney picked it up.

"What've we got?" Franklin asked.

"You aren't going to believe this," said Kearney. He held the clip up. "It's engraved."

"What?" Franklin made it to Kearney's side in three quick steps. He peered at the money clip, shaking his head. "Start interviewing the neighbors. See if they know anyone with the initials *AC*, and"—Franklin started snapping his fingers—"what was the name of Abbott's business partner that dropped by earlier this morning?"

"Mr. Culler."

"That's him. Let's see if he knows anything."

Kearney reached into his pocket and fished out the business card. "Arthur?" he said. "He may know more than he's telling us."

Franklin had begun instructing the officer out front and looked back at Kearney. "Why's that?"

Kearney was staring at the card in frank disbelief. "His first name is Ambrosius."

# CHAPTER TWENTY-EIGHT

## Rendezvous at the Park

### JUNE 1, 1995

Christian knocked on Annie's front door. He'd left a message on her answering machine earlier but never heard back. He knocked again and, after a short wait, decided she must be napping.

Unlocking the door with the spare key she'd given him, Christian walked to the side table in the entryway, where he dropped a stack of mail he found scattered below the mail slot, and headed up the stairs to Annie's bedroom. He tapped quietly. When there was no response, he opened the door and poked his head in the room.

"Annie?" The bed was made—unusual for her, even under the best of circumstances. He headed over to the bathroom, put his ear to the door, and tapped lightly again.

Sitting on the edge of the bed, he gave the situation a general thinking over, and blood rushed to his face. "Oh no," he whispered before streaking downstairs and into the kitchen. As he made for the back door, he spied a piece of notepaper held to the front of the refrigerator by a magnet.

Contrary to her generally slovenly habits, Annie never stuck notes on the refrigerator. She had an organizing tray for that, another of her endearing ironies. She would have put the notepaper on her refrigerator for only one reason—to get his attention. Already knowing what the note would say, Christian muttered several words including "headstrong," snatched the paper from the refrigerator, and started to read.

Christian—

I'm laying odds that you just called me "headstrong." Guilty as charged. I've read through my father's diary and have decoded the secret of the door's operation. I'm off to Kansas to set things right and to attend an auction for the purpose of buying a very odd door. I'll be home soon with details.

Love,
Annie

P.S. You win. I'm starting to hope again. My father solved the bloodline mystery. Note the entry dated May 30, 1894. You love riddles, Christian. Solve this one for me.

P.P.S. Oh, and don't forget that we have tickets to see "The Bridges of Madison County" this weekend.

Christian grunted at the final postscript. Only Annie could combine a request to solve the mystery of time travel with a social engagement. He hoisted himself up to sit on the kitchen counter to scan the diary, meanwhile crumpling her note in his fist. He read several pages before focusing on the May 30, 1894, entry, then walked over to study the door. There was a small stain smeared across the top. Blood?

Wandering back to the counter, he absentmindedly picked up a set of plastic chattering teeth he bought Annie last spring at Fisherman's Wharf. They'd been talking about God knows what while shopping for nothing in particular, and he kept running off on some tangent, despite her attempts to keep him on point. Frustrated, she'd grabbed the toy off the shelf and held it in his face, only to burst into laughter when he lost his train of thought and fell silent. He bought the toy for her as a keepsake, a little reminder of a happy moment.

He stared at the toy, using it to fuel the courage he sought, to do what needed doing, despite being unsure how to go about *doing* it. In the end, the option that entailed direct action won out. He'd need backup, but the only person who could fill those shoes had put a little distance between them since their picnic in the Headlands. The irrepressible Edmond he knew, the one who had a glib response for everything, had gone AWOL, replaced by someone who was… Christian struggled for the proper word. *Careful*, he decided.

This had something to do with his confession at the picnic. Christian was sure of that, but why his memory loss was a problem, he didn't know. Time was wasting, so he stuffed the teeth in his back pocket and picked up Annie's phone to dial one of only two numbers he knew by heart, while thinking that he really needed the old version of Edmond to show up.

"Marden Landscaping."

"Hey, it's me. I'm at Annie's—"

"Ah, the mysterious Annabelle Aster. Say hi for me and tell her that I look forward to meeting tonight."

*Glib is good*, Christian thought. "I would if she were here," he said. "That's why I'm calling."

"Is dinner off?"

"Probably. What are you doing this morning?"

"Babysitting Mrs. Kelly's roses. Why?"

"Can you meet me here in an hour? I have to run an errand, but I'll be back in time to let you in."

"Sure. I'll reschedule with Mrs. Kelly." As Christian was about to hang up, Edmond added, "Annie lives in that big purple and gold Victorian Stick on Dolores by the park, right?"

Christian rolled his eyes. "No, no, no. Don't ever let her hear you call it purple. It's au-ber-gine."

"We need to talk." Edmond blinked, and the thought occupying him was lost when he got an eyeful of Christian standing in Annie's doorway. "What the hell?" he asked, stuffing his hands in his pockets as he gawked at Christian's oddball togs.

"Come on in. I'll explain."

As Christian guided him through the foyer and to the back, Edmond slowed down in the living room and whistled. "Quite a setup," he said. When they reached the kitchen, however, his reaction was altogether different. The color drained right out of him. "I've been here," he whispered.

Christian nodded and gently pushed him into the room. "I suspected as much." He pointed to the door. "And I'm guessing you recognize that?"

"Oh, yeah. That I won't forget." Edmond greeted the door from his dream with silence before allowing Christian to pilot him to the breakfast nook. He watched as Christian went to a cupboard to collect a pair of glasses, filling them with juice from the refrigerator, whatever it was he had wanted to discuss long forgotten.

Handing one to him, Christian dropped into the chair across the table, only to grimace, then reach into his back pocket to fish out the plastic teeth, placing them on the table. "It's time I finished the tale I started in the Headlands," he said.

Edmond listened as Christian recited a long, complicated, and highly improbable story, while absentmindedly winding up the toy. He set it down when he finished and looked at Edmond while the teeth chattered and bounced across the table.

"So, from what I'm hearing—" Edmond pressed his finger atop the toy to help himself think. When Christian placed a saucer over it, Edmond sat back, looking over Christian's shoulder at the door. "I mean, from what you're saying, it wasn't a dream. I visited the past in Kansas, somewhere in the vicinity of 1895."

"Well, that's where things get a little iffy. I don't know what you experienced, but it wasn't *just* a dream. How could it be? You described exactly the same place Annie and I went to."

"And Annie was born sometime in the late eighteen hundreds."

"The twenty-third of June, 1894," Christian said, wincing in advance of the response he expected.

Edmond merely grunted, however. He searched Christian's eyes for any indication of a practical joke before it struck him that Christian was probably incapable of one.

Understanding that words weren't proof, Christian stormed upstairs and returned with something in his hand.

A chill raced up and down Edmond's spine as he scanned Annie's birth certificate and the printed copy. Sitting them on the table, he said, "Okay then," drawing the words out slowly. "There you have it. Annie was born in 1894. Who would've thought?"

Christian scratched his head and leaned on the table. "Don't ask me how it works, but Annie was placed through the door by her father—in 1895 in Kansas City, as a baby—and came out the other side sometime in the late sixties. Here. In San Francisco. Still a baby. Somehow, she skipped those sixty-plus years without aging a day."

Edmond found himself resigned to the improbability of the story and increasingly interested in what would come next.

"Annie's gone back," Christian whispered as if in answer.

"Gone back?"

"In time. To 1895. To Kansas City." Christian threw his shoulder over the bench top and stared at the door. "She's gone through that and is up to something. Her father's murderer probably won't take too kindly to her interference, and she's going to need help." He turned and continued in a quiet voice. "Edmond...she's my best friend."

"I know." Edmond scanned Christian's face. "And you want me to go with you."

Despite it not being a question, Christian nodded.

"Okay." He took a sip of orange juice, then set it down. "Now can you please tell me what you're doing in those stupid clothes?"

Christian pulled self-consciously at the wool trousers and suspenders. "I got them at Prudence Travesty's—the vintage clothing shop in the Haight?" He reached under a chair and pulled out a second pile of clothes—shoes and all. "Two-day rental for forty-eight bucks."

Edmond looked from Christian's face to the second pile and back again. He lurched away from the table, rocking the bench. "Nope. Not a chance," he said. "I agreed to help, but I'm not wearing that."

"Oh, come on! We're going back a hundred years. Don't you think you might stick out wearing a T-shirt with 'Hell no, we won't glow' written on it?"

Edmond pressed his lips into a strained, bloodless line before slumping over the table. He grabbed the shirt on the top of the pile and held it to his nose. "This stuff smells like my grandma's closet," he said. "Not a happy memory, Christian. Grandma was mean." He pulled off his shirt and started to change. "Seriously, do you really think we're going to look the part in these things?"

"Mrs. Weatherall says they're authentic." Christian caught sight of a scar on Edmond's side. "What's that?" he asked.

"Well, if she says so." Edmond glanced at the ceiling with an eye roll, a response to Christian's first question, then back down to his side, a response to the second. He ran his hand along the line of the scar, his eyes veiled, then glanced at Christian as if on the verge of saying something. "Tell you later." Shaking off whatever was bothering him, Edmond continued, "Is it possible she was just trying to make a sale?" He pulled off his sneakers. "Don't answer that," he said. "And do you know when and where we're going to end up once we pass through that door?"

Christian watched as Edmond unraveled a pair of suspenders. "Yeah, pretty sure," he said. "I read through Annie's notes while I waited for you. She's going to an auction. We're doing the same…I think."

"You think?" He gestured toward the door. "After you."

Christian walked to the back of the kitchen and paused, turning to Edmond. "I'm afraid," he said. Not waiting for a reply, he stepped through the door and disappeared.

Edmond looked back to the tabletop. He lifted the saucer, and the toy teeth resumed their fearful chatter.

"Tell me about it," he said and stepped into the void.

Cap'n looked up from under her cap to see what was causing all the ruckus. A handful of ducks were squabbling over the last bits of bread she'd spread around her park bench. On the other side of the pond, however, another cluster of ducks had hit the water, fanning out. At the center of the expanding arc created by their wake stood two men whispering to each other as they studied the stones donated by the Cherokee Council. Dumping the remaining bread crumbs on the ground, Cap'n wandered over to them.

"It d-does say Kansas City on the placard," said the shorter of the two, as if pressing a point.

"Well, that answers the first question. But how do we find out—" The taller one broke off midsentence when he noticed Cap'n's approach.

"Excuse me, mister. Your name Christian?"

He shook his head and pointed to the shorter of the two who looked up from the placard with a start.

"You Christian, mister?"

Christian stared at her, blinking stupidly. He opened his mouth to say something, then changed his mind and merely nodded.

Cap'n relaxed, extending her hand. "I'm Cap'n. Miss Annie sent me here to fetch you."

The taller man cheerfully threw up his hands. "That answers question number two," he said.

Wrinkling her nose, Cap'n looked Edmond up and down before turning to Christian. "Who's the wag?" she asked.

"W-wag? Th-th-hat's—" Christian eyes rolled skyward as he worried his jaw in and out. "Edmmmmond. My friend," he said, smiling apologetically.

Edmond held out his hand, but Cap'n made a show of stuffing her hands in her pockets, eyeing him distrustfully.

She stepped back, assessing the situation. One doesn't survive on the streets very long without being able to read another's character, and she was good at it—very good. Christian was a piece of cake. He was a simple soul. Something in life had bruised him, that was obvious from his speech, but it hadn't twisted him. She'd heard tell of kids who stuttered when schoolteachers forced them to write with their right hands, but she suspected it was more than being a lefty with this guy.

Edmond, however, was a little more complicated. He knew the ropes. She could see it in his eyes. And no one learned the ropes unless they "fell from society's protective bosom," as Fabian used to say. The question was whether Edmond had also fallen from grace. She gave him another once-over, noticing how he hovered near Christian, almost as if protecting him, and she decided he was all right.

"Follow me," she said and led them to the other side of the pond where she crawled up on a small boulder. She pulled off her cap—waiting a moment for Christian and Edmond to adjust to the sight of her pigtails—and made herself comfortable. "Don't worry. Miss Annie's fine, but she's tangling with a couple of rough characters."

Edmond turned to Christian, muttering, "Culler."

"The one and only," Cap'n said. She was about to apologize to Edmond for her earlier rudeness when she saw someone approach from the corner of her eye.

"Pardon me."

The three froze at the interruption, looking up to see a man step off the pathway. He was entirely too polished, too urbane, and, frankly, too pretty in his suit and top hat to feel menacing, but Cap'n immediately slid from the boulder, her eyes darting to Christian.

He shook his head, mystified.

"I apologize for the intrusion," the man continued. "But I was walking by when I heard a name that interests me. Is this 'Miss Annie' you are discussing by chance Annabelle Aster?"

"Doesn't waste any time, does she?" Edmond said, getting a shoulder butt from Christian for his cheek. Cap'n, however, took a more direct approach. "Who wants to know?" she demanded.

The gentleman shifted his weight, clearly uncomfortable. "Well, yes. That does require an explanation. And it's a bit embarrassing, really. Rupert ran off with my hat, you see. A habit of his that, while admittedly irritating, created a happy result..." The gentleman commenced a rambling dialogue concerning Annie and—Christian came to realize—a dog.

The man simply could not get to the point, and there was a quality to his discomfort that Christian recognized. Annie had made an *impression*. Just as Christian began to wonder if his conclusion was as painfully obvious to the others, Cap'n returned his gaze, lifting a brow.

"In all truth, I've walked him several times since then, hoping that our paths would cross again." The man paused, looking startled by his confession. "Anyway, I—"

"Look, Mr. Whoever-You-Are," interrupted Cap'n. "That's a fine story and all, but we ain't got all day here." She held up her hand before he could continue. "Just hold on. Are you Mr. Goodkin?"

"Why, yes!" he said. "I *am*. Nathaniel Goodkin." He searched a breast pocket and pulled out a card.

Cap'n read the name before handing it to Christian. "He's all right," she said and beckoned Nathaniel over. "You might as well join the group. Do I need to make introductions, or did you get our names already?"

Taking a moment to regain his composure after that little barb, Nathaniel finally managed to ask, "Is there trouble? I heard the name Culler mentioned."

Cap'n's eyes strayed to Christian.

*If grabbing a tiger by the tail two thousand miles and a hundred years from home is considered trouble...* "Do you know hoo-hoo-hoo"—he gestured with his hand as if making a comma in the air—"wwwwhere...Annie is?"

"He's just rattled," Edmond said, noticing Mr. Goodkin's confusion.

Christian looked to the ground, then back to Edmond, smiling.

"Yeah," said Cap'n. Having tuned in to Edmond's defense and the nonverbal cues that Christian broadcast, she was suddenly convinced of the story behind his stutter. She smiled back. "Miss Annie's at Pierson's."

"Pierson's?" asked Nathaniel and Edmond simultaneously. Edmond was about to follow up with "What's Pierson's?" but Nathaniel was the first to collect himself. "Is there an auction today?" he asked.

Cap'n nodded. "David Abbott's estate. She's going to buy his door."

"His door? Why on earth... Did she tell you that?" asked Nathaniel.

"Not in so many words."

Christian pulled the hair back from his forehead and turned to Cap'n. "Can you t-t-take us...there?"

She nodded, but obviously thinking better of it, motioned to Mr. Goodkin. "You know the way?" she asked.

He nodded. "Aren't you coming?"

"I'm going ahead to scout," she said.

It was clear from the look on her face that Cap'n had more on her mind than simply getting the lay of the land, and as he watched her cut across a field, Mr. Goodkin said thoughtfully, "I think our good Cap'n is up to something." He turned to gauge his two charges. Gesturing for them to follow, he made for the pathway. "I don't think you were entirely candid back there," he said. "And I suppose I can't blame you. But I'll ask again. Could there be trouble?"

There were a few seconds of silence as Christian waited, hoping Edmond would reply on his behalf. But it wasn't really fair to expect Edmond to respond to something only he could answer, so Christian shrugged, preparing to fight for words that might stick in his throat. "Do you know...this Mr. C-C-Culler?"

"A ruthless man."

"Then-n-n it's quite possible."

The cryptic response left Nathaniel to wonder what Miss Aster's relationship with Mr. Culler might be, while also leaving Edmond to wonder if Christian was being a bit too candid for his own good.

After a couple uncomfortable moments, Nathaniel started to swing his cane in time with his footsteps. "Miss Aster doesn't strike me as a collector," he said.

"No, not"—Christian dipped his head and swallowed, a reflexive action—"really," he said, glaring when Edmond punched his shoulder. He looked around to see that Nathaniel had broken his stride and was staring at him.

"Then why has she gone to the considerable expense and trouble to travel from San Francisco just to buy a stage prop?" he asked.

Nathaniel wasn't intentionally trying to trip Christian up, but his words had the same effect. Christian fumbled unsuccessfully for a response, finally resigning himself to a doleful shake of his head.

Realizing he might be pressing too hard, Nathaniel said, "It must be something very personal," and tactfully changed the subject. "I hope Miss Aster is aware that these auctions are cash only," he said. "I apologize for being so direct, but do you have any money on you, should she need reserves?"

"S-s-some." Christian pulled out a crumpled twenty-dollar bill, picking away the lint before handing it to Mr. Goodkin.

As he was preparing to put the bill in his pocket, Nathaniel paused, staring at it. He surprised Christian by handing it back, then reached into his coat pocket to pull out his wallet, withdrawing several crisp twenty-dollar bills. "May I?" he asked, handing them to Christian.

As the tree line broke, giving them a glimpse of downtown Kansas City, Nathaniel said, "Mr. Keebler, may I recommend you hold on to your cash?" While Christian attempted to determine the reason behind the suggestion, he added, looking unhappy, "The series date is in error."

# CHAPTER TWENTY-NINE

## An Auction

When a person whose world is built entirely on honesty—aside from one or two secrets he keeps from himself—suddenly realizes a lie serves the greater good, he will invariably and carefully weigh the amount of truth he can offer. This can be a considerable undertaking. But when that person also finds himself, on occasion, crippled by words, it can be downright impossible.

Realizing that time was pressing, and not encumbered by such a weight, Edmond dusted off some rusty skills and stepped in before Christian could say a word, speaking casually with Mr. Goodkin. Christian didn't know what Edmond said, but Mr. Goodkin seemed to accept it at face value, leading them through the park without another word.

Chaotic thoughts ran amok in Christian's head, and it was several blocks before he came out of his shell.

They'd broken from the park and onto a city walkway. It was grimy but very much alive with the hustle of everyday life in Kansas City. Christian slowed as they passed a theater for vaudeville, its facade a gaudy display of gold and red, littered with banners advertising, among other things, *Burt Jordan and Rosa Crouch—Sensational, Grotesque, and "Buck" Dancers.*

It was an eyesore on a boulevard of eyesores. But for all the thousand ways this Victorian cityscape varied from the one that Christian knew, one thing remained unchanged—at least for him.

Sitting in a gilded kiosk in front of the theater, the words *Continuous Entertainment for Five Cents* painted over its open window, was his angel. Not even a hundred years could throw her off the scent.

Breaking from his usual policy of turning a blind eye, Christian approached the kiosk, perversely curious. The angel did little to satisfy it, though, merely regarding him with unblinking, oversize eyes, her mouth perpetually agape, and all of her wreathed in sinuous tongues of flame.

Stifling the impulse to speak, he placed his hand, open-palmed, on the glass pane for a moment, then turned to catch up with his companions.

Having witnessed all of this, Edmond hung back to peer inside the kiosk. Finding it empty, he examined the palm print Christian had left—contoured in a film of steam that quickly evaporated—and wondered at what had stoked his friend's furnace.

As he hurried to catch up with the other two men, Edmond overheard Christian ask, "Shall we eat?" while staring through the door of what appeared to be a teahouse. Nathaniel nodded to the hostess as he hooked his arm through Christian's, deftly pulling him away. "Certainly not there," he said.

"Well, I w-wouldn't mind getting a bite to eat."

"That particular parlor satisfies a different type of appetite, Mr. Keebler."

Christian's face colored, and he elbowed Edmond for being a little too entertained at his expense but stubbornly stuck to his original question. "Shall we eat?"

"Shortly. Prudence requires a quick detour."

"To where?"

"To the haberdashery, Mr. Keebler." Nathaniel picked up his pace, leaving Christian and Edmond scrambling to catch up. "It's the clothes, you see." Looking decidedly uncomfortable, he struggled to continue. "Please don't take offense, but…" He scanned their clothes and shrugged, as if to say that words were inadequate.

Edmond took a quick swipe at Christian's ear while mouthing, "Told you," and jumped out of the way before Christian could even the score.

Nathaniel was baffled by the exchange but got into the spirit of things, twirling his cane as he led them to the haberdashery where they purchased clothes. They made their way to Pierson's without further incident, despite the fact that Edmond managed to "talk a load of bull," as Christian put it, the entire time.

"That's it," Nathaniel said, gesturing to a building with a Greek Revival facade, dominated by four Corinthian columns on the portico. Turning around, he studied Christian thoughtfully. "Miss Aster doesn't know you're here?" he asked.

Aside from a "reserved" front row and a smattering of people in the second, the gallery was filled nearly to capacity. With a good number standing against the walls, despite the available seats, Annie guessed that many of the people present were merely curiosity hounds. She took a seat on the aisle near the back of the room.

"Excuse me."

Annie swiveled in her seat and counted out the ten hundred-dollar bills she'd withdrawn from the bank as a gentleman attempted to step past her to claim the seat on the other side. He tripped over her dress and practically fell into his chair. "Terribly sorry," he said.

Annie gathered her skirt and turned to apologize, jumping reflexively. "Mr. Goodkin!" she said, holding out her hand. "I don't think I've ever been so surprised to see anyone in my life!"

Nathaniel cupped it in both of his. "Miss Aster, the pleasure is mine," he said. He collected his catalog, which had fallen to the floor. "Are you here as a spectator or participant?"

"Strangely enough, I'm interested in the last item in the catalog."

Nathaniel flipped to the last page of the booklet. "The door? You wish to purchase Mr. Abbott's magic door?" he asked, waving his hand at a feather that fluttered dangerously near to his nose. It was a stubborn thing, and he snatched at it impulsively, eliciting a squawk from a rather plump woman who had chosen that very moment to sit directly in front of him. Before finding itself in his hand, the feather had been situated atop her hat—an enormous, excessively plumed thing that blocked his view entirely.

Apologies were given all around, and Annie, though secretly enamored of the monstrosity, quietly offered Mr. Goodkin a few inspired suggestions on alternate uses for the plumes, as the woman, suspecting she was the topic of discussion, turned to glower self-importantly. With typical aplomb, Annie rocked forward to compliment the woman's fashion sense and soon had the lady conversing energetically about the millinery on Broadway, even as Mr. Culler worked his way into the room.

He claimed three seats in the front row—for himself, Danyer, and his valise—removing the "reserved" placards and tossing them under his chair. Setting the bag in the seat next to him and indicating for Danyer to take the third seat, Mr. Culler quickly thumbed through his catalog. Spying the final notation, he pulled out his wallet, likewise counting ten one-hundred-dollar bills as the auctioneer approached the podium.

"The items up for auction today come from the estate of the late David Abbott, magician and entertainer," the auctioneer said. As the buzz throughout the room simmered down, he added, "All items in the catalog but the last are available for viewing in the back room. This is a cash-only auction. Credit will not be extended."

Having dealt with the preliminaries, he motioned for the attendant to place a framed composition on the display table. "The first item up for bid is one of ten original drypoint prints created by the American Impressionist Mary Cassatt. Can we start the bid at ten dollars, please? Ten dollars to the man in the corner. Can I hear twenty?"

Annie and Nathaniel spoke quietly in the back of the room as the auction proceeded. To her surprise, Mrs. Fowl, her new friend and style consultant, showed much better taste in art than chapeaus, snapping up all ten drypoints.

One after another, items were brought out for viewing and bidding ensued. Of particular interest to Annie was a lead-glass table lamp designed by Clara Driscoll. She was sorely tempted to bid on it, having heard rumors that it was her designs, not Louis Comfort Tiffany's, that would make his company world famous, but she needed to hold on to her cash. Once again, and to Annie's admiration, Mrs. Fowl gobbled up the piece. Annie patted her shoulder in congratulations, and Mrs. Fowl reached back to rub her hand warmly while preparing for her next battle.

As Annie suspected, many of the attendees were there for the sensationalism of watching David Abbott's belongings be auctioned off so soon after his death. Even so, there were a good many serious attendees, and the bidding was brisk.

A murmur pulsed throughout the room as the final item in the catalog was announced. "While not available for viewing, item number twenty-seven on the manifest is the centerpiece of David Abbott's stage show, designed and made by the man himself."

All business, Annie placed her hand on Nathaniel's arm, forestalling any commentary.

"As described in the catalog, the door is carved with rune signs and astrological symbols and is finished in a unique red glaze, the formula for which was made and kept secret by David Abbott. Can we start the bidding at…one hundred dollars? One hundred dollars for item number twenty-seven."

All eyes shifted to the front row as Mr. Culler nodded.

"We have a bid of one hundred dollars. Can I hear a bid for one fifty?"

A slight woman in the back of the room lifted her paddle. Soon, a few more people joined in and the bidding inched upward.

Annie became impatient at around the three-hundred-twenty-dollar mark and decided to weed out the rabble. "Five hundred dollars," she said, lifting her paddle. As the room gasped collectively—fanning the general hum of anticipation—Messrs. Culler and Danyer spun around to see who had entered the fray.

"Five hundred dollars to the lady in the back," stated the auctioneer.

Mr. Culler turned back to face the podium in a quiet rage, but he couldn't help noticing that Danyer had not and that he was staring at the woman who'd raised the stakes with an almost feral preoccupation. Mr. Culler leaned over, intending to chide his associate for his lack of manners, but Danyer beat him to the punch, whispering in his ear.

He whirled around to fix his gaze on Annie. "Her? From the bank, you say."

Danyer indicated his assent in the usual way, with a grunt, but further speculation was curtailed by the auctioneer.

"The current offer is five hundred dollars. Can I hear a bid for six hundred?"

Still staring at Annie, Mr. Culler held up his paddle. The duel was on.

"Very good. We have an offer of six hundred dollars from the gentleman in the front row. The bid now stands at six fifty. Do I hear an offer for six fifty?"

Annie raised her paddle. "Eight hundred dollars," she said, smiling politely at her opponent.

The gallery relished the tension, glancing back and forth between the two remaining bidders as Mr. Culler turned to face the podium, the back of his neck livid.

"We have eight hundred dollars on the table," said the auctioneer. "Do I hear nine hundred? Anyone for nine hundred dollars?"

Mr. Culler had had enough, bellowing, "One thousand dollars!"

The bid was followed by a gasp, then a general outbreak of pandemonium. The auctioneer struck his gavel atop the sounding board, but the racket drowned it out. Even when the uproar had subsided after several more strikes and a call to order, the gallery continued to ripple with movement as people leaned toward one another to whisper heated comments.

Annie shut out the din, her eyes closed. Her plans had gone completely and unexpectedly awry. But the door on the auction block, the one sitting in her father's living room, also opened to the backyard of her house a hundred years in the future—proof, she thought, that this story had not reached its conclusion. She breathed deeply, willing something to happen.

"We have a bid of one thousand dollars by the gentleman in the front row. The bid now stands at a thousand. Is there an offer for eleven hundred? Eleven hundred dollars, anyone?" When there was no response, Mr. Culler turned around to tip his hat to Annie. "Eleven hundred dollars going once."

A stir of air led her to open her eyes. There were five crisp twenty-dollar bills resting in her lap. Shocked, she looked at Mrs. Fowl who pointed discreetly behind Annie. Looking over her shoulder at her benefactor, Annie did a double take and gasped involuntarily. "Christian!" she said.

Waving shyly from his seat behind her, Christian broke out into a huge grin as he motioned toward the auctioneer with a quick upward nod.

"—twice. Eleven hundred dollars going—"

Spinning around, she shouted, "Eleven hundred dollars!"

The effect of her cry was immediate. The audience burst into cheers, and Mr. Culler's chair toppled over onto his bag as he turned to glare at Annie, his jaw clenching so spectacularly that she wondered if his teeth would chip. With the room in an uproar, he threw his catalog on the floor and manhandled his wallet to thumb through its contents.

"We have a bid of eleven hundred dollars. Anyone for twelve hundred? Is there an offer for twelve hundred? No? Twelve hundred going once. Twelve hundred going twice." With the tables turned, and no benefactor of his own, Mr. Culler listened helplessly as the count concluded. "Twelve hundred going three times. Sold for eleven hundred dollars to the lady in the back!"

At the sound of the gavel, Mr. Culler snatched up his valise and, with a final, venomous glare in Annie's direction, stomped for the exit with Danyer hot on his heels. Head down, he barged directly into a young woman who was standing in the doorway, landing face-first in her bosom.

She grabbed him by his lapels, gave him a shove, and yelled, "Watch it, bub!"

Ripping his coat from her hands, Mr. Culler stormed out without a word.

While applause broke out around her, Annie turned around and grabbed Christian in a tight hug. Abruptly, she held him at arm's length. "You irresponsible, bullheaded—" She stopped short as her mind switched gears. "How did you find me?"

Christian fell back into his chair with a look of satisfaction. "You left a trail of…b-b-bread crumbs."

"I suppose I did," she said before pausing to stare at his clothes. "What on earth are you wearing?"

Christian glanced at Mr. Goodkin as he prepared an explanation. Something in the man's expression, though, led him to perform a second act of mercy instead. "Can you bring her up to speed while I check on Edmond?" he asked.

Annie's brow furrowed as she pointed first to Mr. Goodkin, then to Christian. "You know each other?" she asked. "Wait, did you say Edmond? He's here?"

Christian gave Annie a quick wink, then cocked his head toward Nathaniel. "You might thank Mr. Goodkin for the money, by the way."

She watched as Christian was swallowed by the swarm exiting the building, then turned to meet Nathaniel's gaze. "Mr. Goodkin." An unexpected heat rose to her face. Flustered, she opened her purse and pulled out the checkbook, but Nathaniel placed his hand over hers.

"Can you—" He broke from his thought, sounding tentative. "Can you not do that and simply let me take you to dinner?" he asked.

He couldn't have been any more charming, and Annie hesitated, wanting to say yes. "My situation is complicated," she said after a moment.

Glancing toward the exit, Nathaniel quietly asked, "Is this regarding Mr. Keebler?"

"No." The nuances behind the question tickled Annie and she smiled. "Christian is a dear friend."

Rallying as only a true gentleman could, Nathaniel stood, offering his arm. "With your permission then, I'd be pleased to escort you back to the hotel."

"That is an offer that I can and will gladly accept," she said.

Noticing the clerk who was waiting patiently at the end of the aisle, Nathaniel gestured in his direction and said, "Shall I meet you outside?"

After Annie signed the necessary paperwork to complete the sale and learned from the clerk that the door was not available for immediate delivery, being part of a crime scene, she pulled a scrap of paper with an address written on it from her purse. She stared at it while deliberating how to ensure that the door would ultimately be delivered to a little antique store in San Francisco. Borrowing a pencil from the clerk, she turned the scrap over and wrote a note—her plan in full swing.

The wild card of that plan, in the form of Ambrosius Culler, paced furiously outside the auction house. He pulled Danyer out of view behind a large column, whispering fiercely. "Our plan is unraveling, Mr. Danyer. First, Mrs. Grundy; now this. I'm open to suggestions."

Ever thrifty with words, Danyer uttered only four.

"Get rid of her?" Mr. Culler looked to the entrance, pondering the advice. "Point well taken. But let's see if we can reason with her first."

Danyer grunted. Coming from him, it was a veritable treatise on the pitfalls of Mr. Culler's soft heart.

A gentleman sitting on the steps directly below the column lowered the paper he'd been reading and watched as Mr. Culler headed to the entrance of the auction house. Hearing his name being called, he stood.

"Edmond!"

Christian and Mr. Goodkin hurried over. Christian started in on a progress report when Edmond interrupted him with a gesture. "We have trouble," he said before repeating the conversation he just overheard.

"And you heard them discussing Miss Aster?" asked Nathaniel, as Christian sunk to the stairs, visibly shaken.

"Yes, clear as a bell."

"Where are they now?"

"One walked off. I think the other is still back there." Edmond gestured over his shoulder.

Nathaniel wandered in the direction of the column, paused, then turned to Christian and Edmond with a quick shake of his head. "Miss Aster is settling her account," he said as he returned to the huddle. "Would you mind keeping an eye open for Cap'n while I escort Miss Aster to her hotel?"

It seemed a simple enough request to Edmond, but the look of delight that stole across Christian's face, replacing his earlier chagrin, told a different story. Edmond glanced quickly at Mr. Goodkin, noticing that his ears were beginning to color.

"Would you prefer—"

"No!" Christian said, startling both men with his interruption. "No, that's fine," he added.

A smattering of applause broke from the top of the stairs, and the three men looked up to see a small crowd gather around Annie as she emerged from the door.

She hadn't made it past the landing, though, when an arm slipped under hers, roughly guiding her down the steps.

"Allow me to congratulate you on your purchase, Miss Aster. The name is Ambrosius Culler."

The mention of that name had an electric effect. Annie's heart started hammering as if someone had floored her accelerator, but she played it cool, smiling as she unwound his arm from hers. "It may surprise you to learn that I'm not one for being manhandled, Mr. Culler," she said.

Expecting a watery response and receiving the opposite, Mr. Culler halted, indecisive. He plucked a business card from his breast pocket, and Annie couldn't help but notice two things as she took it from his hand: there was a gunpowder burn on the side of his neck she suspected was courtesy of Cap'n's hand-rolled cigar, and the end of his left pinkie finger was missing.

He caught her staring and his eyes darkened. "You're very observant," he said. His remaining fingers twitched randomly, as if itching to slap her, and it was clear to Annie that Mr. Culler was seething. She could almost feel the heat of his anger creeping up the length of her arm from where he'd grabbed her, lodging the taste of fear in the back of her throat.

"How can I help you?" she said.

"The better question is how you can help yourself, I think."

"Neither am I fond of being patronized," she responded crisply. "Now if you'll excuse me, I'll be on my way."

Her fright gave way to outrage when he grabbed her arm as she turned to leave. Annie wrenched it free, rounding on him. "Be warned, Mr. Culler," she spat.

Not put off in the least, Mr. Culler merely smiled, his eyes dancing. He put his hand in his pocket, toying with something while studying the ebb and flow of the crowd, its leading edge now within earshot. He collected himself. "Miss Aster, that door is, I assume, nothing more than an amusement to you," he said. "It is, however, extremely important to me. Therefore, I'm ready to make your investment immediately profitable. I would like to purchase it from you for two thousand dollars."

"You'd like to what?" she asked. Taken off guard by the offer, she found herself at a sudden loss for words. Recovering quickly, she added, "Well, Mr. Culler, I can't help but wonder at the true value of the door when you offer almost twice my bid." She held up his business card. "We'll be in touch."

There was a flurry of movement, followed by a crack and a grunt, but the only thing Annie could focus on was the stinging sensation in the palm of her hand. She stared at it uncomprehendingly and looked over to see Mr. Culler rubbing his cheek—a scarlet relief of her palm raising itself on the surface of his skin. Her face flushed with color to match it when she realized she'd slapped him as he'd attempted to bar her exit by stepping into her path. Christian's warnings that her temper would trip her up some day passed through her mind as she watched Mr. Culler's expression galvanize into something unutterably cold.

Before she could say a word, he chuckled. "Please don't apologize, Miss Aster," he said. "It will only spoil the fun. But I'm afraid I will be retracting my offer. Such a shame, really." He stepped aside.

Galled by his self-assurance and her own weakness, Annie could only glare at him.

"Ah, Miss Aster."

Looking up, she spied Nathaniel walking over at a leisurely pace. Relief gave way to impudence and Annie stuck her tongue out at Mr. Culler before beating a hasty retreat. Given a moment to collect herself, she might have even thrown in a big, old raspberry to boot, but she was suddenly overcome by a wave of fatigue.

Taking her by the arm, Nathaniel glanced over his shoulder at Mr. Culler, who regarded the two of them while massaging his cheek. Suddenly Mr. Culler smiled, tipped his hat to Nathaniel, and turned to walk off. "I don't trust that man," Nathaniel said.

Annie followed his gaze, watching Mr. Culler disappear into the crowd. "Not a very pleasant fellow," she said while rubbing the palm of her hand.

Though he didn't consider himself much of a mathematician, Nathaniel could add two and two as well as the next guy. By all accounts, it looked as though Miss Aster had slapped the man. He looked to her for an explanation but, receiving none, guided her back to the portico of the auction house.

Standing unnoticed to the side and watching the entire exchange was the young woman whose bosom Mr. Culler had accidentally pawed. "Good for you, Miss Annie," she said under her breath. With Miss Aster seemingly out of danger, she turned to skip down the steps to the street and past a kid—their hands touching briefly as they continued in separate directions.

At a bend, Cap'n stopped to examine the thousand dollars picked from Mr. Culler's coat pocket by Belinda, Tater's older sister and another seasoned veteran of the con game. Between Miss Annie and herself, she thought wryly, there had been a substantial drop in Mr. Culler's net worth lately. And she didn't intend to let up. She was going to plague the man until he was dead and buried.

She made a mental note to hold on to a hundred bucks for Belinda. The rest would go into the gang's fund. She looked back at the auction house, her lips pursing when she saw Annie and Mr. Goodkin walking away from a noticeably flushed Mr. Culler.

"Are you all right? You look terribly pale," said Nathaniel, looking back to make certain they weren't followed.

Waving off his concern, Annie paused to catch her breath. "Your timing is impeccable," she said.

Nathaniel turned, preparing to ask her meaning, and stopped dead in his tracks. "Did he strike you?"

"No. Why?"

In answer, he fished a kerchief from his pocket and held it to her nose. "Are you sure you're all right?" he asked.

She tilted her head back, glancing sideways at him.

"I know of that man," he said, watching her closely. "He's dangerous, Miss Aster."

"Is that the voice of experience?"

"After a fashion," he replied. "And I must admit to a certain bias. His former employer, a client of mine—Mr. Raven—died under circumstances entirely too convenient for Mr. Culler."

Annie recalled the name with a shudder. She also recalled the pinkie finger it belonged to. Struggling to keep the conversation light, she said, "That's not encouraging at all, but I'm certain it has nothing to do with me." She folded the kerchief and handed it back to Nathaniel, nodding congenially to a couple offering a congratulatory word.

"The conversation Mr. Marden overheard between Messrs. Culler and Danyer does, I'm afraid. I fear they mean you harm."

"Mr. Marden?" Annie frowned. "Oh, Edmond! But, Mr. Goodkin, be sensible. What can they do when I have three capable men at my side?"

"They're also plotting against a Mrs. Grundy. Does that name mean anything to you?"

Nathaniel couldn't have been more effective in getting Annie's undivided attention had he stuck his cane between her feet. She stumbled and looked at him in horror. "We must hurry," she said as she spied Christian standing next to Cap'n and another gentleman she assumed to be Edmond.

Annie hurried to their side, giving Cap'n a quick hug, then turned to Edmond. "Mr. Marden," she said, "will you forgive me if I postpone the small talk? There is something that I'd like to discuss with you and Christian."

Before Annie had a chance to say anything more, Cap'n took Mr. Goodkin by the hand, leading him down the stairs. She looked back and winked.

When they were out of earshot, Annie turned to Christian. "I understand that Edmond overheard Mr. Culler say something about Elsbeth?" She pressed her lips together when they confirmed her fears. "Christian, I hate to ask this of you, but—"

"You want me to warn her."

"Whatever restrains me has to do with bloodline," she explained.

"But you're coming home with us, aren't you?"

"I think Elsbeth is still in the city. If she is, with the help of my little confederate, I'll get a note of warning to her." When that didn't convince him, she added, "I'm also making arrangements for the door's delivery."

Christian stared at the pavement. "Annie, I'll go to Elsbeth's," he said, clearly unhappy. "But Edmond and I will wait here for you to take care of this business with the door, then I want you coming back with us." Before she could argue, he added, "If El is in the city, Cap'n can warn her just as easily as you."

Caught off guard by Christian's logic, Annie almost relented. "There's a sandlot next to Womack's Hardware at Third and Broadway," she said. "Cap'n knows about it. Wait there. If I'm not there in three hours, please go home and warn Elsbeth." Knowing he wouldn't be happy with the compromise, she grabbed his hand. "Please. I promise I won't be far behind."

"Three hours," he said, then hesitated, his face blanching. "There is one more thing I think you should know. There's a potential p-problem with Mr. Goodkin."

"He *does* seem a little smitten."

Christian touched her arm. "I gave him a twenty."

The seeming non sequitur made her pause. "I'm not sure I—"

The next words fell from his mouth like a brick. "It was newly minted."

At first there was nothing, no response, then the gap between Annie's brows dimpled, and she stepped back reflexively, looking down the stairs where Cap'n and Nathaniel were in earnest discussion. "Oh dear," she said.

Nathaniel looked up, his smile fading when he noticed her expression. He squeezed Cap'n's elbow, pointed to Annie, and the two of them returned.

After a brief exchange, Cap'n took off for the sandlot with Christian and Edmond, leaving Nathaniel alone with Annie. "The Broadway is not far," he said, offering his arm.

Paradoxically aware that Miss Aster was disinclined to speak for some reason, yet unaware that Danyer had detached himself from the side of a building on the opposite side to follow them, Nathaniel led her down the street.

They made it several blocks before either spoke. Finally, Nathaniel broke the silence as they neared the hotel. "You must understand that Messrs. Culler and Danyer have a savage reputation. If they want Abbott's door, and it is clear that they do, they will stop at nothing to get it."

"I'm counting on exactly that," Annie said.

The comment so astonished Nathaniel that he lost his balance and had to use his cane to keep from falling. Annie said it so witheringly that he wondered if he'd heard her right. After all, it sounded like a challenge, and he couldn't, for the life of him, imagine why anyone would want to provoke those two men.

For her part, Annie was equally surprised by the comment. It wasn't until the words were uttered that she realized that had been her intention all along. But to what end, her subconscious hadn't revealed.

Ducking into an alley across the street, Danyer watched them pause in front of the Broadway. He pointed in Nathaniel's direction, then lowered the brim of his Stetson over his eyes and disappeared into the shadows. A second man emerged from the alley, pulled a beret from his pocket, fit it over his head, and crossed the street.

Inside, Annie walked directly to the reception counter while Nathaniel headed upstairs. "Pardon me," she said. "I was wondering if you have a guest in residence by the name of Elsbeth Grundy?"

The expression on the duty clerk's face was difficult to read, but the topic seemed to be objectionable. He responded woodenly, "She checked out, ma'am."

"Are you certain?"

"Quite," he said. "She left without settling her bill."

For the sake of his wounded pride, Annie tried to look scandalized, but she couldn't vouch for the effectiveness of her performance. She reached into her bag to pull out the note she'd written at the auction house, as well as the receipt of sale for the door. Grabbing an envelope from the counter, she slid both inside, gave directions for it to be delivered to an Arthur Langley at the Antiquarian, and headed to her room. Nathaniel was waiting in the hallway. She handed him the key, since Christian had left strict instructions that he was not to allow Annie in her room until it was inspected.

Rolling up his sleeves—a gesture Annie found mildly amusing—Nathaniel quickly unlocked the door and disappeared inside. Almost immediately, she heard a loud bang followed by a moan. She leaped through the door to find him leaning against a wall, laughing mirthlessly as he rubbed his head. On the ground by his feet was a large wooden clock, its glass casing knocked off center.

He looked at Annie, bemused, as a welt appeared on his forehead and pointed to the shelf by the bed. The wood panel was hanging loosely. "I tripped," he said.

"That's going to leave a nasty bruise." Ducking into the bathroom, Annie grabbed a washcloth and soaked it in cold water. Wringing it out, she folded the cloth into thirds and pointed to the bed.

Nathaniel obeyed but started to fidget as Annie placed the compress on his forehead. "Ants in your pants, Mr. Goodkin?"

He stopped squirming long enough to frown. "Miss Aster, I'm not certain it is proper that I be alone with you in your room." He started to sit up, toppling the compress.

Exasperated, she pushed him back on the bed and tucked a pillow under his head. "I'm confident my virtue will weather the storm, Mr. Goodkin, but if you think I'm going to let you trot off with a possible concussion, then you don't know me at all." She tenderly repositioned the compress. Then, motioning for him to move over, she sat on the bed beside him, folding her hands in her lap.

His charms were winning her over, and her gaze, uncertain where to settle, rested awkwardly on his arm. It seemed so solid—opaque—compared to the translucence of her own. She had a sudden desire to trace the length of a ropy vein as it meandered through the swirling patterns of hair on his forearm.

Seeing where her gaze lingered, Nathaniel turned on his side, putting his weight on his elbow. He tried to catch her eyes, but she wasn't having any of it.

It wasn't that she was unaware of what was transpiring. Annie wasn't naive, but neither was she prepared. So, she sat there, at something of an impasse.

There was a certain kind of beauty in the awkward moment that followed, and Annie would later recall every detail—her refusal to meet his gaze, his hand stretching out to lightly touch her leg, her sudden fixation with his lower lip.

And in that moment, what passed for good sense in Annie's mind told her to get up, to walk around, to do anything but return Nathaniel's gaze so that the lump and thump of her emotions could cool. Good sense lost. Meeting his eyes, she sighed and said, "You've become a very pleasant complication."

And he didn't disappoint, startling her with a whisper-soft touch to the cheek. As her eyes fluttered shut, he leaned forward and brushed his lips against hers—featherlight—his breath causing the hairs loosened from her chignon to ripple.

On later recollection, Annie could not decide whether the world had tipped on its axis or Nathaniel had gently laid her against a pillow, but she did remember his mouth covering hers, sending a heat throughout her body that burned away the remainder of her restraint and left her falling, falling, falling…

So it was a bit of a jolt for her when he got up without saying a word and walked drunkenly to the bathroom sink, placing the washcloth across the spigot.

"Nathaniel?"

"I've never done that before," he said, leaning against the basin, breathing heavily. He turned his head to the side to meet her gaze, looking bewildered as he added, "I don't know what's come over me. I honestly don't. One minute I want to cradle you like a baby in my arms, and the next I want to wrestle you down, pin your arms overhead, and crush your lips with mine." He pushed away from the sink to stand in the doorway, looking at the floor. "It's a condition I've lived with since the moment we met," he confessed.

A pillow bounced off his chest, landing on the cold tile at his feet.

"Did I somehow leave you with the impression that I didn't love every moment of what just happened?" Annie asked. She stiffened, sounding almost insulted when she added, "Or for that matter, that I'd let you do something I didn't wish for?"

"It isn't proper," he said, leaning over to pick up the pillow.

"Well, thank God for impropriety!"

As he stepped to the bed to lean the pillow against the bolster, Annie gathered her dress and patted the space next to her. Waiting for him to get comfortable, she said, "Now that that's settled, would you do me a favor and take it from the top?"

# CHAPTER THIRTY

## Johnny Parker

"It was only a kiss," Annie reminded him a second time.

Nathaniel turned in the doorway. "Why do you keep saying that?"

"Because"—she clenched her fists—"I'm going to be so *angry* if you discover your misplaced masculine scruples after the fact and pretend nothing just happened."

Nathaniel shook his head.

"I'm serious, Nathaniel! You'd better not."

Looking at the clock, he said quietly, "The letter?"

"Hmm?"

"You wanted me to wait while you wrote a letter to your grandmother."

"Oh!"

As Annie scrambled to the desk, he added, "I'll be in the library at the end of the hall."

May 30, 1895

Dear Elsbeth:

Men! Why is it that even the best of them only find their virtue after the conquest? It's exhausting just thinking about it. All that push and pull. Women are so much more sensible.

I've just left the auction house after bidding successfully on the door. It's safe for the time being. I suspect, however, that I am not. Mr. Culler is something of a sore loser—more on that later.

As for the door, it will remain at my father's home for now. I intend to have it delivered to the owner of the Antiquarian, one Arthur Langley who happens to be the great-great-grandfather of the man from whom I bought the door, with the receipt and a copy of the article. I'm meticulously duplicating the events that move the door from Kansas City in 1895 to San Francisco of 1995.

I can't tell you how strange it feels, bidding on an object I already own so that I can leave it in a place where I will find it and unknowingly purchase it yet again.

I have a "partner in crime," a young lady with certain talents that have proven to be indispensable. She was able to "pinch" a money clip that displays Mr. Culler's initials and planted it on my father's body. It should be in the hands of the authorities by the time you read this letter, that is, if you don't read about it in the paper first.

Christian won't be pleased, but I've decided to wait for tomorrow's paper to confirm that Mr. Culler has replaced you as the primary suspect in the murder before making my way back home.

Be careful! Once he's implicated, it's your testimony that will convict him of the murder. I'm sure he'll come to the same conclusion.

Your granddaughter,
Annabelle Abbott Aster

Annie wandered down the hall to find Nathaniel dozing in a leather armchair, a copy of the paper in his lap.

She was tempted to let him sleep in peace, but lowered herself to sit on the armrest of his chair and stirred him awake with a kiss. "Give this to Christian for me," she said.

Glancing at the name on the envelope, Nathaniel rubbed an eye, looking confused. "Elsbeth Grundy. *She's* your grandmother?"

Annie nodded.

Nathaniel stood, straightening his jacket. "Will you please do me a favor and lock your door?" He turned to leave, but quickly spun around to reach behind her head, pulling her close. He kissed her lingeringly, then put his lips on her forehead and breathed deeply before walking out the door without another word.

He headed out onto the busy street, his head so full of the "push and pull" of masculine contradictions, as Annie would put it, that he hardly watched where he was going and almost flattened a poor fellow. "Pardon me!" he said while bending over to pick up the beret he'd knocked from the stunned man's head.

Looking quite shaken, the man collected his hat and mumbled, "No harm done."

As Nathaniel walked off, the man's look of shock slowly gave way to sober reflection, and he looked down at his stolen booty. He shook his head and wandered to the alley running the length of the Broadway.

Danyer stepped from the shadows to give the man a ten spot in exchange for a letter and wallet he'd pinched off Nathaniel. He dropped them into a valise and walked across the street into a tavern.

"What have we here?" Mr. Culler said, glancing at the valise at the foot of the table. He dug around inside and retrieved the stolen items. Taking a slug from his beer, Mr. Culler quickly pocketed forty dollars from the wallet's inner sleeve before pulling out a business card. "It appears that Miss Aster's escort is a Nathaniel Goodkin," he said, looking at Danyer. "Does that sound familiar?" Tossing the wallet back in the bag, he held up the envelope. "And what's this?" He turned it over and stared at the addressee's name before unsealing it.

After a lengthy pause, Mr. Culler said, "Well, well. It seems that Mr. Abbott is having a last laugh at us from the grave." He handed the letter to his associate and lowered his head to stare at beads of moisture sliding down his sweating beer stein. Taking a quick gulp, he looked into the mirror above the bar. Danyer's reflection stared back at him, waiting.

Mr. Culler began to speak in fragmented sentences, broken thoughts, almost as if to himself, knowing his associate would follow the thread. "Abbott must have been warned somehow," he said. "Tucked her safely away... If the door could place a child forward in time, then we must assume it can also... That would explain her presence at the auction..." He turned to Danyer, awe-struck. "We've underestimated this woman."

He got up and began to pace, peanut shells crunching under-foot. "What next, what next," he mumbled.

Knowing where Mr. Culler's mind was going, Danyer nodded, his pitch so deep as he mumbled that the two words he spoke registered more as thought than sound.

"Mrs. Grundy, indeed," answered Mr. Culler.

Danyer snarled, his meaning clear. Mr. Culler waved off the implied question. "Yes, yes, Miss Aster will have her turn," he said. "But we need to make ourselves scarce for the time being, and going to Pawnee County kills two birds with one stone, so to speak." He reached into his breast pocket. A flicker of doubt crossed his face as he turned the pocket out. Finding it empty, he slumped back on the bar stool to slowly down the remainder of his beer.

When the stein was emptied, he exhaled and looked into the mirror to peer at his reflection. It stood and took three steps in his direction. Slowly, a smile formed over its features, its eyes alight and wild as it ran a finger across its own throat. Without the slightest change of expression, he heaved the mug into the glass. Glancing at the stunned bartender, he rolled his shoulders, cracked his neck, and said, "Bill me."

# CHAPTER THIRTY-ONE

## And the Truth Comes Tumbling Out

It is a universal condition among males of the species that those who are smitten have little use for the obvious, and in that regard, Nathaniel Goodkin kept good company.

He was laboring to make sense of it all as he made for the sandlot at the corner of Third and Broadway—the mystery surrounding Miss Aster, the baffling power she had over him, and his willingness to involve himself in her affairs without explanation. His subconscious would sort through the irrelevancies, expose the glaring truths, and generally take him in hand later. At the moment, he had a letter to deliver.

Christian and Edmond were sitting in the dugout of a small baseball diamond talking to Cap'n, their eyes following his every step as he walked up and sat down on the bench.

"Where's Annie?" Christian asked, breaking the silence.

Nathaniel peered over the sandlot. "I left Miss Aster in her hotel room with instructions not to answer the door except for one of us." He reached into his pocket. "She wrote a letter addressed to an Elsbeth Grundy and asked that I deliver it to you." Frowning, he switched his hand to the other pocket before taking the coat off and turned the pockets inside out to check them more thoroughly. "I don't understand," he said as he reached into his pants pocket. "My wallet is missing."

Cap'n, who had been watching the production with more than

a hint of skepticism, shook her head. Being quick on the uptake and possessing a greater reservoir of experience in certain matters than the present company, she'd already come to the conclusion Nathaniel was gradually working his way toward.

"That man," he said, sounding thoughtful. "The man with the beret!" He palmed the top of his head, his expression reflecting the shock in his voice. "I think my pockets have been picked."

"This ain't good."

Edmond turned to Cap'n. "What's not good?" he asked.

"I should've seen it coming." She held her up a finger, indicating that she'd get to Edmond's question shortly. "Mr. Goodkin," she said. "Was this guy blond and short, with a baby face?"

Nathaniel's mouth flew open, confirming Cap'n's suspicion.

"It was Johnny Parker. I'd bet my bottom dollar on it." She grabbed some sunflower seeds from her pocket and popped them in her mouth. "Johnny Parker's a professional pinch," she explained. "Usually works solo but pulls the odd job for Mr. Culler now and then. It's a good bet old man Culler has your wallet and the letter."

Christian groaned, leaning forward to put his head in his hands.

"Is Annie in danger?" asked Nathaniel.

Christian looked up, peering at Nathaniel between outspread fingers, and nodded.

Annie tossed and turned, caught in a dream where her father was standing over her crib with a tiny baseball mitt in his hand, saying, "I always wanted to teach you how to play ball." He started to put it in her hand when the sound of gunshot cracked from somewhere behind, and—

Annie sat up in bed, trying to regain her equilibrium, when she heard another bang, this time coming from the door.

"Miss Aster, are you in there?"

Recognizing Nathaniel's voice, she stumbled to the mirror and adjusted her hair. After running her hands down the length of her skirt, she gave up and opened the door. Her half-formed smile faded when she saw that Christian, Edmond, and Cap'n had accompanied him.

"Thank goodness," Nathaniel said. "May we come in?"

They were all breathing heavily, and Annie searched for a clue to what had them so tightly wound as they filed into the room.

Cap'n, all business, headed for the bed and placed a pillow in her lap, while Christian leaned forward to stare into Annie's eyes. "You look exhausted. How long have you been asleep?"

"A hundred years, I think."

Nathaniel looked at her quizzically, then surveyed the hallway to confirm no one was watching. He closed the door and turned to Annie. "Miss Aster, I think it would be wise for you to share the contents of your letter."

Annie looked anxiously from one face to another. "Is there a problem?" she asked.

"I'm afraid it has most likely found its way into the hands of Messrs. Culler and Danyer."

Annie's hand flew to her mouth, and she began to chew on the end of her thumb. "Are you certain?"

"I am," said Cap'n. "Remember me telling you about Johnny Parker? From the look of things, Mr. Culler hired him to find out more about Mr. Goodkin and got your letter to boot. Just plain old bad luck."

Annie sighed, rocking her head back to thump lightly against the wall. "Oh dear." She began to pace about the room while the others made themselves comfortable.

"I suppose it's time for an explanation." She picked up the clock sitting on the desk, staring at its face. "Heaven knows you're due one. The truth, I fear, will be difficult to understand." Setting the clock aside, she retrieved her handbag from the closet, rooting around until she found a piece of yellowed paper. Sitting on the edge of the bed, she held it in her lap with both hands.

"You too," she said to Christian.

He looked at her, surprised, then sheepishly reached into his pocket to pull out the twenty-dollar bill.

Annie gave the piece of paper in her hand to Nathaniel, motioning for Christian to do the same.

Looking very uneasy, as if knowing there would be no going back once he learned its secret, Nathaniel inspected the bill, while Cap'n scrambled to her knees to peer over his shoulder. "Who is Mary Ellen Withrow?" she whispered. He shook his head, not wanting to speculate.

"Can you tell me the series number?" Annie asked.

When Nathaniel didn't respond, Cap'n peered at the corner of the bill. "It says 'series 1994.'"

"And what about the other one, Mr. Goodkin?" Annie gestured to the document on his lap.

Nathaniel handed the bill to Cap'n and picked up the document in question. "It's an article from the *Star*," he said. He rubbed his thumb over its surface. "It's quite weathered," he added, looking for the date. Inhaling sharply, he looked up. "It's tomorrow's edition."

As Cap'n scrambled to his side for a better view, Annie said, "To answer your question, Cap'n, Mary Ellen Withrow will be the Unites States Treasurer in the year 1994."

Nathaniel gave no indication that he'd heard Annie, but Cap'n's head snapped up. Her expression gave the appearance of someone on the verge of understanding, but Nathaniel merely closed his eyes and placed his forehead in the palm of his hand.

Picking nervously at a loose thread on the cuff of her sleeve, Annie pressed on. "I am…from San Francisco as you learned in our first meeting, Mr. Goodkin," she said. "But before I made my way to Kansas City, it was May thirty-first in the year 1995."

Nathaniel remained withdrawn—Annie wasn't even certain

he was listening—but Cap'n's response was a pleasant surprise. Illustrating the credulity of youth, she simply said, "Well, I'll be."

Annie smiled at her before continuing. "I live…in your future. I am here, I suppose, because of a peculiar door I purchased and installed in the back of my home—Mr. Abbott's door. Somehow, it found its way over time to me. The door is, as he claimed in his show, a time-travel conduit. Through it, I became pen pals with Elsbeth. Because of it, I learned of Mr. Abbott's murder and rashly asked El to intervene. She attempted to do so and was hidden in his closet while he was murdered."

Cap'n dropped to her seat and crossed her legs, spellbound.

"Unfortunately," Annie continued, "El was seen leaving Mr. Abbott's home by a neighbor and was implicated as the primary suspect. I took it upon myself to correct the situation. In the course of doing so, I have learned that I am not only Elsbeth's granddaughter, but also the daughter of David Abbott."

Nathaniel jerked upright. "What?"

Reaching over to put a reassuring hand on his leg, Cap'n turned to Annie. "You?" She took a second to make certain she understood what Annie had shared. "Are you saying you're the baby that was reported missing?"

Nathaniel leaped to his feet.

Annie ignored him for the moment, focusing on her confederate. "Yes, Cap'n. I'm the child reported missing yesterday," she said, glancing at Nathaniel. "I'm Annabelle Abbott Aster, and the door didn't end up in my possession by accident. Something larger is at work."

Cap'n, to her credit, was doing her best to take everything Annie said at face value, but the math escaped her. "How?" she asked. "Abbott's daughter ain't even one year old yet."

Annie studied Nathaniel carefully before turning back to Cap'n. "Yesterday, on your timeline, just before he was murdered, my father transported me, his one-year-old daughter, through the door and into the future where I grew to adulthood completely unaware of my past," she said. "In that one day that has passed for you, I traveled forward in time seventy-odd years and have lived two and a half decades since." She paused, thinking, and pulled a pouch from her bag. Inside it was a syringe. She held it up. "This is erythropoietin. It is medicine from the future that stimulates the production of red blood cells and helps me to manage a little medical problem."

Unable to contain her curiosity, Cap'n held out her hand.

"I have a lifetime of memories, not all of them happy," Annie said, looking at Nathaniel as she gave the syringe to her little confederate. "I remember sitting alone in the corner during my eleventh birthday party, my godmother teaching me to shoot skeet, my adoptive parents' funeral, meeting Christian at the park"—she paused, glancing at Nathaniel—"and my first kiss." Still, he didn't respond, so she marched on.

"With the door's aid, I came back in time to Kansas City hours before my father was murdered. Our meeting in the park, Mr. Goodkin, and our meeting on Broadway, Cap'n, were on my first day in Kansas City as an adult. However, while I met the two of you, I was simultaneously asleep in a bassinet in my father's home in Westport."

Cap'n seemed to absorb the information as easily as a sponge, nodding throughout Annie's tale. Nathaniel swallowed mechanically, but to Annie's relief, he finally spoke. "There were so many peculiarities I couldn't explain," he said to himself, sitting on the edge of the bed. He looked up as if about to say something more, but whatever it may have been died on his lips when Christian spoke up.

"Annie," he said. "What was in the letter?"

"Everything," she said. "With the least bit of imagination, Mr. Culler will figure everything out—that I am David Abbott's daughter, that my grandmother is a witness to the murder..." She took Cap'n's hand in hers, holding it gently while she looked in her eyes. "I wrote that my 'confederate' stole a money clip from Mr. Culler and helped me plant it on my father's body. It won't be hard for him to deduce who that is."

"Do you think he'll believe it?" Christian asked.

Cap'n lowered her feet and hopped off the bed. "He'll believe it." She stood up and faced Annie. "It's not safe here for you no more," she said.

"Me? What about you?" Annie's question was full of apologies, guilt, and the memory of the mementos she and Cap'n had found in Mr. Culler's office.

Cap'n's laugh had a sarcastic ring to it. "I can run rings around him, but you need to disappear," she said. "And the way I see it, there ain't no better place to hide than through that door."

No one picked up where her comment left off, so Cap'n removed her cap, considering the menu of options. She placed the pillow against the headboard. "Miss Annie should head home soon," she said: "And I expect she'll be heading to the park."

When Annie nodded, admitting that she wasn't certain how to find it, Cap'n turned to Christian. "Can you get there from here?"

He looked at Edmond, then shook his head.

"What about you?" Nathaniel asked when she turned to him.

"I got something to do," she said, "but I'll catch up with you shortly."

Nathaniel looked at Annie, his expression unreadable, and nodded to Cap'n. "I'll take them."

While they had been making plans around her, Annie had quietly slipped to the desk and written a note. She folded the paper in thirds, placed it inside her bag, and retrieved her suitcase from the closet. "I suppose I'm as ready as I'll ever be."

As everyone headed for the door, Annie reached out to touch Nathaniel's hand. "Can you wait a moment?" she asked.

Unwilling to meet her eyes, he walked back into the room without comment.

Annie turned to Christian and said, "I'll meet you downstairs," closing the door before he could respond.

She turned, searching Nathaniel's face. "I suppose I should have told you before we…" Her voice trailed off as she sought the right words. "Before we kissed. I tried to tell you as we walked to the hotel, but—" She stopped, horrified by his expression.

His lips were bloodless, compressed in a chalky line, and he was breathing heavily, as if struggling against some frightful impulse. "You think that's what bothers me?" he asked.

She stepped back, holding up her hands defensively, as he leaped forward, grabbing her roughly. He shook her until her head bobbled loosely. "Annie!" he cried, shaking her some more. "Do you think that's what bothers me?" Suddenly, his features crumpled. "You're going someplace I can't follow." He crushed her against his chest, rubbing his face in her hair. "I can't bear it."

# CHAPTER THIRTY-TWO

## Good-Byes

Don't leave without saying good-bye!" Cap'n scampered down the street as Annie reached Christian's side, her arm entwined with Nathaniel's.

Before she was out of earshot, Edmond cupped his hands around his mouth and yelled, "Watch yourself!"

Without breaking stride, Cap'n spun around and, running backward, saluted.

When she turned a corner, Edmond folded his arms across his chest and turned to Christian, grinning. "She's something else, isn't she." As always, Edmond's inflection made it clear this was a statement, not a question.

Annie laughed quietly as she sorted through the pair of messages left in her inbox.

Dear Miss Aster:

Mr. Langley accepts delivery of the door and will have it shipped to the San Francisco location as you requested, though he did express some confusion as to how you were made aware of a store that won't be opening until this fall.

Sincerely,
Thomas Gophe, Manager, the Broadway Hotel

Attached to the message was a receipt signed by Mr. Langley. Annie wondered for a moment what his future ascendant, the surly owner of the Antiquarian, would say if he knew of her shenanigans. She started to laugh again, but her smile quickly faded as she flipped to the second message.

Miss Aster:

Or should I say, Miss Abbott?
The first round goes to you, but the game is far from over.

Ambrosius Culler

Nathaniel was the first to catch the change in Annie's mood. "Annie?" he asked. "What's the matter?"

She handed him the note and watched as his face darkened. "We must get you to the park immediately," he said.

Christian was about to question Annie regarding Nathaniel's comment, but she rushed forward, grabbed Edmond's arm, and began a spate of trivial chatter, glancing back at him with a barely detectable shake of her head.

He held back, thinking he'd corner Nathaniel. Instead, he found himself on the receiving end of something he half expected and dreaded.

Nathaniel pocketed the note. "I'm going with her," he said. When there was no immediate reply, he repeated himself, looking very determined.

Christian shoved his hands into his pockets and looked ahead to make sure Annie was outside earshot. "You mustn't," he said. "It'll put Annie in the terrible position of having to refuse you." Before Nathaniel could protest, he added, "And not for the reasons you think. It's clear that she cares for you a great deal. That's the problem, strangely enough."

Nathaniel grabbed Christian by the arm. "How can love in any way be a problem?" he asked.

The question was inevitable and deserved an answer, but the story behind it was not Christian's to tell. "She refuses to be a burden to anyone," he whispered. Looking from Nathaniel's hand, wrapped firmly around his bicep, and into his eyes, Christian sighed. "She's an orphan, Nathaniel. She knows what it's like for those who are left behind." Having said that, he removed himself from Nathaniel's grip and, leaving the man to ponder his meaning, hurried to catch up with Annie and Edmond.

As they approached the pond, Annie slipped her hand into Christian's and gave it a squeeze. "Would you mind?" she asked, glancing Nathaniel's way.

After a few parting words and an embrace, Christian and Edmond made for the other side of the pond and a pair of stones.

Annie watched them leave and turned. Before she could say a word, Nathaniel put his hand over her mouth, holding it there until he could see the beginnings of a smile from the set of her eyes. Satisfied, he lowered his hand and wrapped her in his arms. As she laid her head against his chest, he rested his chin atop it, and looking out over the pond, he decided to test the waters. "Do you really think I'll let you run off without me having a say in it?"

"You're an attorney, Nathaniel. I could hardly keep you from it." Annie looked up, grinning, before settling back against his chest. "I have to go," she whispered, simultaneously fearing and hoping he'd press his suit and ask to follow.

Whatever else she might have said—ambiguous arguments, insincere denials—was forgotten as Nathaniel lifted her chin with a finger to caress her upper lip. He worried her mouth open with his tongue to kiss her with greater promise, his fingers snaking through the hairs at the nape of her neck. He stopped long enough run his thumb along the length of the vein that pulsed like a drumbeat and cupped her face in his hands to kiss her again.

A sudden gust of wind swept past, buffeting their bodies with cotton-ball clouts that stirred the surface of the pond. From behind them, Annie heard a series of rapid-fire crunches and broke away to see Cap'n pelting up the path.

"Wait up!"

Reaching their side, Cap'n dropped something in Annie's handbag and leaned over with her hands on her knees, panting. "It's…it's a mock-up of tomorrow's article," she said.

Annie turned to Nathaniel. He reached out, placing his palm on her cheek, and offered her a broken smile. He shook his head and turned to walk down the path.

She almost called out to him, but he disappeared behind a thicket, and it was too late. She closed her eyes, praying she'd made the right decision. After a moment, she opened them to look across the pond.

Cap'n followed her gaze to find Christian and Edmond sitting on a log, their backs to them. She straightened, smiled, and, uncertain what to do, looped a thumb through her suspender and started grinding the gravel on the path with the toe of her shoe.

Annie noticed there was a hole in it.

Finally, Cap'n said, "Well, I guess I won't be seeing you no more, huh?"

"Come with me."

Words are like rivers, constantly altering the landscape, and those three words produced a remarkable result within Cap'n, eroding the remainder of her distrust, the thin veneer of her self-reliance crumbling alongside it.

It was a considerable shift, but the only evidence of the change Annie witnessed was the fluttering of Cap'n's eyelids—that is, until she suddenly rushed forward, throwing her arms around Annie's waist.

Annie dropped to her knees and began to cry, as words and half words reflecting loss and love tumbled from her mouth, words she wished she'd also shared with Nathaniel. She rocked until both were able to regain their self-possession.

Cap'n stepped back to toy with the lace on Annie's bodice, then shook her head, smiling—her cheeks shiny and pink. "I can't," she said. "There's the gang to look after."

Annie nodded. "I know, I know, I know..." she said as she straightened Cap'n's cap. She struggled to her feet, studying the girl's face, committing it to memory. Then she withdrew a slim booklet from her handbag and held it out.

"What is it?" Cap'n asked, accepting it with as much grace as she could muster. She flipped through the pages before looking up into Annie's eyes, her own wide with shock. "Your checkbook?"

"And a letter of transfer."

Cap'n gawked at the sum and, in a gesture that reflected the shine beneath the spit, handed the booklet back to Annie. "I can't take it," she said.

"It's of no use to me where I'm going." Annie gently folded Cap'n's hand around it. "I can't give you back your mom—lord knows, I wish I could—but, one way or another, I am going to make sure you have a home," she said.

Cap'n took off her cap, her pigtails tumbling down her back, and fidgeted with its brim as Annie continued. "Listen to me," she said. "I don't know if what I'm about to tell you is wise. Tinkering with time has proven to be a tricky proposition. So, to ease my conscience, I'm going to give you a riddle to solve." Something in the tone of Annie's voice made the little hairs on Cap'n's arms stand on end. "I made certain Mr. Culler bet on the wrong horse." Annie raised an eyebrow and added, "And it's only a two-horse race."

Cap'n seemed confused at first. After a moment, she looked at Annie, her lips forming a perfect O to match the roundness of her eyes.

The wind chose that moment to pick up again. A gust swirled around them, lobbing a leaf into Cap'n's hair. It perched just above her ear, quivering erratically, as if it alone found the humor in goodbyes. Annie plucked it, watching as it dipped and swayed until alighting atop the pond. Sighing, she said to no one in particular, "It seems the west wind is calling me home." She reached for the cap and placed it on her tiny confederate's head. "You"—she brushed Cap'n's nose—"watch out for yourself."

"Bye," said Cap'n, the word popping out her mouth like a hiccup.

"Bye."

Finding no other excuses to remain and feeling a little lost, Annie touched Cap'n's shoulder and drifted toward the pond.

"Wait!"

Cap'n pounded after her, stopping a few feet away, suddenly too embarrassed to look Annie in the eye. She took the cap from her head and worried it into a tube, clutching it to her chest. "This was Pepper's," she said. "He gave it to me when Fabian made me Cap'n." She held out her hand, offering her greatest treasure.

Annie took it in both of hers as if it were the Eucharist. Wise enough to know that there are some gestures you can't ignore, gifts you can't refuse, she reverently placed it atop her own head.

Cap'n nodded, giggling at the sight, and gestured for Annie to kneel so she could rework the brim. She whispered in her ear, "Don't forget me."

And then she was gone, running down the path—a jackrabbit in overalls.

When Cap'n had disappeared from view, Annie broke down. Loss hurts, and hers was doubled. Blotting her eyes with a tissue, Annie circled the pond to the log where Christian and Edmond were seated.

Christian stood to give her a hug. "You okay?" he asked, staring at the cap atop her head.

She looked across the water, then back to him. Without a word, she crossed the lawn to stand before a pair of boulders draped in night-blooming jasmine and altissimo roses.

Christian and Edmond stood behind her to stare at the gateway through which they'd stepped into Kansas. The sun was sitting in the sky at that perfect angle, illuminating the flowers in such a way that they seemed to create a border of fire around the stones.

"Is it going to take us home?" Edmond asked.

"It brought us here," Annie said. It was the best she could offer.

"That's great, but did you book a round-trip ticket?"

*Thank goodness for Edmond*, she thought. She looked across her shoulder, grinning at his attempt at levity, and stared at the stones with the honeysuckle halo. "Let's find out," she said. Hooking her arms around both Edmond's and Christian's like Dorothy with the Scarecrow and the Tin Man, she led them through the brush between the stones.

When their heads stopped spinning, they found themselves looking around a very familiar place—Annie's kitchen.

She closed the back door and peered at the clock above the sink. "Well, we're home. The question is when?"

"I can answer that," said Edmond, looking stunned. He pointed to the breakfast table where a set of chattering teeth bounced across the surface and over the edge onto the floor.

Annie leaned over to pick them up, looking first to Christian, then Edmond as the toy slowly wound down in the palm of her hand. She set it aside before settling into the breakfast nook to unfold the sheet of newsprint Cap'n gave her. It was identical to the yellowed clipping from the Antiquarian, but she could now read the text made illegible by age. The paper reported that the money clip was found in her father's hand and that Culler was wanted for questioning. Even better, there was no further mention of the elderly woman who had been seen leaving Abbott's home.

Scanning through the remainder of the article, she found the other item she was looking for:

> Even more chilling is the fact that nothing has been discovered regarding the location of Annabelle Abbott, who appears to have disappeared into thin

air. The case of the missing daughter is turning out to be more mysterious than Mr. Abbott's murder…

"Thin air," Annie whispered. "I suppose that's exactly what I did."

Christian read the article from over her shoulder while Edmond wandered across the room to raid the refrigerator. He laid his hand over her tapping forefinger to get her attention. "Mission accomplished. Elsbeth's off the hook. What's next?"

Annie stood and peered out the kitchen window, noting that one of the solar lamps she'd installed the year before had fallen over. She wandered over to rest her hands on the sill. "Christian?" she asked. "Don't you find it odd that we can see my English garden from here, but only Elsbeth's back forty the minute we step outside?"

He joined her at the window as a flash of iridescence zipped across the pane. "Look, a hummingbird."

After the bird caromed over the fence and out of view, Annie turned to Christian. "What's next? I think you should go home and get out of your play clothes while I write to my grandmother."

Edmond closed the refrigerator door and caught Christian's eye. He shook his head slowly. "The bad guys?" he mouthed and began applying mustard to slices of wheat bread before heaping deli meat and some cheese on top.

Taking the hint, Christian turned, leaning against the sill with his arms crossed over his chest. "Annie, I'd rather we stay here tonight, if you don't mind."

"Is this about Mr. Culler and his odious friend?" she asked. "How do you propose they find their way to San Francisco with the door safely tucked away and under guard? The only other way to get here is through a pair of stones they know nothing about, or a misplaced house in the middle of a wheat field."

Far from certain that Mr. Culler lacked the cunning to ferret out Elsbeth's address, Christian started to protest, but Annie cut him off by pushing him toward the breakfast nook. "Eat up and let me get on with the business of writing to El. She needs to be warned."

Edmond passed out the sandwiches, along with potato chips, sliced tomatoes, and lemonade, and the three set to it with gusto, not having eaten all day. Wiping mustard from his hands with a napkin, Christian watched Edmond clear the dishes and broke the silence. "Leave your cell phone on," he said.

CHAPTER

# THIRTY-THREE

## A Bad Investment Decision

### MAY 30, 1895

The secretary for the investment division of New York Life was stewing in her juices, or, as her daughter would put it, "positively wild." Her anger was so palpable that the night guard and janitor, usually up for a good conversation, were keeping a wide berth.

Mr. Adcock, her boss, had once again left early to meet the head of the division at the Gentleman's Club where they would no doubt smoke their expensive cigars, sip their twenty-year-old port, and congratulate each other with a slap on the back. The liquidation of Mr. Culler's orders and subsequent purchases in Tesla Electric—as well as the run Mr. Adcock had created by talking up investment opportunities with the company's elite clientele who were more than willing to jump on the insider bandwagon—had surpassed their quarterly quota, spelling big commissions, not that she'd see a penny of it.

She slammed her desk drawer closed and began sorting through carbons while assigning the two men their proper roles in the animal kingdom. The head of the division was definitely an orangutan—a gluttonous, obtuse orangutan—while Mr. Adcock was a... What was he? He was a weasel, that's what he was—a corporate-climbing little rodent who'd step over anyone's back to reach the next rung. His avariciousness was going to land him in hot water one day, and she was going to buy a front-row ticket for the show. Take

Mr. Culler, for example. No one in his or her right mind would handle *that* man's money. He was a wolf, and Mr. Adcock was going to get bitten one day.

It tickled her sense of the ironic to know that Miss Aster had pulled a fast one on them. She wasn't sure how, but she was certain that neither the head of the division, her boss, nor Mr. Culler was going to be very happy when Miss Aster's high jinks saw the light of day. An unhappy wolf meant a hungry wolf, and when wolves were hungry, they hunted weasels.

So it was with a feeling of grim satisfaction that she saw Mr. Culler stride through the entry as if on cue, his posture broadcasting that Mr. Adcock was on the menu.

He wandered directly to her desk and tapped it with his forefinger. "Is Mr. Adcock in?"

The secretary looked up from her desk with a smile, determined to squeeze as much entertainment out of the exchange as possible. "I'm afraid he left early today," she said. "You might find him at the Gentleman's Club with our division head. Perhaps I can help?"

"Not unless you can explain why my cash account is empty."

"Oh yes," she said, sorting through several files. She withdrew a stack of carbons from one, holding them out for Mr. Culler. "Mr. Adcock left these for you."

"What are they?" he demanded as he snatched them from her hand.

"Your sale and purchase orders, of course."

The corner of Mr. Culler's left eye spasmed at her response. It was the work of only one muscle, and a tiny one at that, but it was enough for the secretary to confirm her suspicions. She'd obviously poured a little gunpowder on his day and decided it wouldn't be complete without lighting a match. "The ones delivered by your secretary, Miss Aster?" she added sweetly.

The explosion took place out of sight—in Mr. Culler's gut—but the secretary was certain it had packed quite a punch, judging from the silence that followed.

It took a supreme effort of will for Mr. Culler to marshal his expression, as he'd experienced a disconnect—a flutter of uncertainty—while considering the possibility that he was simply outmatched by Miss Aster. He quickly discarded the notion, making a pretense of examining the carbons, all the while deciding his next course of action.

"Thank you. Tell Mr. Adcock that I will follow up with him very soon."

He marched out the building and onto the street, just as the evening edition was being delivered to the corner stand. It landed in a heap of paper and twine, the headline reading "Suspicious Shift in the Abbott Murder."

Mr. Culler looked up as Mr. Danyer arrived—surprisingly calm. "Get the horses."

"I thought we were going to Pawnee by train."

Mr. Culler pointed to the paper. "Change of plans."

# CHAPTER THIRTY-FOUR

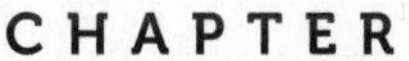

## Into the Frying Pan

Elsbeth was having a difficult time of it.

She could hear the kitten mewling under her cabin but couldn't see it anywhere. Two had already been collected and were resting in a large crate sitting by the rocker she'd filled with hay. Looking under the floorboards with her back end wagging in a most undignified fashion, Elsbeth was finally able to nab the rogue kitten before it could back farther under the steps. She held it up with one hand as it spat and batted at her with its paws.

Cackling as she walked onto the porch, Elsbeth said, "You are a feisty little one, aren't you? Noisy too. I'm going to call you Bristle." Holding it up, Elsbeth added, "A boy... Makes sense." She wandered into the cabin and placed the little gray-and-black ball of electric fur into the crate.

Ordinarily, Elsbeth would have left the kittens under the porch. Their momma would be more than capable of taking care of them. However, she'd found a dead cat by the road, and the kittens had been mewling for more than a day. These kittens were clearly orphaned, and it tickled Elsbeth to take care of them—especially since she and Annie had traded barbs on just such a topic.

She dropped heavily into her rocker and reached for a basket of yarn as Bounder, the great-great-granddaughter of Tom's favorite hunting dog, ambled over to see what all the fuss was about. Bounder sniffed at the kittens, prompting Bristle to stand on his back legs, waving his front paws like a prizefighter. Undaunted, Bounder nudged him with her muzzle, and Bristle tumbled over backward, only to right himself and get ready for another go.

As Bristle straddled Bounder's snout, hissing and clearly thinking she would shortly succumb to his death grip, the dog looked morosely at Elsbeth, who said, "Don't look at me. Solve your own problems." So she did. Stepping delicately into the crate, Bounder circled a few times before settling down with her body wrapped around the kittens. Bristle, who had tumbled onto his brother and sister, hissed one more time for good measure, then, thinking better of it, started to knead at Bounder's belly.

Elsbeth placed the basket of yarn in her lap and was beginning to wade through its contents when she heard a low rumble. Looking over to see Bounder staring at the window, she lowered the basket to the floor and eased herself out of the rocker. Pushing the curtain aside, she noticed a cloud of dust and the faint outline of what appeared to be a horse as it worked its way up the road toward her cabin. *Well, that didn't take long*, she thought.

She stepped over to the crate, petted Bounder on the head, and went to the closet to unwrap Tom's old shotgun. Fishing the cigar box from under the floorboard, she loaded a couple shotgun shells into the double barrel, stuffed another handful into the pocket of her frock, and eased back into her rocking chair to wait.

Elsbeth glanced uneasily toward the door when Bounder's hackles started to rise. "Easy now," she said.

The dog gazed at her mistress, then lowered her head to rest on the corner of the crate with a quick huff of air.

Mr. Culler directed Danyer to the side of the cabin and headed for the front door as soon as they saw the rusty mailbox with *Grundy* painted on it. When Danyer was in position, Mr. Culler tethered his horse, unclasped the holster of his gun, and knocked on the door.

There was a scuffling sound and the dull clank of a metal latch releasing. The door opened a few inches, and a shotgun snaked out to tap Mr. Culler on the forehead, causing him to look almost cross-eyed as he tried to focus on the barrel. He heard the click of a trigger being cocked as a disembodied voice floated from inside the cabin.

"If this were a rifle, I'd try parting your hair down the middle and not lose a minute's sleep if I missed. Now turn around and head back the way you came."

"Madam, please!" Mr. Culler could barely see the little woman peering through the sight of the shotgun. "Is this how you treat all your guests?" he asked.

Elsbeth threw the door open and took a quick step forward into the door frame, firing a shot that cracked through the air, causing Mr. Culler to stumble back with a hand to his ear. It came away with blood on the fingertips of his riding gloves.

"Is that more to your liking, *Mr. Culler*?"

Called out, he smiled and started to lower his hands.

Elsbeth cocked the second barrel with a quick swipe. "You lower those hands any farther, young man, and I'm going to blow a hole in your britches so big you'll need a ladle to take a piss." She lowered the barrel, training it on the area in question.

Mr. Culler's arms shot up. "Please, call me"—he flinched as she nudged his privates—"careful!"

"Son," she said, prodding him a second time. "I'm more likely to call you a mortician, if you don't do as I say." She looked over his shoulder. "I hear you come as a team. Where's your lackey?"

Mr. Culler stole a quick glance to his left. As Elsbeth followed his gaze, a hand snaked out from the right and grabbed her gun by the barrel.

She let out a scream, and there was an explosion of sound as the shotgun missed its target, shredding a hole in the eaves of the porch above the door. Mr. Culler ripped the weapon from her hands, shoving her into the cabin so hard she fell against a wall—her spectacles tumbling from their perch and onto the floor. He wandered across the threshold with Danyer, as always, shadowing his steps, while checking the barrel of the gun to make sure the shells were spent.

He tossed the gun onto the table, along with his riding gloves and jacket, and turned to study Elsbeth as she fumbled about for her glasses. Kicking them out of reach, he slid down with his back against the wall until he was sitting next to her. He draped his forearms over his knees, letting his eyes wander across the room. "Charming." He slapped her leg affectionately. "I love what you've done with the place."

Bounder, growling the minute Elsbeth hit the floor, chose that moment to let out an ear-shattering bark, and Mr. Culler reached for his holster.

"Down, girl," said Elsbeth as she struggled to get up.

Bounder let out a shrill whine and settled into the crate.

"Where are my manners?" Mr. Culler stood and dusted off his pants. Reaching under her armpits, he lifted Elsbeth and deposited her roughly into the rocker. "You will behave now, won't you." He wagged his finger. "No, don't respond. That wasn't a question."

He fished a letter from his pocket and dropped it onto her lap. "It's from your granddaughter," he said. "She sends her love, by the way." Grabbing the armrests of the rocker, he leaned in so close that Elsbeth caught an overpowering whiff of tobacco mixed with stale cologne. "What a tangled little mess we have here. You, Miss Aster—or should I say, Miss Abbott, a dead man, and a door." Cupping her chin between his thumb and forefinger, Mr. Culler lifted Elsbeth's face until their eyes met. "Miss Aster has run me a merry chase. You should be proud."

He gave her chin a little shove and walked halfway around the rocker while running his hand along its rim. "The last few days have been most illuminating, though I still haven't figured out one thing.

It's my hope you will be able to shed some light on the subject." He crossed his arms on the back of the rocker, towering over her. "How did she learn to operate the time-travel conduit without instructions?" he asked.

Elsbeth motioned for him to lower his head and said, "I have some carbolic toothpaste in the back and an extra brush. It may not move the conversation along any more quickly, but it'll certainly make it more pleasant."

A current ran across Mr. Culler's face and down his arm—not that Elsbeth could see it. He shook his hands loosely. "I see," he said. "I was hoping that you would be more…pliable." He gave the rocking chair a nudge and began to search the cabin.

"What exactly are you looking for, Mr. Culler?" asked Elsbeth.

Peering in a cupboard above the stove, he said, "It's obvious that you and your granddaughter have communicated. It's also obvious she knows how to operate the door. That suggests to me that either you or she has my late business partner's diary." He looked over his shoulder. "Perhaps you can save me the trouble?"

"Were you dropped on your head as a child?"

Ignoring the taunt, he said, "Letters then?" Seeing that he'd scored a hit, Mr. Culler added, "Oh, come now. I showed you mine. Now show me yours."

When Elsbeth remained intractable, he sucked air between his teeth. "You disappoint me, Mrs. Grundy." He wandered to the back door and glanced outside before motioning to Danyer. "Will you be so kind as to see if there are some chairs in the barn," he said under his breath. "I think that we will be spending a bit more time with Mrs. Grundy than anticipated."

He watched Danyer make his way across the yard, then stalked over to stand in front of Elsbeth.

She closed her eyes as he leaned in, his tobacco breath steaming her cheeks. "Don't toy with me."

At close range, she couldn't miss the shift and boil of his features.

Quickly as that, his face settled back into a blank mask. But in that moment, Elsbeth knew what she was dealing with. She whispered, "Lord have mercy," following his gaze as it settled back on the crate.

He tapped it a few times with the toe of his boot and looked at Elsbeth, his mouth curving in a wicked smile. "Let's leave him out of it, shall we?" He reached in, picked up one of the kittens, and walked over to the stove, setting it on a burner. The kitten lowered to a crouch, mewling, as Mr. Culler checked the contents of the oven belly. Finding it empty, he grabbed a couple logs from a basket in the corner, looking up in time to see Danyer walk in empty-handed, his face turning dark.

Anticipating a scene—Danyer had an inexplicable soft spot for kittens—Mr. Culler scampered to the door with his hands held out placatingly. He guided Danyer onto the back porch, where he found himself pressed against the wall, flinching against the expected aggression. When none was immediately forthcoming, he opened an eye to find Danyer staring at him—his face, as usual, a blank canvas.

Sighing in exasperation, Mr. Culler adjusted his collar, then leaned over to speak quietly in Danyer's ear. "Just a little persuasion, Mr. Danyer. That's all. Don't embarrass me in front of Mrs. Grundy." He glanced through the door at Elsbeth, who was listening to the muffled exchange with obvious distaste. "I wasn't going to harm it, honestly," he said, turning back to his associate.

Whatever else Mr. Culler was going to say was immediately forgotten when Danyer pointed across the wheat field. Striding past the watering well, Mr. Culler spied a purple Victorian house on the horizon. Even at a distance, he could make out an unmistakably red door blazing in the Kansas sun. Taken aback, he looked at Danyer, who nodded in agreement, then wandered over to the well to collect a coil of rope before stepping inside the cabin.

Elsbeth didn't move a muscle as Mr. Culler dropped the kitten in the crate and sauntered behind the rocker to whisper in her ear. "It seems you have a reprieve." He began securing her arm to the rocker, looking up occasionally to roll his eyes at Danyer who sat on the ground at the edge of the crate with a kitten in his lap.

Mr. Culler repeated the exercise with Elsbeth's other arm and both legs until she was effectively trussed, then motioned for Danyer to put the kitten down and follow him outside. They stood on the porch, taking in the peculiar sight, then walked through the wheat field to pause at a picket fence surrounding a rose garden. The door—their prize—sat at the end of the pathway. There was no mistaking the unique hue and perplexing carvings. This was the door that Abbott used in his magic show.

Even so, they hesitated. Both were uneasy. For neither Mr. Culler nor Danyer was a particularly courageous man. They were resourceful. They were mean. But their fortitude was based upon the certainty of an outcome for which they had stacked the cards in their favor. Walking through that door would be as uncertain a prospect as they had ever encountered. In the end—spurred by greed—Messrs. Culler and Danyer swung the gate open to walk up the gravel pathway to Annie's home.

Unaware of her guests a few paces and a century away from her home, Annie sat at the rolltop desk writing a letter to El. While she had written to her several times since returning from her misadventure two days ago, the letters had been primarily of the "Let me know you're okay" variety. It was time, she decided, to ask her grandmother's opinion regarding a certain gentleman. She heard a faint sigh, like air released from a balloon, coming from the back of the house and laid down her pen, looking nervously in the direction of the kitchen. Acutely aware of every wheeze and mumble put off by the house since she'd returned home, Annie strained to hear other telltale sounds, but there was nothing more.

She picked up the pen and twiddled it in her fingers as Mr. Culler and Danyer crept through the back door and into what Mr. Culler decided could have only been dreamed up in an opium-induced fantasy from Alice's Wonderland. There was a switch on the wall, and like Alice with the bottle, Mr. Culler couldn't help himself. He flipped it, flinching when recesses in the ceiling cast the entire room into brilliant illumination. There were strange metallic objects riddling every surface that took his likeness, morphing and melting it into ugly caricatures, before throwing it back at him.

He looked away, not being a fan of reflections, and headed for a doorway, slapping Danyer's hand as he reached for something. It was a conical gewgaw that appeared to be filled with coffee beans. But again, temptation overcame Mr. Culler. He opened the lid and smelled them. Replacing the lid was not easy, and he used a little more force than intended. Quite unexpectedly, the beans bounced in a noisy frenzy, and he knocked the object over, watching stupidly as half-ground beans spilled over the counter and to the floor.

In the other room, Annie leaped from her chair, her heart thumping. She threw open the desk's center drawer and grabbed a letter opener—a frightful thing she'd purchased at a garage sale, only to later learn that it was a British no. 4 spike bayonet from the early 1940s. She clutched it to her chest as her eyes darted around the room. Stealing across the floor, she plucked her cell phone and house keys off the table in the foyer, dropped them into her purse, and hurried to the front door. She'd released the bolt and was easing the door partially open when she heard a very unwelcome voice.

"You should have sold the door to me when you had the opportunity, I'm afraid."

Annie caught a glimmer of sunlight coming from outside as the door slowly swung shut, barring her escape. A hand reached over her shoulder and threw the bolt closed, leaving Annie with only two options. Not being a quitter, she chose the second. Chancing a glance at the arm blocking her escape, and before indecision rendered her immobile, Annie pivoted recklessly and buried the letter opener in the soft meat of Culler's shoulder, screeching hysterically. Startled by her own audacity, she met his eyes and, lacking other avenues of escape, dashed up the stairs just out of Danyer's reach, knocking over a decorative table holding a large vase.

Mr. Culler gurgled in outrage before the pain registered, at which point he let out a bellow. As Danyer gave chase, Mr. Culler clenched the letter opener in his fist and tugged at the handle—his hand vibrating with fury. There was initial resistance, as if his flesh didn't want to give up the blade, but then it began to ooze outward. As the tip slid from his shoulder, the skin closed over the wound like Jell-O. Three counts later, it began to discharge a stream of blood. He tossed the letter opener aside and, alerted by a deep, resonant thumping noise, looked up the stairwell to witness Danyer, a table, and a vase tumbling over one another down its length.

Leaping out of the way, he watched in morbid fascination as Danyer landed in a heap on the hardwood floor at his feet, the vase careening down the stairs to land on his gut. It knocked his breath out before rolling quietly onto a carpet runner at the base of the stairs where it spun lazily to a stop.

A phone plummeted over the railing, the receiver bouncing up and down on the coiled cord.

Wheezing, Danyer picked himself up and leaned against the wall by the stairs.

Mr. Culler gritted his teeth as he pressed a kerchief against the shoulder laceration. "Are you well?" he asked.

Danyer coughed, running a hand across his mouth as he nodded.

"Good, because I'd like you to check on Mrs. Grundy," Mr. Culler said. Certain that Danyer would object, he added, "I know it's your place to deal with unpleasantness, but I'm feeling uncommonly motivated."

Danyer expressed disapproval with an animal-like grunt, but lacking a rebuttal that didn't include his love affair with brutality, he made himself scarce, even as Annie threw open the utility room door, frantically scanning for something with which to defend herself. Her eyes locked onto a fire extinguisher. Ripping it from the wall, she rushed out of the room and stole down the hall to her bedroom, where she peered out the window. With the garage occupying the first floor, she was essentially thirty feet up.

She looked over her shoulder at the stairwell before backing into her bedroom closet and closing the door, then set the fire extinguisher aside to put her eye to the keyhole. A repetitive thud tickled at the edge of her hearing, and Annie spun about wildly before realizing it was the throb of her own heart. She whined in fear and frustration and pressed her fist over her mouth to dampen the noise while bracing her other hand against her thigh.

A single, lucid thought broke through her panic, and Annie wrestled the cell phone from her purse, attempting to punch in a number.

"Shit. Shit," she whispered, as it began to slip from her sweat-slick hands. She squeezed, causing it to emit an electronic squeal. Roughly pushing her hair out of the way, Annie flipped the lid shut to disconnect the line, reopened it, and tried to punch in the correct code using her thumbs, saying the numbers out loud in quick gasps. "Eight, six, seven—"

The ringtone of an incoming call startled her, and the phone tumbled from her hands to rebound off the wall and land inside one of a pair of stiletto heels. She wasted precious seconds frozen in disbelief before grabbing the shoe to shake her phone loose. Jamming the shoe in a pocket, she punched in the numbers.

"Please answer. Please," she hissed.

The line connected and she cupped her hand over the receiver to whisper in short, hoarse bursts. "Christian, he's here!" she said. "In the house. Culler—"

"… come to the phone right now. Please leave your name and number. I'll get back to you as soon as I can. Have a good day. Oh, and wait for the tone."

She threw the phone against the wall with a shriek and slapped her thigh over and over in frustration. Unbelievably, she heard a beep. Snatching it off the floor, she whispered, "Christian, I'm in big trouble. Come—"

Her words ended with a scream as the closet door flew open. Reacting with fear-drenched speed, she grabbed the extinguisher, pulled the pin, and showered Mr. Culler from head to foot in white, foamy fire retardant.

He stepped back, thrashing his arms wildly about. She darted for the bedroom door, but he recovered quickly, diving for her legs. As he grabbed hold of an ankle, Annie stumbled and fell, banging her head on the floor as the stiletto tumbled from her pocket.

She rolled onto her back—pain lancing through the ankle in Mr. Culler's grip—and tried to yank free while kicking at his face and arms with the other foot. He released his hold, bellowing as the heel of her loafer grazed the side of his head above the ear, raking out a slice of skin.

Both shoes flew from her feet, bouncing against the wall.

Howling murderously as blood ran from the gash down the side of his head, Culler scrambled on top of Annie, clamping her legs together between his thighs. He reared up and slapped her hard across the face as she fought to turn over, then grabbed both of her flailing arms, pinning them to the floor above her head. As she struggled for breath, he smirked, slowly sliding his legs back to press the full weight of his torso against hers, a shudder of pleasure rippling down his body as he let out his breath with a very Danyer-like grunt.

He hunched over Annie—his shoulders knotted, his chest heaving—aroused by her helplessness. He grunted once more while slowly lowering himself to run his chin roughly across her cheek before locking his mouth onto hers. He kissed her savagely, breathing so heavily he almost whined.

Revulsion triggered another wave of adrenaline, and Annie bucked so violently that he almost lost his purchase atop her. Feeling his grip ease, she ripped a hand loose, seized the stiletto that had settled by her ear, and thrust her arm forward with a dreadful whimper to bury its heel into the wound in Culler's shoulder. She ground it back and forth, her face frozen in a rictus of hatred, until he howled and fell to the side.

Panting and light-headed, she lurched to her feet and stumbled down the stairs, only to trip over the cord holding the phone that was swinging from the railing. She crashed back and forth between the railing and the wall and tumbled into the foyer.

For a moment, she was as still as a corpse. Then her eyelids fluttered. Moaning, she opened them to see Mr. Culler lumbering down the stairs with a gun in one hand and his other fist pressed against his shoulder, the corner of his mouth rolled up into a sneer. He fired a warning shot.

"Believe me, there is nothing I'd enjoy more than slicing your neck from ear to ear, Miss Aster, but I think it best to put both hens in one coop for the time being."

Mr. Culler descended the remaining steps and nudged her with his boot. "Get up," he said.

As she struggled to her feet, he smiled sweetly and, with little warning beyond an explosive tremor rippling across his features, backhanded her across the cheek so hard she fell into the wall. "Move," he said, gesturing toward the back of the house.

When they arrived at the entry to the kitchen, she stopped, resting her chin on her collarbone.

"You know where we're going." Clutching his wounded shoulder, Mr. Culler prodded her in the back with the barrel of his gun.

Coffee beans crunched under Annie's bare feet as she stumbled across the floor. She stepped outside, squinting under the glare of the sun as she cupped her hands over her eyes.

"If you please," he said. After a second, less gentle prod, Annie started in the direction of the cabin with the muzzle of Mr. Culler's gun in her back, a single thought charging into her head like discharge coughing from an exhaust pipe. *The door repels bloodlines.*

Annie casually reached up to remove a hairpin, scraping it across the palm of her hand to draw several pearls of blood. Desperation left little room for doubt, and she whirled around to slap Mr. Culler across the face.

Caught off guard, he blinked. Laughing, he grabbed a fistful of her hair. Giving it a yank that brought her to her knees, her eyes watering, he said, "Perhaps I deserved that." With her hair still knotted in his hand, Mr. Culler wiped his face with the other hand and stared curiously at the blood on his palm. "Go on now," he said, lifting her upright by her hair.

They had left the wheat field for the grounds surrounding Elsbeth's cabin when Annie noticed a change in the air. The skirt of her dress clung to her legs, and she experienced the first wave of the telltale dizziness.

As they approached, the horse in the corral tossed its mane and started running around the perimeter, clearly agitated, while the pigs shifted from one side of the sty to the other in a restless display. A pair of crows landed atop the barn, watching them with flapping wings. A third perched atop the cabin roof, as still as if carved from its beams.

Annie braced herself as Mr. Culler reached for the handle to the back door of Elsbeth's cabin, feeling the ground jerk violently when his hand made contact. She found herself thrown to the dirt beside the well.

Recovering quickly, she jumped to her feet and dashed into the field.

Mr. Culler wasn't quite as quick on the draw. He shook his head and sat up, clearly befuddled. The shoulder wound had begun to bleed again, and dirt mingled with the blood on the side of his face—the last stubborn clumps of foam retardant still clinging to his shirt. He spat grime from his mouth, blinking stupidly as he watched Annie run across the wheat field. Gathering himself, he looked about, finding his associate peering from the cabin door. He wagged his hand in the direction of the field. "Follow," he rasped. Grabbing Danyer's collar as he passed, Mr. Culler added, "Alive."

Danyer stared at the rapidly diminishing figure running in the wheat, then turned to Mr. Culler, nodding. He set out after Annie, favoring his left leg.

When Danyer disappeared into the wheat, Mr. Culler grabbed his gun and plodded to the well. He drew a bucket of water and cleaned the wound above his ear and shoulder as best he could. Dipping a kerchief in the bucket, he scrubbed the grime from his face and hands before continuing on to the cabin.

His voice boomed as he threw the door open. "Mrs. Grundy!"

Elsbeth looked up from the chair to which she was hog-tied and squinted. Even from across the room she could tell Mr. Culler was alone. She panicked. "Where's Annie?"

That was the wrong question to ask. Mr. Culler stormed across the room and backhanded her with a palpable smack—another tactical error on his part. Bounder knocked him over before he knew what had happened, clamping her jaws around the meat of his calf and shaking her head so violently he flopped to the floor. Apparently, payback was not simply a two-legged concept. Mr. Culler howled and inched across the room on his rump, pulling the snarling dog with him, and reached for the gun that had been knocked from his hand.

Elsbeth shouted, "Bounder, out!" as Mr. Culler's hand closed around the handle. The dog released Mr. Culler's leg and leaped through the door as a gunshot splintered its frame.

Mr. Culler scrambled after the dog to release four wild shots from the porch as she disappeared behind the barn. Cursing, he limped to the bedroom, where he ripped a length of cloth from a pillow cover and wrapped it around his lower leg to contain the bleeding. He hobbled to the rocking chair. Spittle flew like scattershot from his mouth as he leaned over Elsbeth, dotting her cheeks with flecks of his derangement. “Now…I’m angry,” he said. He looked outside, calculating, and snatched his coat from the table before hobbling out the door to follow Danyer’s limping form.

# CHAPTER THIRTY-FIVE

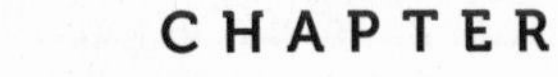

## And Out of the Fire

Annie rushed into the house, slamming the door behind her with her back. She breathed rapidly while going through the details of the plan she'd formulated as she escaped through the wheat field.

A strange alchemy was reworking the fear and helplessness that had so completely disabled her earlier, and the constant drip of adrenaline, like nitro in her veins, left her hyperalert, yet coolly detached.

Running was out of the question, as was seeking help—not with her grandmother in danger and time running out. It must end here, and she had to do it.

Her eyes darted from the counter to the cupboard, the solarium, and the entryway, recalling the outrageous pranks she and her godmother would play on each other when she was a little girl. One of her favorites was dubbed "mousetrap," and she intended to pull off a variation that made use of her knowledge of basic chemistry. The thing about mousetraps, though, was that they needed bait. And she planned to offer herself up as the cheese.

But first things first. She ran to the refrigerator, grabbing a vial and a thirty-gauge needle from behind a panel on the door. Pulling a healthy dose of the liquid into the syringe, she hiked up her dress to expose her thigh. Her quadriceps was covered in tiny, mottled bruises, some of them going yellow around the edges. She chose an unblemished spot and injected the solution before tossing the vial and syringe in the trash.

That done, she ran to the counter to collect a rubber ladle and a ball of twine from a utility drawer, tying off the latter to the former through a hole in the handle. She looked around, drumming her fingers on the counter, then threw open the cupboard door below the sink. She grabbed several items, placing them on the countertop—a large Mason jar, an emptied jar of jam, a bottle of window cleaner, and a plastic jug of Clorox.

Working with rapid, nervous movements, she poured the window cleaner in the emptied jar of jam and Clorox in the other. Capping the lid to the first, she dropped it inside the half-full Mason jar of Clorox and sealed its top. Tucking a rolling pin and the jar under her arm, she started across the room but paused, turned around, and looked back toward the kitchen sink. She wandered back to peer into the utility drawer a second time and seized a final item that she deposited in her pocket on the sly, almost as if its existence was an embarrassment.

She navigated her way to the back side of the solarium and placed everything on the floor. Circling back to the front, she used the ladle to wedge the solarium door nearest the kitchen open and stepped inside to grab a bag of cocoa-bean husks propped up by the door. She walked briskly around the room, emptying the bag. Darting to a small shelf, she seized a bag of fertilizer, ripped a hole in the plastic, and spread the granules evenly over the floor. With that done, she strode through the near door and around the sidewalls, playing out the twine attached to the ladle until she reached the door on the opposite side. It was a silly prank, she thought, but it would have a nasty kick.

Outside, Mr. Culler had caught up to Danyer as he opened the gate to the picket fence, wrenching his associate's dagger from its scabbard without missing a step. As they approached the door, he put his hand on Danyer's chest and shook his head.

Annie was propping open the far door of the solarium when he burst into the kitchen, bellowing her name. He dragged the edge of Danyer's blade across her kitchen countertop, creating a chilling sound reminiscent of a pair of charged socks being pulled apart. His eyes narrowed as he scanned the room.

At the sound of his voice, Annie ducked under the pane of glass at the opposite end of the solarium. She rested her back against the wall, letting its coldness soothe the fire that had been stoked under her skin. A thought edged into her head—*This is a bad idea*—but it was a little late for regret. The sound of coffee beans being crunched underfoot brought her back into the moment. Her head jerked up, following Culler's progress through the kitchen. She waited.

Despite her misgivings, the distinct pop of the cocoa husks brought a fierce grin to her face. She counted four steps, then reached for the twine, giving it a good yank. The ladle under the door at the opposite side sprang free, bouncing off the wall. As the far door slammed shut, she leaped up to throw the Mason jar into the solarium, shattering it on the concrete floor.

Culler stared at the shards of glass in momentary confusion, watching as rivulets snaked around the seed husks to disappear down the drain in the cement floor. Looking up, he saw Annie standing in the open door at the far end of the solarium with a rolling pin in her hand, a strange smile on her face. He roared, lunging for her as she heaved the door shut and slid the large metal bolt in place. She backed away, watching as he crashed into the door with a heavy thud, its impact absorbed by the metal struts.

While he pounded impotently, Annie stepped forward to observe him, as if he were some ape in a cage.

Unnerved by her calm, he went still, returning her gaze. His eye twitched once, then he shrugged, turned, and lazily wandered to the far door. He reached for the doorknob. As it came off in his grip, he turned to watch her shake her head. "Should have gotten that thing fixed," she yelled.

Throwing the doorknob to the ground, he slowly made his way

over to stand in front of her. He sneered contemptuously as his hand thrust up to clank the dagger against the glass, holding it in place with his open palm. The glass chirped and stuttered like a deathwatch beetle as he rubbed the knife slowly up and down against the pane. His eyes were dead, but his message was clear.

They stood face-to-face, inches apart, and Mr. Culler opened his mouth to breathe heavily on the glass. He scrawled the word *whore* in the resulting fog.

As the word faded, he coughed once and rubbed at his eyes. He reached for a handkerchief, only to pause when he noted Annie's peculiar smile. It was out of place, and his mind ticked off a warning. She pointed over his shoulder, saying something he couldn't hear. He coughed again, this time deep in his chest, and followed her gaze to an empty bag of fertilizer on the floor—*chemical hazard, combustible, poisonous fumes* written in bold print on its warning label.

He looked from it to the broken Mason jar, and his eyes widened in alarm. She waved, an impudent gesture, and followed his example by fogging the glass before writing a word of her own, spelling it backward so he could read it easily—*loof*. Once done, she held up her hand, slowly lowering the index finger with which she'd written and raising her middle finger in its place.

He coughed again, this time so violently that spittle clung to his chin, and stumbled to the center of the room, his throat and eyes on fire. Swaying, he dropped to a knee, the knife clattering to the floor, and leaned against a wrought iron table to keep from toppling over. He began to scratch at his throat.

Annie turned to leave as Mr. Culler slowly folded over the table like a leaking tire. She only caught his final act of desperation from the corner of her eye.

Screaming, she knelt reflexively, covering her head as he hurled the table—an explosion of glass scattering overhead to ricochet off the far wall and cascade around her.

Before she could grab the rolling pin that had scuttled across the floor, Mr. Culler reached through the broken pane and grabbed her by the hair. Taking in huge bites of air, he wound her hair around his hand and wheezed, "I'm…going…to…peel you like a grape."

She arched her back, trying to ease the pressure as she reached for his wrist with one hand, her other hand scouring the floor until she came across a large piece of glass. She raked it across Mr. Culler's forearm, slicing open the palm of her hand in the process. Blood sprayed from his gash in a delicate arc to splatter across her cheek. She raked again and again, creating crimson spumes, until he released her with an agonizing howl. Scrambling across the floor on her belly, Annie got within a hand's breadth of the rolling pin as Mr. Culler crashed through the broken pane and yanked her to the side.

"You bitch," he bellowed as he rolled on top of her, wrapping his hands around her neck. He started to squeeze even as he lifted himself up to a sitting position, straddling her body. His forearms were whipcord strong and slick with sweat, and Annie couldn't get a grip, not that it mattered. With mass and leverage on his side, her bucking and squirming were useless, becoming more pathetic until finally she reached up to place a trembling hand on his chest. It kneaded weakly over his breast pocket before reaching to the ceiling. The fingers splayed briefly, trembling, then her arm fell limply to the side.

Mr. Culler continued to squeeze, his face expressionless, even as sweat beaded on his forehead, and the muscles in his back and neck bunched and quivered. After a moment more, he released his grip, taking in a shuddering, almost sensual breath, and shifted his weight to get more comfortable. Telltale bruises, like livid sausages, were already starting to form on Annie's neck. Satisfied, he removed a pair of surgical scissors from his pocket and peered at her face. Giving it a light smack, he said, "Wake up,

Miss Aster," and watched as her eyes began to roll from side to side under their lids.

She gasped, not so much from the lack of air, but from the memory of his hands around her neck. Her hands flew up, clawing at his eyes, but he caught one in midmotion, and while she looked on in horror, waved the surgical scissors with his other hand. "This might be a bit premature, but I wanted you to watch the show." As he forced her pinkie between the blades, he added, "This is going to hurt...a lot."

"Yes, it is," Annie replied as she shifted her weight. A hum, like a current coursing through a wire, traveled up Mr. Culler's torso, causing his back to arch in a spasm and his jaw to lock before he collapsed to the side.

Pulling herself out from under him, Annie raised the Taser that was in her skirt pocket. "Welcome to the twentieth century, asshole."

She threw the Taser aside and began kneading her neck. Retrieving the rolling pin, she crawled to Mr. Culler's side, watching dispassionately as his muscles seized, sending him into a full-body cramp. She struggled to her knees, lifted the rolling pin over her head with both hands...and froze.

There comes a moment, a precise instant, when your next move redefines you, erasing everything before it. You are a tablet upon which the future course of your life awaits instruction. This was Annie's moment. As she knelt with the rolling pin hovering above Mr. Culler in judgment, prepared to snuff out his inhuman light, Christian's face appeared in her mind's eye and she began to sob. It started as a little thing, a hiccup of sorrow, but as her exhaustion mounted, it overcame her, and she broke into tears.

Even so, there was a job to finish. And despite the kinks, it was still going according to plan. She looked down, allowing malice to etch her features one more time, and shuddering in revulsion, slammed the pin down with all her strength, connecting with the meat of Culler's thigh just above his kneecap. "That'll leave a bruise," she said under her breath.

"Wake up, Mr. Culler."

Ambrosius moaned, cracking open an eye to see a trio of images that eventually merged into the figure of his associate. Mr. Culler closed his eye and swallowed thickly. As Danyer leaned over to shake him, Mr. Culler grabbed the offending arm and croaked, "Don't do that." He extended his hand, allowing Danyer to help him to his feet where he teetered for a moment, his muscles still rebelling under the influence of Miss Aster's electric device. His head was pounding.

When Danyer opened his mouth, Mr. Culler held his hand up, motioning for silence. Hearing nothing, he took a single step toward the living room before reaching for his leg with a gasp. "Bravo, Miss Aster." He pulled out his gun, motioned for Danyer to follow, and limped through the living room.

Entering the kitchen, he noticed that the back door was ajar and turned to Danyer, curiosity turning into something more urgent. "Did you leave the door open?" he asked.

Danyer shook his head, staring at it suspiciously.

"She's going for her grandmother! Damn!" Mr. Culler exclaimed. "If they get to the horses, we're lost."

Danyer ran to the back door with Mr. Culler limping behind him. He turned to say something, but Mr. Culler's leg seized up and he stumbled, sending both of them crashing through the door.

The dead silence that followed was soon broken as the pantry door creaked open, and Annie peered into the kitchen. Seeing no one, she crawled out of the cupboard to close the back door just in time to hear a banging noise at the front of the house.

"Annie!" Christian shouted, bursting through the front door. "Annie! Where are you?"

They found her in a pile on the kitchen floor. Her hair was a mess, a spray of blood was on her face, and she was covered in dirt. She was pressing a dish towel against the palm of her hand, and her body was trembling.

"Annie!" Christian hurried over to kneel in front of her while he looked madly about the room. "I'm so sorry. I just got your message. Are you all right? Did Culler do this?"

Annie nodded—tears forming parallel streaks of grime on her cheeks—and pointed to the backyard.

Christian and Edmond scrambled for the door. As they yanked it open, Annie screamed, "No!" They turned to face her. "No." She shook her head and gathered herself. "I reset it."

# CHAPTER THIRTY-SIX

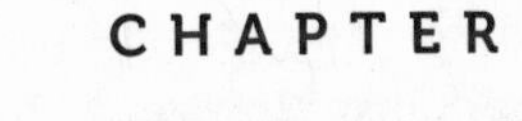

## Curtain Call

Something was wrong.

Mr. Culler sensed it immediately. He picked himself up from atop Danyer to look around but could make out very little in the dim light. The only thing he could say for certain was that they were not in the rose garden behind Miss Aster's house.

They appeared to be in a living room. The shades were drawn and the only sound to be heard was a barely audible drone. As they stepped farther into the room, flies—hundreds of them—lifted from the floorboards, swarming around the two men. Culler stared at the stain that had attracted them and began to speak softly so as not to aggravate the pounding in his skull. "That damn woman," he said.

Danyer turned, making his plodding way back to the door through which they had tumbled, but Mr. Culler grabbed his arm. "Not just yet," he said. He tightened the tourniquet on his leg, checked the state of the cuts on his forearm, and turned to stare at it. "We killed a man for that," he said.

The air seemed to close in with Mr. Culler's comment. Then, as if the silence had been stretched to the breaking point, twin explosions cracked through the darkness. Mr. Culler jerked involuntarily at the sound, blinking in confusion at a stain spreading across Danyer's chest. He looked down and dropped to his knees. There was a stain on his chest to mirror Danyer's. He covered it with his hand, looking up when he heard the tread of shoes on wood.

A match was struck, its flame bobbing and flickering before merging with the glow of a gas lamp.

A figure emerged from the shadows.

"You!" exclaimed Mr. Culler. He wagged a bloody finger, his mind struggling to make sense of the image resolving before his eyes. He coughed, and a fine red mist sprayed from his chest, settling to a gurgle that leached into the cotton of his shirt, the stain swelling to merge with the dried blood he'd acquired at the hand of Miss Aster.

Twirling a gun, the assailant walked across the room and sat on the sofa. He crossed his legs and rested his arms over the backrest, the gun dangling from the index finger of his left hand.

"But you're dead," Mr. Culler blurted.

David Abbott considered the bloodstain on the floorboards. "Indeed, it appears that I was." He lifted his head to return Mr. Culler's gaze. "It should follow then that I will be again. But who knows? At the present, I am very much alive." He lifted his chin. "It's your mortality we should be discussing at the moment."

Mr. Culler watched as Danyer lowered himself to the floor, bracing his torso with one arm, his unencumbered fist pressed into a bullet hole to slow the bleeding. "How can this be?" Mr. Culler asked. "I saw you fall. I watched as your blood spilled." He glanced at the fly-infested stain, heedless of the fresh one being created as his blood dribbled beneath him.

David leaned forward to confide in Mr. Culler. "I have no knowledge of it," he said. "You see, whatever you may have done in your mean, petty little way is yet to transpire for me."

Mr. Culler blinked. "I don't understand."

"Don't you?" David leaned back against the divan and managed to look almost offended. "It's quite simple, really. I was forewarned of your intent and skipped through time even as you knocked on my front door. I'm sure you know by what means." David turned to gaze pensively at the door standing in the corner. "But I must give my creation its due. It chose the perfect time and place for me. For here you are, and I've exacted my revenge for a murder that is yet to take place." He whispered, "It's my intent, even now, to cheat death, though"—his eyes lost focus as he tried to understand something that was just out of his reach—"I wonder…" He cut the sentence off, smiled, and returned to his dialogue.

"Death is the greatest illusion. Perhaps I've mentioned that before?" He paused, allowing Mr. Culler the space to respond. When none was forthcoming, he continued. "And am I not a master of illusions?" he asked. "You should know that your eyes can be betrayed by someone possessing the requisite skill. Think of this"—David extended his arms flamboyantly—"as my command performance. My final curtain call." He stood to bow before dropping back onto the divan with a chuckle. "I'll understand should you not feel compelled to applaud."

Pulling the gun from his holster, Mr. Culler pointed it at David with an unsteady hand, the mad spark in his eyes dulled by pain. "Not many people can boast that they killed the same person twice," he said.

David shrugged, throwing his arms across the back of the sofa. "To what end? Am I not already dead?"

Unruffled by the comment, Mr. Culler attempted to train the barrel of the gun on David, but it swayed and teetered across the intended target. Steadying the revolver with both hands, he focused on the gun sight and pulled the trigger. It clicked dully. With his mind on the weapon, Mr. Culler didn't notice as David flinched imperceptibly before a glimmer of a smile passed over his features.

Mr. Culler pulled the trigger again and again as David looked on with increasing mirth. Mr. Culler paused, puzzled. Then he remembered. A shot to warn Miss Aster. Another shot as Elsbeth's dog escaped through the door. Four more as it ran behind the barn. He'd emptied the chamber of his six-shooter and forgotten to reload.

He ran numb fingers over his gun belt.

David leaned forward and put his forearms across his knees to study Mr. Culler's actions.

The man's vision was becoming as unreliable as the legs that gave out beneath him, so he simply knocked a bullet from its loop on his holster and watched stupidly while it rolled across the wooden floor. He fished for it drunkenly before finally collecting it between forefinger and thumb.

Opening the cylinder to his pistol with a shake, Mr. Culler dumped the spent shells on the rug and tried to insert the bullet in a chamber but gave up when his hand spasmed and the room began to spin.

He smothered a cough. Feebly wagging the gun at David, he turned to his companion. "Mr. Danyer?" he asked.

David followed Mr. Culler's gaze, then turned back, entwining his fingers under his chin. "Mr. Danyer?" he said. "Oh yes, your hatchet man." After a moment, he dropped his head between his shoulders. Tears of laughter wet his eyes when he looked up, and his next words sliced through the room like a scythe. "There is no Danyer here."

CHAPTER

# THIRTY-SEVEN

## Danyer Reprised

Danyer returned Mr. Culler's stare, his eyes full of pity.

Something in his expression reminded Mr. Culler of his childhood—admissions he'd buried, confessions he'd never spoken. It struck him suddenly how much Danyer's eyes were a reflection of his own, almost like a mirror—the very things he avoided like the plague. Mr. Culler's eyes jerked toward David before resting once again on his partner. His whisper became husky, urgent. "Mr. Danyer!"

Danyer only shook his head in response, causing Mr. Culler's eyes to dilate as confusion gave way to panic.

In sudden comprehension, David said, "Ah, I see now. What a pitiful state of affairs." He walked over to crouch in front of Mr. Culler, canting his head to the side before following the man's gaze. He stood abruptly and strode across the floor.

Mr. Culler watched as Danyer averted his eyes, raising his arm as if to ward off the very devil himself, but David walked right through him as if he were made of vapor.

David turned. "You see? It seems that there never was a Mr. Danyer. And that makes you something of an illusionist yourself, Mr. Culler—a kindred soul." He crossed his arms. "It appears you've been doing your own dirty work all along."

Teetering and dangerously close to collapsing, Mr. Culler spoke with childish petulance. "You lie." He turned back to Danyer, the muscles of his eyes tight. "This is no time for your usual reticence, Mr. Danyer," he said and reached feebly for his associate, who simply shook his head and spoke words only he could hear. "I'm sorry, Mr. Culler."

Those words, sounding so final, broke the spell. Danyer raised his palm to his maker and faded away.

Mr. Culler blinked slowly, and his head rocked backward before he retrained his eyes on the spot where Danyer had disappeared. He screamed Danyer's name only to notice in some small part of his awareness that the sound rolled out of his mouth as a whimper. Stifling a sob, he repeated the same declaration over and over: "No. No. No—" as if his associate, his constant shadow, would be resuscitated by it.

Instead, his denial did something more insidious, unlocking long-suppressed memories and observations. Even as he tried to block them, to shove them back into his subconscious, they eluded his grasp and overwhelmed his mental barriers.

They blinked like tiny sparks before his mind's eye as they were lifted from his memory. Danyer's uncanny talent for going unnoticed in a crowd. His almost pathological fear of physical contact. His hesitance to speak in the presence of others. Their absolute disregard for him on the occasions he did. Sparks flew as a spool of scenes played out in Mr. Culler's mind—gaining momentum, swelling. Recent scenes involving Annabelle Aster, David Abbott, and Elsbeth Grundy burst like fireworks inside his head. He could recall no direct interaction or contact with Danyer in any of them. None.

A tattered valise leaped into Mr. Culler's consciousness—the one he kept at his side but never opened. In it were a duster, a Stetson, spectacles, and a costume beard that he donned from time to time to carry out his more vile tasks. Finally, as if to bind the images together in a single piece, a blinding light swept across Mr. Culler's inner vision as his memory trailed back to his childhood and to a case of the mumps that had left him sterile and his twin brother, Chauncey, dead from encephalitis.

A sigh escaped Mr. Culler's lips, and he found himself looking at David in shock. A flicker of movement captured his attention then, and his eyes wandered to his own torso.

At first, he thought he saw caterpillars inching up his trunk, but his heart thudded, trying to escape his chest when he recognized the various pastel shades. Terrified, he tried to brush them off—the pinkie fingers of his victims—but they merely melted into his clothes, resurfacing seconds later to continue their progress.

He clawed at his shirt, trying to rip it off, but they continued their irrepressible march, crawling up his neck and into his mouth, between his teeth and gums, under his tongue, down his throat, filling him to the gagging point until he was certain he'd drown in the flesh and bones of his victims. Then, as the chug of his heart became labored and his blood thickened like porridge, Mr. Culler arched his back and screamed, dying not so much from his bullet wounds, but from fear.

David watched the man's fit with a strange detachment, wondering what plagued him. When Mr. Culler's life finally fled, David leaned forward on the sofa to rest his elbows on his knees, covering his head with the palms of his hands. He rubbed his temples with his thumbs, then stood up wearily and walked past the side table. A clock captured his eye. On an impulse, he paused to stop the hands and turn the clock facedown.

Satisfied, he circled the den and stood before the red door. He hesitated for a moment. Staring at the dried bloodstain and struggling with the inevitability of what was to come, David began to tap out instructions on its facing. He paused and, with a look of rebellion, altered the commands at the last minute. As he disappeared into the doorway, David smiled while considering a dim prospect. *I may elude it yet.*

The door flew open and he stepped back into the room only

to hear tapping coming from the front of the house. Startled, he pivoted sharply and looked at the door. "I didn't—" He added in a whisper, "Ah, you are a fickle friend."

Gathering his resolve, David said, "I am the master here, and I determine the outcomes." He walked through the living room but slowed to reflect on the fact that his former associate had vanished and the room was free of bloodstains. It was as though the murders—his and Mr. Culler's—never happened…or had not yet happened. Time had been placed out of order yet again by the peculiar faculty of the door.

Remembering his unwelcome guest, David's gaze flicked to the closet and its cantankerous contents. He lifted his hand and waved, a sad gesture, before crossing the room. A moment later, his voice carried weakly from the foyer. "What an unexpected surprise. Please come in."

# CHAPTER THIRTY-EIGHT

## Sacrifices

### JUNE 3, 1995

That cut looks pretty bad," Christian said, examining the laceration on Annie's hand.

"Christian, listen to me." Annie put her good hand over his and squeezed to get his attention. When he looked up, she locked on to his eyes and said with deliberate slowness, "He said he was going to put both hens in the same coop."

"Who? Who said that?"

"Mr. Culler."

It took a second for the words' meaning to sink in. "Elsbeth!" he gasped.

Annie nodded. "I can't go," she said. "You know I can't."

He shook his head firmly. "Annie, no, not now. I need to get you to a doctor. And what happens if—"

"I'm fine!" More gently, she repeated, "I'm fine. And I don't think Mr. Culler will be coming back."

"You don't know that!" He closed his eyes, starting over. "That hand needs stitches, and you've been seriously traumatized. Your health is delicate at the best of times. I'm not taking a chance."

"But, Christian, you—"

He was about to shut her down when he heard, "I'll go."

Edmond lowered to a crouch in front of them. "I'll go," he repeated.

Annie looked to Christian. When he nodded, she wrapped

the towel around her hand and struggled to her feet. The worry lines that had appeared on her forehead eased, and she embraced Edmond while taking care not to mark him with her blood. She stepped to the door and tapped out a complex pattern, watching from the corner of her eye as Christian drifted to the other side of the room. "Thank you," she said, turning back to Edmond.

He reached for the doorknob.

"Hey!"

Edmond looked over his shoulder to find Christian fussing with a drawer by the refrigerator. "Be careful," he said, glancing at Edmond from under his brow as he rummaged noisily through its contents.

The color returned to Edmond's face as he prepared a goofball response, but something in the moment, maybe something in Christian's remote expression as he said, "Be careful," stopped him. Edmond glanced at Annie, who regarded him with an apprehensive, hopeful smile. He looked back to Christian, who had chosen that moment to inspect a pair of scissors, and marveled yet again at the man's absolute willingness to lay himself open—to risk mockery—with such sincerity. And that he was able to do so with two simple words.

Ill-equipped to express what he'd learned in the blink of an eye, Edmond did the only thing he could think of. He disappeared through the door.

Annie closed it behind him and turned to regard Christian. She reached over, cupping her hand lightly against his cheek.

"What?" he asked, flustered.

"I didn't say anything."

Christian rubbed the heel of his hand against his brow and went to the pantry to pull a medical kit from the shelf.

While he washed her hand in the sink, Annie said, "You have a courageous heart, darling man."

Ignoring the comment, he began to rewrap her hand with gauze, but Annie was not willing to let him withdraw. "And you mustn't worry about Edmond," she added.

The comment surprised Christian, but he nodded stiffly before cutting several strips of tape with the scissors.

"You've given me a gift, you know." She watched as he placed them in parallel lines across her palm. "Hope."

Christian looked up from his task and searched Annie's eyes, clearly mystified.

She gathered her skirt and walked to the kitchen window, where she leaned against the sill. She beckoned to him and, when he joined her, took his hand in hers and said something unexpected—something that perhaps only the two of them could understand.

"You sacrifice too much. You always have."

If he suspected her meaning, he gave no immediate indication. Presently, however, the muscles around his eyes began to tighten, and the warm kitchen light played off a translucent line of moisture collecting on each of his lower lids. "I don't—" He swallowed, looking for words.

Annie shook her head, interrupting before he could say anything else. "Listen to me." She sounded almost angry. "You can spend all the time given you on earth making terrible sacrifices for others who, without ever having walked in your shoes, presume to decide right and wrong on your behalf—people who want the world only on their terms, parading their intolerance, their ignorance and narrow-mindedness while calling it morality. Or you can set your own course." She held his hand up. "You know right and wrong, Christian—better than anybody. It's your particular genius."

Confused and very near to tears, Christian attempted one last little rebellion. "Annie, you're d-doing it again. I duh-don't…understand."

It was clear from his broken speech that she'd upset him, but it couldn't be helped. Some things simply needed to be said. She leaned over and kissed him on the cheek. "Yes, you do, my dear, dear friend. You're a good man with a huge heart. Let it choose for once."

Christian had been running his arm across his nose. He froze, staring at her, then at his shirtsleeve—horrified.

"Promise me you won't sacrifice your happiness for something as cheap as acceptance," she begged as he backtracked to the refrigerator. "Find your courage, Christian. To hell with everyone else."

He nodded, though not sure why, and reached for the refrigerator door. At first, he thought the sigh was simply air decompressing as he opened it, but the sound came from behind him. He turned in time to hear Annie say, "Christian?" She stared at some blood on her hands while a steady stream of red ran over her lips and down her chin and neck to bloom across the cotton appliqué of her bodice.

He stormed across the room as her eyes rolled into the back of her head, but he was one step too slow. Her head bounced off the counter ledge with a sickening crack just as he wrapped his arms around her to break the fall. She collapsed into his lap, even as he fished his phone from his pocket, dialing. "I n-n-nuh—" He hit the back of his head against the counter. "Need!" He gulped air and continued. "An am-ambul-lul-lul—"

Precious time was being lost as he tried to communicate with emergency services. He became frantic, sobbing into the phone. And by the time the operator could successfully repeat the address and dispatch a vehicle, several more minutes had been lost. He hurled the phone aside and, gathering Annie against his chest, started rocking. "I'm sorry, I'm sorry, I'm sorry," he cried, over and over again.

While Christian streaked recklessly down Dolores Street in Annie's Mercedes, following the ambulance, Edmond leaned over her picket fence to stare at a cabin in the distance. A warm breeze ruffled his hair. He glanced up. A crow circled overhead before descending to perch on the letter box—its eyes turned to him, button-black and impervious. It cawed, the sound eerie and mournful.

"Quite a day, huh?" Edmond said, not that he expected much conversation in return.

Indeed, the crow was unmoved by his question, and Edmond was reminded of his first conversation with Christian. Christian, the crow…who became an eagle that said, "Be careful."

Be careful.

Unlatching the gate, he trekked through the field—the rippling wheat making the sound of a broom sweeping sand as it slapped against his legs. Or perhaps a sigh. Regardless, with each step he took, the wheat whispered, "Be careful."

"Be careful of what?" he demanded, throwing his hands in the air. Was this about Christian? There were things Edmond had yet to say to him, because he didn't know how, but that was a poor excuse and a dangerous game to play. Regardless, it was his choice, and the wheat field could go stuff itself, he decided. "Busybody!" he yelled.

The only response was a distant caw. He looked up to see the crow spiraling overhead. Then he looked to his destination. As in his dream, Edmond's depth perception was on the fritz, and the cabin appeared to loom larger, rather than closer, as he approached.

The spell broke when he crossed in front of the barn and heard a wet whimper. A dog appeared from around the corner and let out a bark. "Hey, big fella." Edmond squatted down as the dog trotted up to sniff him. Its tail started to wag as it put both front paws on his shoulders. "Okay, okay, that's nice," he said as it licked his face. Standing up, Edmond wiped his sleeve across his cheek and stared at the cabin.

The dog jumped back, barking excitedly, then loped to the porch. It looked toward the closed door, then back at Edmond, and began to whine as it scratched at the door frame.

Edmond dusted off his pants, stepped onto the porch, and opened the door. A wisp of a woman sat motionless in a wooden rocker on the far side of the room, her arms and legs bound.

Looking at Edmond with rheumy eyes, she said defiantly, "Alone again, Mr. Culler?"

"Mr. Culler?" responded Edmond, uncertain whether to move. "Oh no. No! I'm not Mr. Culler."

Elsbeth strained to focus on her visitor, but the sun shining behind him left little more than a silhouette. She heard a familiar bark, recognizing Bounder circling his legs, and relaxed. Bounder had good instincts. "Well, don't just stand there. Either shoot me dead or untie me, for heaven's sake!" she said, grumbling as Edmond leaped into motion. "And don't step on my spectacles!"

The words brought Edmond skidding to a stop. He spotted her glasses on the floor by the cabin wall. Cleaning them with the tail of his T-shirt, he placed them across Elsbeth's nose.

She looked him up and down. There was something fundamentally different about this one, though she couldn't put a finger on it. An impossible notion entered her mind, but all she said was, "You aren't from these parts."

Chuckling at the understatement, Edmond agreed. "No, ma'am, I'm not." He began to untie her arms as Bounder made a nuisance of herself, trying to crawl into Elsbeth's lap. He said, "My name is Edmond Marden," before dropping a bomb. "Annie sent me."

Elsbeth stiffened. "Annie?" she said.

"Yes."

"Is she safe?"

He nodded. "But she's a little shaken up. Christian's taking her to a doctor."

Elsbeth patted Edmond on the arm with the hand he'd just freed. Then, in an apparent effort to reassert her gruff exterior, she adjusted her spectacles and cleared her throat. After a pause, she opened her mouth, but Edmond anticipated her next question.

"A nasty gash on her hand that will need stitches," he said as he unbound her legs. "Other than that, a few bruises. She went through quite an ordeal, but she should be fine. It's you I'm worried about," he said, glancing at her cheek.

The blood had started to pump back into Elsbeth's hands,

causing a dull ache. She rubbed her wrists, saying, "What of Mr. Culler?"

Edmond shrugged. "Annie did something," he said. "Don't know what." He freed her legs, then examined the side of her face. "That doesn't look so good."

Elsbeth wagged her hand, dismissing his concern. When he straightened up to cross his arms, she gave him her best schoolmarm stare, the one that had a 100 percent success rate in quelling mutiny among her students. He merely rolled his eyes.

"Fine," she groused. "There's some willow bark in the cupboard above the stove. Stir a teaspoon or so in a cup of water."

Edmond combed through the cupboard and pulled out a tin of white powder. He held it up to Elsbeth. When she nodded, he poured a small amount in a cup, added water, and stirred. "Bottoms up," he said, handing it to her.

Shaking her head, Elsbeth mumbled something about being treated like a child, but she knew when she'd met her match. She downed the tea, peevishly holding the empty cup out for Edmond's inspection.

"Where would you like me to begin?" Edmond said, satisfied.

"Did Mr. Culler—" Elsbeth broke off midsentence at the soft rapping that came from the front door.

"Are you expecting company?" Edmond asked.

"Expecting company? Me?" Elsbeth stood and made her way to the table, grousing. "No, I'm not expecting company," she said. "Indeed, I've had more company this day than in years. Most of it unwelcome."

Edmond grinned as she hobbled across the floor. She seemed to have recovered quite nicely. The rap on the door became more insistent, and Edmond, looking for a weapon, grabbed a broom.

"What are you going to do? Sweep them into submission?" Elsbeth asked. "Put that down before you get yourself hurt." She was a step ahead of him anyway, having grabbed her shotgun and loaded it with a pair of shells. "I'm getting entirely too much use out of this thing today," she muttered. She stepped past him and made her way to the door. Cracking it a bit, she slid the barrel through the opening. "State your business and make it snappy!"

"Madam! I apologize for the intrusion, but I assure you I mean no harm."

Edmond's head jerked when he heard the voice. He reached over and slowly lowered Elsbeth's rifle. Then, to her surprise, he pushed the door wide open and yelled, "Nathaniel!"

# CHAPTER THIRTY-NINE

## Out of Options

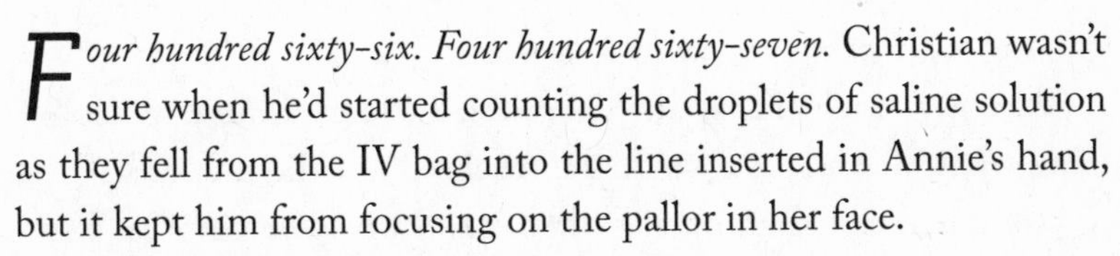

*Four hundred sixty-six. Four hundred sixty-seven.* Christian wasn't sure when he'd started counting the droplets of saline solution as they fell from the IV bag into the line inserted in Annie's hand, but it kept him from focusing on the pallor in her face.

*Four hundred sixty-eight.*

Her vein had collapsed after the nurse's first few attempts to insert the needle into her forearm, so there was now a butterfly needle in the back of her hand, as well as an ugly bruise radiating out from the insertion point.

*Four hundred sixty-nine.*

Christian leaned back in the chair, rubbing the exhaustion from his eyes. He ran his palm over a day's growth on his chin, then pulled at his cheeks before leaning forward to rest his elbows atop his knees. She looked so frail in her hospital gown—her joints so pronounced, like a little girl—and he wondered why he hadn't noticed before.

What kind of a friend misses something like that? Annie had always seemed so substantial in her mounds of crinoline and sateen, he thought defensively. A better friend would… His mind emptied. What would a better friend do? That he even had to ask himself the question implied that he'd failed as one. Annie deserved better, deserved someone better.

*Four hundred seventy-two.*

He released his death grip on the guardrail and shook his hand, hating himself for his thoughts.

*Four hundred seventy-four.*

Solitude…that he understood. He was good at it. And he understood the whys and wherefores behind his. There was no blame. Few people had the patience for his sluggish speech, the tortoise-like roll of his words. Invariably, they wanted to finish his sentences, take ownership of his unexpressed ideas, and move on. Everyone was in such a hurry.

Except Annie.

*Four hundred seventy-nine.*

Except…Annie. He studied her face. Then, without even realizing what he was about to do, he reached over the rail, tucked a wayward tendril of hair behind her ear, and whispered into it. "I'm here," he said, his doubts gone.

Her eyelids fluttered as if in understanding, and he sat up, breathing deeply while he checked the clock on the wall for the time. There were some hard realities to face. Annie was sick, sicker than he'd thought, sicker than she'd led him to believe. He broke from his train of thought when she shifted restlessly, murmuring something in her sleep. He placed his hand on her forehead. That seemed to settle her, and she went still, breathing shallowly.

*Four hundred eighty-six.*

There was also their last conversation to consider. She'd talked about things—about Edmond and sacrifices and hope. And something else… He couldn't get to the heart of it. Even so, it made him anxious, especially the part about Edmond.

As if hearing his name in Christian's thoughts, Edmond appeared in the doorway. "How's she doing?" he asked.

Christian didn't even bother to look up. "She could have died by the time I got the fu-fu-fucking words out," he said, stuttering intentionally.

Edmond didn't need to ask what he meant. The message

Christian had left on his answering machine was agonizingly long, though it only managed to convey that Annie had been taken by ambulance to San Francisco General.

Christian looked up finally to find Edmond still standing outside the doorway. He held a spray of periwinkles that burst in a free-for-all of green and violet from a porcelain container shaped like a teakettle. *Annie's going to love that*, Christian thought, motioning Edmond inside. "She's sleeping."

Edmond stepped across the room and placed the arrangement on the sill. "That's a lot of blame to take on all by yourself," he said while he pinched off a few tired buds. "Imagine what would have happened if you *weren't* there."

Edmond's point was clear, and Christian acknowledged it with a quick nod, though it didn't really make him feel any better. "Annie's uncle came by earlier." He looked up, meeting Edmond's eyes. "I didn't even know she had one," he said. "The man's in shock. Annie never told him a thing."

Edmond grunted, grabbed a chair from the corner, and carried it across the room to sit next to Christian.

Neither said another word—keeping vigil.

At around the five hundredth drip, Edmond put his arm across Christian's shoulder and gave it a light squeeze. It was only meant as a little kindness, but the gesture seemed to break the membrane of Christian's composure, and he rocked forward, folding his arms tightly across his chest, his back rising and falling silently until a single, lonely sob broke from his lips.

It was a heartbreaking sound, but Edmond knew as well as anyone the healing power of a good cry. He'd been there time and time again. And he knew what had to be done. He pulled Christian even closer, intending to repeat the usual platitudes, beginning with "She's going to be fine," but there was a rap at the door, and Christian leaped to his feet, wiping the tears from his eyes before a word had been said.

"Is this a bad time?" asked the attending physician as he poked his head in the door.

Edmond cursed silently, wanting to tell the doctor to come back in a few minutes, but Christian shook his head, and the doctor entered the room, flipping through the pages on his clipboard. He leaned over the bed to check Annie's pulse against his watch and made a quick notation before peering under the bandage on her forehead.

"As best we can gather from Annie's blood work," the doctor said, "an enormous amount of adrenaline was dumped into her bloodstream. Her delicate system couldn't cope and simply shut down." He paused, letting Christian digest the information. "Do you know anything about that?" he asked.

"There was an intruder," Christian said. "When can she go home?"

"I'd like to keep her under observation for another day or so."

"Why?"

The doctor clicked his pen and slid it into his shirt pocket, a gesture Christian came to learn through experience meant bad news. "She's not doing as well as I would've hoped." He motioned for Christian and Edmond to sit. Taking the chair against the wall, he added, "She needs a bone-marrow transplant. And soon."

"Are you sure?" It was the only thing Christian could think to ask.

"No, we're not," he said, shrugging. "We've never been sure. Her condition has characteristics of myelodysplastic syndrome, or MDS—a sort of preleukemia, but there are anomalies."

"If you're not sure, then why take the risk?" Edmond asked.

The doctor simply stared through Edmond, his expression promising more bad news. "She's run out of options." He stood and made for the door, only to pause. He turned around. "There's one more thing," he said quietly. "And I'm not certain it's my place to tell you."

Christian was fussing with the bedspread and didn't hear him.

Edmond touched his hand and pointed to the doctor.

When he had their attention, the doctor said, "Miss Aster's hemoglobin level was elevated—extremely elevated." The comment obviously puzzled them. "She's showing signs of an erythropoietin overdose."

"Epogen? Her medication?" Christian asked. "But why would she do that?"

"I was hoping you'd tell me," the doctor said as he leaned against the door frame. "Was she planning to enter the Tour de France?" he asked half-jokingly.

"What do you mean? I…I don't know what you mean."

"It gives you the stamina of a race horse." The doctor paused. "It also puts you at risk for heart failure," he added. "A risk Miss Aster is well aware of."

He grabbed the handle and started to close the door behind him but looked back over his shoulder. "What I'm trying to say is that whatever happened back there, at Miss Aster's home"—he jiggled the handle with his index finger before looking at Christian somewhat sheepishly—"she planned for it."

# CHAPTER FORTY

## Auntie Liza

A dream is a slippery thing, plucking and bending and toying with our memories, sometimes acting as a bridge between the living, the loved, and the loved no-longer-living, but more often than not acting as a lesson not quite learned. Yet, despite the enormity of a dream's purpose, this particular one happened to be nothing more than the necessary but gentle nudge that lifted a very sick young lady from death's slumber into a wakeful world.

"Wake up, birthday girl."

Annie didn't question the fact that the person belonging to that voice was long dead and opened her eyes, grinning as Auntie Liza ran a finger down her nose. She pulled the duvet over her head and squealed before peering out from above the covers to reveal a mound of flyaway auburn hair and a pair of hungry eyes. The day was only a few seconds old, yet already promised to be quite excellent, she thought.

"Have you given some thought to what you'd like to do?"

"Well," Annie said, shoving the duvet aside and putting on her most adult face. "Now that I'm eight and very nearly a grown-up"—she pursed her lips, glancing sideways at her godmother—"I think it's time I kiss a boy."

Auntie Liza grabbed a length of chiffon from the bed's canopy and tossed it around her neck, eliciting a giggle from Annie. She leaned against the headboard, nodding gravely. "I think that's an excellent idea," she said. "But—"

Something in the way Auntie Liza said the word *but*, drawing it out, was so impossible to ignore that Annie couldn't help herself. She sat up, toppling her pillows. It would never do to overlook Auntie Liza's suggestions. They were… She searched for the appropriate word. Singular? No. Exceptional? Inadequate. Avant-garde? Yes, that was it! That was just the most perfect word. Avant-garde.

"But," Auntie Liza continued, breaking Annie from her thoughts, "if you're willing to be flexible…"

"Yes?"

"How would you feel about a spitting contest?"

"A spitting—" Annie smacked her bedcovers. "I'd rather kiss a boy, if you don't mind," she said, not even trying to mask her annoyance. Annie knew her godmother too well, however. There was more to this than met the eye.

"Even if it's off the Empire State Building?"

"What?"

"Tonight, under the stars, so get dressed. The airport limo will be here in an hour." Auntie Liza turned on her heel and disappeared into the hallway, only to poke her head back in around the door frame a second later, grinning impishly. "And don't bother to pack. First stop, Bergdorfs!" she added.

That settled it. Boys would have to wait, Annie decided as she pelted into the bathroom.

The day was a deluge of firsts, from the flight—first-class—to stargazing from atop the Empire State Building, and Annie was full to bursting with happiness. Her new ballet slippers—autographed by Melissa Hayden, no less—dangled from the back of her chair, while five Bergdorf bags and a second edition printing of *Pride and Prejudice* rested at her feet. She was so transfixed by the kaleidoscopic stained glass ceiling in the Russian Tea Room that she didn't even notice the waiter until he flambéed the cherries jubilee. As the brandy burned off, Auntie Liza explained that the recipe was credited to Auguste Escoffier for Queen Victoria's Golden Jubilee of 1887.

Annie scooped a glossy mound onto her fork and took a bite. She closed her eyes, sighing, before saying the strangest thing. "This tastes even better than the first time I turned eight." She savored another bite. "Birthdays were never the same without you, Auntie Liza. Remember Sassafras?"

"That gorgeous piebald Arabian horse I gave you for your tenth birthday?"

Annie nodded, not thinking it the least bit strange to discuss something that wouldn't happen for two years as if it were a memory.

"I almost forgot about him. Your father was furious. Said I was spoiling you." Auntie Liza paused with the glass of Sauternes hovering under her lips. Her eyes crinkled. "Of course I was spoiling you!" She took a sip. "Sassafras was sent to a stud farm," she added. "I daresay that was one happy horse."

One by one, they took turns opening their memories together, precious little chestnuts, and Annie found herself asking, "And what about my fourteenth birthday when I insisted—"

Auntie Liza interrupted her. "I'm afraid I was in heaven by then, dear."

"Oh, that's right." Embarrassed, Annie swung her legs under the chair and stirred crimson curls of cherry puree through the melting ice cream. She smiled, her lips angled slyly, one eye half shuttered. "I know this isn't real."

"Of course you do. You're very smart."

"Then why are we here?"

"Just a little healing, dear. You were starting to slip, you see, and we can't have that. You have a difficult task ahead of you."

"What task?"

"Life, dear. Life. Now wake up. Christian's worried sick. He blames himself, you know."

# CHAPTER FORTY-ONE

## Plan B

With the all-too-obviously love-struck Nathaniel back in Kansas City, and word from Edmond that Annie was on the mend, Elsbeth was getting back to business as usual. She waved in the direction of the plume of dust kicked up by Amos's wagon as he headed back down the road to Sage.

Going inside, she began to put away the provisions he dropped off and noticed a copy of the *Sun Sage* in the bottom of the bin. Forgetting the remaining perishables, she grabbed the paper and dropped into her rocking chair. Bristle, never one to wait for an invitation, jumped in her lap, purring before he even settled down.

Unfolding the paper, she read the title of the lead article and froze. After scanning it, she picked Bristle up, grabbed a quill and paper, and walked over to her breakfast table. Dropping the kitten back in her lap, she began to write.

*Dearest Annie:*

*You'll find this article to be of interest.*

*I have no sympathy for the man. Anyone who delights in terrorizing kittens deserves his fate.*

*Love,*
*El*

Annie was in the solarium pruning when Christian burst through the door. He startled her so badly that she dropped the gardening shears onto a bottle of fertilizer, spilling the solution on the tips of her suede shoes. Accustomed to his talent for bedlam, she simply sighed and rubbed her cheek with her forearm, leaving a bit of soil on the side of her nose.

"You have mail," said Christian. "From Elsbeth."

Annie ran to the kitchen alcove, throwing the gloves in the sink on the way. She ripped open the envelope and breezed through the note before unfolding the enclosed article.

> A new chapter has been written in what may go down as the most bizarre murder case in Kansas City history.
>
> The body of Ambrosius Culler was found today in the very living room where he was suspected of murdering David Abbott. It was in the early stages of decomposition, a condition much maligned by a neighbor, Evillene McCready, who'd complained to the police about a strange odor coming from the Abbott estate the day before.
>
> How he got into the home, and why he is dead, remain a mystery that threatens to topple a few heads within the police force, including the chief of police himself.
>
> The cause of death appears to be two gunshot wounds to the chest. However, there were also severe lacerations above the left ear and on the right forearm, a puncture wound in the right shoulder, and an apparent dog bite on the right leg.
>
> A pistol, confirmed as having been owned by

> Ambrosius Culler, was found next to the body, along with six expired shells and a single bullet…

"He's dead," she said.

"Who's dead?" asked Christian as he snatched the article from her hand. He laid his hand atop his head as he read. "I can't believe it."

"I can."

Christian looked up, studying Annie's face. She spoke as if she'd expected the outcome. She'd been acting differently of late. He couldn't put his finger on it, but he was fairly sure it had to do with the Culler nightmare. That seemed obvious. It was equally obvious that she was hiding something. Before he could speculate further, she handed him Elsbeth's letter, stood up, and headed to the counter.

He scanned it quickly, chuckling despite his concern. "The man almost kills you, and Elsbeth worries about kittens."

"An inside joke," Annie said.

Christian went back to the article. "What about Danyer?" he asked, setting it aside.

Annie reached for her stack of linen napkins, wandered back to the breakfast nook, and sat down—looking pensive. "I don't think there ever was a Danyer."

"Annie, you saw the man!"

"No." She shook her head. "I saw *someone*," she said. "And as I recall, Edmond never actually saw Danyer at the auction house. He overheard a conversation." She started folding the napkins, while giving Christian a brief description of what she'd found at Mr. Culler's office—his curiosity cabinet, his "collection," and what she'd found in his closet. "Now that I've had time to think about it, I'm certain it was a costume beard."

"You aren't suggesting—"

"I *am* suggesting."

Christian stared at her blankly. "Split personality?" he asked.

She shrugged, a gesture that suggested they might never learn the truth, and marched upstairs with Christian just behind her. Reaching under the bed, she pulled out her old suitcase. It was already packed.

"You can't be serious, Annie. You just got out of the hospital. You're not well enough to travel."

She dropped it on the bed, wrinkling her nose as she inspected its contents. "I'm well enough for this," she said and disappeared into the bathroom.

Christian sat in the side chair, tapping his foot nervously, but he got up and walked downstairs as soon as he heard the shower water begin to hiss. Some thirty minutes later, Annie breezed into the kitchen wearing, oddly enough, a high-waisted sundress that reached to her ankles. It was a babbling brook of a piece—cornflower blue—and so airy it rippled in the air-conditioning.

She lowered the suitcase by the kitchen counter and wandered over to stand behind him at the breakfast nook. Before he could turn in his seat, she wrapped her arms around his chest from behind and placed her head against the side of his. "There's one more thing I must do to close out this chapter," she said. "I'll be gone a few days at most. Would you and Edmond mind terribly keeping an eye on the place?"

"But, Annie—"

"I have to do this," she said, silencing his protest with a kiss atop his head. "Is he still acting strangely?"

The question was about Edmond. "A little." Christian shrugged as he added, "I'll see you out." He stopped short when he saw her dress. Its color set her honeypot eyes ablaze, but it was her bonnet that made him grin. This one was another Annie classic—a lemon-colored safari hat that was adorned with a repeating pattern of pink and white roses. It was outlandish and, therefore, perfect.

Annie pulled the brim over her ears, bending a knee coquettishly just to get a rise out of him, then reached for her handbag and hurried downstairs to the garage.

Christian followed her with the suitcase, throwing it into the trunk as Annie turned the ignition over. He waved his hands in a vain attempt to clear the exhaust that burped from the car.

She rolled the window down. "Three days at the most," she said.

"Annie?" Christian placed his hand over the top of the window before she could close it.

The tone of his voice left her uncertain as to whether she wanted to meet his eyes. She gripped the steering wheel for support.

"Why didn't you end it? You know, when you zapped Culler. You had the rolling pin."

A shadow crossed over her face. "I was going to," she said after a moment.

"Why not then?"

"I suppose, in the end, it came down to you."

"Me?"

She nodded. "I was afraid—" Her voice broke, and she started again. "I was afraid you would never look at me the same way again."

Christian thought about the response before smiling in that particular way of his—confused, a little sad, yet deeply touched—then tapped his fist three times over his heart before pointing to hers.

She repeated the gesture.

As she pulled the car from the garage and disappeared from view, he pulled out his cell phone.

"Edmond here."

"She's gone."

"Well, you expected it. Did she say where she was going?"

"She didn't have to. She was wearing a sundress and espadrilles."

"So..."

"So, I'm going home to pack."

# CHAPTER FORTY-TWO

## Something Simple

Christian headed upstairs to Annie's living room, slowing when he spied David Abbott's threadbare diary on the coffee table. It made him uncomfortable, seeing it. It could well hold the answer to everything—uniting Annie with her grandmother, providing a donor for a bone-marrow transplant, and healing some old hurts.

He'd stared at it until he was blue in the face over the last few days and had yet to come any closer to solving the riddle of why Annie and Elsbeth's shared bloodline seemed to make the magic of the door go haywire. He sighed, deciding to give it another go. Sitting on the sofa, he picked up the diary and began to read through the notations, focusing on the entry from the thirtieth of May, 1894, where Abbott claimed he'd solved the bloodline riddle.

Christian emptied his head, and as he did, bits of conversations with Annie and Edmond and passages from the diary began to bump and collide until they formed a single piece—an answer. Before it could lodge itself in his brain, however, the pieces drifted apart. He clutched at the solution, trying to hold it together, but failed.

Frustrated, he pored through the diary in the hope that the elusive thought would surface once more. Getting nowhere, he picked up Annie's phone, put it on speaker, and leaned forward with his forearms on his knees, waiting for the familiar click on the other end of the line.

"Hey," he said.

"What did you forget? Wait, did you change your mind?"

"No, no. I had something for a split second. Now it's gone."

"What? What are you talking about?"

"I don't know for sure. Just bear with me. It has to do with the whole bloodline mess."

Christian's exasperation was plain to hear, so Edmond decided to pull in the reins. "Calm down and start at the top. What were you doing when the thought slipped to the surface?"

"I was reading the entry in Abbott's diary where he said he solved the problem of the bloodline."

"Yeah? So?"

"He didn't write his solution down. Don't you find that strange?"

"Well…didn't he want to keep it secret?"

Christian balled his fist in his hair. "Yes, but if he wanted it kept secret, why mention it at all? Why tease us by saying that the answer was within his reach and so simple?"

"I don't know."

"What are we missing?"

"Don't know."

Christian let go of his hair and sighed. He repeated the words out loud. "Something simple. Something within reach." His voice trailed off. Suddenly, he sucked in air, and his eyes widened. He started to laugh.

"What?"

"It can't be that easy," he said to himself. "But I think it is!" He took the phone off speaker and held the receiver to his ear. "Listen, do you remember what that crazy shaman specter said to you?"

"Of course. I'll never forget that."

"Good! Stay put. I'm coming over!"

"What's up? What are you thinking?"

"I'm thinking"—Christian paused to stare at the diary—"you're a lousy translator of Cherokee."

# CHAPTER FORTY-THREE

## Periwinkles and Sunflowers

Annie knew what she was going to do the moment she read the letter from El. Like Edmond, indecision was foreign to her nature. While not certain her plan of action was wise, she wasn't swayed in this particular case by wisdom. Annie was interested in closure.

She found herself on a plane bound for Kansas City while considering the hubris of Oscar Wilde. *I can resist anything but temptation.* Like him, she had chosen to succumb to it.

After picking up her luggage from the carousel at Kansas City International, Annie walked curbside and grabbed a shuttle to the rental car station. A half hour later, sitting in the car, she pulled out a map and a notepad with notes scribbled over several pages. At the top of the fourth page was a set of simple directions. She studied them before pulling out of the lot to follow the street signs to the on-ramp of the freeway where she was soon put into a trance by the metrical pulse of passing telephone poles. The sign for exit ramp 168 took her by surprise, and she churned up a little gravel from the soft shoulder while exiting onto the feeder road.

She pulled up to a stoplight and turned left onto the main street of a small roadside city. *Welcome to Sage* drifted across the marquee for a drive-through bank on the right. A neighborhood of brick, ranch-style houses to the left looked like a slice of Americana. Each was encircled by a chain-link fence and boasted one or more of the following: a Slip 'N Slide, swing set, trampoline, or inflatable pool. In one yard, an explosion of freckles, pigtails, and high-octane squeals played freeze tag in a brazen choreography of youth.

Driving past a strip mall, Annie pulled into a Sinclair gas station where she idled the car to speak to the mechanic.

"East?" he said. "I don't think there's much of anything out there but wheat. Sage Road is just past the next rest stop, but the entrance is blocked. You can't drive it."

Thanking him, she returned to the car and drove a few miles before pulling into the rest stop.

Parking her car by some picnic tables, Annie reached into the rear seat to grab her backpack. Hoisting it in place, she popped the floral-patterned safari hat on her head, secured the chin cord, and started walking in an easterly direction on a little-used dirt road. Unnoticed, a tiny flicker of black—a tear in the daytime sky—streaked overhead. It croaked once, and Annie looked up. Circling her in a lazy pattern, the crow broke off, flying east. *Five miles due east of Sage as the crow flies*, she thought, following it.

After a hike of half an hour, Annie stopped to slip the pack from her shoulders. She pulled out a bottle of water and a granola bar, scanning the landscape. The stark beauty of the wheat waving in the sun was broken by a grove of trees and the plume of dust kicked up by a tractor some half mile from the road. She was thinking about the heat and the enormity of silence when an unearthly sound broke her reverie.

Another crow, easily as big as a terrier, sat on a barbed wire fence not ten yards away, cocking its head sideways to stare at her. It flapped its wings several times while bobbing up and down on the wire before majestically lifting into the air. Annie never thought she'd admire a crow, but the bird was striking, with its silky, black feathers carrying a hint of violet in the reflected sunlight. It too flew east, and she scrambled to keep up, shoving the bottle and wrapper in her backpack as she walked.

Just as the unchanging vista started to become tiresome, Annie found herself gazing at a sign atop a post in the distance. She picked up speed and arrived out of breath. It read: *Welcome to Pawnee County, Kansas. Population 23,076. Five Miles Due East of Sage as the Crow Flies.* A rendering of the state of Kansas sat above the wording with the perimeter of Pawnee County outlined within.

It was not what she was looking for, but a dozen yards away, listing wearily to the side, stood another pole, marking where a barely recognizable path joined the road. On top was a solitary piece of wood three feet across by eight inches wide. The plank was bone-dry and looked like it would splinter in her hands. She could just make out the faded words *Crow Flies.*

Annie looked up the path, beyond a mailbox so rusty it was riddled with holes, and her breath caught at the first glimpse of her destination. Tired and missing several pieces of timber, it was a dilapidated shadow of its former self. Hearing a rustling noise and feeling a suggestive turbulence of air, Annie watched a pair of crows settle on the signpost a few feet away, bold as brass. She waved before walking up the path to the cabin.

The front door was askew, having broken away from a rusty hinge, and the overhang above the small porch had a large hole with splintered edges. Annie grabbed the doorknob and jumped back as the door clattered to the ground. Dust plumed upward, flaring in the sunlight that sprayed into the room from behind her.

She stepped through the door, coughing.

*This is not a home; it's a mausoleum,* she thought. It was bleak and colorless—a husk—and no echo remained of its former life. All the joy and woe of Elsbeth, Tom, and Beth Anne had dried up over the years and turned to dust.

Annie tried to picture the cabin as it might have been in another day and age. She circled the room once, then placed her palm on a wall, hoping to tease out a few memories. She closed her eyes, emptying her head. At first, there was nothing. Slowly, though, the cabin started to shake off its lassitude, sharing sounds from the four chapters of Elsbeth's life.

It began with the tinkling laughter of a little girl, bacon sizzling on a skillet, and voices exchanging love and contentment in wordless riffs that faded eventually to silence. Out of the hush, a dog barked in the distance, and whispered words—"Help him, Mommy"—lifted from the floorboards to be replaced by the somber tones of a eulogy: "Ashes to ashes, dust to dust."

Hurtful words battled prideful ones after that, and the finality of footsteps running out the door echoed through the cabin. Then, before the ghostly music could play itself out, it performed an uncanny finale. The sound was distinct and unmistakable. It was the creaking of a rocker as it swayed slowly back and forth in time to the rasping wheeze of a turned page—the sound of Elsbeth's loneliness.

It was almost more than Annie could bear, that sound, knowing there was nothing she could do to ease it. Love could be a painful thing, she realized, especially when family is suffering. And Elsbeth had spent far too many years as a member of the lost and lonely club. Annie might not be their patron saint, but she was certainly a sucker for them, having experienced firsthand how cruel people could be to misfits—the square pegs in a world of round holes.

She took her palm off the wall and opened her eyes, looking for the sound's source. And there it was, sitting under the windowsill, covered in cobwebs and dust. She wandered to it and sat down. Presently, she began to rock while considering the life of a schoolmarm in a cabin resting under the endless Kansas sky.

The chair's shadow had marched across several floorboards before Annie gathered herself. She grabbed her hat and stepped out the back door. Just off the porch grew four fiery sunflowers. She decided that the number was fitting—one for her grandfather, grandmother, mother, and herself. Searching the pack for her Swiss Army knife, Annie reached down and cut three stalks off near the ground. With the sunflowers in hand, she walked across the yard to pause at a ramshackle well. Resting the sunflowers on the ledge, Annie leaned over to stare into the void. "Hellooooo..." she called.

"Loooo...looo...loo...look," billowed up from the cheerless hole.

"Look where?" she asked. Dropping a pebble down the well, she turned, holding her hand over her eyes to cut out the glare of the sun and saw a wheat-covered rise in the distance. A gnarled old oak stood sentry on its crest.

Annie climbed the hill and looked about as a gust of hot wind threatened to make off with her hat. Placing her hand atop her head, she pirouetted slowly, like a porcelain ballerina on a jewelry box, as she memorized the sparseness of her grandmother's world. She scanned the horizon until the oak niggled at the periphery of her vision and she finished her climb.

She leaned against its trunk and saw what she had come across half the country to find—two small, wooden grave markers with wording burned onto their surfaces. The first read *Thomas Grundy, 1829–1867*. Catching her breath, Annie looked to the second. It read *Elsbeth Grundy, 1832–1927*. That last number held the answer she sought, the source of her temptation. Content, Annie released her breath. Fodder for a fool. But she decided that the world could do with a little more foolishness. She laid a sunflower next to each grave and sat down in the ample shade of the tree to look out over the cabin before digging pen and paper from her backpack.

Dear Nana:

I like that word—Nana. Let me know if it suits.

I'm writing this letter from Pawnee County, Kansas, while sitting under an old oak tree that is kind enough to offer me some shade. Just to my right is your grave, and I'm looking back on a forlorn little cabin. Clearly it misses your company.

There were sunflowers growing off your back porch. I hope you don't mind, but I gathered a few and laid one next to your marker. It didn't seem right that I should visit you for the first time without a gift, and a sunflower seemed to me to be the perfect reflection of the occasion.

I have so many questions for you, Nana. I hardly know where to begin. You told me once that honeysuckle was my mom's favorite flower. What about yours?

Mine is the periwinkle.

Grandfather's marker is here as well. And even though hers is not, I've laid a sunflower between your two markers for my mama. For Beth Anne. For Florence.

Your old rocking chair is still in the cabin. I sat in it briefly, imagining you rocking back and forth while reading my first correspondence. I laughed at the memory. You were so insulted, and we got off to such a questionable start.

You'll be happy to know that the well is still out back, at least a good part of it, and I gladly confirmed that there were no remains of drowned kittens, only a few tumbleweeds.

Please don't be cross with me for coming here. I'm struggling so badly with the space between us and did what I could to spend a moment in your company.

So, I will sit here and share this beautiful day with you for a while before heading home to drop my letter in the same letter box sitting at the bottom of the rise.

I didn't intend to travel across half the country to write so little, but I suddenly find myself at a loss for words. Only three remain.

I love you.

Annabelle

Annie put the pen down and looked back at the cabin. A shadow drifted over her shoulder as if pushed along by the breeze. Without looking up, she said, "How did you know where to find me?"

Christian sighed, sliding down to sit beside her. He leaned over to whisper into her ear. "Where else would you go?"

Leaning her head against his shoulder, Annie spied a pair of crows drifting on the air currents above the barn. "I'm glad you're here."

Christian didn't need to respond. He watched the crows spiral up and away.

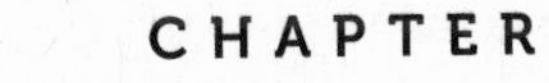

# CHAPTER FORTY-FOUR

## Wrapping Up Loose Ends

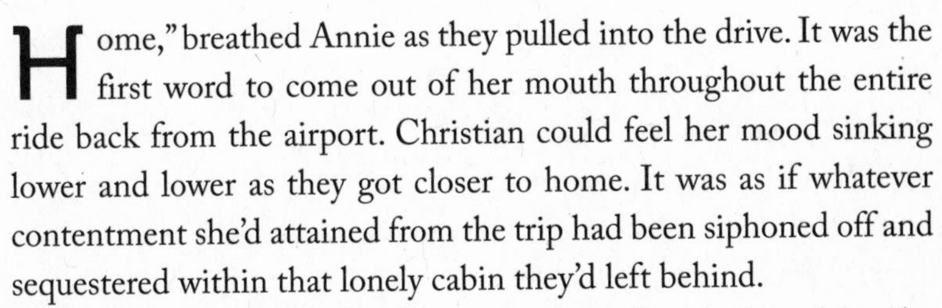

Home," breathed Annie as they pulled into the drive. It was the first word to come out of her mouth throughout the entire ride back from the airport. Christian could feel her mood sinking lower and lower as they got closer to home. It was as if whatever contentment she'd attained from the trip had been siphoned off and sequestered within that lonely cabin they'd left behind.

He was afraid that Annie might have been infected by the cabin's loneliness, destined to waste away like some Dickensian character over time. *That's good*, he thought as he turned off the ignition. *Maybe I should write it down before I forget*. He popped the trunk and glanced through the jagged edges of light cutting through the rear window at Annie, feeling guilty that he'd used her misery for some less-than-literary inspiration. She hadn't moved from the passenger seat, and the refraction left her looking broken—only half there.

He started to organize the luggage under his arms and in both hands while Annie stared at the front of her house. Through the confused light of the pane he saw her shake her head and step out of the car. She followed him up the stairs to the front door, where he waited for her to pull out her keys, but she appeared to be in another world. Lowering the luggage, he fished his set from a back pocket and unlocked the door. Reorganizing the suitcases, he nudged the door open with his foot and carried the luggage into the entryway.

Arranging the bags next to the stairwell, Christian looked back at her. She was hovering in the doorway uncertainly and seemed terribly, terribly lost. "I'm going to run you a bath," he said.

Annie looked at Christian, and the corners of her mouth lifted with a hint of humor in them. Her smile broadened as she placed her palm on his cheek. "That sounds divine. I'm just going to drop this letter in the mailbox for Elsbeth, and I'll be right up."

She moved through the entry to the living room, letting her thoughts drift as she ran her fingertips along the back of the sofa. She wandered lazily in the direction of the kitchen, listening with half an ear as a pair of warm, contentious voices drifted toward her.

"You bet all your chits on a pair of sevens?"

"I was bluffing."

"You're letting me win, you ingrate."

A belly laugh rolled across the room as Annie stepped into the kitchen while tapping the envelope lightly over her mouth. She glanced at Edmond, sitting at the breakfast nook, and waved.

He stood up abruptly, causing the bench to scrape loudly across the floor.

She continued on to the door and was about to turn the knob when it finally hit her that he wasn't alone. She turned. "Where on earth are my manners?" she said.

A mousy little woman sat at the table with several playing cards fanned out in her hand. *Gin rummy or maybe crazy eights*, Annie thought. The woman was staring at her in obvious fascination. Annie altered her course, heading for the breakfast nook to make the woman's acquaintance, and amid the variety of thoughts flickering in her mind, there came quite clearly the image contained in a faded photograph. Annie's gait slowed as she looked more closely at the guest—muslin work skirt, cotton blouse, wooden buttons—and she froze, letting the letter slip from her fingers before raising her hand to cover her mouth.

She gasped, and the moment slipped from the stream of time. "I think I know you," she whispered, breaking the spell. "From a letter or two, perhaps? And from a photograph."

The slight figure nodded uncertainly.

"Elsbeth?" Annie stifled a sob. "Nana?"

The little woman placed her hand of cards down, braced herself against the table, and, with a little assistance from Edmond, slowly righted herself. She stood still as a board. Her features didn't shift as she returned Annie's gaze, though unshed tears from a hard life—tears that had been years in the making—gathered on her lower lids before spilling onto her cheeks. She walked stiffly toward Annie. Stopping in front of her, El reached out a mottled hand to touch Annie's cheek and said, "You have her eyes, you know… Beth Anne's." She caressed an auburn strand. "And her hair."

Ever so slowly, Elsbeth mustered her courage and gathered Annie in her arms. She held her close, and Annie began to cry. "There, there, my baby girl. My little Annie," she crooned while rubbing her back.

Annie stepped back, wiping a tear from her face with the back of her hand. "How?" she asked.

That one word sufficed. Elsbeth looked over her shoulder to Edmond as Christian secreted himself in the kitchen to stand against the back wall.

Seeing all eyes on him, Edmond straightened the bench and placed the cards he'd picked up from the floor onto the table. Uncertain where to begin, he turned over a card. It was the joker. "I found a book at the library where I work," he said, rubbing his hand over the back of his arm. "A treatise on Native American spirit journeys and shamans in the Cherokee tribe called 'chosen ones' or 'keys.'"

Edmond looked anxiously at Christian, who encouraged him with a lift of his chin. "This won't make much sense," he said. "But I fell asleep while I read it and dreamed that I was walking through a kitchen." He paused, looking almost apologetic. "This kitchen." Allowing Annie a moment to recover, he nodded toward the back door.

"Outside was"—he shook his head—"a strange world, all black and white, and I saw this guy in a breechcloth who spoke a phrase to me in a Native American tongue that I later translated as 'You are the key.' Next thing I knew, I was wandering through a rose garden, across a field, and around a cabin. There was a mailbox with the name Grundy written on it. Then I woke up and found myself back in the library." Edmond's face turned crimson. "I took the book."

He picked up a leather-bound volume that was sitting on the breakfast table. "I thought the man was telling me that I was a 'chosen one' as described in this."

Annie struggled to comprehend what Edmond was sharing, but failed. "I don't understand," she said.

Christian interrupted her. "Your dad wrote in his diary that the solution to the bloodline problem was within his grasp all along, remember?" When Annie nodded, he shrugged. "He meant it literally."

"What do you mean…literally?"

Christian pushed away from the wall. "Edmond's translation was wrong," he said. "The shaman hadn't said, 'You are the key.' He'd pointed to the book in Edmond's hand and said, 'You have the key.'" Christian took the book from Edmond's hand. "It's the book, Annie. The diary mentioned that your father made the door…and its codex. He'd made two books. We forgot about that. This"—he held up the book—"is the codex. The magic behind the magic of the door. As long as the codex exists, the door will allow you to travel through time." He opened the book and flipped through a few pages. "It also happens to short-circuit the bloodline anomaly for some reason."

Annie looked at her grandmother. "Then you just—"

"Yeah," Edmond said, completing her train of thought. "It was that simple. I went to the cabin and gave Elsbeth the book. She tucked it under her arm and walked right through the door into your kitchen." He grinned at Elsbeth, looking more like himself as he said, "Well…okay, she didn't just waltz in, but she did put on quite a show."

"Edmond," Elsbeth said in warning.

"Well, you poked it with your cane!"

Elsbeth grumbled. "The entire episode was undignified."

"For who? You or the door?"

"It's 'for whom,' you literary lion."

Annie and Christian were mesmerized by the natural exchange and obvious affection between the two, heckling one another as only people of long acquaintance knew how.

When they'd finished trading one-liners, Christian turned to Annie. "There's something else," he said. "The book is the something 'more' that Abbott talks about in the diary. What else it is, I don't know. Maybe it's like a hard drive. Or a memory chip. But it's powerful enough that your father felt the need to hide it in the only place he felt it would be safe."

As his meaning became clear, Annie gasped. "In the future. In a library."

Christian smiled. "Exactly."

Dumbstruck, she turned to Edmond. "How did you find it? The book, I mean?"

"Albert Einstein said coincidence is God's way of remaining anonymous." Christian stopped flipping through the pages of the codex, blushing when he realized that everyone was staring, waiting for him to continue. "Sorry, don't know why I said that."

Edmond wasn't so sure, having learned from experience that some of Christian's greatest wisdom was downplayed as impulse. "I was chasing down a coworker to ask if he would trade shifts," he said. "Followed him to the end of a bookshelf but lost him. I found the book where he was standing."

"A coworker?"

Annie's question was meant to be rhetorical, an indication of her disappointment, but Edmond surprised her. "Maybe not," he said.

"Did you know that the diary entry where your father said he had to hide the codex was dated May 30, 1894?" When Annie nodded her assent, he added warily, "Is it a coincidence then that I found the book on a May 30 also?"

"You're going to catch a fly with that," Christian said, pointing to Annie's gaping mouth.

She shut it, took the book from Christian's hand, and stared at the cover. It was titled *Hidden Doors: Hidden Magic*. "Are you trying to say that"—Annie looked up—"you saw my father?"

Elsbeth led Annie to the breakfast table as Christian fetched a glass of water. Moving over to make room for Edmond, Annie picked a playing card off the floor, looking self-conscious. She also retrieved the envelope while she was down there and handed it to her grandmother. "I visited your cabin," she said.

"Edmond told me. I'm not sure it was wise," Elsbeth said as she opened it.

Annie tallied up the chits on the table while her nana read the letter, smiling at the ample pot—Edmond's bluff cost him dearly. The doorbell rang, and she looked from the front of the house to Christian.

"I'll get it," he said.

There was a bit of a commotion coming from the front, and Christian returned to the kitchen, looking a bit baffled. "Annie, y-you have a...visitor," he said.

She looked up with a start. Something had cracked Christian's composure. "I'm not expecting anyone," she said. Sighing at the unwelcome intrusion, she headed to the front door after Elsbeth gave her a smile and waved her on.

A smartly dressed, sturdy woman stood just outside the door. A quick glance at the warmth in her face told Annie that she wore good humor a cut above her Armani suit. As they made eye contact, the woman did something completely unexpected. "Oh...my... Lord! You've hardly changed," she bellowed.

"I beg your pardon?" Annie almost turned around to see if someone was standing behind her.

"Wow, I wasn't expecting—" Startled by her own brashness, the woman regrouped. "That was pretty rude," she said, tapping her forehead. "Whatever goes in my head tends to pop out of my mouth. Runs in the family." She broke from her outburst to gaze fondly at Annie. "It's no surprise you don't remember me after all these years," she said. "I've put on a few pounds." And once having said that, she executed a series of odd hand movements, grinning all the while.

To anyone else, they would have meant nothing. But to Annie, it was a ritual—bound by spit, a "hope to die" oath, and mutual regard—that was conceived in a candlelit tent pitched on the Persian rug in the living room and shared between a little girl, her beloved godmother, and her godmother's great-granddaughter.

"Elizabeth?" Annie asked.

The woman reached for Annie's hand. "It's been a while," she said.

Annie stared at the hand holding hers with a look that could easily have been mistaken for aloofness, but she was experiencing a disconnect that was only broken when Elizabeth said, "May I come in?"

Shaking her thoughts out of the past, Annie blanched. "My lord, I'm so—" She practically pulled Elizabeth inside. "Come in, come in," she said.

Edmond appeared in the foyer, looking concerned. "Annie?" He nodded politely to Elizabeth. "I'm sorry to interrupt, but Christian wanted me to remind you that you have company inside."

He was about to say something more when Annie gestured toward her guest. "Edmond, I'd like to introduce you to my godmother's"—she turned to Elizabeth—"great-granddaughter?" When Elizabeth nodded, Annie continued, "We were childhood friends."

Elizabeth extended her hand to shake Edmond's. "Elizabeth Strathmore. Nice to meet you."

Annie put her hand on Edmond's back and gave a gentle shove.

"Would you mind whipping up some of that lemonade you made the other day?" she asked.

Taking one last befuddled glance at Elizabeth, Edmond headed to the back, passing Elsbeth and Christian, who were peering through the kitchen door as Annie ushered her guest into the living room. At a nod from her, they came in and sat down.

When everyone was introduced, Elizabeth reached into her purse to pull out a large manila envelope that she held in both hands. She smiled a child's smile as she held it, recalling to Annie's mind a little girl who would turn her upper eyelid inside out, then collapse on the bed in squeals of laughter.

"This is for you," Elizabeth said and handed the envelope to Annie. "It's from Grandma Liza," she added, chuckling quietly when Annie almost dropped it in surprise.

"I know. Crazy, huh?" she said. "There's something else, something I didn't learn until recently. Grandma Liza was the one who saw to your adoption. Did you know that?"

Perhaps it was one revelation too many for a single day. Dumbstruck, Annie shook her head. She stared at the envelope, almost afraid to open it.

Elizabeth, however, didn't share those scruples. "Go on!" she said. "I can't stand the suspense!"

That was definitely the girl Annie remembered. She grinned and started to tear open a corner, but hesitated once again. "Why now?" she asked, her eyes glued to the handwritten letters on the envelope's face. "After all this time."

"I'm really not sure." Elizabeth crossed her arms, leaning back in the chair. "From what I can gather, it has to do with Grandma Liza's will and a final stipulation regarding the maintenance of the family trust," she said. "But why after all these years? Open it and let's find out."

Annie peeled away the lip of the envelope to reveal a few sheets of paper. She withdrew one and stared at it for a heartbeat before gasping.

Christian looked over her shoulder. "Annie? What is it?" He looked closer, reading a single line loud. "General Electric?"

"What! May I?" asked Elizabeth.

Annie handed her the document, warming to an impossibility.

"That's an original GE bearer bond," said Elizabeth, confusion written on her face. She took a moment to gather herself. "They're the cornerstones of the family fortune." She pointed to the remaining pages. "What does the letter say?"

Annie read aloud.

*June 22, 1980*

*Hello, dear.*

*Your Auntie Liza here. Today is the eve of your thirteenth birthday, but circumstances are such that I won't be able to celebrate it with you in person. And while I regret it more than you can know, I will be there in spirit. I am a venerable woman of ninety-seven years, my dear, and must confess that as stubborn as I am, the universe will not bend to my will and see me to my ninety-eighth.*

*So I'm sending your present by mail. And as it is my intention that this letter not be delivered to you for many years, I won't be spoiling the surprise by telling you that it is that darling little pearl choker we found at Prudence Travesty's to go with your Easter dress.*

*But this letter isn't about birthdays. I have something important to tell you, my darling Annabelle—a little confession I must make, and one that may be hard for you to understand.*

*While I've had the incomparable pleasure of being your "Auntie Liza," watching you grow up these last twelve years and loving you as only a mother can, you will also come to know me for a brief while by another name.*

*For you see, my dear, I am also Cap'n.*

*Yes, I know. It must come as quite a shock to learn that the little girl you befriended not so long ago is also the godmother who took you stargazing atop the Empire State Building when you were eight. But time, as you know better than most, has a funny way about it.*

*Kindness is the antidote to an indifferent world, my dear, and you always did have a tender spot for strays, bringing home an endless parade of broken wings to mend. I think it was because you began life as one. And what was I or Christian—or Edmond, for that matter—but another chick that had fallen from the nest? You saved me from my circumstances and became the mother I never had, if only for a brief while.*

*So when you left that day with my cap atop your head, I already knew what I was going to do. We orphans must stick together, after all.*

*I solved the riddle you put to me. The enclosed token proves that. And I became very wealthy indeed—wealthy enough to live an extraordinary life that should not have been obtainable by someone of my rank and file, let alone a woman, all the while biding my time until I would lay eyes on you some seventy years later, see to your adoption into the family of friends, and have a hand in your raising.*

*So, here we are at the end of our story, except for one more little thing. It has something to do with a secret I stirred into the stream of our shared lives. A little paradox we created together. If you should think of me from time to time and find that your smile is more expectant than nostalgic, darling Annie, I offer a simple explanation.*

*We meet again.*

*Love,*
*Auntie "Cap'n" Liza Tolliver*

# CHAPTER FORTY-FIVE

## Fire and Fate

Did you get that chocolate syrup for El?" Christian yelled, looking around the empty room. Getting no response, he lowered his duffel bag to the ground and walked to the back. "Hey!" he shouted, annoyed to find Edmond sitting on the edge of his bed—his shirt unbuttoned, an open carry-on sitting on the floor—and staring at the wall with a strange sort of preoccupation.

Christian grabbed a pile of clothes from the floor. "Get a move on!" he said. "We miss the flight, we miss the concert."

As he prepared to drop them in the suitcase, Edmond reached down, closing the lid.

"Come on, we don't have time to kid around," Christian said, lifting the cover with his foot.

"Christian." Edmond put his own foot on the suitcase to get his attention. "I can't go." He walked out of the room without another word, leaving Christian to stand there with his arms full of clothes.

Christian sat on the bed in the exact spot Edmond had just vacated, the clothes piled in his lap. While he fretted, his eyes wandered to the bedside table, a bubble of shock teasing at his spine when they drifted across something familiar. It was his bookmark—the one Edmond rescued from the street corner the day they'd met. The clothes in his lap tumbled around him as he reached for it, finding a list written in Edmond's bold hand on the back.

1. BE PATIENT. (IT TAKES COURAGE TO FACE THE THINGS WE HIDE FROM OURSELVES.)
2. ASK FOR FORGIVENESS.
3. MAKE AMENDS. (HOW?)

This was something very personal, something he wasn't supposed to see. Feeling like a voyeur, Christian flushed and placed the bookmark back on the table where he'd found it. What the words meant, however, he couldn't fathom. But courage—that word seemed to dog him lately. Annie had also said something about courage the day he and Edmond had found her weeping on the kitchen floor after her encounter with Mr. Culler. Edmond had just disappeared through the door on his way to check on Elsbeth. "Promise me you won't sacrifice your happiness for something as cheap as acceptance," she'd said. "Find your courage, Christian. To hell with everyone else."

He dropped back on the bed and placed a pillow over his head to stifle a scream. Her meaning eluded him, but that wasn't unusual. Annie loved to torment him with innuendo. He had the vague notion, however, that it had something to do with Edmond and what was playing out at this very moment.

He lay there, the familiar smell of Edmond's aftershave drifting off the pillowcase, thinking back to the first time they'd crossed paths. He'd been on his way to Annie's and had almost collided with Edmond at the corner of Church and Twentieth. Storm clouds were gathering on the horizon, he recalled—a prelude to the "uneasy itch" he'd experienced for the first time as Edmond walked past. He'd put it down to déjà vu that day, fearing that Edmond might belong to the world he'd left behind in Texas. The itch never went away, however, only growing stronger as their friendship cemented itself—a curious thing he'd never stopped to reflect upon.

*Courage*, Edmond had written. And *courage*, Annie had said. But he had so little of it, being better acquainted with fear. It bullied him—dictating his life, driving his choices. And as he thought about courage, something else Annie had said that same day began to slowly tease itself from memory—something about, something about...

He sat up with a quick intake of air. "It wasn't déjà vu," he whispered to a pair of socks swimming in the carpet. Despite the fact that they were mismatched, he rolled them into a tube and dropped them in a drawer. "Annie knew all along," he said. Suddenly panicked, he snatched the bookmark off the table and rushed into the living room, breathing a sigh of relief when he found Edmond sitting on a bar stool, nursing a diet cola. Not waiting to collect his thoughts, he blurted, "I've been af-af—" He closed his eyes. Accepting the inevitable didn't make it any less frustrating. He fought with the word *afraid* some more. "—all my life."

Edmond's chin dropped, resting on his collarbone for a fleeting instant before he shook his head. "Stop," he said weakly.

Determined, and deaf to anything but the sound of his own voice, Christian marched on. "I always kn-knew I had to make s-s-suh—"

"Stop!"

"—saaaa...crifi-fices. I'm sorry," he said. His hand rose, and Edmond groaned as it took charge with nimble movements. "To be forgiven for my sins."

"Sins?"

The word, sounding like a clap of thunder, broke through Christian's barriers where the others hadn't. He winced, his hands dropping to his side, and he looked up, surprised to find Edmond standing stiffly in front of the bar stool, his fists clenched, white-knuckled.

"I've lied to you, Christian." There was a wildness about Edmond, a magnetic desperation in his features that caused the hairs on Christian's neck to stand on end. "I've been lying all along." He opened his shirt, exposing the scar Christian had first noticed when they were changing clothes before going off to rescue Annie. "You asked me about this," he said, his lips rounding in an angry knot. "Do you know how I got it?"

Unbalanced by Edmond's anger, Christian stared dumbly at the puckered line that ran from the bottom of Edmond's rib cage to his hip.

"Shrapnel." Edmond hugged himself, as if the act of remembering left him cold. "It was a Sunday morning—early. My ex and I had been partying. There was so much noise and heat and metal... *He ran; Isaac ran!*" He yelled the last two words and dropped back onto the bar stool, shocked into momentary silence by his reaction. "I caused an accident, Christian. I was high as a kite, and I walked across the street against the light and caused an accident. Someone was hurt bad, real bad."

This was important stuff, and Christian wanted to keep up, but he was disoriented, having been pulled from his own confession, and he found himself only able to lock onto a single pronoun, the word *he*. It was the fuse to a powder keg, being part and parcel of a conversation the two men never had on a topic Christian didn't fully understand—not until a moment ago, anyway. Edmond had been content to keep the peace, and so had he, but now it brewed such a storm in his head that he had difficulty following where Edmond was going—that is, until Edmond turned him inside out.

"You could've died."

Three words—a piece of dark magic that tilted the floor underneath Christian. He lost his balance, reaching for the door's threshold to steady himself.

Seeing that, Edmond's head dropped again and began to swing back and forth, as if suddenly too heavy a burden for his neck. "My God, the fear. I'd never seen anyone so afraid in my life. You asked me—" His voice caught. "You asked me to s-s-stay with you." He ground the heel of his hands into his eyes and moaned.

"I covered you during the explosion, but I was young, and there was so much blood, and Isaac had run off, and I was afraid and stupid, and I was high as a fucking kite!" The words sputtered from his mouth, as if the engine driving them were on vapors. "I ran when I heard the sirens." He made a wet sound, a gurgle. "I left you there to bleed all over the sidewalk."

And that was it. Edmond had run out of words.

"You?" So many pronouns. So much meaning. An image formed in the back of Christian's mind, superimposing itself over his hallucinations, all eyes and golden hair surrounded by a halo of flames that writhed from the twisted steel of a car in the background—golden hair that matched his mother's but, more importantly, matched the image in a Polaroid paper-clipped to the sun visor in Edmond's truck. And, for the first time, he heard the echo of a voice talking to him, a man's voice, comforting him as strong hands pulled him from the wreckage.

He only heard Edmond weep words about the impossibility of their paths crossing again with half an ear. Others like *fate* and *atonement* slid over the surface of his consciousness as if it were made of glass, because all he could focus on was that face and the voice that had been pulled from the lost and found of his mind. "I've got you," it said. "Don't worry, I've got you."

"You're the angel?" Christian slid to the ground, his back supported by the door's threshold, and began to pick at the carpet. "You're the angel," he repeated, but as a statement this time. It was painful, letting go of the certainty that he'd been saved by his mother, accepting the truth of it, and he rocked, a lumbering to-and-fro motion as he ran his hands through the carpet's weave to ease the pressure. "How long have you known?" he asked, immediately banishing the question with a wave of his hand before going completely, catatonically still—frozen under the weight of it all.

From where Edmond sat, Christian's eyes betrayed nothing. It wasn't so much that the spark animating them had gone out, he thought, as it was that the source of that spark had retreated to a place where he wasn't invited. "Step nine," he said, his voice tired. "It's all about making amends, asking for forgiveness. But how can I ask for something I know I don't—"

"I forgive you."

The words might as well have come from a stone, as Christian hadn't budged from his huddle, but before Edmond could protest, he repeated, "I forgive you," only louder.

Sometimes, mercy burns with a white-hot flame, and the flesh along Edmond's jawline seemed to ripple from the heat it gave off. He gritted his teeth. It was too much, too generous, and too soon. He put his head in his hands, the same ones that had saved Christian's life, and let Christian's grace wash over him as he quietly fell apart.

And as he wept, Christian said, "What's left for me if I don't, Edmond? A lifetime of broken m-muh-memories and fear?" There was a smudge on the wall opposite him. He concentrated on it as his hands awakened to form a channel in the carpet that alternated between dark and light shades of gray with each swipe. "I'm good with fear—a real pro. I've been badgered my whole life by it, starting with something, something I never wanted, something I—"

His eyes closed, pulling at an invisible stitch that gathered the skin around them into folds, as he shared something he'd never dared voice, not even to Annie. "There's a thing inside me, Edmond. And I can't get rid of it. I've spent a lifetime trying." He rubbed his hands through the carpet's weave as if it were a drug. "The church, my family, everyone says I'm not trying hard enough. And I would take a knife to it for their sake, I would, but it's tied to..."

He broke. The words were gone.

The talk of knives had unsettled Edmond, however. "But it's what?" he asked, dropping his hands from his face, only to clench at the bar stool's seat. "What's inside you?"

"Don't you know?" Christian asked. When Edmond didn't respond, his face crumbled, and his hand, the one that often spoke for him, started to pound at his chest, as if to beat whatever was inside him into submission.

It was intolerable, what Christian was doing, and Edmond found himself storming across the room, unable to bear it, yet also drawn to it. He dropped to his knees. "For their sake?" he asked, trembling with anger and fear and anticipation. "They did this to you? Tormented the kindest man I've ever known so badly he finds himself completely unable to speak?" He seized Christian's hand before he could harm himself further, squeezing. "It's not sin, what's inside you," he said. "I promise you it's not."

And having said that, Edmond kissed him.

It was a chaste thing, though earnest, for all that it was impulsive, and Edmond expected resistance. When there wasn't any, he closed his eyes and pulled back a hair's breadth, feeling strangely vulnerable as he asked again, "What is it tied to, Christian, that thing inside you?"

And he waited an agonizing wait until he felt a faint stirring and heard…

"You."

# CHAPTER FORTY-SIX

## Where the Door Is Concerned

### SIX MONTHS LATER

Annie slid a pen under the scarf wrapped around the top of her head, scratching at her scalp as she stared at the door her father had made and she'd acquired a century later. It had become something of a bad habit since losing her hair. The bone-marrow transplant had been a breeze, and her grandmother had pulled through like a trouper, but the chemotherapy accompanying it had left Annie with a spate of skin rashes, mouth ulcers, and…a bald head.

The night Annie's hair fell out was something of an emotional roller-coaster ride, and her memories were still partitioned into two spheres—those of her loss itself and those of how very special Christian really was. She'd been taking a bath in her eagle-claw tub, her head half submerged, when she'd opened her eyes to find a clump of hair floating across her field of view.

Christian had come flying into the bathroom at her scream and had found her sitting up in the tub, sobbing, with strands of hair draped over both her hands like ribbons. He'd thrown both arms around her as she'd completely lost herself in self-pity, assuring her it was just temporary. When she'd gotten hold of herself, he had her lean back so he could gently sponge away the remainder, collecting it all in a plastic bag.

It was what he'd done next, however, that made it all

bearable—almost. He'd told her to close her eyes and disappeared downstairs. She wasn't at all happy with his brief absence—vulnerability was a new experience for her—but he'd returned quickly and, after ensuring her eyes were still shut, had begun to brush the top of her head with the tenderest strokes. The sensation was so soothing that she'd simply given in and quietly let him apply his "therapy," as he'd called it.

She had no idea how long he was at it—at least an hour—before he'd ran to her vanity, smiling self-consciously when he returned. He'd held up a mirror for her inspection. "You always wanted to go blond, and I thought..." He'd let the remaining words drift away and waited for her response. She'd gasped at her reflection and had broken into further tears, not because of her loss, but for what he'd done. Christian had painted the most beautiful golden curls all over her head to replace the hair she'd lost.

"I can wash it off. I can wash it off right now," he'd said, panicking at her reaction.

Had anyone else done it, she would have been horrified, but it was the perfect expression of who Christian was that he'd planned for this moment, thinking of how to spare her pain. So she'd done the only thing she could, putting her hand over his mouth to cry and cry and laugh and swear she loved them before crying some more.

When she was all played out, he'd pulled a gift-wrapped box from underneath the tub, explaining that it was a gift from everyone—him, Edmond, and Elsbeth (who was recovering in her cabin under Edmond's watchful eye). Inside were a good dozen of the most extraordinary silk Chanel scarves she'd ever seen. He'd had her pick one, and then, having assured himself that his artwork was dry, had wrapped it around her head in a retro style taught to him by Mrs. Weatherall.

His artwork had faded over the next few weeks and her hair was growing in nicely, but it itched like the devil all the time.

Annie withdrew from the memory, and her eyes returned to the door. They fixed on the bloodstain she'd put in the top left-hand corner before her first foray into the past, trying to decide whether or not to share her suspicions with her grandmother. She couldn't even bring herself to tell Christian that she knew Mr. Culler had been murdered well before Elsbeth confirmed it. That when she couldn't decide how or where to banish him, couldn't think beyond her outrage in that critical moment he was lying unconscious on the floor outside her solarium, the door seemed to take matters into its own hands, showing her an image of her father exacting revenge. It was a ruthless image, and she'd accepted it greedily in that moment, knowing it would come to pass.

In the quiet days that followed, as she slowly put her life back together, Annie pretended that it had all been the workings of her overactive imagination and that she didn't really know she'd sent Mr. Culler to his death. But the minute she opened the letter from Elsbeth and saw the article, she knew what it would contain. So, Mr. Culler's demise remained a mystery that only she, her father, and the door knew the answer to.

*Yes*, she thought, *the door*. There was more to it than the magic of time travel. It weighed on her mind, and she began to suspect, as her father did before her, that it was inhabited by an intelligence.

And what were the implications of her suspicions? She couldn't accept that it was evil, because that would require her to destroy it. The door had brought her precious cargo in the form of her grandmother. And in many ways, it had fostered an extraordinary family—her, Elsbeth, Christian, Edmond, and Cap'n—misfits one and all, alienated by society and perfectly suited for each other's company. Certainly, something capable of creating such beauty couldn't be evil. And, after all, Mr. Culler's death was justifiable.

Not comfortable with her conclusions and not wanting to frighten anyone, Annie decided to keep her speculations to herself. She was preparing to write *Love, Annie* at the bottom of the letter she'd been writing when she heard the sigh of a door hinge and the murmur of voices in the kitchen, signaling that the boys had just come in from the back. Edmond had been whipping the rose garden into shape all week. He'd recruited Christian to help, and it had worked out well enough, though Edmond refused to allow him near anything that conducted electricity or had sharp edges. Knowing Christian as she did, Annie applauded Edmond's good horse sense.

"Take off your shoes," she yelled.

She'd scribbled her name and folded the note into thirds when a hand rested on her shoulder. "Give me a second," she said and reached up to pat it, even as she felt the light pressure of a kiss atop the scarf on her head.

Her smile faded. Whether by instinct or intuition, she couldn't tell, but she was infallibly certain that the hand belonged to neither Christian nor Edmond. And she was equally certain to whom it did. *But it's not possible*, she thought, the shock jump-starting her heart to thump in its chest cavity. And, just as quickly as that thought passed through her mind, she realized that the door made anything possible. She held her breath as a cheek brushed against hers, not daring to move.

"You'll find me not so easily dispatched this time, Miss Aster."

The voice, hauntingly familiar, spurred Annie into motion. She sprang from her chair, pivoted, and launched herself at her uninvited guest even as he said, "Why, you don't look at all happy to see me, Ann—"

Her name was cut short by a grunt as the two landed in a mound of flailing limbs that led inevitably to Annie's arms being pinned above her head. She had little time to recall the irony of the last occasion in which she'd found herself in that position before a pair of lips crushed hers. She struggled, to be sure, but the nature and duration of her struggle was altogether different this time. It was brief and ended with her returning the kiss with a passion that would do credit to all Catholic schoolgirls everywhere. But as their tangled bodies uncoiled and an elegant hand reached for the scarf, she recoiled.

"Don't," she said, shaking her head.

Nathaniel brushed his lips across her nose before resting them on a brow and, ignoring her plea, drew the scarf away. He rested on his elbow to take her in, his eyes swelling in a manner that very nearly broke Annie's heart.

"It'll grow back in," she said.

He put his hand over hers as she struggled to replace the scarf. "You mistake me, madam." He tossed the scarf aside and gently fingered an angel-fine strand of hair. "I didn't think it possible, but somehow you are even more beautiful than I remembered."

As Annie pulled him to her, and they reacquainted themselves with certain laws of attraction wholly unrelated to physics, Christian peered into the living room from the kitchen. Satisfied, he disappeared.

Elsbeth doffed her nightgown and replaced it with her frock. Grabbing her spectacles, she wandered to the stove to boil some milk. She opened the cupboard and reached between a sack of flour and a tin of lard to retrieve something that had no business being there. Chuckling indulgently, she squeezed some of its contents into the pan, watching as the goop spluttered and bubbled out.

Making a mental note to have Edmond pick up some more chocolate syrup, she poured herself a steaming cup of cocoa and headed to the mailbox with a familiar pop and snap. She stared about at the austere landscape and took a sip before lifting the lid to the box to withdraw a letter. It had become part of her daily routine. Shuffling back to her rocker, she began to read.

December 7, 1995

Dear Nana:

I had the strangest dream last night in which I awoke to find a woman sitting in my dressing chair, watching me. She was petite and beautiful, wore a period piece that turned me to pudding with envy, and smelled heavenly, though I couldn't put my finger on the fragrance. I was completely at ease. We sat on the floor like two little girls to play chess, as if it were the most natural thing in the world, with a set made from the most ridiculous pieces imaginable. The pawns were toads, the king a crow, and the queen—that fabulous queen—a brightly colored totem pole.

She talked and talked as we played, saying how proud she was of me, that she admired my strength, but that it was time for me to give up my "silly, self-imposed isolation," as she put it, and not waste the family of remarkable misfits that had been given me.

When I woke this morning, it was to that last thought and the almost overpowering fragrance of honeysuckle. Then, suddenly, I remembered something. That scent has been following me everywhere since the surgery. I woke to it when I was in the recovery room—I don't know how I could have forgotten that. I've also caught a whiff of it from time to time in my quieter moments, while reading a book or flipping through channels. Isn't that odd?

I've given it some thought. It's my mother, isn't it? You wrote that she loved honeysuckle, chess, and crows.

I'll do as she said. And she's right, you know. We are misfits, one and all, thrown off by society for our perceived slights—eccentricity, age, addiction, orphanhood, and well, I've already discussed Christian's perceived slights with you, though Edmond seems to have cured them quite nicely.

For starters, I've invited my neighbor over for tea—the one who bought the house three doors down. Christian, no doubt, will like her instantly.

Before I forget to mention it, the auction of the bearer bonds turned into a bloody field day. I can't even process what it all means. The investment division at the bank is seeing to the transfer and investment of the funds.

It goes without saying that Doctor Gow is pitching a fit over our plans, insisting I haven't convalesced long enough, but he relented under pressure. Paris for the holidays—imagine that. I've already had some dresses made in your size.

Love,
Annie

P.S. I burned the cookies again. Edmond had the cheek to say they were an improvement over the prior batch.

P.P.S. See if you can coax Bristle through the door. This house needs a cat.

Elsbeth put the letter down and chuckled. "Well, I'll be damned," she said. Finishing off the cocoa, she disappeared into the bedroom, banging about and making a terrible ruckus. Moments later, she placed a cigar box on the table and sat down. Inside, nestled between shotgun shells and fishing wire, was an assortment of knickknacks.

One in particular caught her eye. She held up a bracelet made of twine, remembering that long-ago night when Tom had given it to her. He'd sat her on the swing under the oak at her parents' house, pulling out two pieces of twine—one red, one white—and had begun wrapping them around each other, tying seven knots along their length. With each knot, he'd made her a promise, ending with a pledge at the seventh to replace it with a proper wedding ring when he was able. He'd tied it around her wrist, and they were married within a fortnight. Three years later, he'd given her a simple silver band—the one she still wore. It dawned on her suddenly that Tom had kept every promise, including "until death do us part."

She laid the bracelet aside and retrieved another trinket from the box. Tom had carved this one for Beth Anne. It was an odd little thing, painted in clashing bright colors and looking more like one of those Tootsie Rolls Amos sold at the Hay and Feed than a chess piece. It was Beth Anne's favorite. The white queen—the totem pole. She wrapped it in a piece of newsprint, tied the bracelet around it, and wrote a quick note.

*Annie—*

*I think your mother would want you to have this.*

*Nana*

"Nana?"

"Hmm?"

"You're hogging the popcorn, the afghan, *and* the couch."

"Sorry, baby girl." Elsbeth started to move her feet out of the way, but Annie lifted them onto her lap instead. Better situated, Elsbeth wiggled the bunny slippers she'd taken to wearing 24-7, while pointing to the television set as closing credits scrolled across the screen. "What was the name of this show again?"

"*The Golden Girls*."

"That's it." Elsbeth crammed a handful of popcorn in her mouth and said between chews, "Sophia rules, but I have a hankering to powder Blanche's bottom."

"Rules?" Annie palmed her forehead, immediately aware of the dreadful slang's point of origin. "Edmond," she said, shaking her head at the obvious. Theme music filled the room as she watched scene after scene in which Bea Arthur displayed an incredible range of expressions that commingled exasperation and disbelief in varying ratios, most of which were aimed at Rose, all the while trying to figure out what had gotten her grandmother's goat. Elsbeth was being positively fidgety. Annie had a sneaking suspicion why, but wanted to hear it confirmed.

"What's wrong, Nana?" she said finally. "What's got you so touchy?"

Elsbeth tucked the afghan around her sides, the corners of her lips slouching for a second before she asked, "What's today's date, again?"

"That's the third time you've asked. It's the ninth. What's going on?"

Elsbeth pulled the afghan up to her chin. "The Great Caruso debuted in Milan yesterday," she said. And while her comment was almost wistful, she still managed to glance at her granddaughter with perhaps a wee bit of petulance.

Feigning boredom, though the tic in her cheek nearly gave her away, Annie paused the video and reached between the sofa cushions to pull out a pair of tickets that she dropped into her grandmother's lap. "Happy birthday."

Elsbeth peered at them, uncertain how to handle the turn of events. Feeling slightly embarrassed, yet annoyed that Annie had drawn out the suspense, she finally sat up and held them at arm's length, staring over her spectacles. "But…" she said, glancing at Annie, then back to the tickets. "But we're too late. It's over. The canary sang and flew the coop."

Annie grabbed a handful of popcorn before gesturing toward the kitchen with her thumb where a very peculiar door stood and said, "You're kidding, right?"

# Reading Group Guide

1. If you had Annie's time portal, when and where would you go?

2. Who is your favorite character in the novel? Why?

3. Imagery adds depth to the written word in literature. There are several repeating images in *The Lemoncholy Life of Annie Aster*, one of which is that of a crow. What do you think the crow might represent? Did you notice any other significant images? What might they mean?

4. Roses, particularly, have been a bonanza for symbologists throughout history. What do roses represent to you? What do you think the roses that appear behind Annie's house represent?

5. Déjà vu is defined as the illusion of having previously experienced something. Christian fears that he may have met Edmond before but doesn't remember. In the end, did he experience déjà vu, or was it more complicated than that?

6. As a society, we are undeniably judgmental about drug abuse. Did your impression of Edmond change when you became aware that he struggled with drug addiction? Why or why not? Do you think drug addiction is a disease or a choice?

7. Cap'n was shocked by how the world treated her when she lost her family and home. Fabian said that homelessness and poverty made her invisible to the world, because otherwise people would have to "face their own pettiness." Do you think that is a fair comment?

8. "I'm not proud of what I done, but pride ain't really something I can afford." Cap'n says this after admitting to Annie that she steals, and her point is clear. While she is mindful that theft is wrong, she's not going to suffer too many scruples about it when her survival is at stake. What is the measure of this sin (stealing) when it is held up against survival? Whose sin is greater: Cap'n's for stealing, or society's for creating the circumstances that forced her to steal?

9. *The Lemoncholy Life of Annie Aster* is, at its heart, a novel about five misfits—Annie, Elsbeth, Cap'n, Christian, Edmond—that explores the concept of marginalization through their experience. What do you think were the qualities or circumstances that led to each of the protagonists' marginalization?

10. Edmond says, "It's not sin, what's inside you. I promise you, it's not." His comment addresses one of today's hot-button topics—homosexuality as a sin. Is it?

11. Do you think homosexuality is a choice? Does the fact that LGBT youth are four times as likely to attempt suicide as their heterosexual counterparts (eight times as likely if they've experienced rejection from their family) affect your determination as to whether or not homosexuality is a choice?

12. Does our concept of what constitutes sin evolve over time

as we gain a better understanding of the forces behind it? (Example: slavery.)

13. In the novel, the author toys with the concept of fate as a physical force of the universe, not unlike gravity. Just to make things complicated (he loves complications), he stirred in two other powerful forces—love and time—binding the three together. Which of these three forces—love, time, or fate—played the greatest role in uniting Annie and El? Which of these forces played the greatest role in uniting our other protagonists?

14. Danyer is a figment of Mr. Culler's imagination that allows him to do evil without feeling the weight of guilt or the need to take personal responsibility for his actions. Basically, Mr. Culler blames Danyer for his own bad behavior. What are some common scenarios in which people blame others in order to deny personal responsibility today?

15. Courage and sacrifice often go hand in hand. Annie begs Christian to find his courage and be true to himself, and he does, but he has to sacrifice everything he was taught to do so. What other acts of courage did you find in the book, and what sacrifices did they require?

# A Conversation with the Author

**Is "lemoncholy" even a word?**

Well, sort of. I'd been browsing through an online dictionary of Victorian slang (I can go to extreme lengths to avoid actual writing) and discovered that it was used as a synonym for "melancholy" back in the day. The word was too perfect for my purposes, and I decided to give it new meaning by combining the phrase "If life gives you lemons…" with the word "melancholy" to characterize the state in which someone makes the best of a bad situation.

**Did you base any of the characters in the manuscript off people in your life?**

My best friend, Steve, is an acquired taste. He's a loner with a wicked tongue, a cantankerous and, on the odd occasion, tactless eccentric who will, if you give him half a chance, win you over with his loyalty, tender heart, and generous nature. All I had to do was imagine him in a cabin surrounded by a sea of wheat to breathe life into Elsbeth.

Edmond was drawn almost entirely from another friend. Let's call him "Sam" for anonymity's sake. Aside from his extraordinary charisma, his fascination with dream catchers, and his unique ability to like absolutely everyone, Sam had a demon—drug addiction. He'd rise and fall over and over, but always in good cheer.

I received an email from his sister last year, not four weeks after Sam and I spent an hour on the phone planning his first international trip to visit me in New Zealand. He'd died of an accidental overdose, she wrote. What can I say? There's not a day that goes by that I don't miss him.

And finally there's Christian. I'll keep that one short. I'm him and he's me, only without the debilitating stutter. Mine's pretty mild by comparison.

**What did you want to accomplish by writing *The Lemoncholy Life of Annie Aster*?**

More than anything, I hope to give the person reading my book something of the same experience my favorite authors give me. I love to be charmed by a story—not just by its premise, but also by the words within it. If I can evoke the wonder of A. A. Milne's Hundred Acre Wood in any way, or the magic of Erin Morgenstern's *The Night Circus*, gifting someone with a smile as they read, then I feel I've accomplished something meaningful.

**What was the seed of inspiration behind *The Lemoncholy Life of Annie Aster*?**

A botched first date—I kid you not.

I thought everything was going fine until my date proclaimed, "I think we're destined to be great friends." Not the response I had in mind, let me tell you.

Behind every failed date lies an opportunity, I always say (just made that up, actually), and I concocted a pair of characters while driving home with my tail tucked between my legs—Annabelle Aster (her last name was Biddleton at the time) and Elsbeth Grundy, pen pals who write one another between contemporary San Francisco and Victorian Kansas, depositing their letters in a brass letter box that stands in some magical common ground between the two.

When I got home, I whipped up a letter from Annie to Elsbeth in which she asked for advice regarding her love-struck friend—me—and emailed it to my date.

Within a couple hours, I received a call. Apparently my email had done the rounds at my date's office and was a bit of a hit. More were demanded. I responded, "Sadly, I cannot, at least not until Elsbeth writes back." Within the hour, there was an email in my inbox with Elsbeth's name in the subject line. And thus began what I dubbed the "Annie El" letters.

The date? Who was the date, you ask? It was Sam, the man who inspired my character Edmond.

**You mentioned New Zealand earlier. What gives?**

Mike, that's what. He's a Kiwi. (That's what New Zealanders call themselves.) We met eight years ago and said our vows before family and friends in the rotunda of San Francisco's City Hall on October 8, 2013.

The path to our happy union was a little bumpy, to say the least. When we made the decision to share our lives, I was unable to sponsor Mike for U.S. residency due to the Defense of Marriage Act, which prohibited same-sex unions until it was declared unconstitutional last year. New Zealand, however, was a different story, and I moved here when Mike sponsored me for residency five years ago.

Today, we own a lovely 1920s bungalow in Auckland, with a huge backyard that I'm not allowed to mow. Apparently, I don't do it right. (It may or may not be true that I cultivated this deficiency intentionally.)

**If you could travel back in time, when and where would you go?**

Middle-earth. That's kind of cheating, but I'm sticking to my answer. I've read Tolkien's Lord of the Rings trilogy at least fifteen times—the first when I was thirteen.

Keep this little secret under your hat. When I was a kid, there were ten members in the Fellowship of the Ring, not nine. Take a stab at who the tagalong was. If you're still not sure, I'll help. I even memorized the elfin poetry, not that I suggest you request a recitation. You might get a tomato thrown at you. Regardless, it started me on a sci-fi and fantasy binge that easily spanned a thousand books.

**If you cut your teeth on science fiction and fantasy, how did you come to write a commercial fiction novel?**

It all started with those Annie El letters I wrote, of course, but it was also fueled by a challenge. My mom hates fantasy and science fiction. I mean, she has a deep-down-in-the-bones loathing for it. I wanted to see if I could change her mind by wrapping a fantasy premise inside some good, old-fashioned commercial fiction.

**Did it work?**

Nope.

**How would you describe your writing process?**

It is said that there are two types of writers—"plotters" or "pantsers"—and never the twain shall meet. A plotter plans, researches, outlines. They're methodical, flushing out their story before putting a single word on the page, and I hate them. (Just kidding!) I fall firmly in the latter camp, sitting in front of my laptop waiting to be surprised by what I put down.

Being a pantser (writing by the seat of your pants) is not a strategy for the faint of heart, I can tell you. On an average writing day, when not typing, I talk to the computer screen, fully expecting it to talk back. I fidget, I pace, I doodle. I stare outside and sigh at the futility of it all an awful lot.

**Tell us something no one knows about you.**

Well, I'm pretty much an open book, but here's something very few people know. I was a national titleholder in the sport of gymnastics. And, as the result of a gymnastics-related accident in which my left arm was, for lack of a simpler explanation, severed at the elbow—yep, you read that right—and reconstructed through surgery, it's about an inch shorter than my right arm. Weird, eh?

**Anything else?**

I've eaten the same breakfast every day for the last seven years—steel-cut oats and a six-egg-white, one-yolk omelet. I am such a gym fanatic that I even work out while on vacation and can still do a standing back flip at the ripe old age of mumble, mumble. Oh, and I do a "morning dance" every day while making breakfast. Video confirmation is forthcoming.

# Acknowledgments

Look, I need to come clean. When you succumb to the impulse to write a piece of fiction from scratch, without a clue as to how you actually go about it, yet find yourself many years later in the surreal position of having to write a dedication and acknowledgment to something for which the pages of its first draft are on suicide watch (yes, it was that bad, people), a little reflection makes it painfully clear that you'd never have gotten to that bizarre point without the support of a pretty crazy cast. So, without further ado:

Mom and Dad, seriously? I still can't wrap my head around the unwavering support you gave me from the moment I took this outrageous leap of faith. Just know that I love you to pieces and will do everything I can to pay you back for those comped meals, and the cumulative total of around three hundred bucks Dad slipped into my pocket in an endless parade of tens and twenties each time we hugged good-bye at airport curbside. Okay, fine! It might have been closer to eight hundred.

Steve. Without you, there'd be no Elsbeth, and for that inspiration alone, I'm eternally grateful. Studies show that if you manage to remain friends for seven years, you'll be friends forever. Frankly, I knew *that* would be our destiny when you so charmingly (and creatively!) insulted every last thing I'd cooked during our first meal together fifteen years ago. Too many carbs. The chicken was dry. And while I can't remember what you said about the asparagus off the top of my head, who actually bothers to notice the sodium content of sparkling water? It was Perrier, for heaven's sake!

Jennie, Tee, Heather, Ian, and Peggy. Why did I choose you to critique, edit, and cajole? You're all way smarter than me, that's why—a quintet of unsung heroes who saved me from myself time and time again with wisdom, enthusiasm, and a remarkable level of restraint, considering my chronic obtuseness.

Barbara. I was powerless to go anywhere else for agency representation when, after asking in a tremulous voice if I was speaking to *the* Ms. Poelle, you hollered, "I better be! I'm wearing her pants!"

Shana and Anna. You're editors. No one can make that funny. All kidding aside, you are the two most incredibly insightful, meticulous, supportive, and driven professionals who squeezed the very best possible version of *Lemoncholy* humanly possible into the light of day, while also being as close to funny as a pair of editors can be.

And, finally, I tip my hat to you, Sidney and Reid. If it wasn't for that mean little push you gave me way back when, I'd never have found the courage to walk away from one career and embark on another.

# About Scott Wilbanks

Photo by: Charles Thomas Rogers

They say, "Write what you know." Who "they" may be still remains a mystery, but I took the advice to heart when I wrote a book about five misfits who found themselves walking a path I trod daily, seeking understanding in an indifferent world—but more on that later.

With my life constantly pushed and pulled by a pair of opposing bugaboos—ADD and drive—I surprised myself by graduating summa cum laude from the University of Oklahoma while also garnering a handful of titles in the sport of gymnastics.

Life-changing accidents, lost loves, and an unremarkable career path followed, that is until a lawsuit and Mike changed everything. The lawsuit motivated me to step away from my career. Mike added the extra push, convincing me to take a leap of faith and move to the country of his birth, New Zealand, while also encouraging me to "see where this writing will take me."